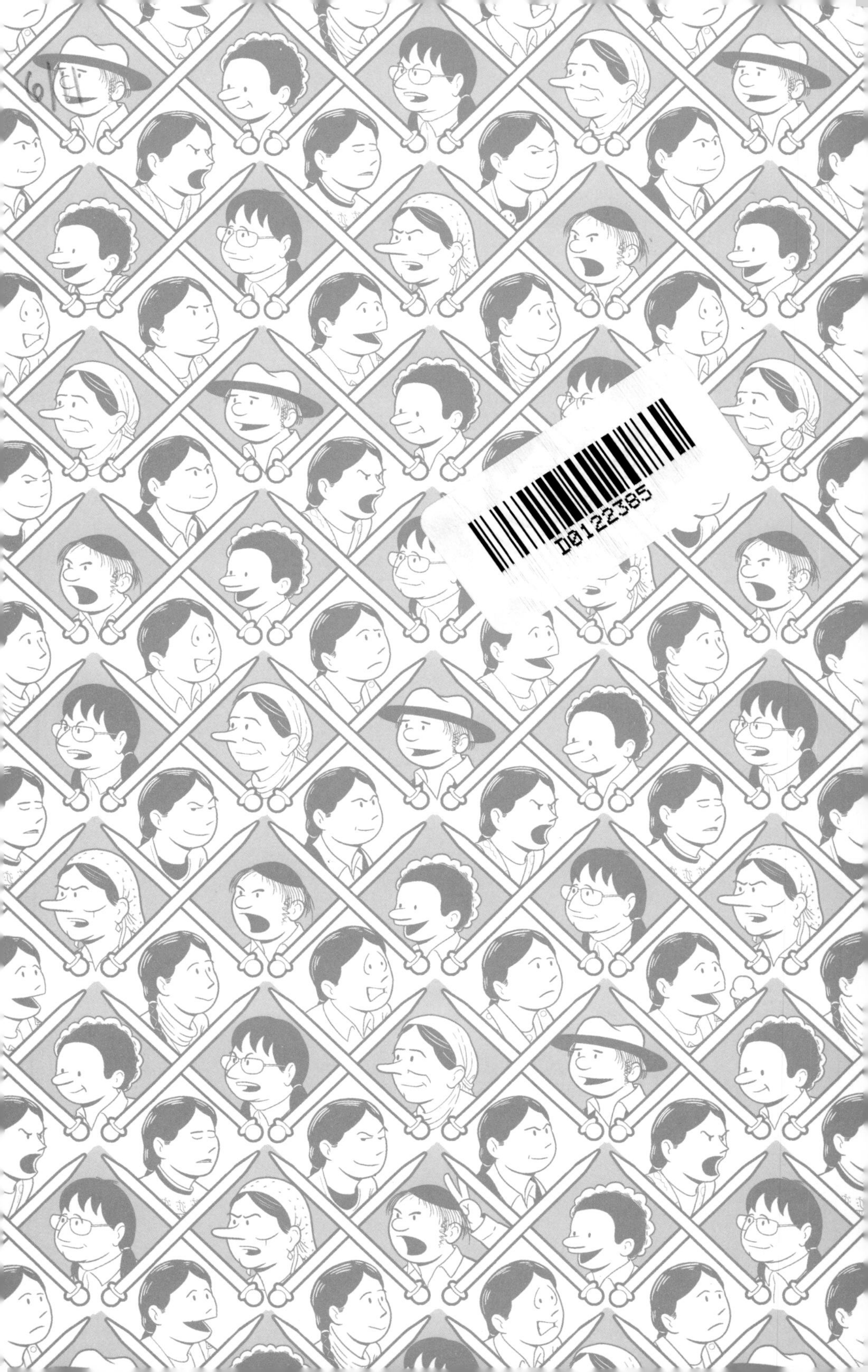

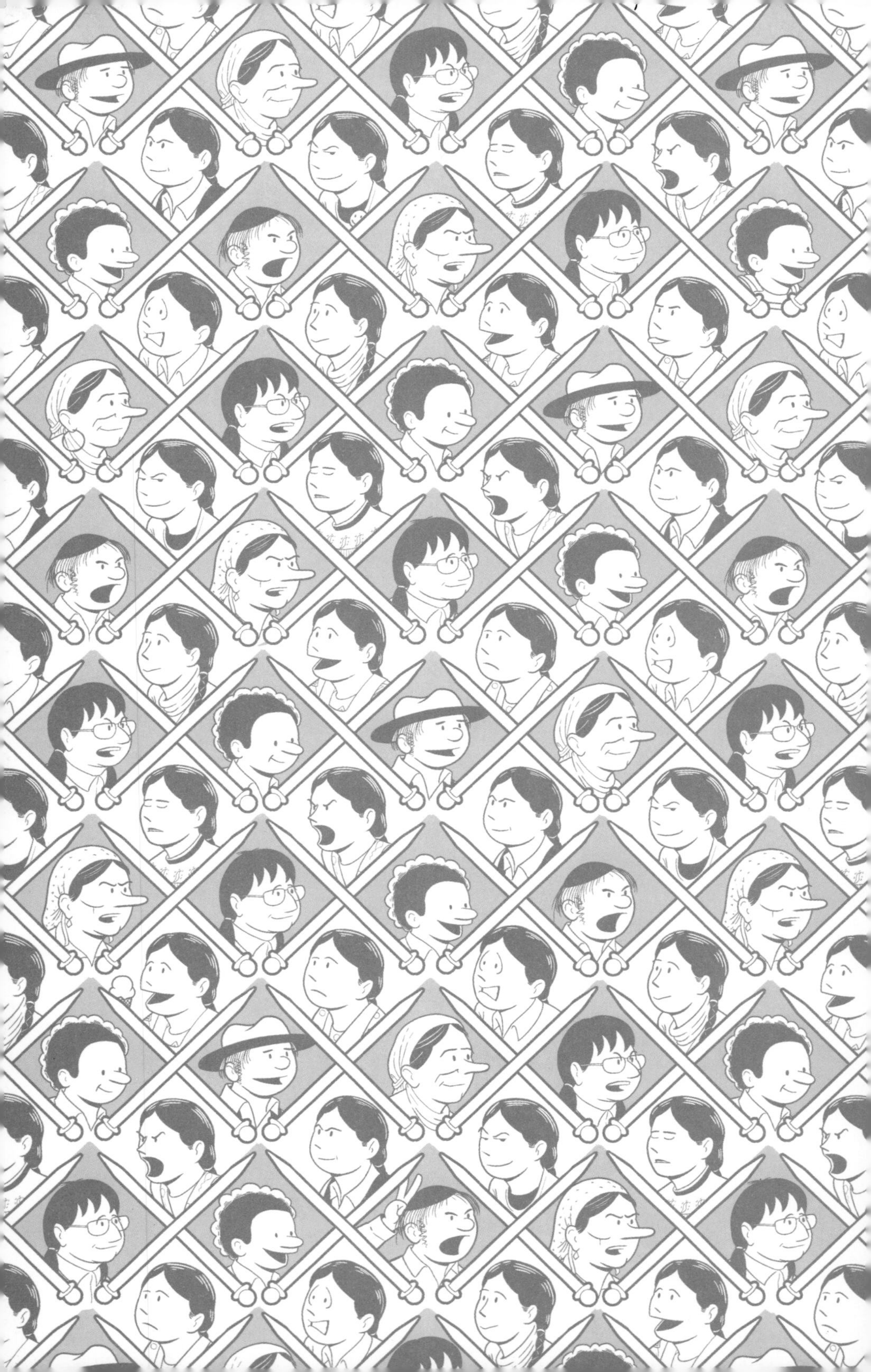

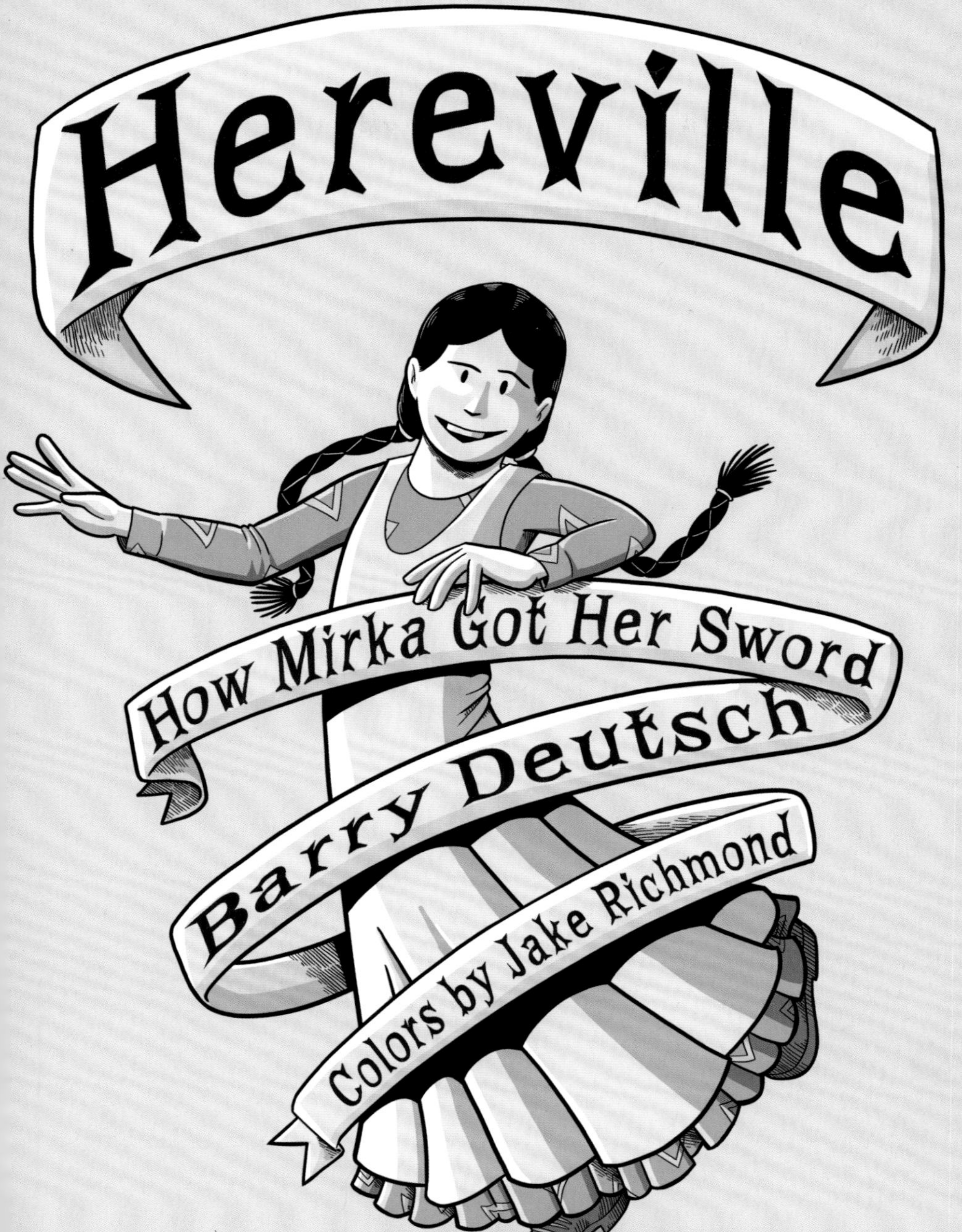
Hereville
How Mirka Got Her Sword
Barry Deutsch
Colors by Jake Richmond

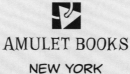

AMULET BOOKS
NEW YORK

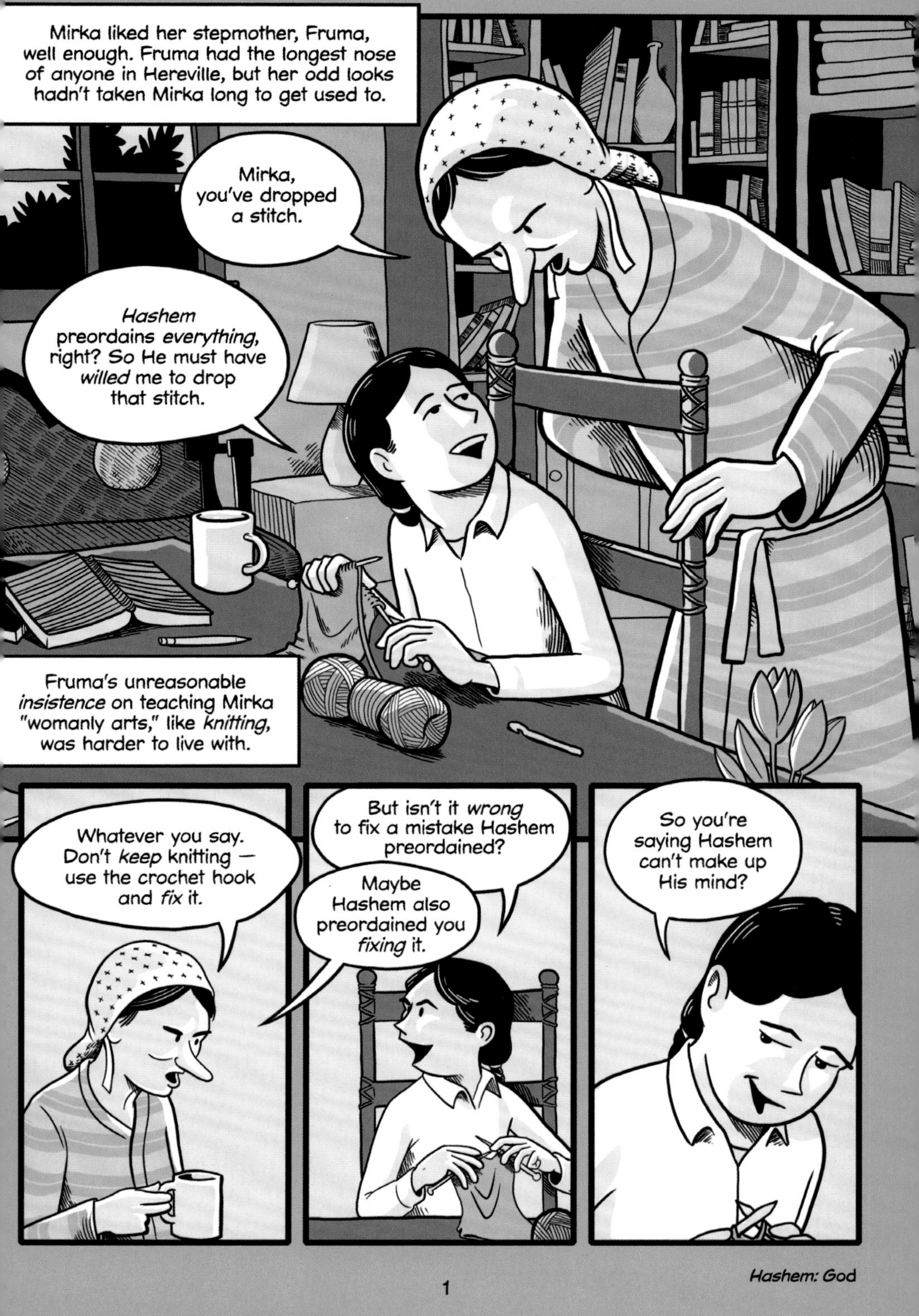
Mirka liked her stepmother, Fruma, well enough. Fruma had the longest nose of anyone in Hereville, but her odd looks hadn't taken Mirka long to get used to.
Mirka, you've dropped a stitch.
Hashem preordains *everything*, right? So He must have *willed* me to drop that stitch.
Fruma's unreasonable *insistence* on teaching Mirka "womanly arts," like *knitting*, was harder to live with.
Whatever you say. Don't *keep* knitting — use the crochet hook and *fix* it.
But isn't it *wrong* to fix a mistake Hashem preordained?
Maybe Hashem also preordained you *fixing* it.
So you're saying Hashem can't make up His mind?

Hashem: God

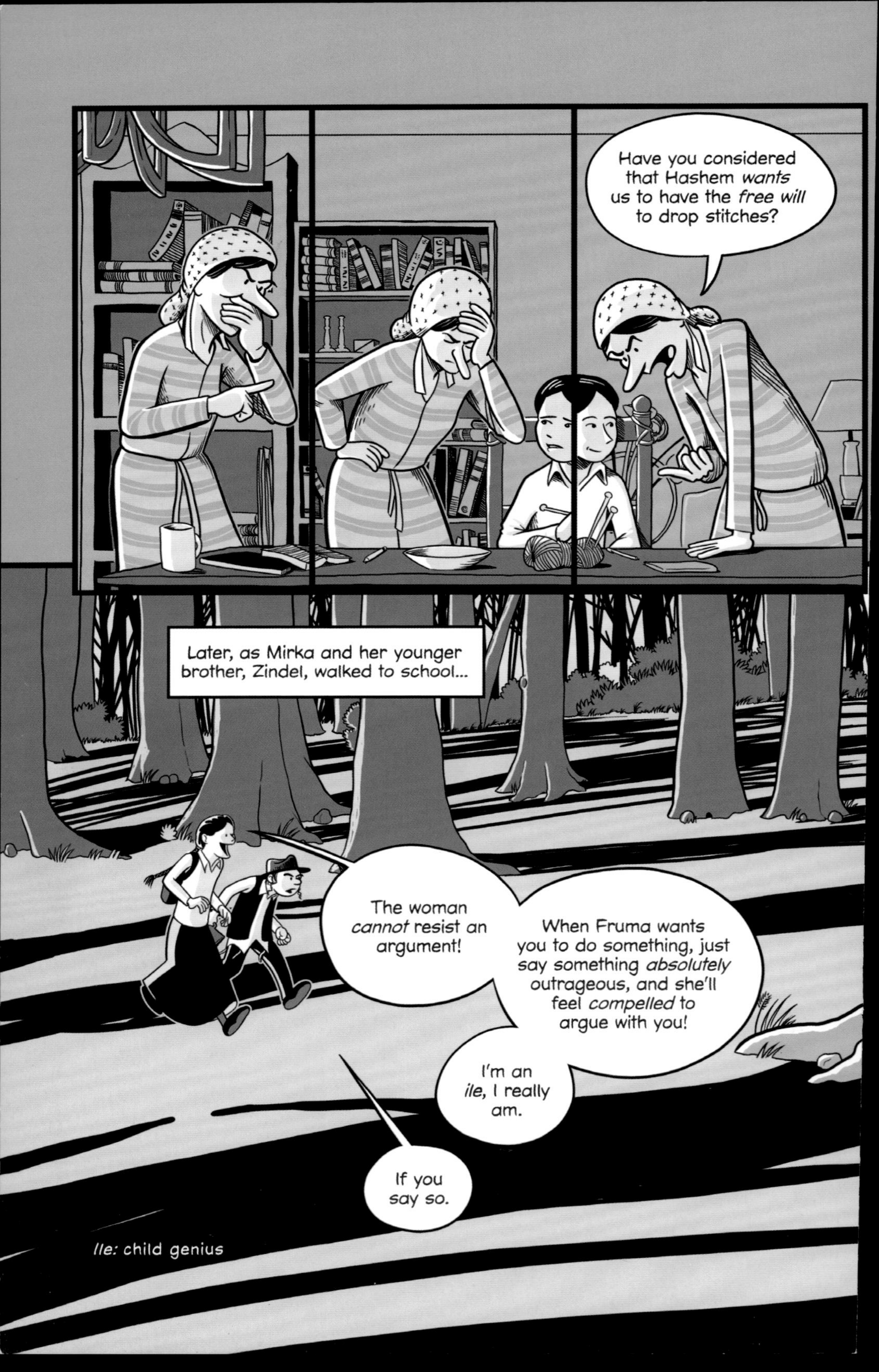
Have you considered that Hashem *wants* us to have the *free will* to drop stitches?
Later, as Mirka and her younger brother, Zindel, walked to school...
The woman *cannot* resist an argument!
When Fruma wants you to do something, just say something *absolutely* outrageous, and she'll feel *compelled* to argue with you!
I'm an *ile,* I really am.
If you say so.
Ile: child genius

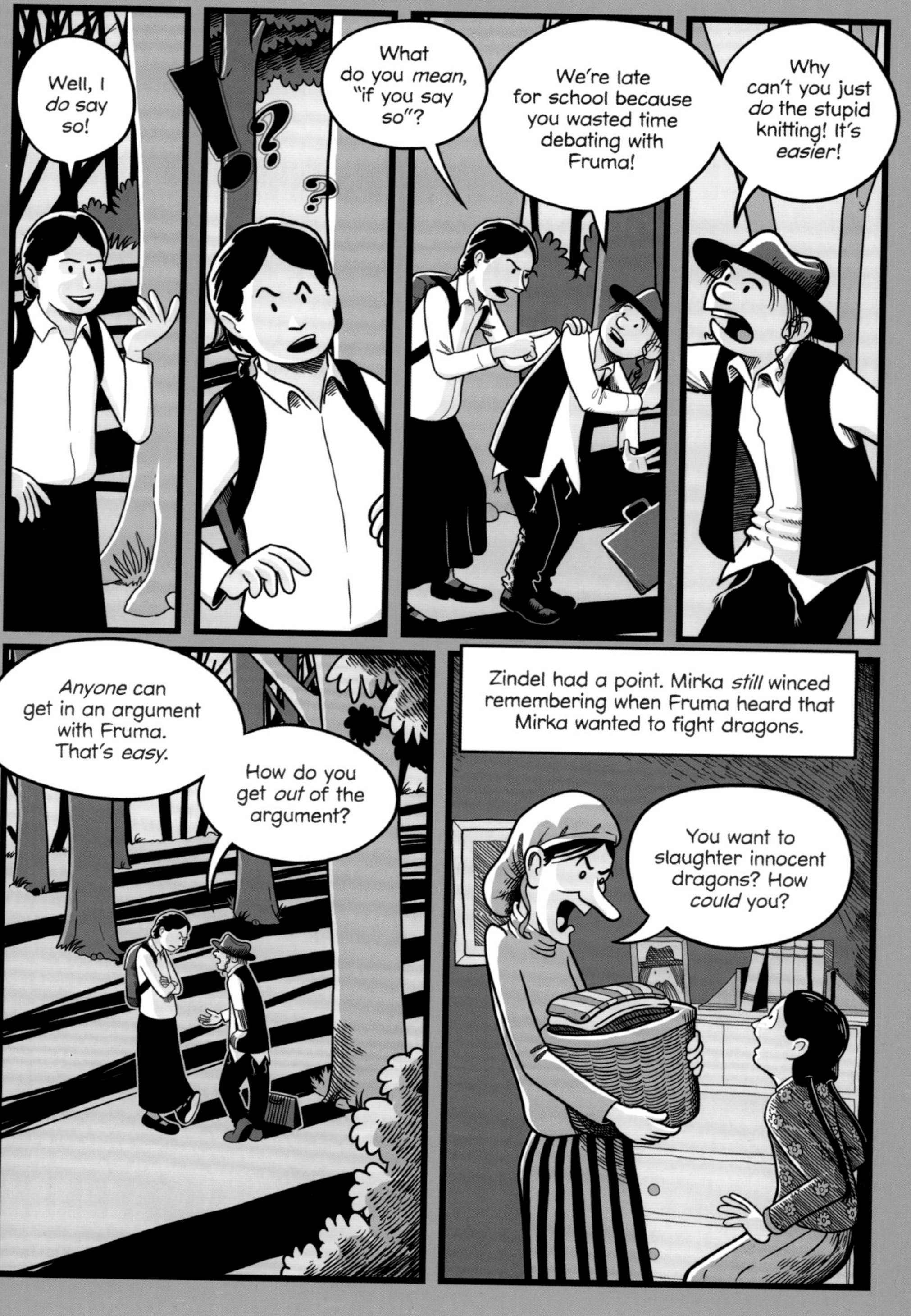
Well, I *do* say so!
!??
What do you *mean*, "if you say so"?
We're late for school because you wasted time debating with Fruma!
Why can't you just *do* the stupid knitting! It's *easier*!
Anyone can get in an argument with Fruma. That's *easy*.
How do you get *out* of the argument?
Zindel had a point. Mirka *still* winced remembering when Fruma heard that Mirka wanted to fight dragons.
You want to slaughter innocent dragons? How *could* you?

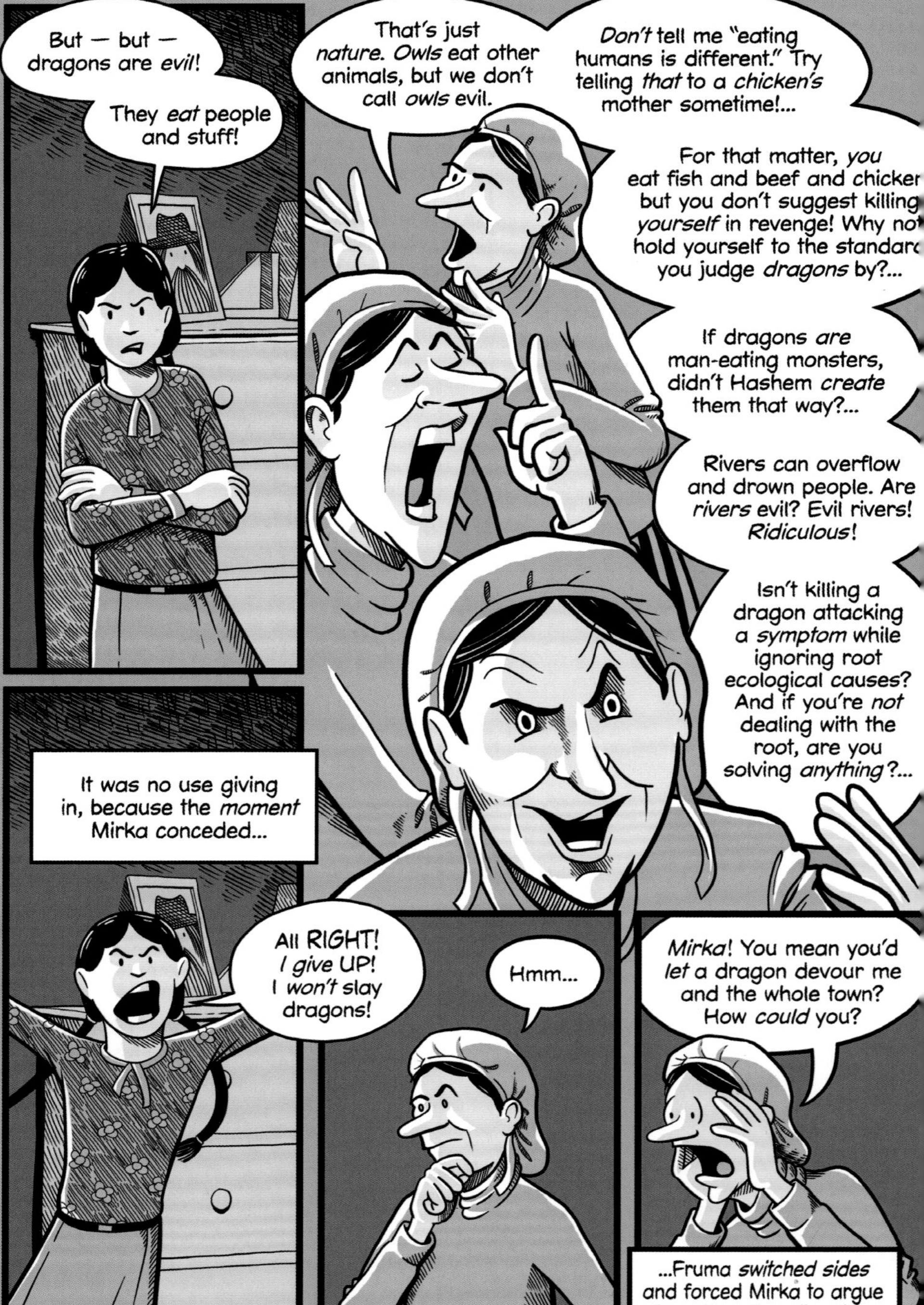
But — but — dragons are *evil*!
They *eat* people and stuff!
That's just *nature*. *Owls* eat other animals, but we don't call *owls* evil.
Don't tell me "eating humans is different." Try telling *that* to a *chicken's* mother sometime!...
For that matter, *you* eat fish and beef and chicke but you don't suggest killing *yourself* in revenge! Why no hold yourself to the standar you judge *dragons* by?...
If dragons *are* man-eating monsters, didn't Hashem *create* them that way?...
Rivers can overflow and drown people. Are *rivers* evil? Evil rivers! *Ridiculous*!
Isn't killing a dragon attacking a *symptom* while ignoring root ecological causes? And if you're *not* dealing with the root, are you solving *anything*?...
It was no use giving in, because the *moment* Mirka conceded...
All RIGHT! *I give* UP! I *won't* slay dragons!
Hmm...
Mirka! You mean you'd *let* a dragon devour me and the whole town? How *could* you?
...Fruma *switched sides* and forced Mirka to argue from the other direction.

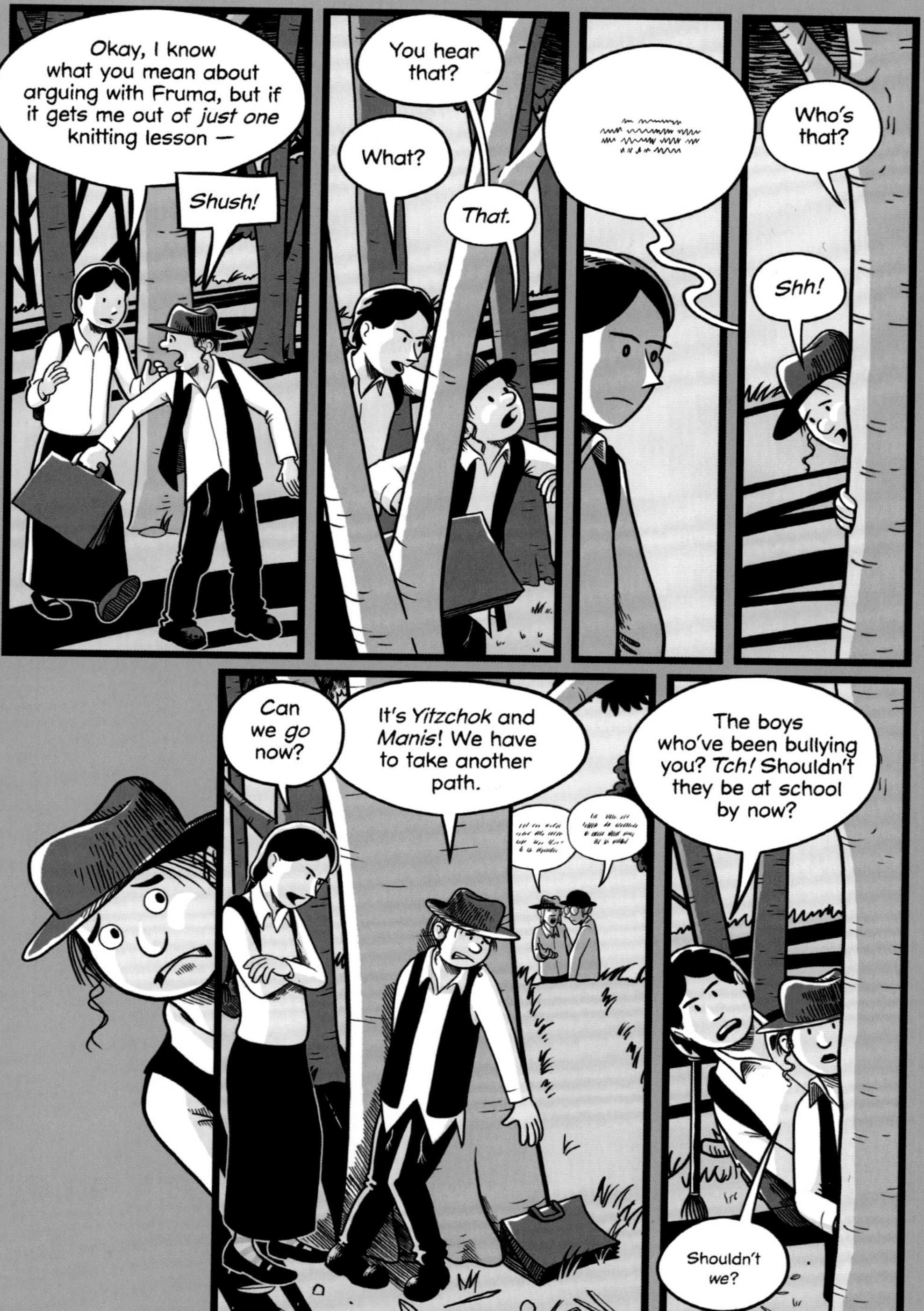

Okay, I know what you mean about arguing with Fruma, but if it gets me out of *just one* knitting lesson —
Shush!
You hear that?
What?
That.
Who's that?
Shh!
Can we *go* now?
It's *Yitzchok* and *Manis*! We have to take another path.
The boys who've been bullying you? *Tch!* Shouldn't they be at school by now?
Shouldn't we?

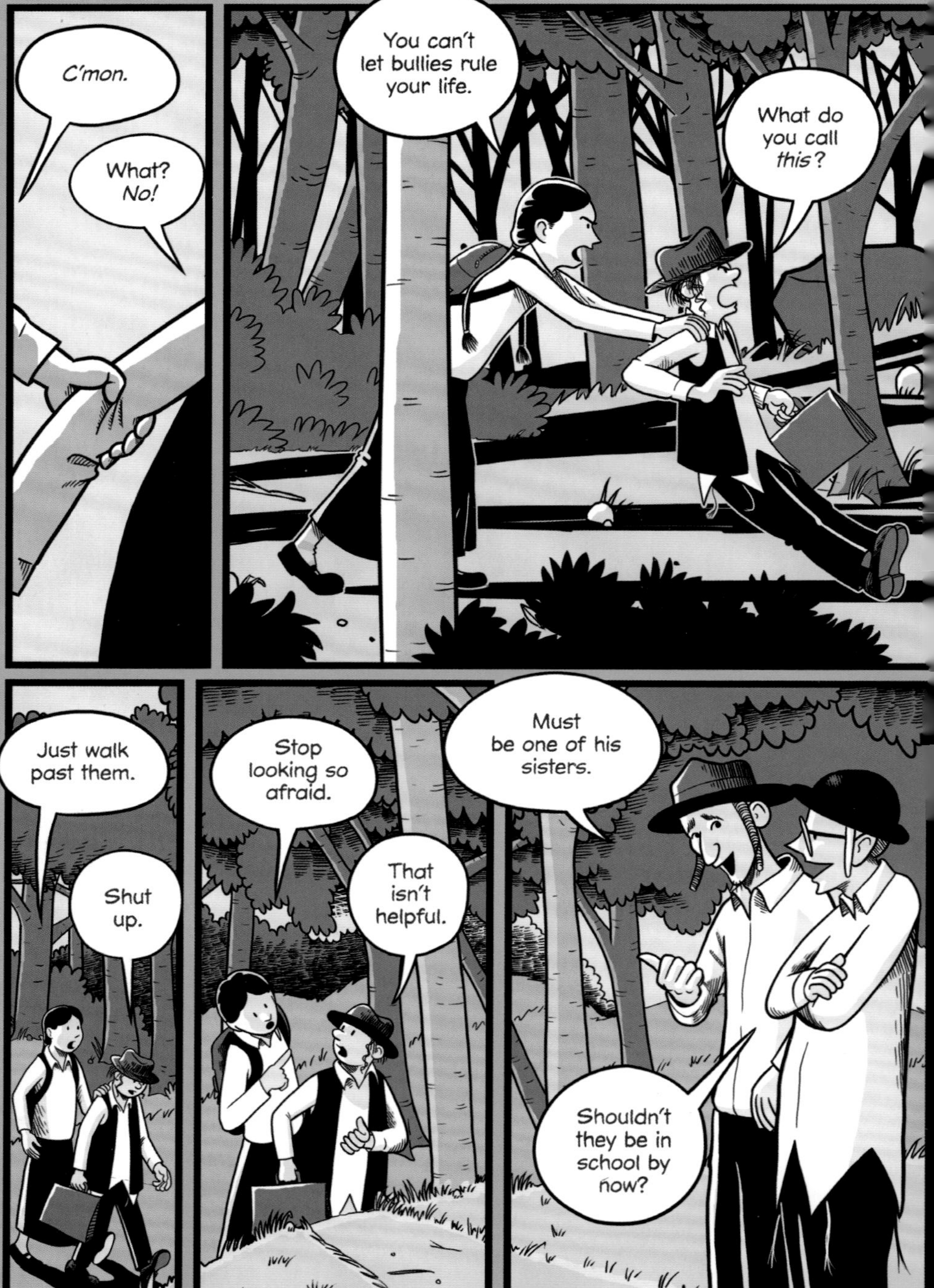
C'mon.
What? No!
You can't let bullies rule your life.
What do you call *this*?
Just walk past them.
Shut up.
Stop looking so afraid.
That isn't helpful.
Must be one of his sisters.
Shouldn't they be in school by now?

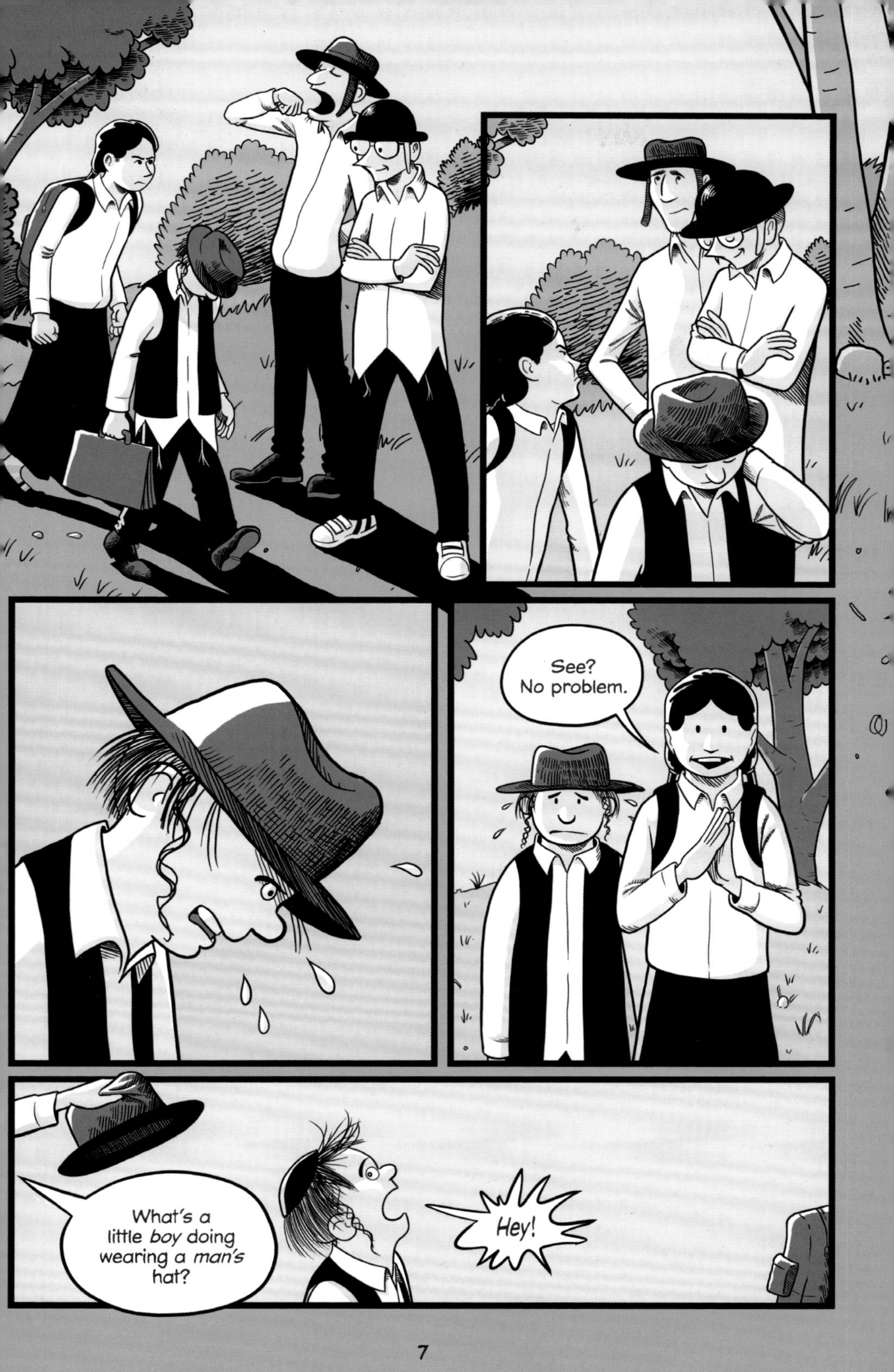
See?
No problem.
What's a little *boy* doing wearing a *man's* hat?
Hey!

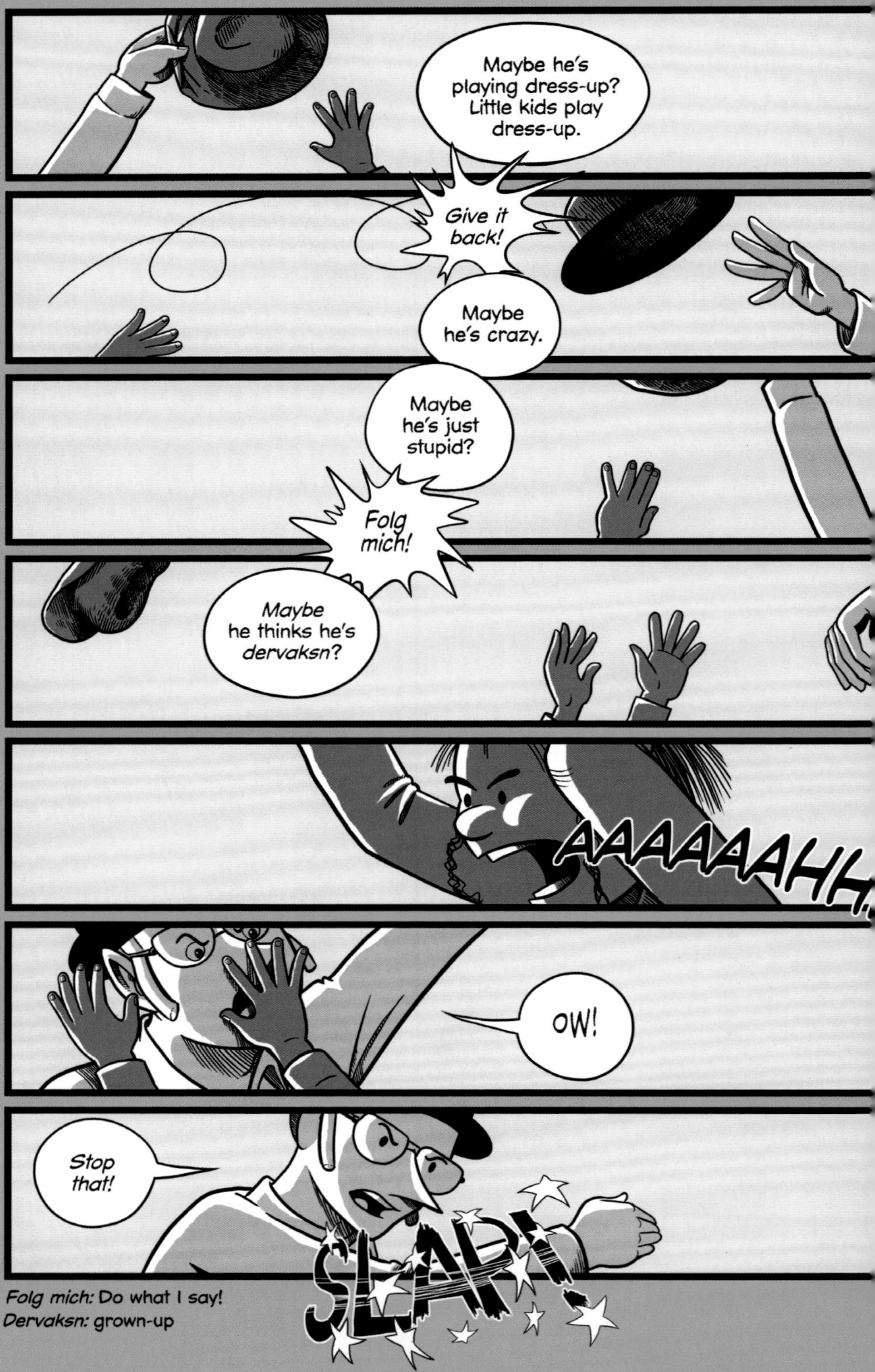
Maybe he's playing dress-up? Little kids play dress-up.
Give it back!
Maybe he's crazy.
Maybe he's just stupid?
Folg mich!
Maybe he thinks he's *dervaksn*?
AAAAAAHH
OW!
Stop that!
SLAP!

Folg mich: Do what I say!
Dervaksn: grown-up

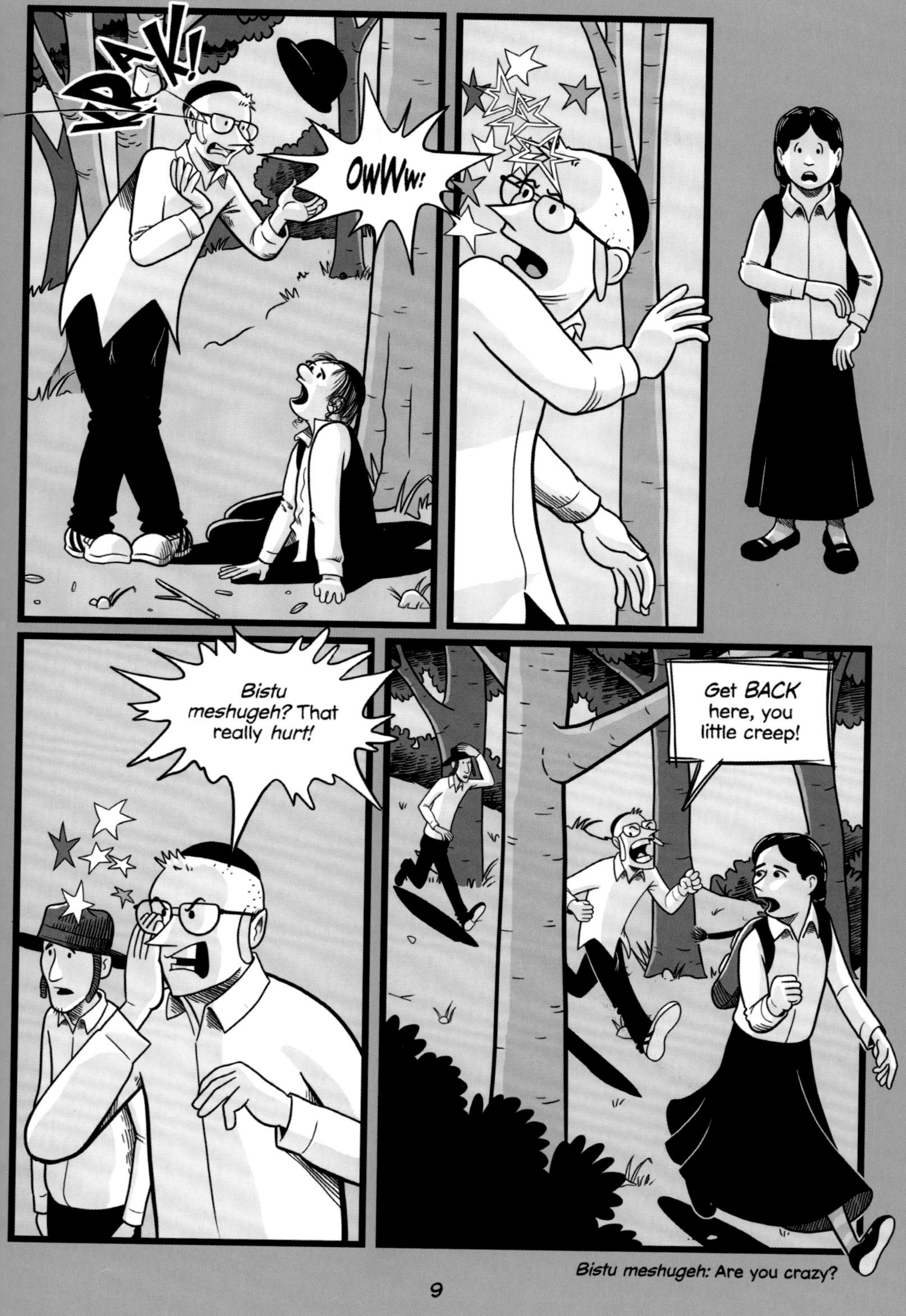
KRAK!
OWWw!
Bistu meshugeh? That really hurt!
Get BACK here, you little creep!

Bistu meshugeh: Are you crazy?

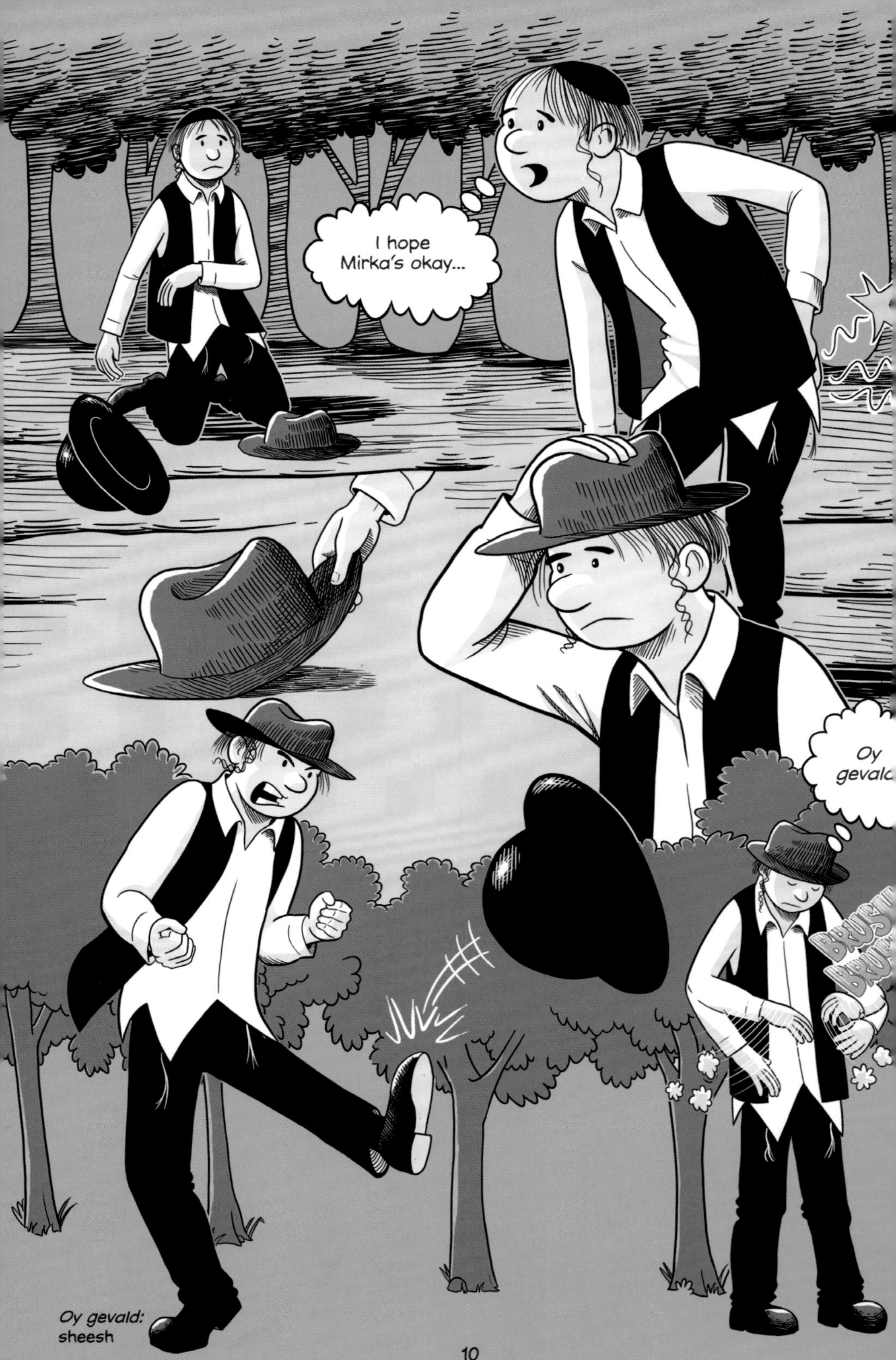
I hope Mirka's okay...
Oy gevald

Oy gevald: sheesh

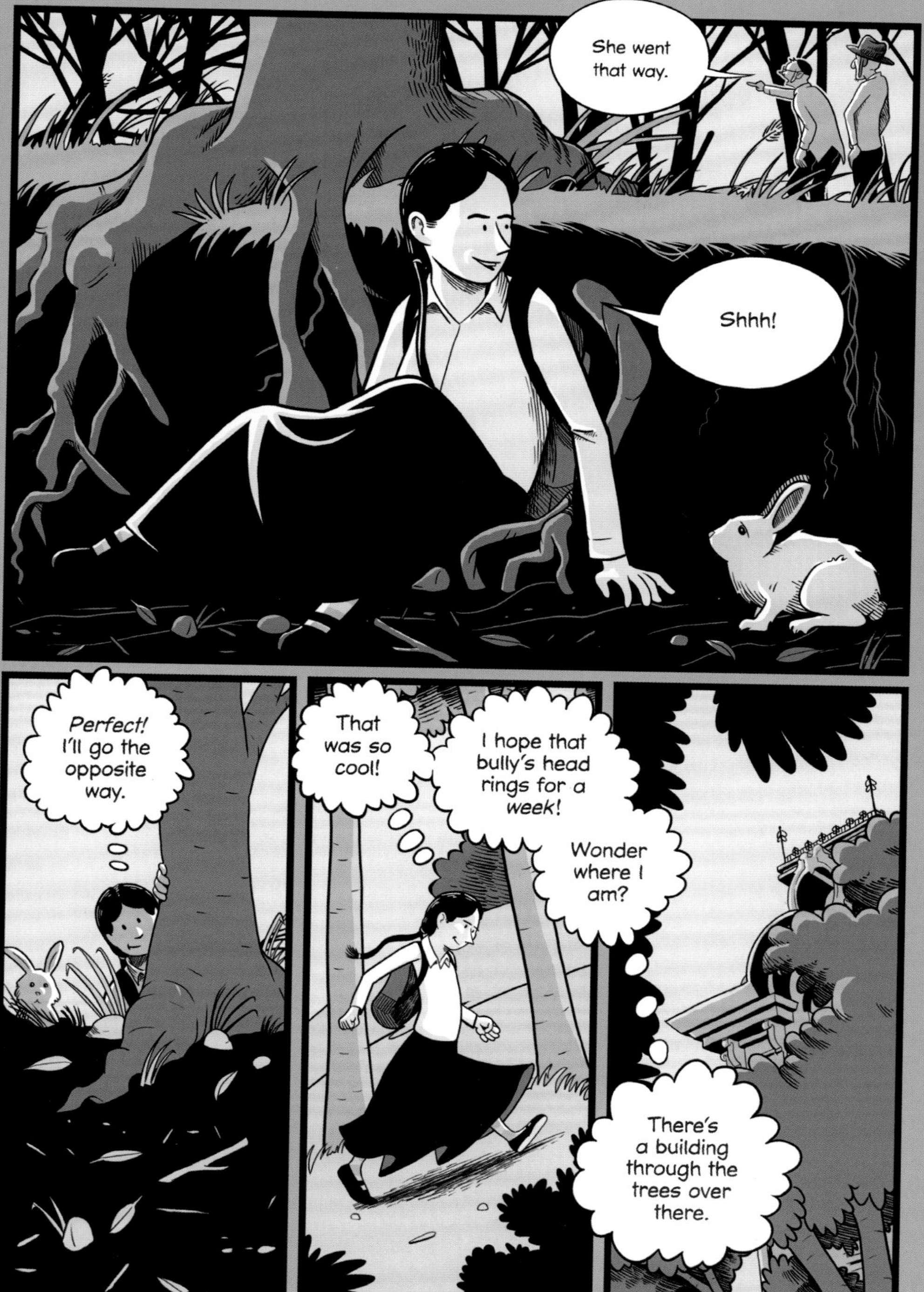
She went that way.
Shhh!
Perfect! I'll go the opposite way.
That was so cool!
I hope that bully's head rings for a *week*!
Wonder where I am?
There's a building through the trees over there.

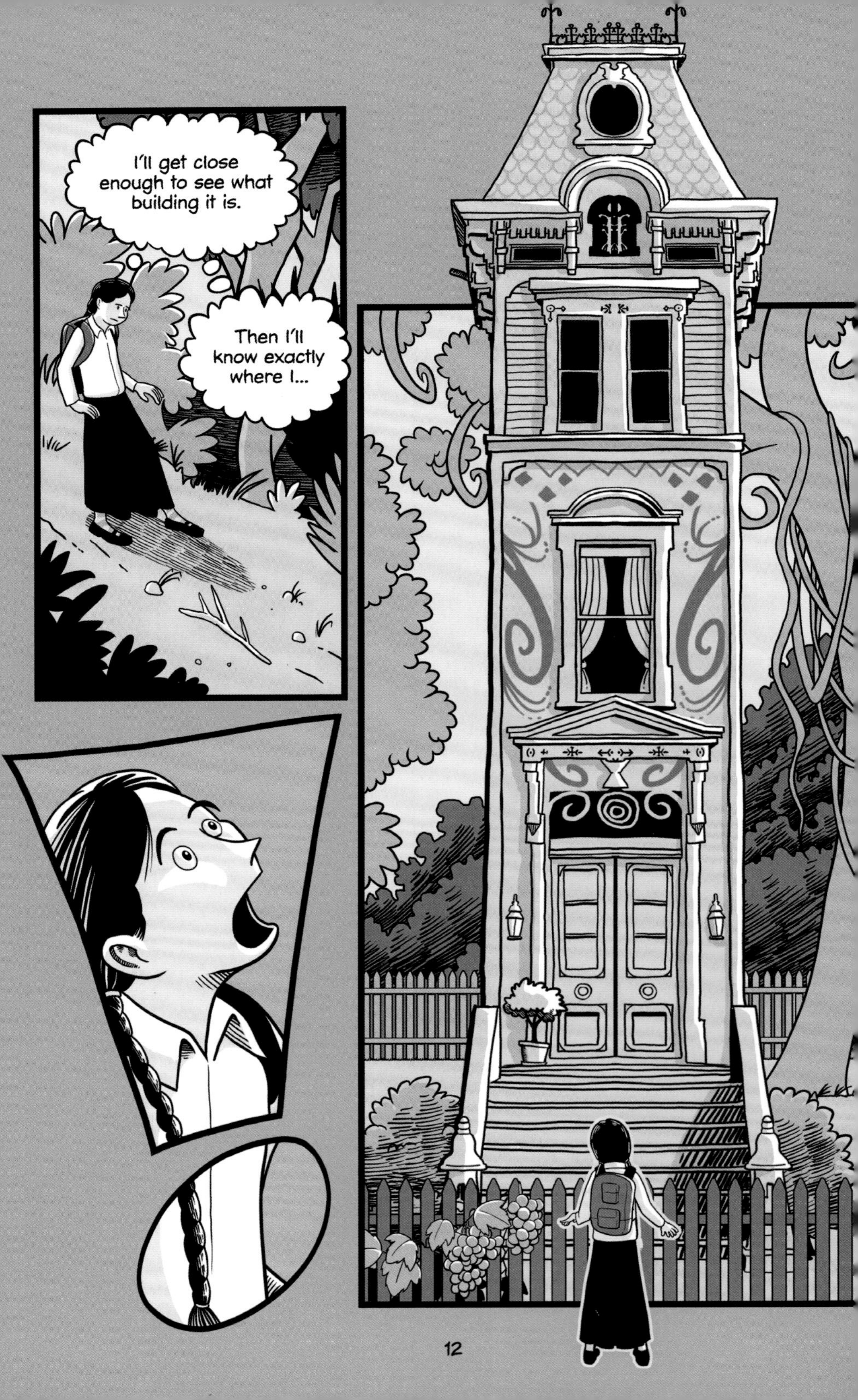
I'll get close enough to see what building it is.
Then I'll know exactly where I...

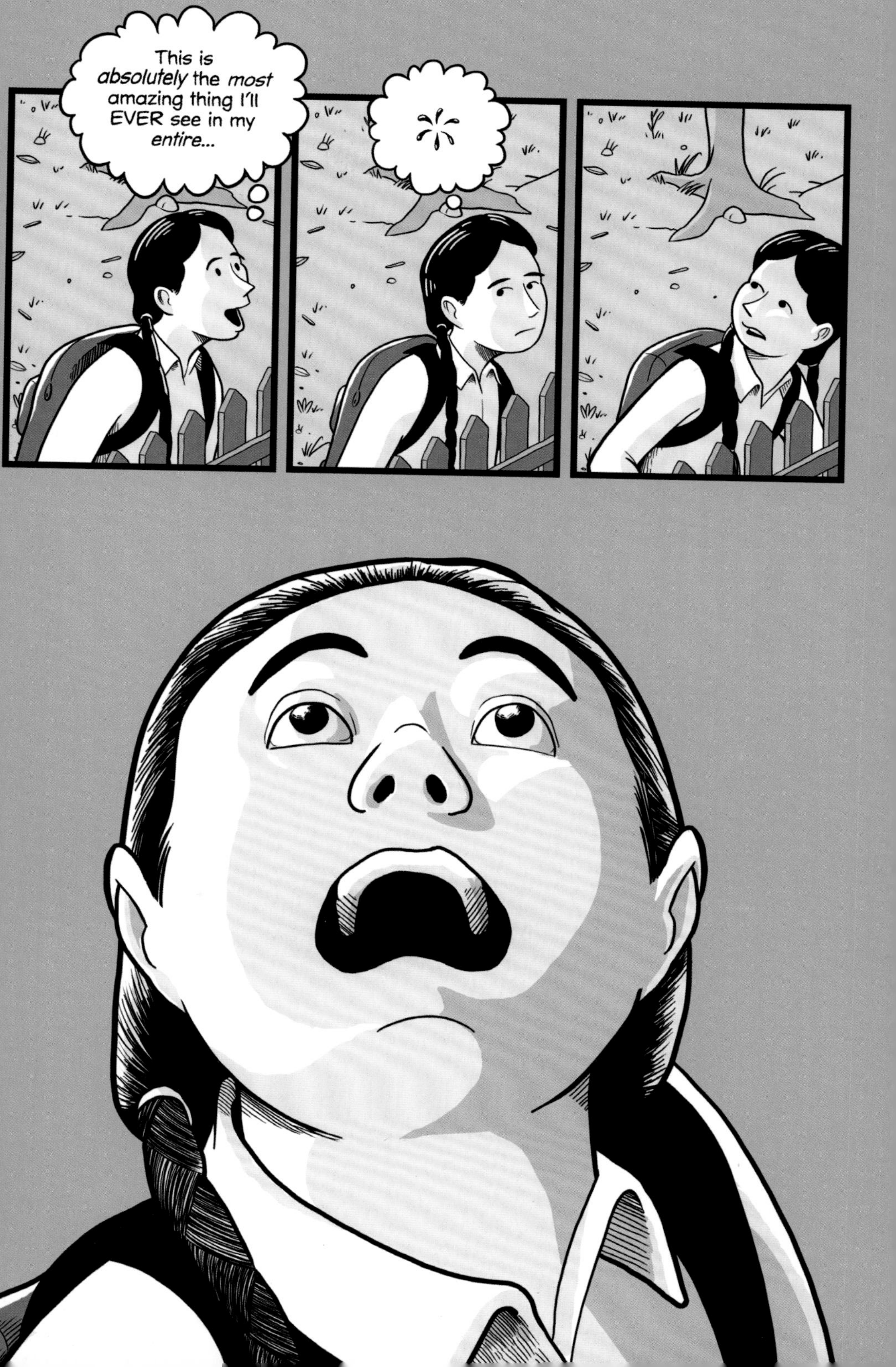
This is *absolutely* the *most* amazing thing I'll EVER see in my *entire*...

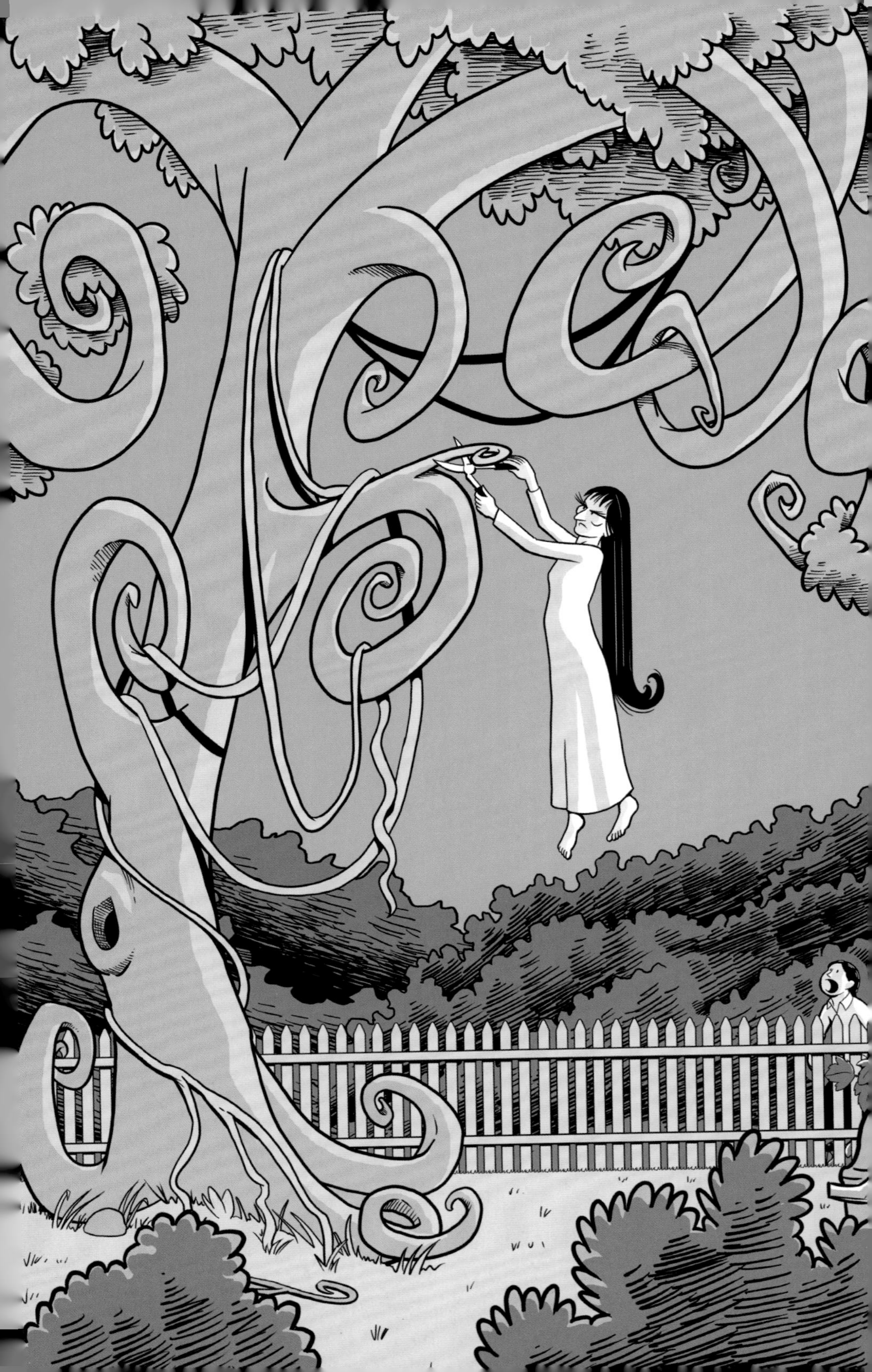

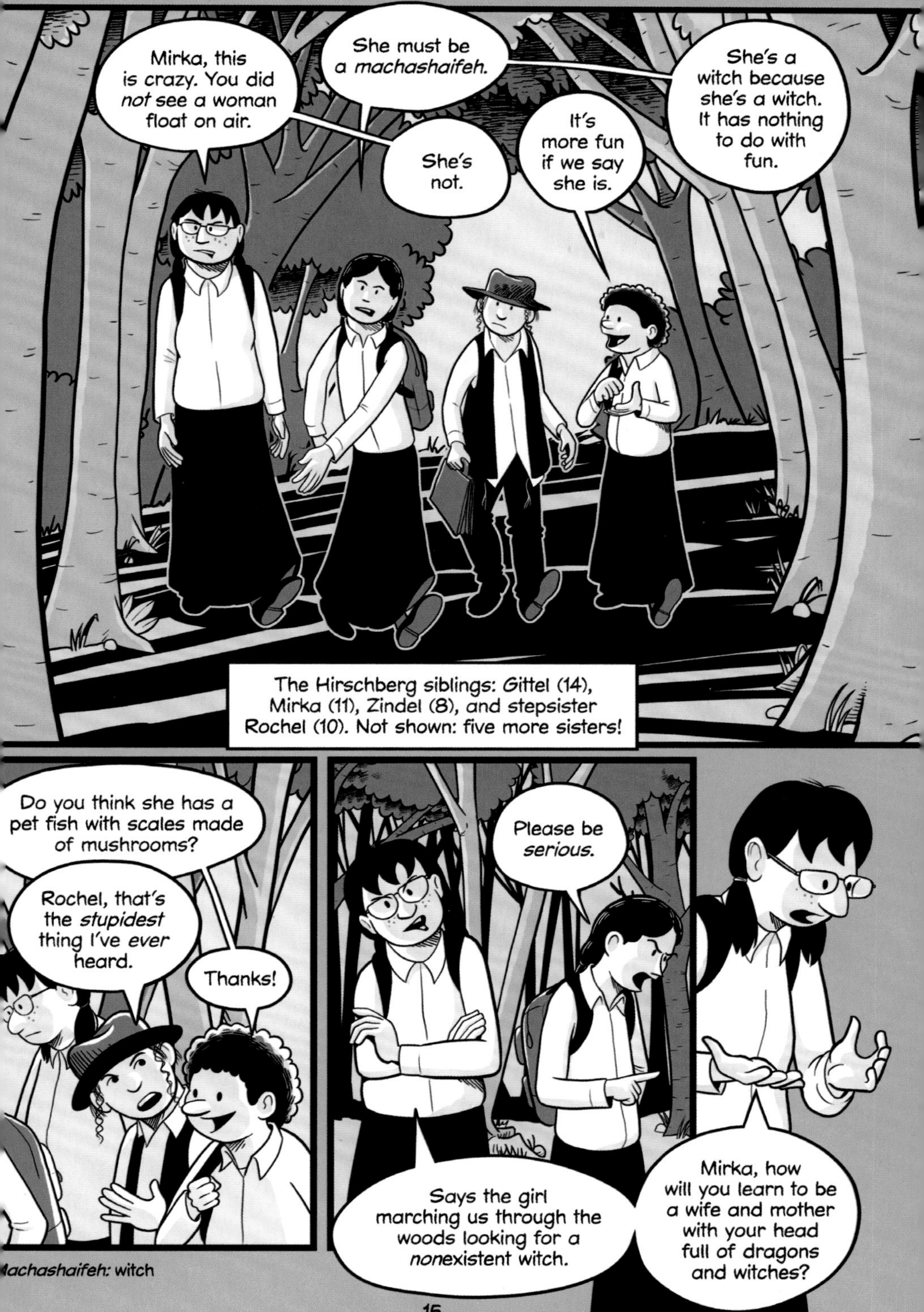

Mirka, this is crazy. You did *not* see a woman float on air.
She must be a *machashaifeh.*
She's not.
It's more fun if we say she is.
She's a witch because she's a witch. It has nothing to do with fun.
The Hirschberg siblings: *Gittel* (14), Mirka (11), Zindel (8), and stepsister Rochel (10). Not shown: five more sisters!
Do you think she has a pet fish with scales made of mushrooms?
Rochel, that's the *stupidest* thing I've *ever* heard.
Thanks!
Please be *serious.*
Says the girl marching us through the woods looking for a *non*existent witch.
Mirka, how will you learn to be a wife and mother with your head full of dragons and witches?

Machashaifeh: witch

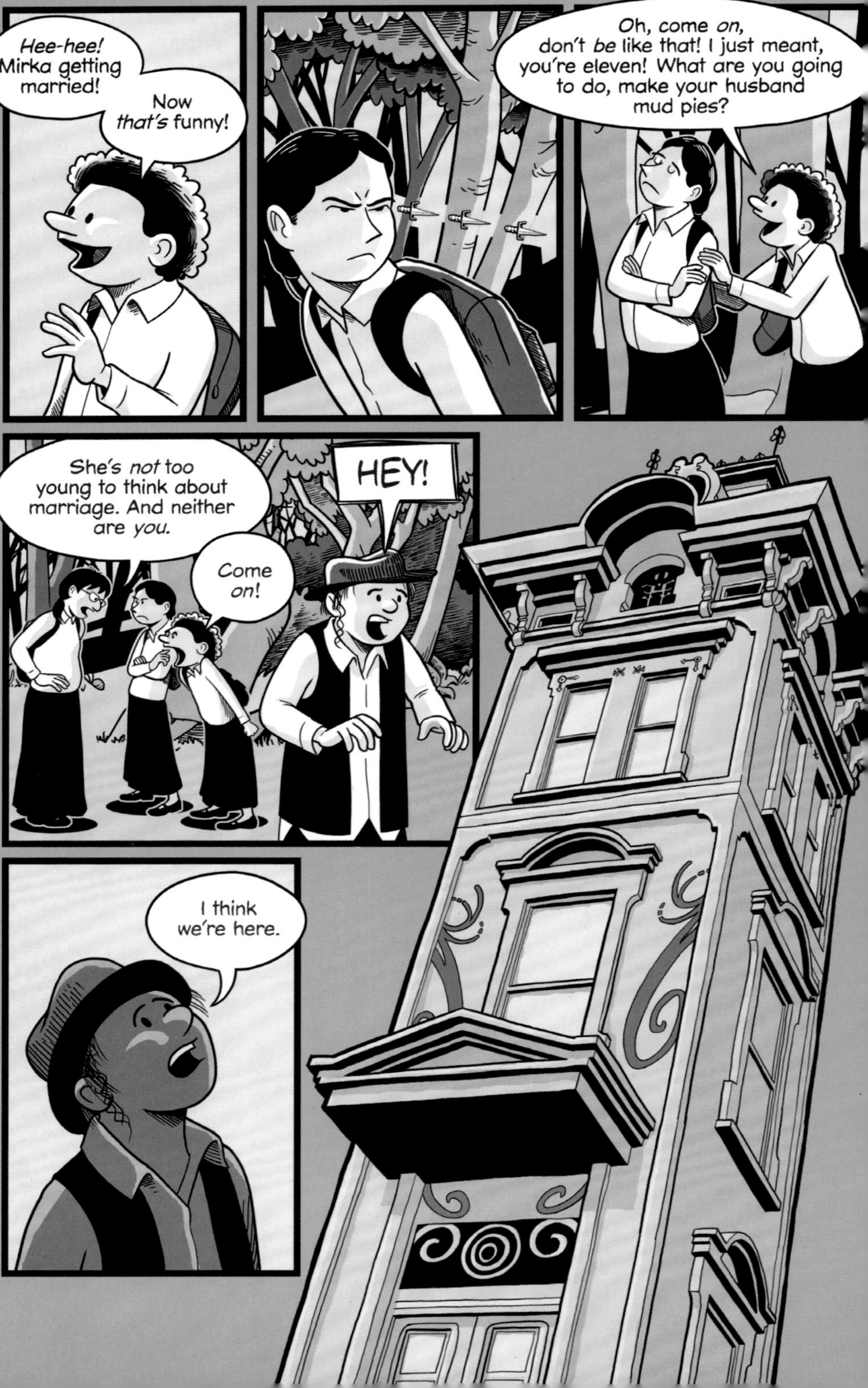
Hee-hee! Mirka getting married!
Now that's funny!
Oh, come on, don't be like that! I just meant, you're eleven! What are you going to do, make your husband mud pies?
She's not too young to think about marriage. And neither are you.
Come on!
HEY!
I think we're here.

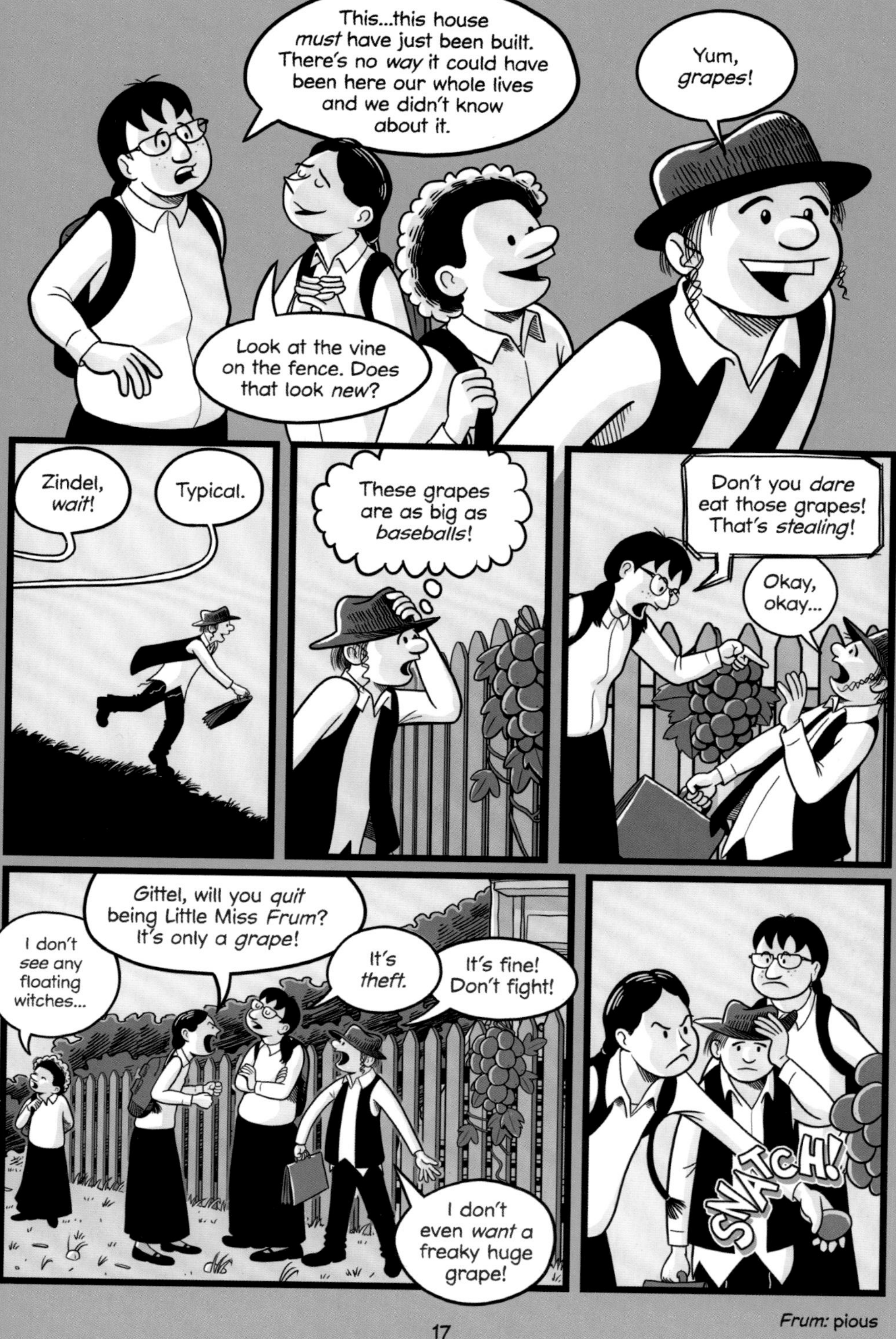
This...this house must have just been built. There's no way it could have been here our whole lives and we didn't know about it.
Yum, grapes!
Look at the vine on the fence. Does that look new?
Zindel, wait!
Typical.
These grapes are as big as baseballs!
Don't you dare eat those grapes! That's stealing!
Okay, okay...
Gittel, will you quit being Little Miss Frum? It's only a grape!
I don't see any floating witches...
It's theft.
It's fine! Don't fight!
I don't even want a freaky huge grape!
SNATCH!

Frum: pious

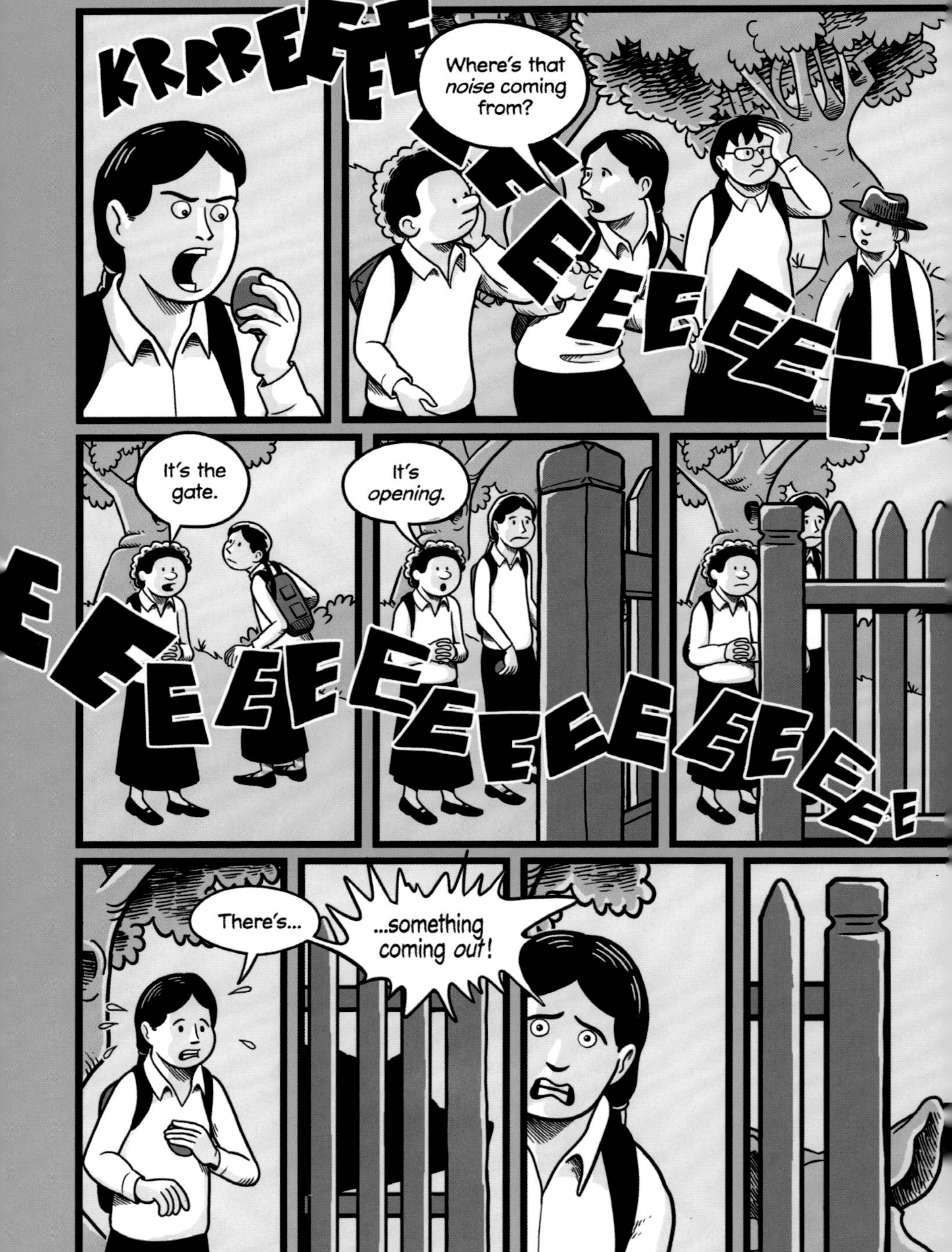
KRRREEEEE
Where's that *noise* coming from?
EEEEEEEE
It's the gate.
It's *opening*.
EEEEEEEEEEEEEEEEE
There's...
...something coming *out*!

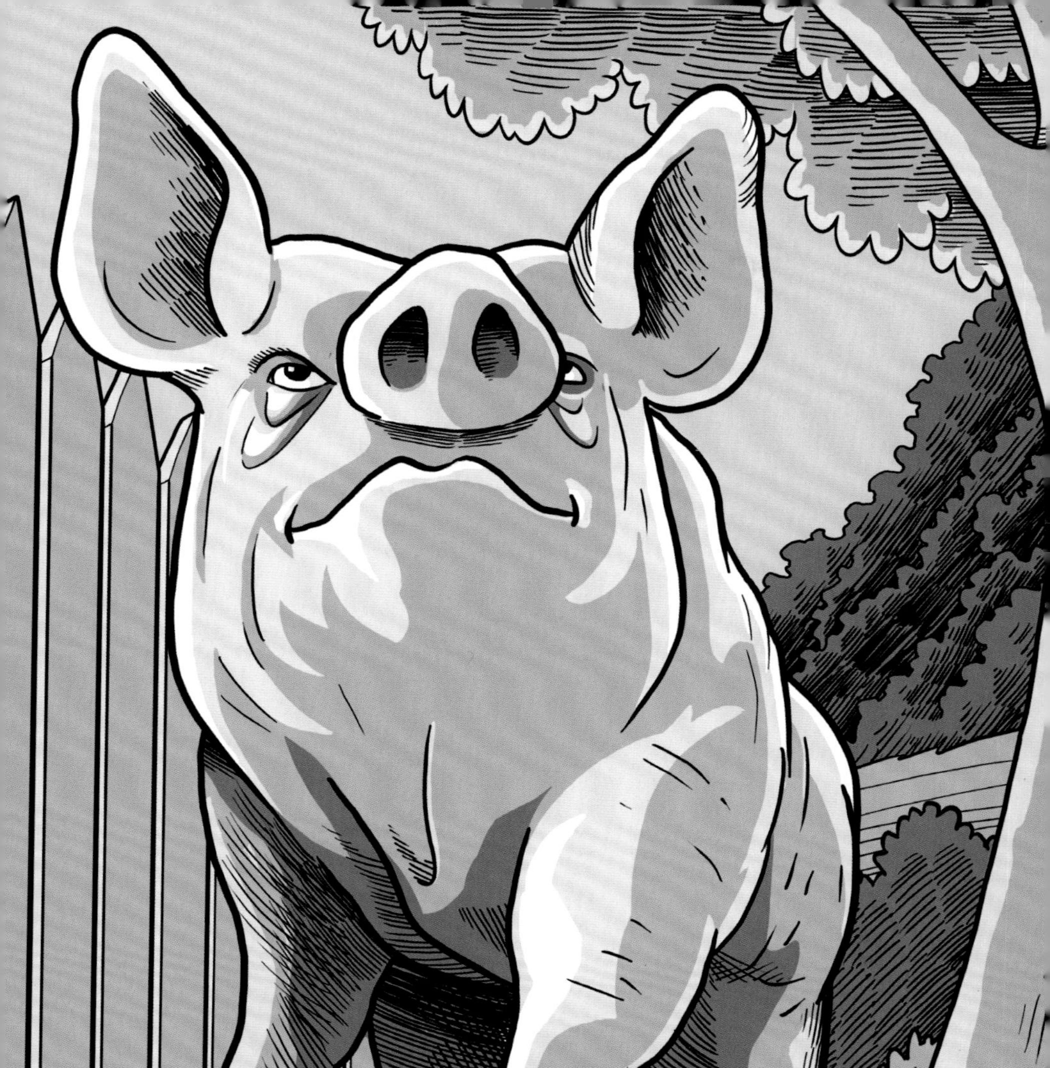

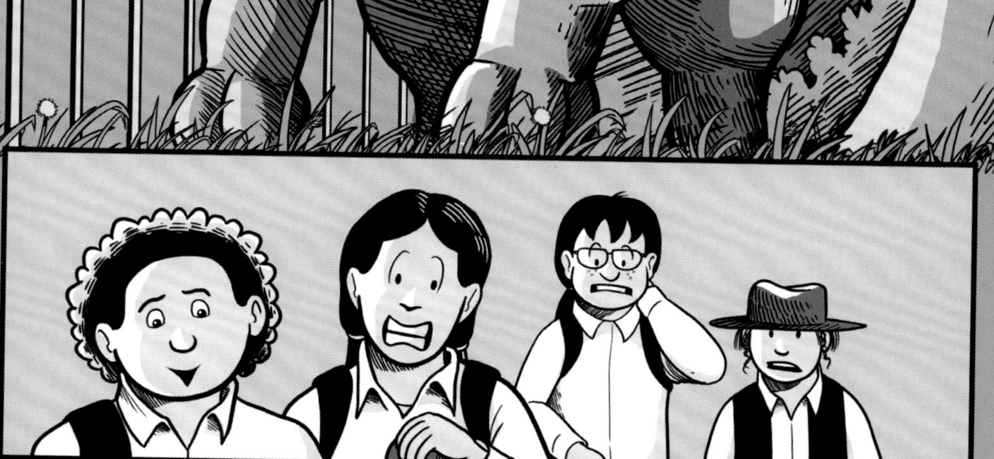

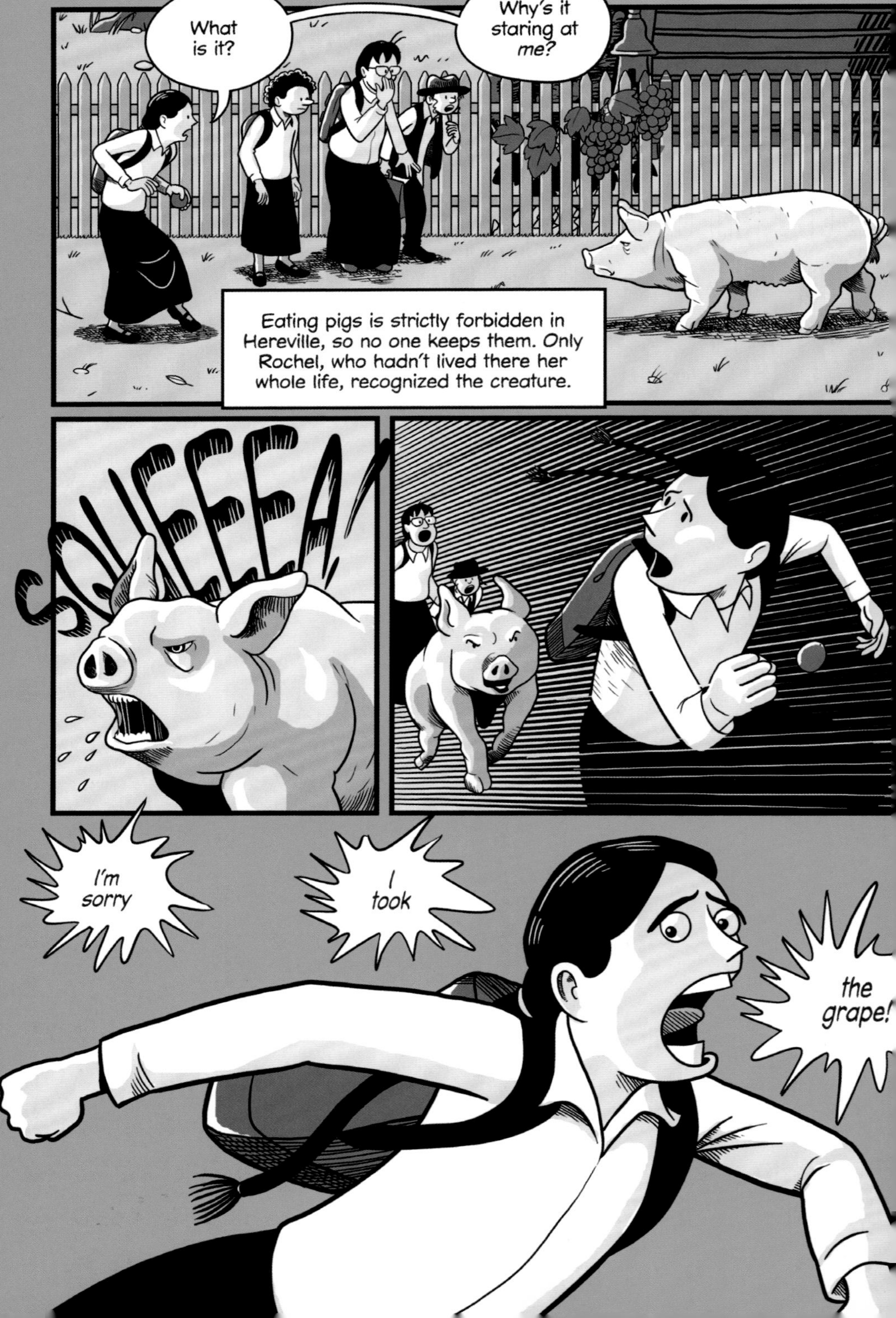
What is it?
Why's it staring at *me?*
Eating pigs is strictly forbidden in Hereville, so no one keeps them. Only Rochel, who hadn't lived there her whole life, recognized the creature.
SQUEEEA!
I'm sorry
I took
the grape!

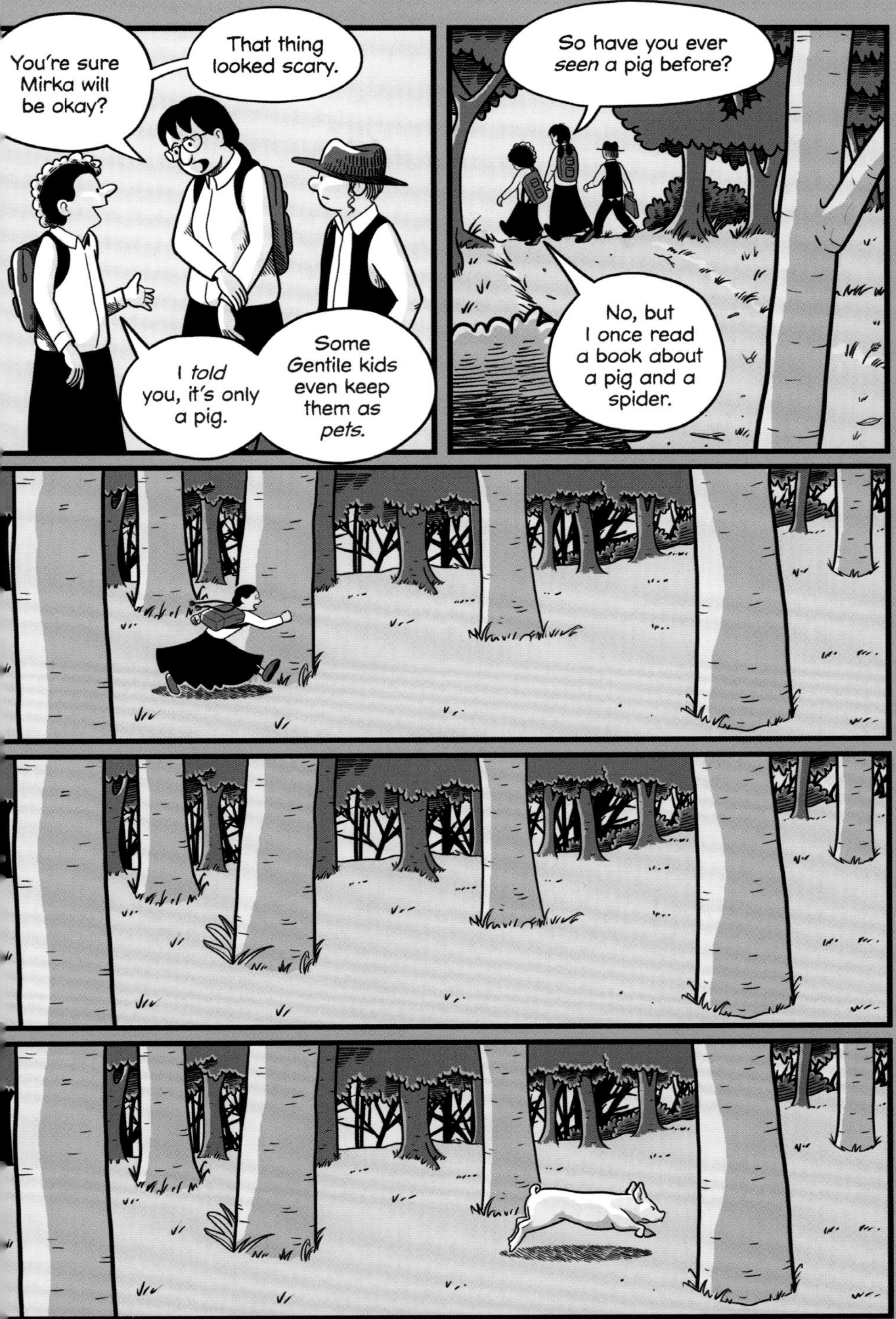
You're sure Mirka will be okay?
That thing looked scary.
I *told* you, it's only a pig.
Some Gentile kids even keep them as *pets.*
So have you ever *seen* a pig before?
No, but I once read a book about a pig and a spider.

Gentile: non-Jewish

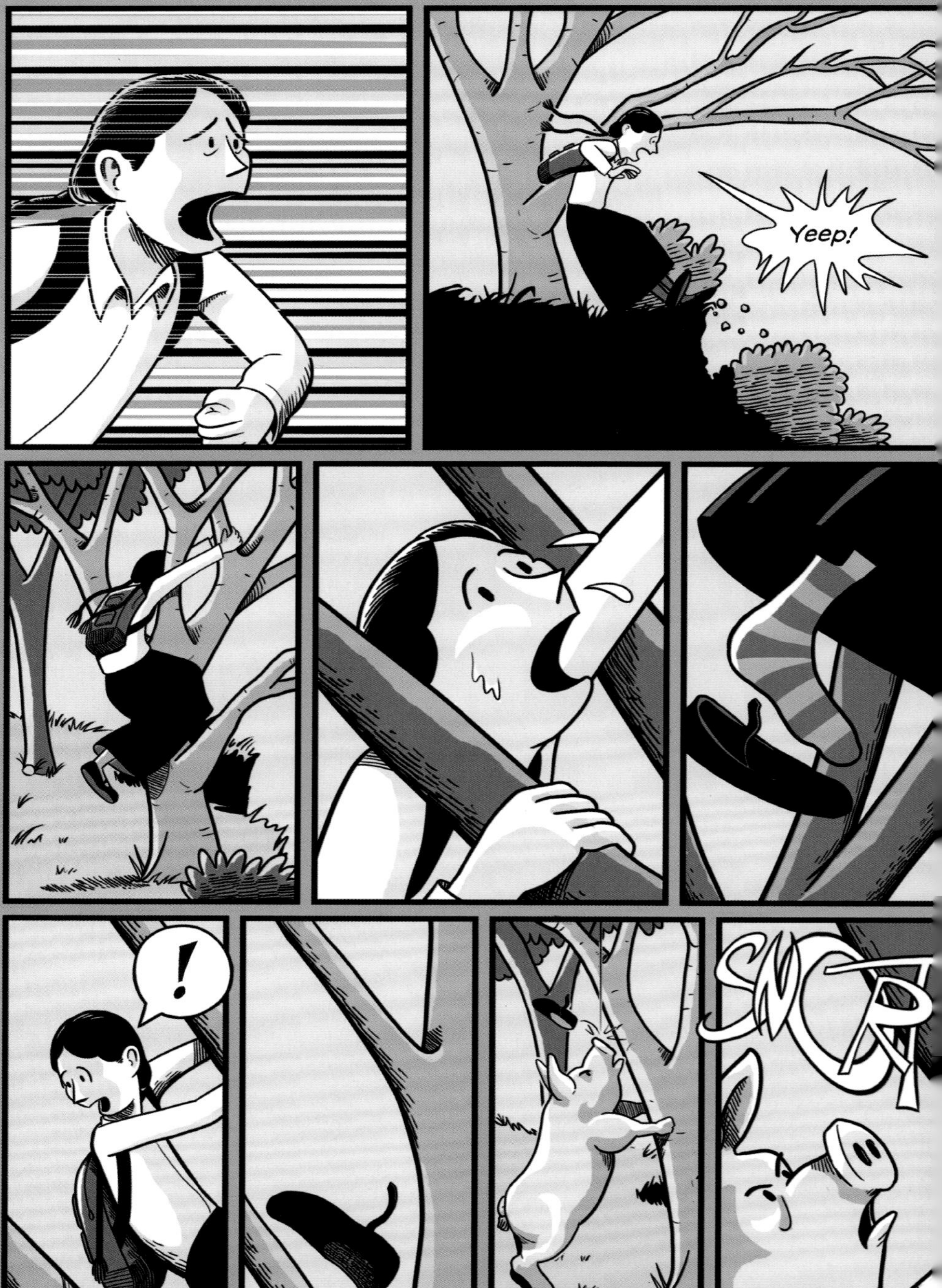
Yeep!
!
SNORT

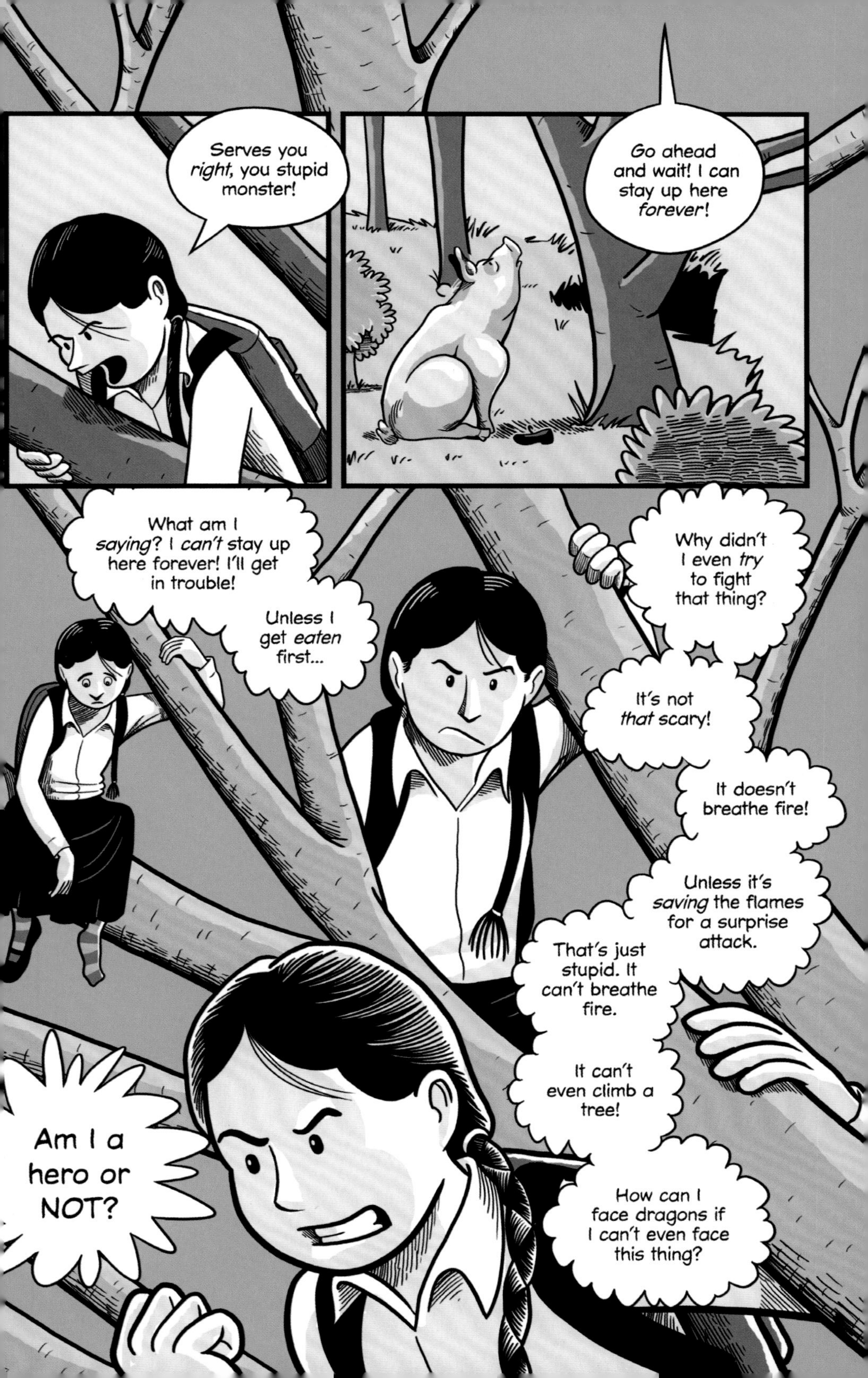
Serves you *right*, you stupid monster!
Go ahead and wait! I can stay up here *forever*!
What am I *saying*? I *can't* stay up here forever! I'll get in trouble!
Unless I get *eaten* first...
Why didn't I even *try* to fight that thing?
It's not *that* scary!
It doesn't breathe fire!
Unless it's *saving* the flames for a surprise attack.
That's just stupid. It can't breathe fire.
It can't even climb a tree!
Am I a hero or NOT?
How can I face dragons if I can't even face this thing?

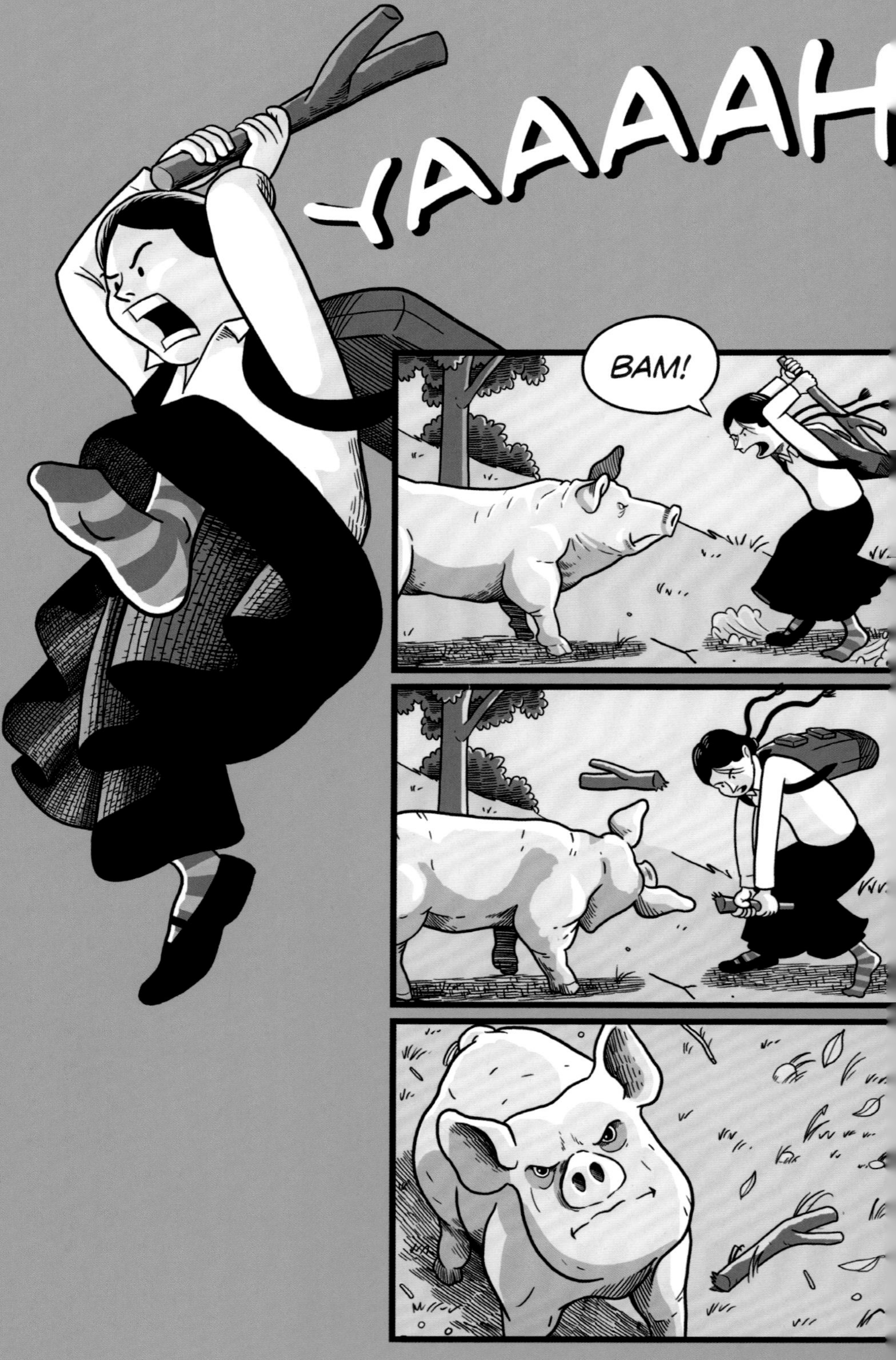
YAAAAAH
BAM!

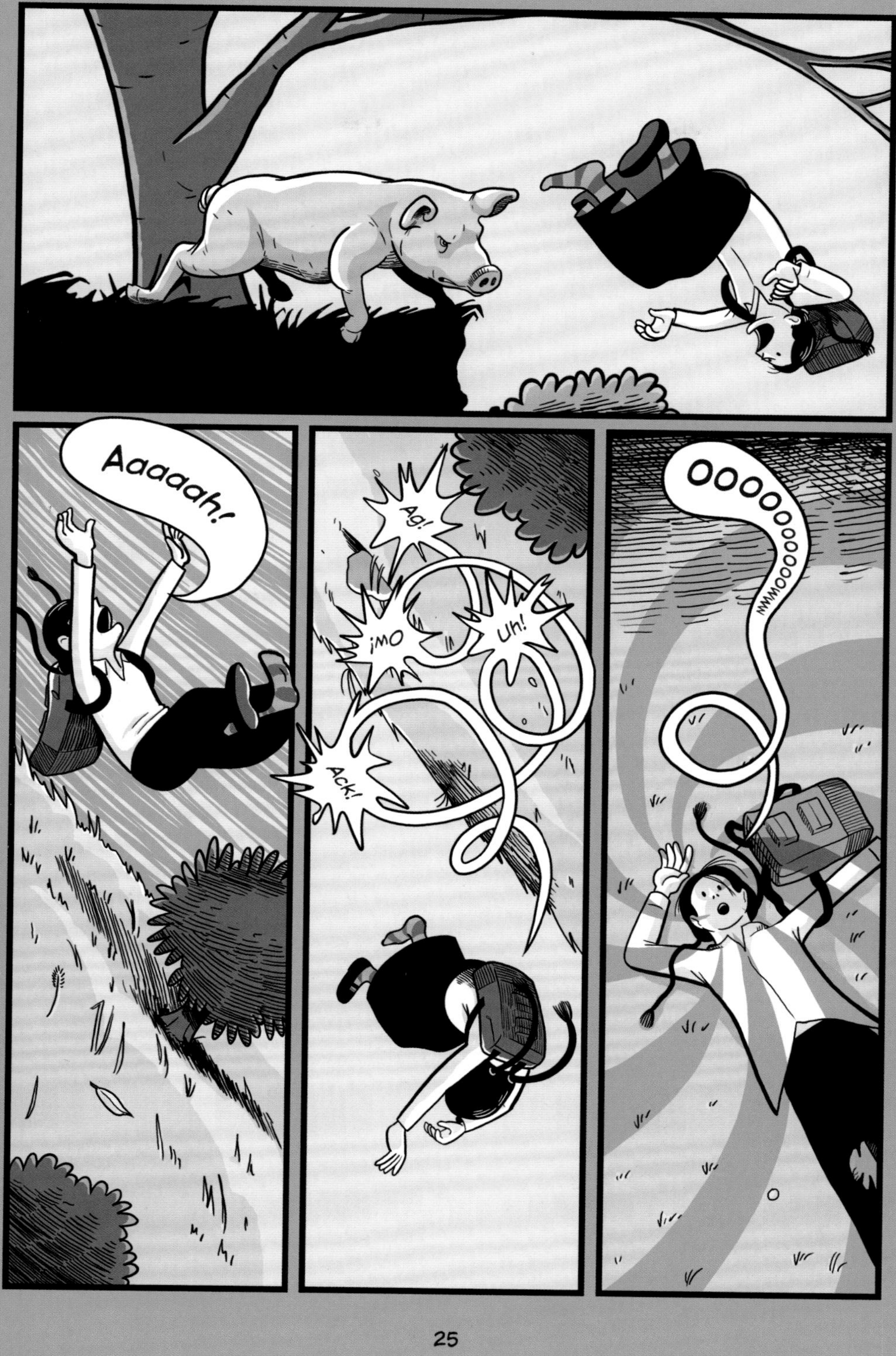
Aaaaaah!
Ag!
OW!
Uh!
Ack!
OOOOOOOOOOMMMM

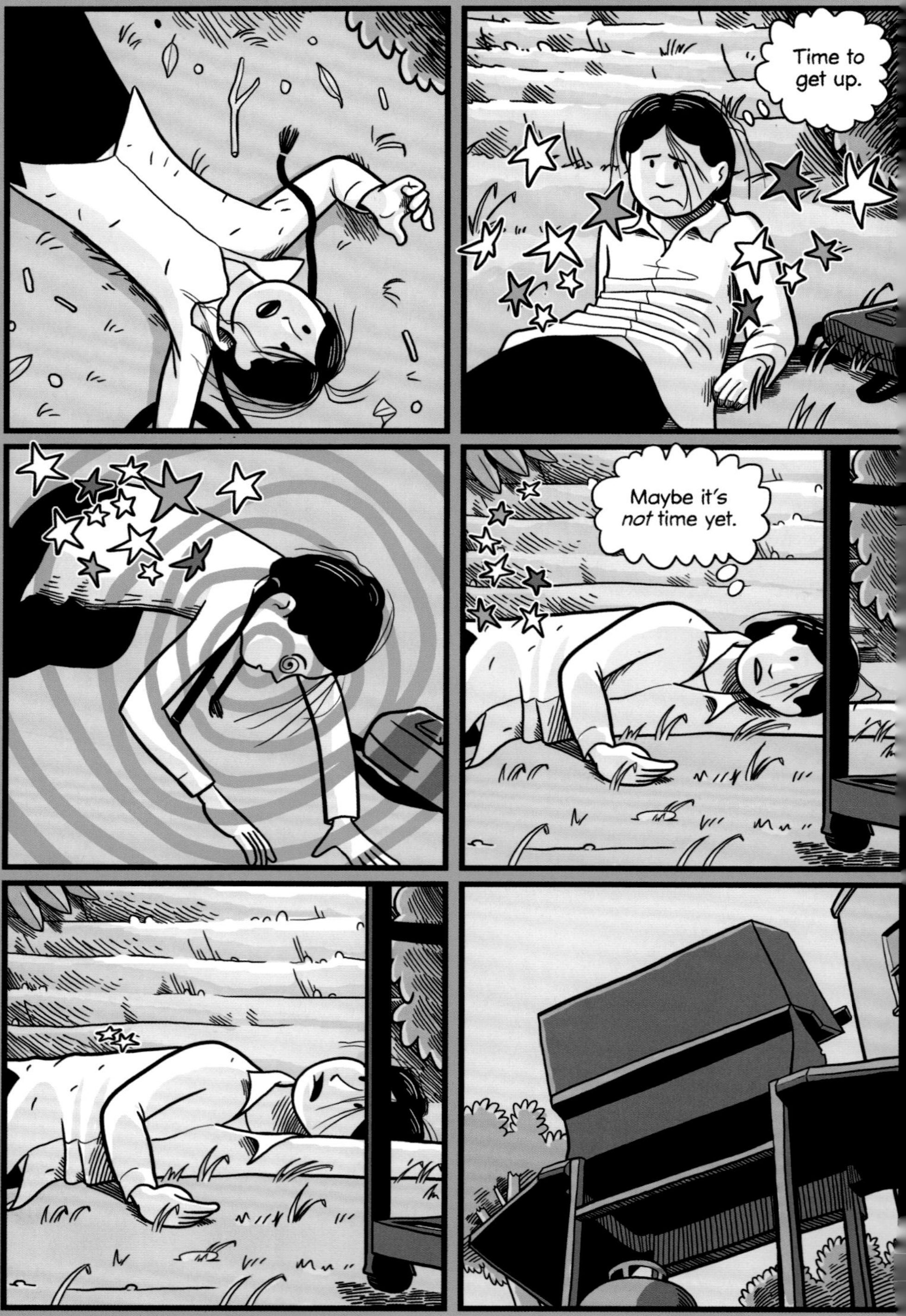
Time to get up.
Maybe it's *not* time yet.

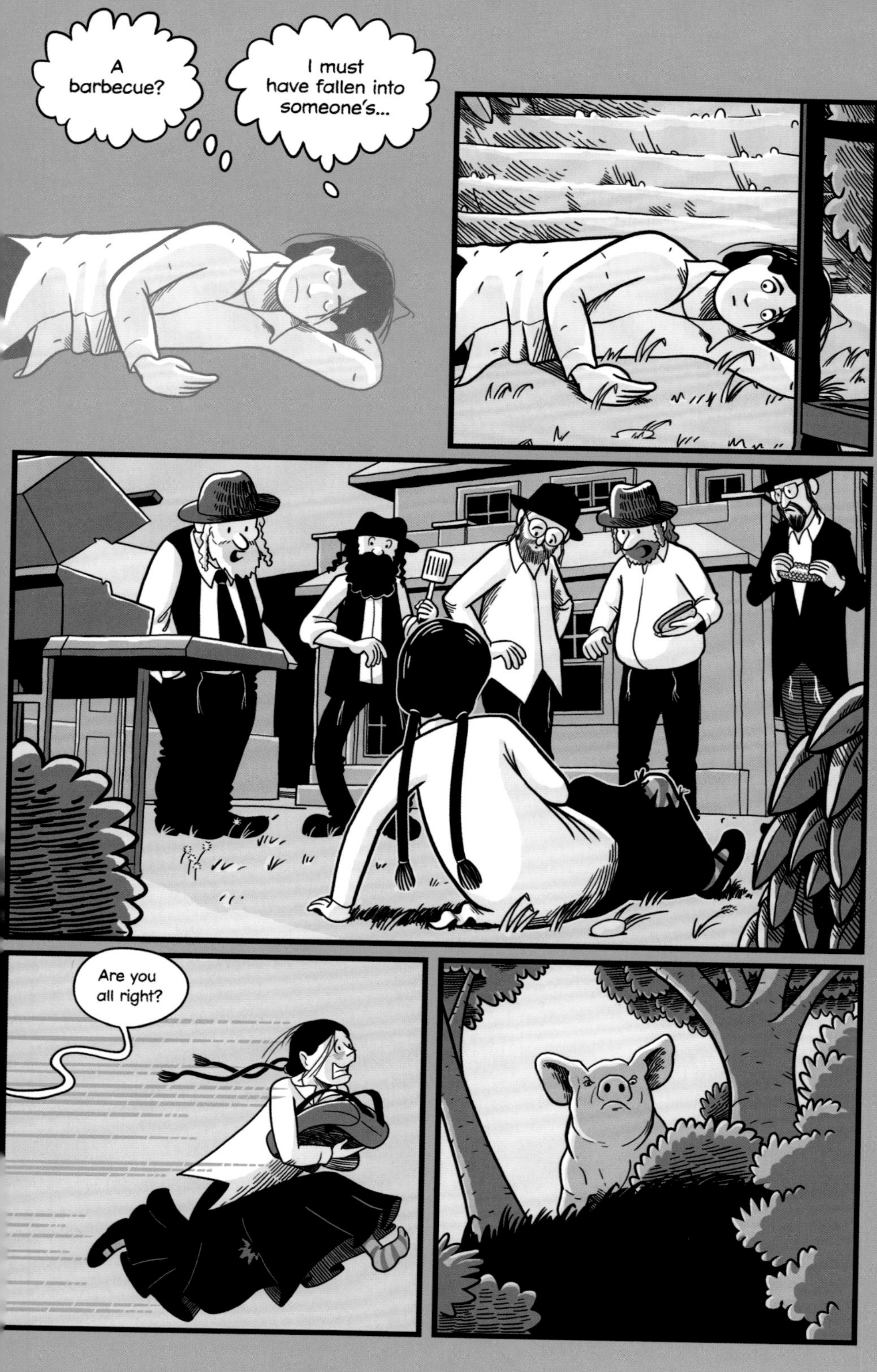
A barbecue?
I must have fallen into someone's...
Are you all right?

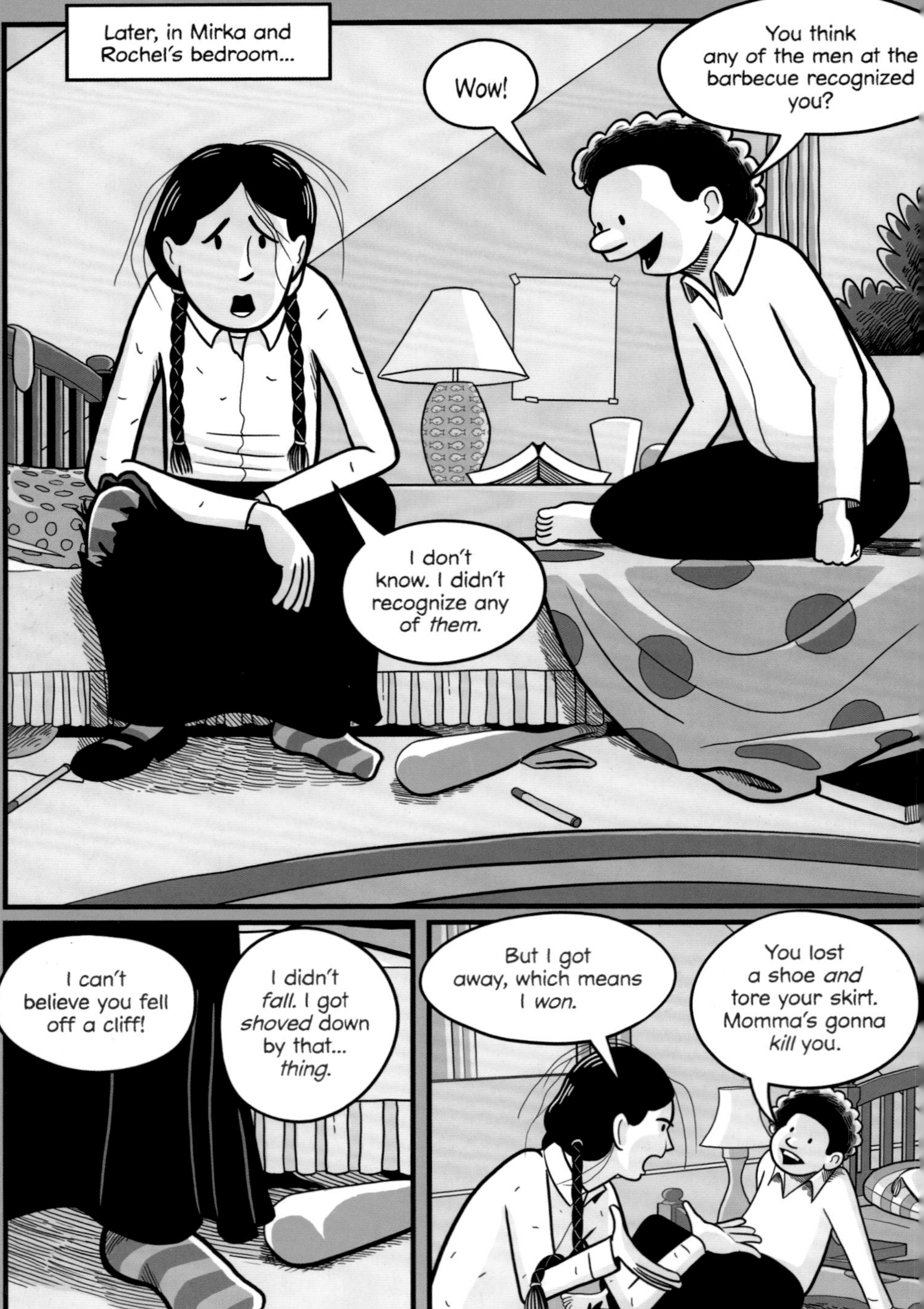

Later, in Mirka and Rochel's bedroom...
Wow!
You think any of the men at the barbecue recognized you?
I don't know. I didn't recognize any of *them.*
I can't believe you fell off a cliff!
I didn't *fall.* I got *shoved* down by that... *thing.*
But I got away, which means I *won.*
You lost a shoe *and* tore your skirt. Momma's gonna *kill* you.

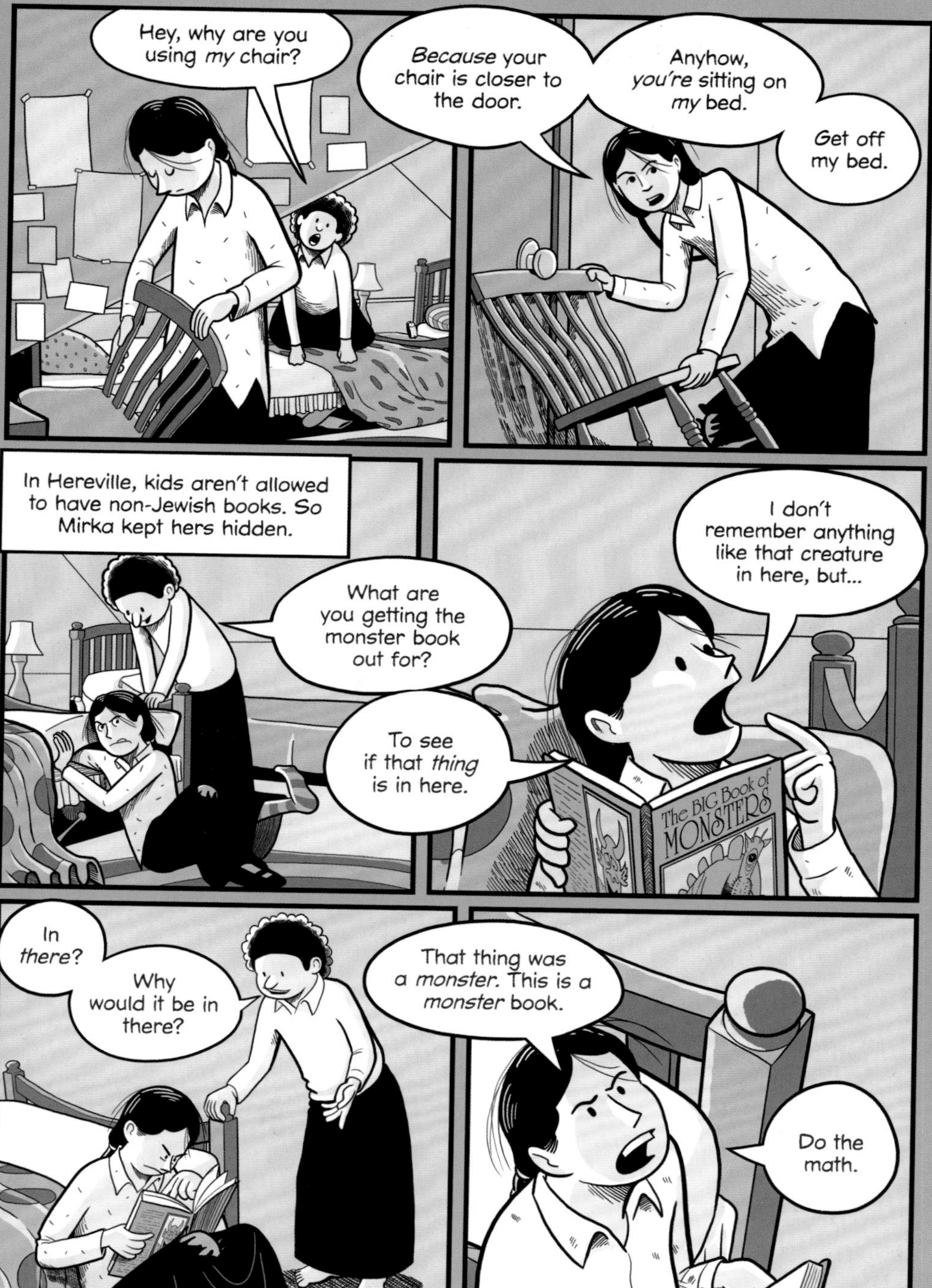
Hey, why are you using *my* chair?
Because your chair is closer to the door.
Anyhow, *you're* sitting on *my* bed.
Get off my bed.
In Hereville, kids aren't allowed to have non-Jewish books. So Mirka kept hers hidden.
What are you getting the monster book out for?
To see if that *thing* is in here.
I don't remember anything like that creature in here, but...
The BIG Book of MONSTERS
In *there*?
Why would it be in there?
That thing was a *monster*. This is a *monster* book.
Do the math.

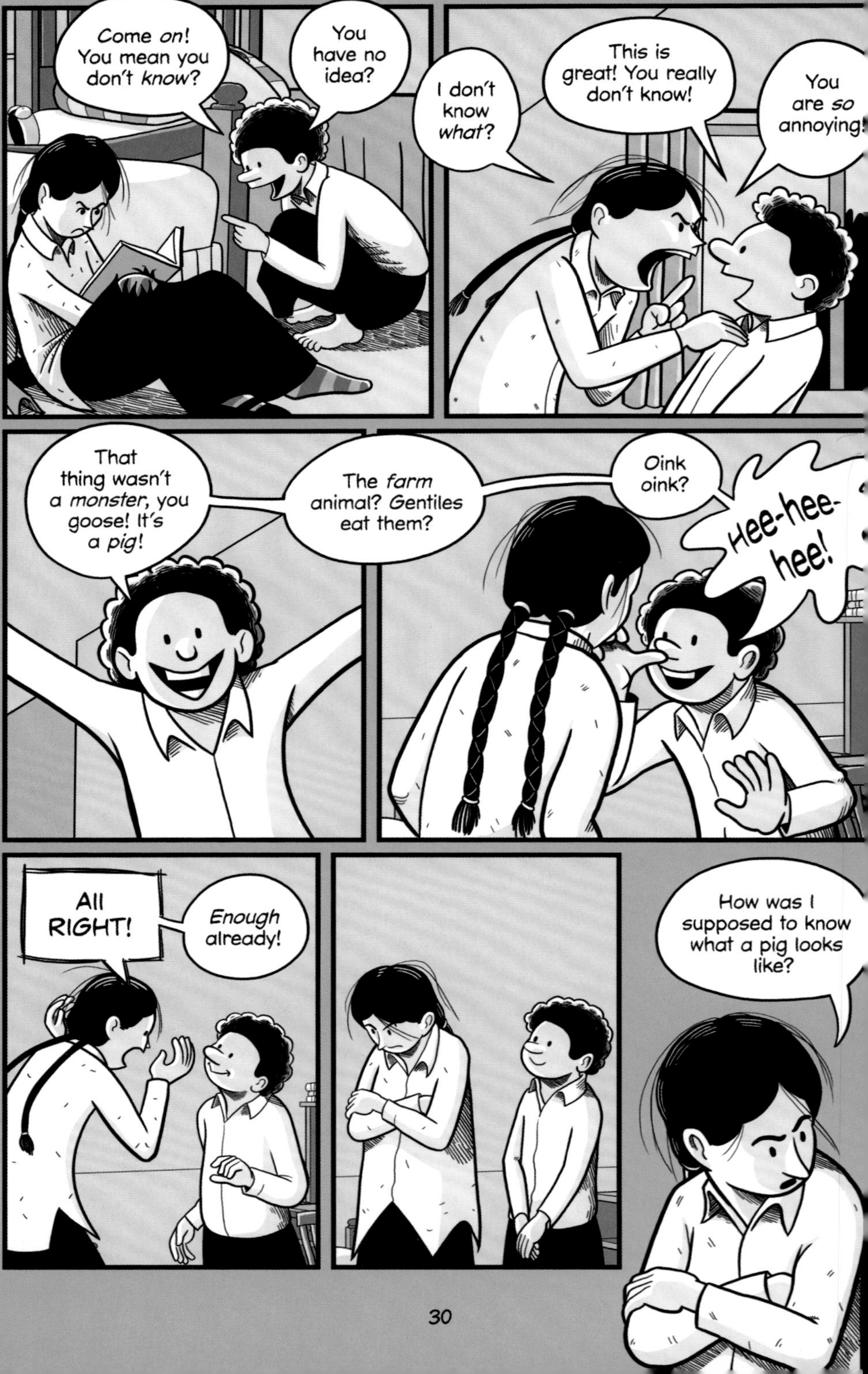
Come on! You mean you don't know?
You have no idea?
I don't know what?
This is great! You really don't know!
You are so annoying!
That thing wasn't a monster, you goose! It's a pig!
The farm animal? Gentiles eat them?
Oink oink?
Hee-hee-hee!
All RIGHT!
Enough already!
How was I supposed to know what a pig looks like?

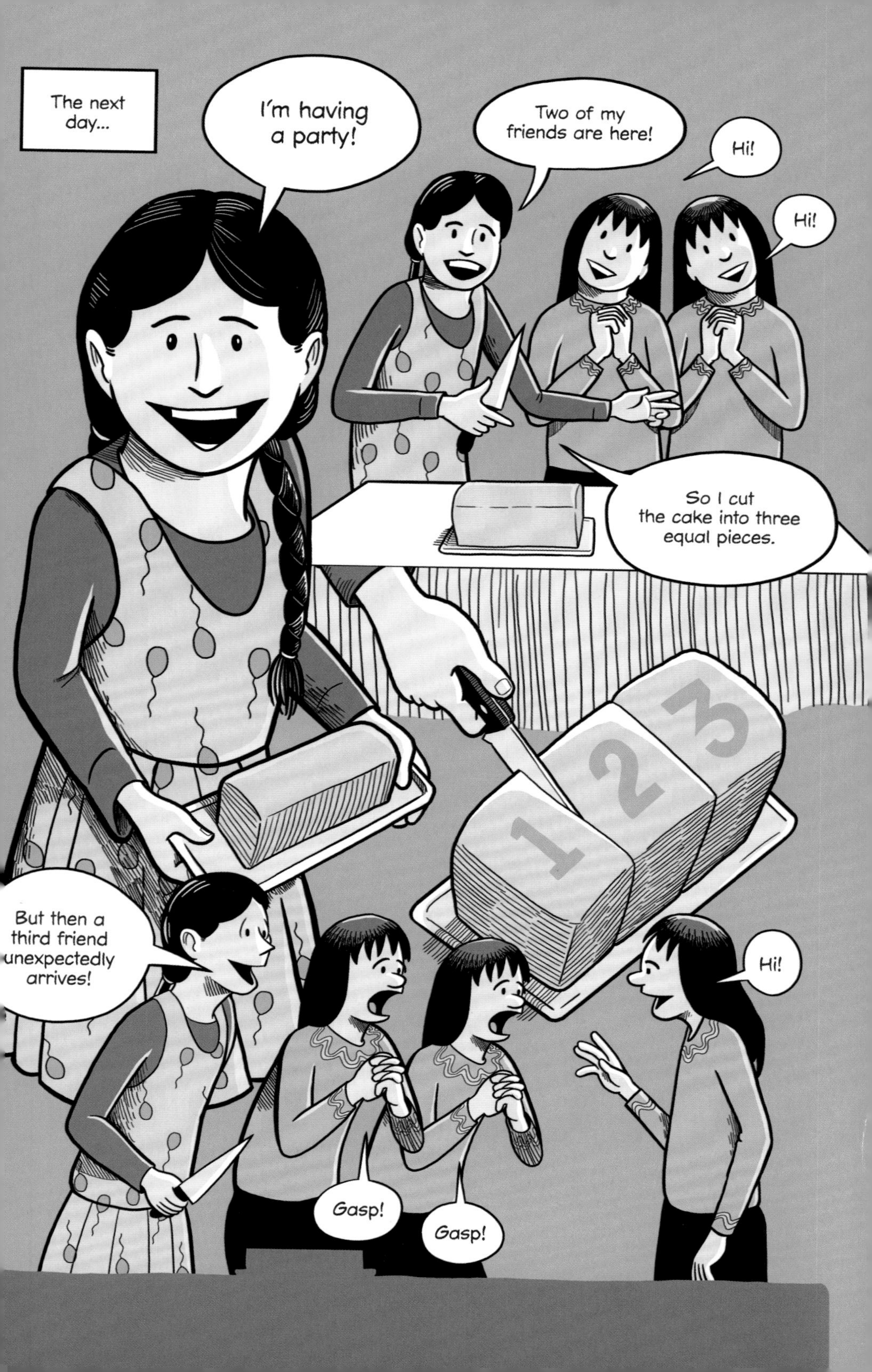

The next day...
I'm having a party!
Two of my friends are here!
Hi!
Hi!
So I cut the cake into three equal pieces.
1
2
3
But then a third friend unexpectedly arrives!
Hi!
Gasp!
Gasp!

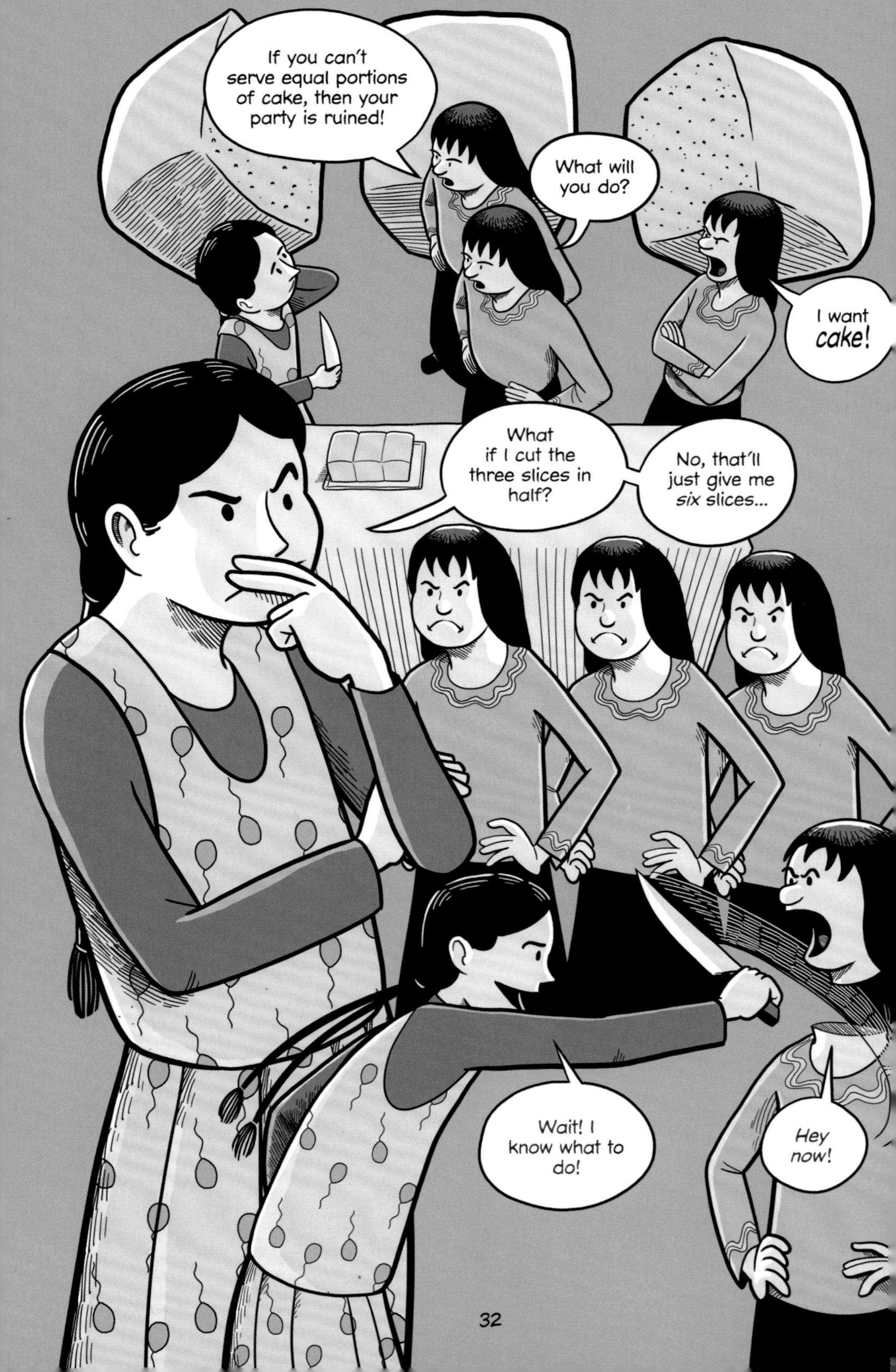
If you can't serve equal portions of cake, then your party is ruined!
What will you do?
I want *cake*!
What if I cut the three slices in half?
No, that'll just give me *six* slices...
Wait! I know what to do!
Hey now!

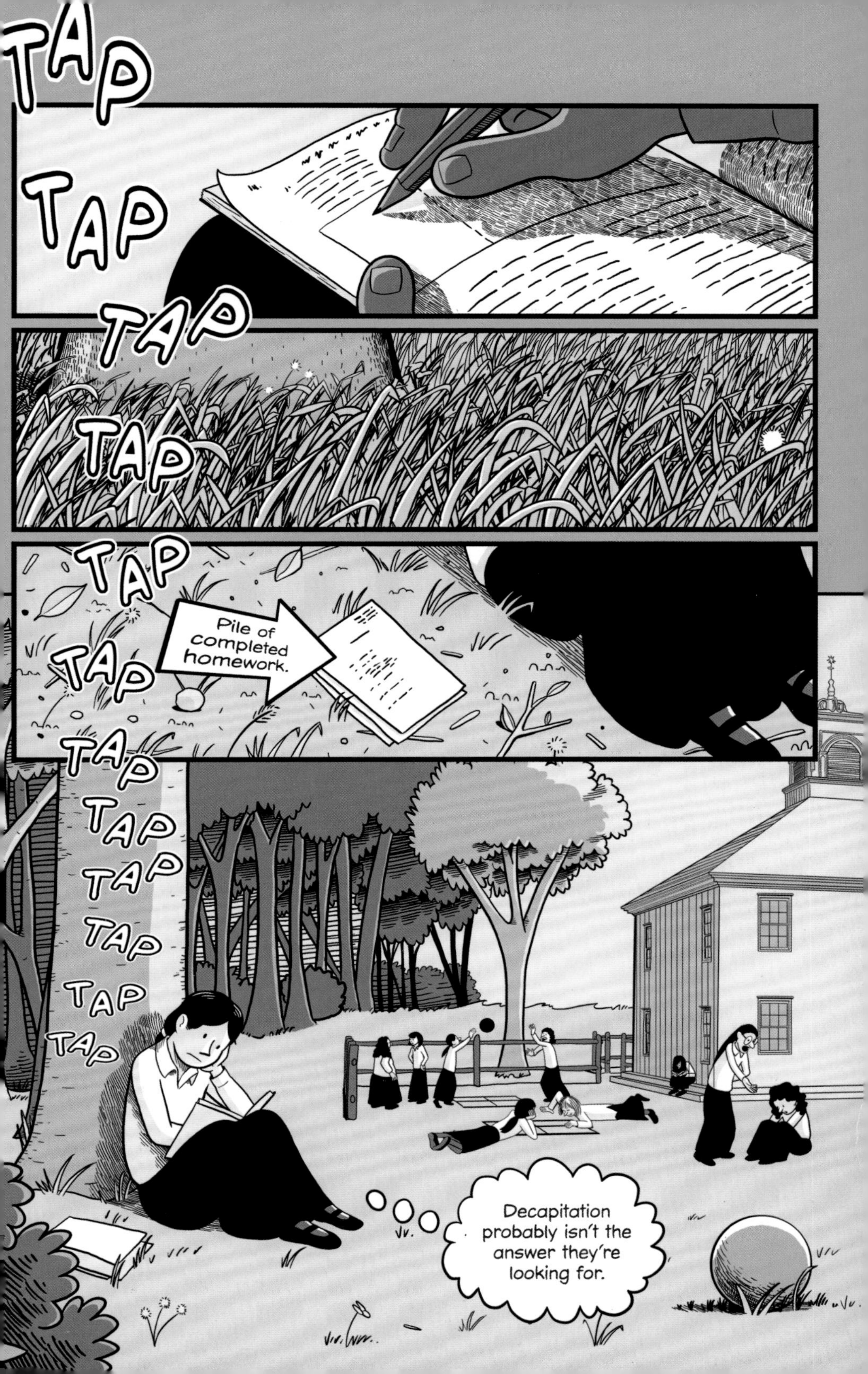
TAP
TAP
TAP
TAP
TAP
TAP
TAP
TAP
TAP
TAP
TAP
TAP
Pile of completed homework.
Decapitation probably isn't the answer they're looking for.

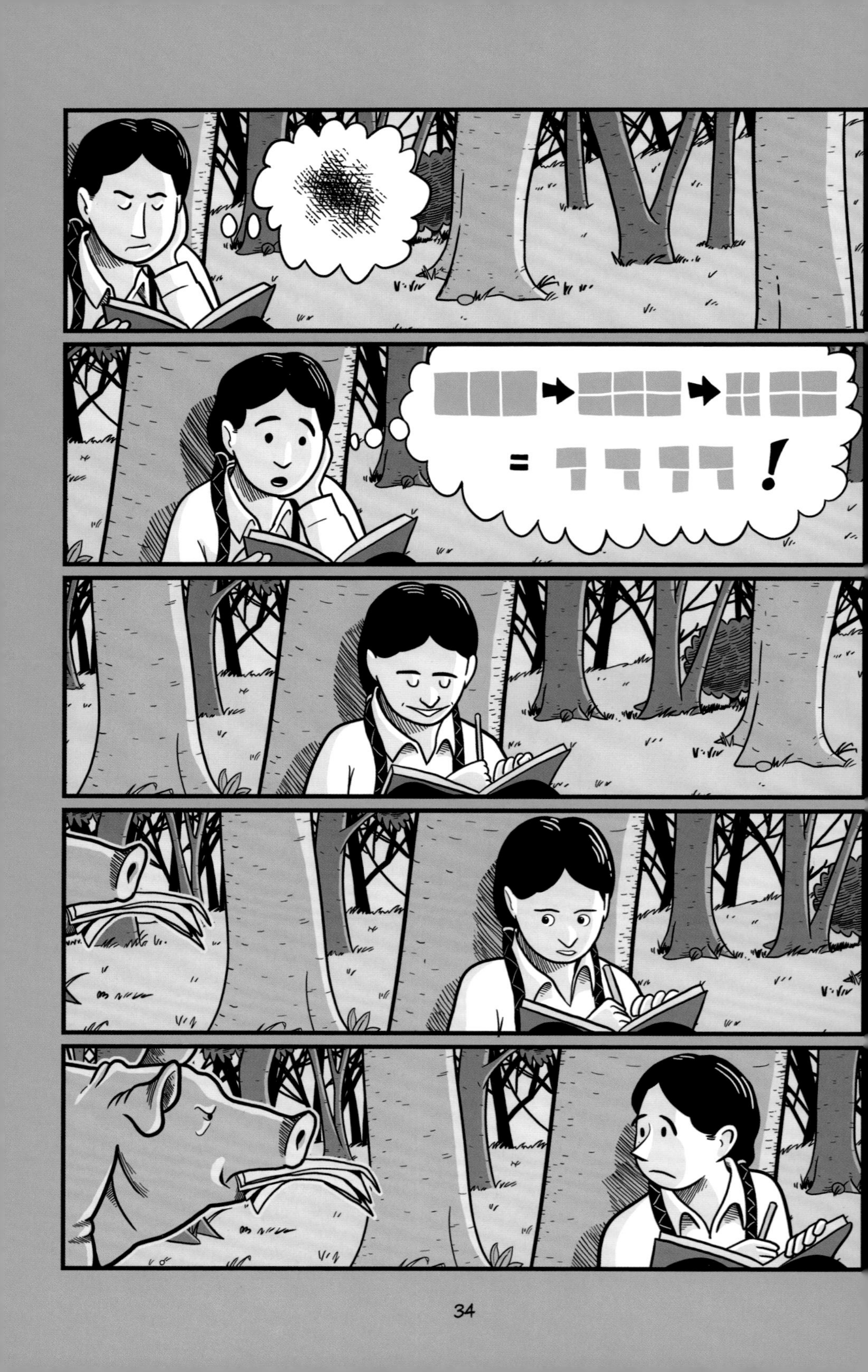

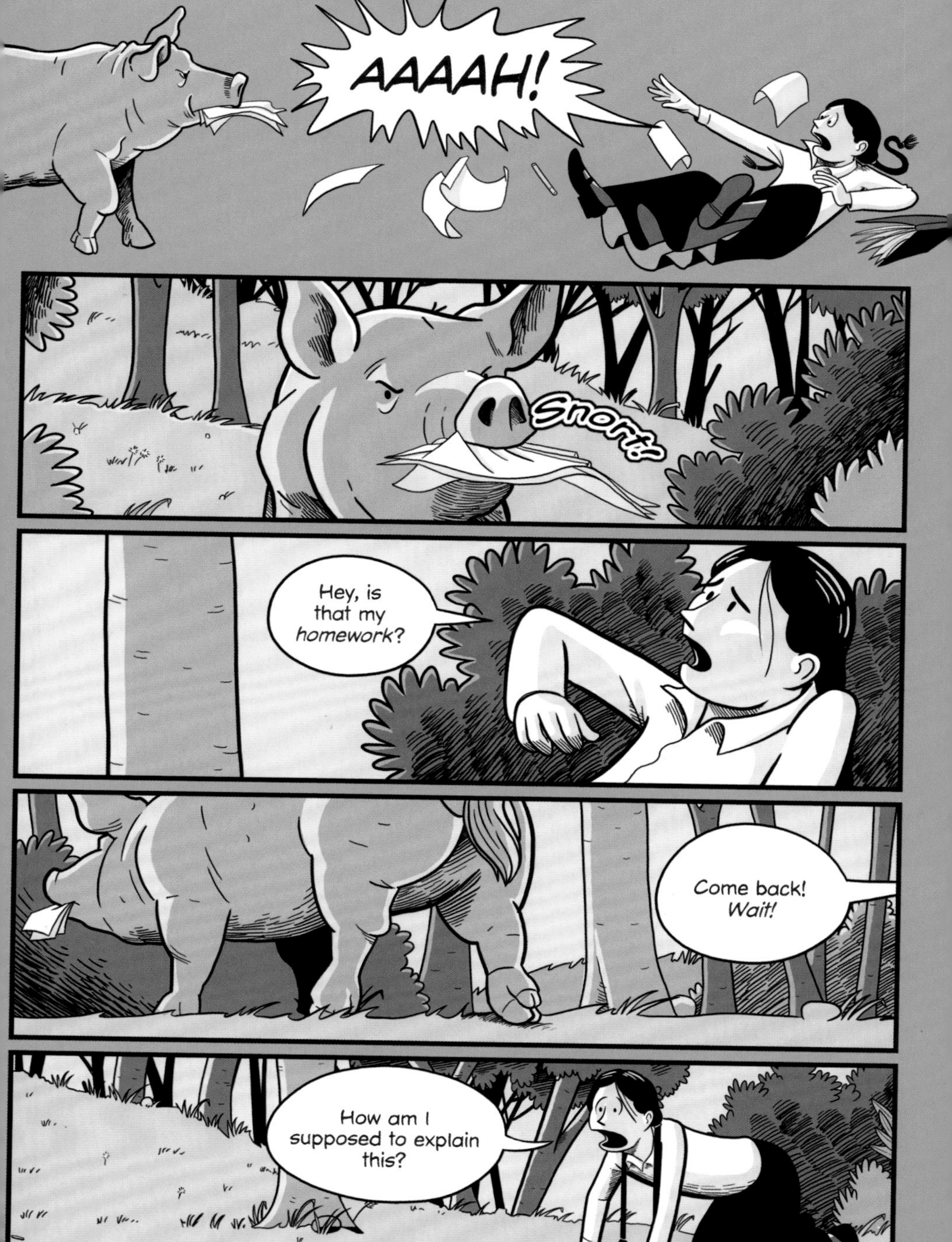
AAAAH!
Snort!
Hey, is that my *homework*?
Come back! *Wait!*
How am I supposed to explain this?

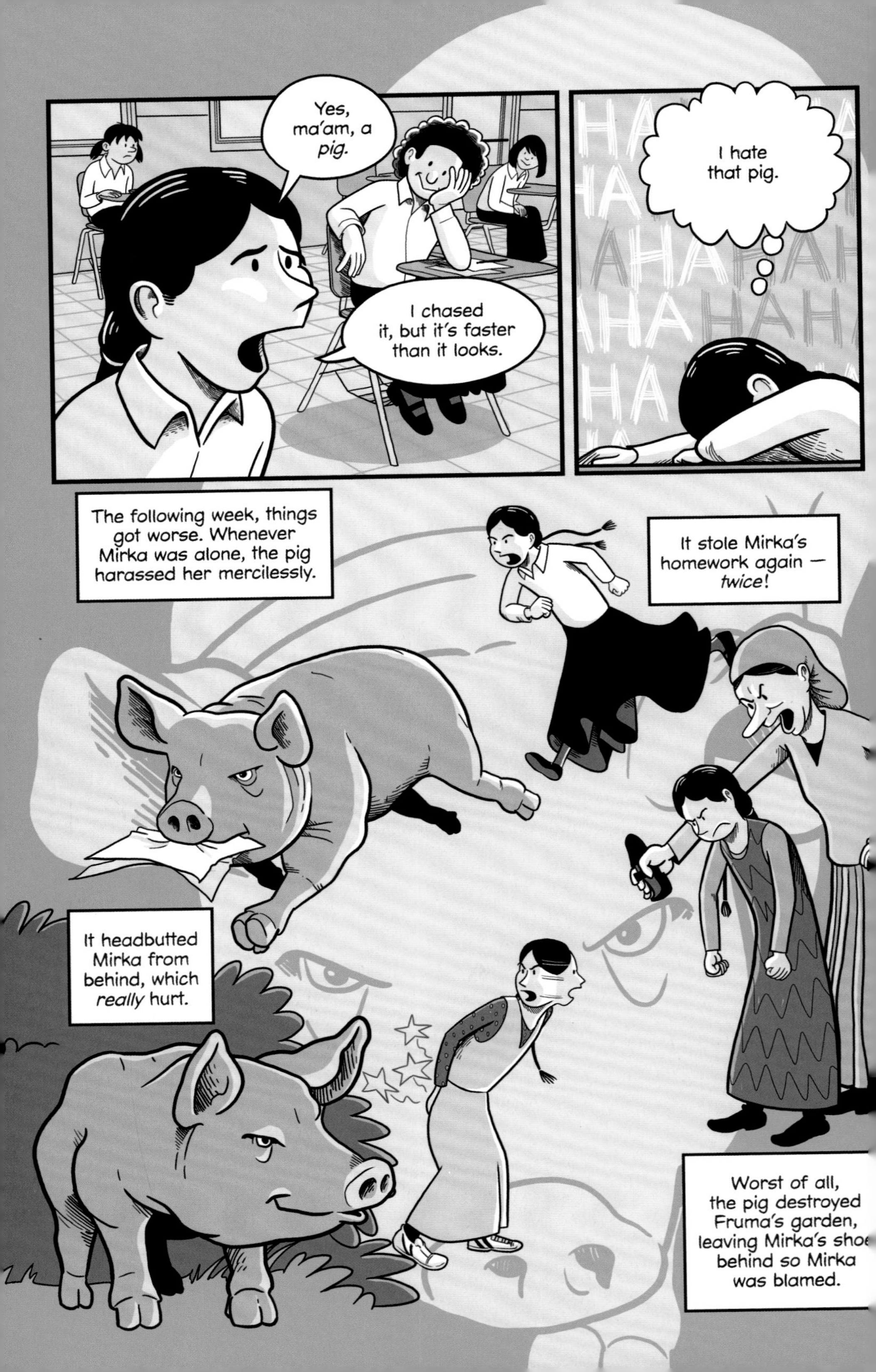
Yes, ma'am, a *pig.*
I chased it, but it's faster than it looks.
HAHAHA
I hate that pig.
The following week, things got worse. Whenever Mirka was alone, the pig harassed her mercilessly.
It stole Mirka's homework again — *twice*!
It headbutted Mirka from behind, which *really* hurt.
Worst of all, the pig destroyed Fruma's garden, leaving Mirka's shoe behind so Mirka was blamed.

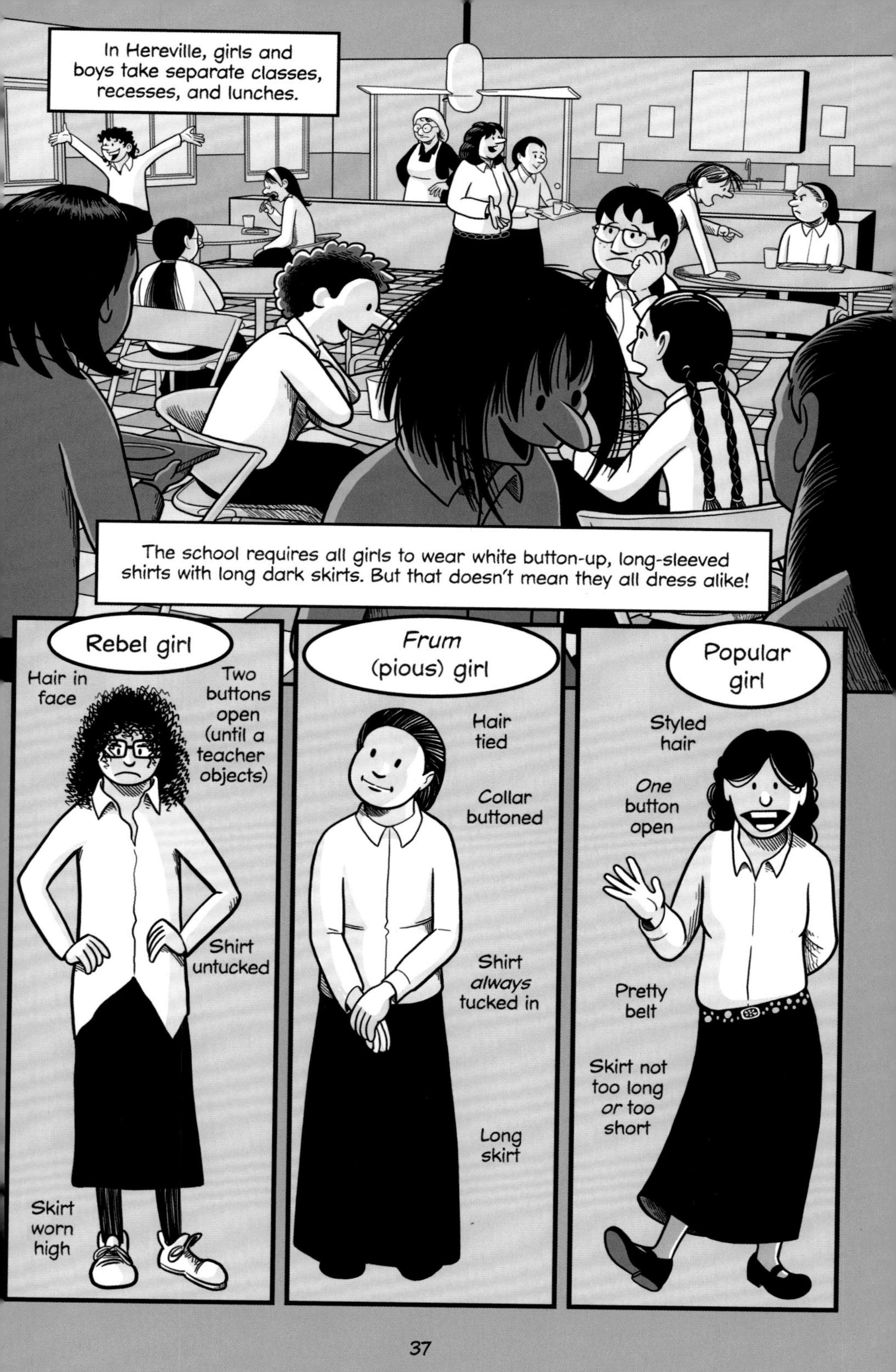
In Hereville, girls and boys take separate classes, recesses, and lunches.
The school requires all girls to wear white button-up, long-sleeved shirts with long dark skirts. But that doesn't mean they all dress alike!
Rebel girl
Hair in face
Two buttons open (until a teacher objects)
Shirt untucked
Skirt worn high
Frum (pious) girl
Hair tied
Collar buttoned
Shirt *always* tucked in
Long skirt
Popular girl
Styled hair
One button open
Pretty belt
Skirt not too long *or* too short

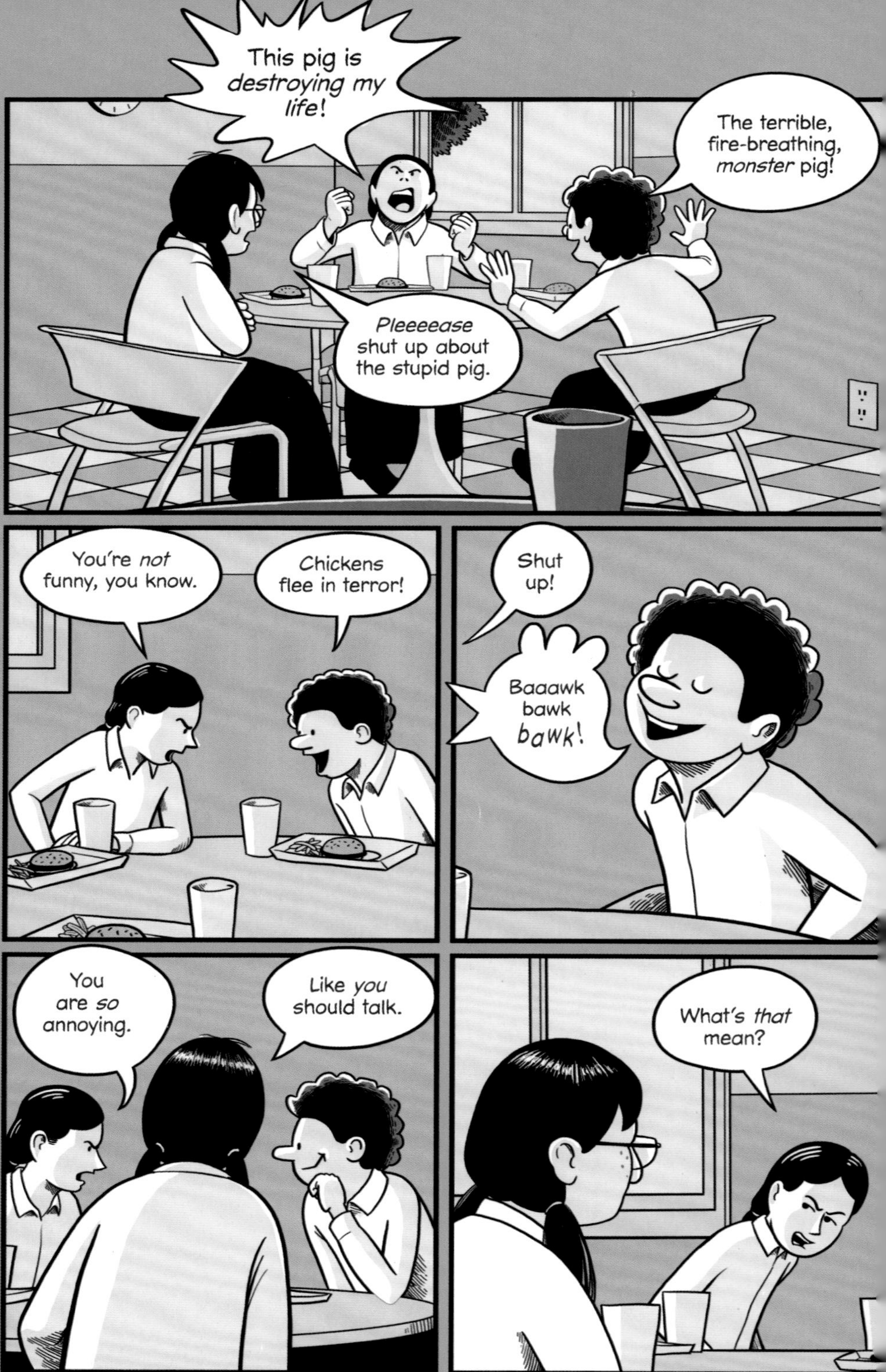
This pig is *destroying my life*!
The terrible, fire-breathing, *monster* pig!
Pleeeease shut up about the stupid pig.
You're *not* funny, you know.
Chickens flee in terror!
Shut up!
Baaawk bawk bawk!
You are *so* annoying.
Like *you* should talk.
What's *that* mean?

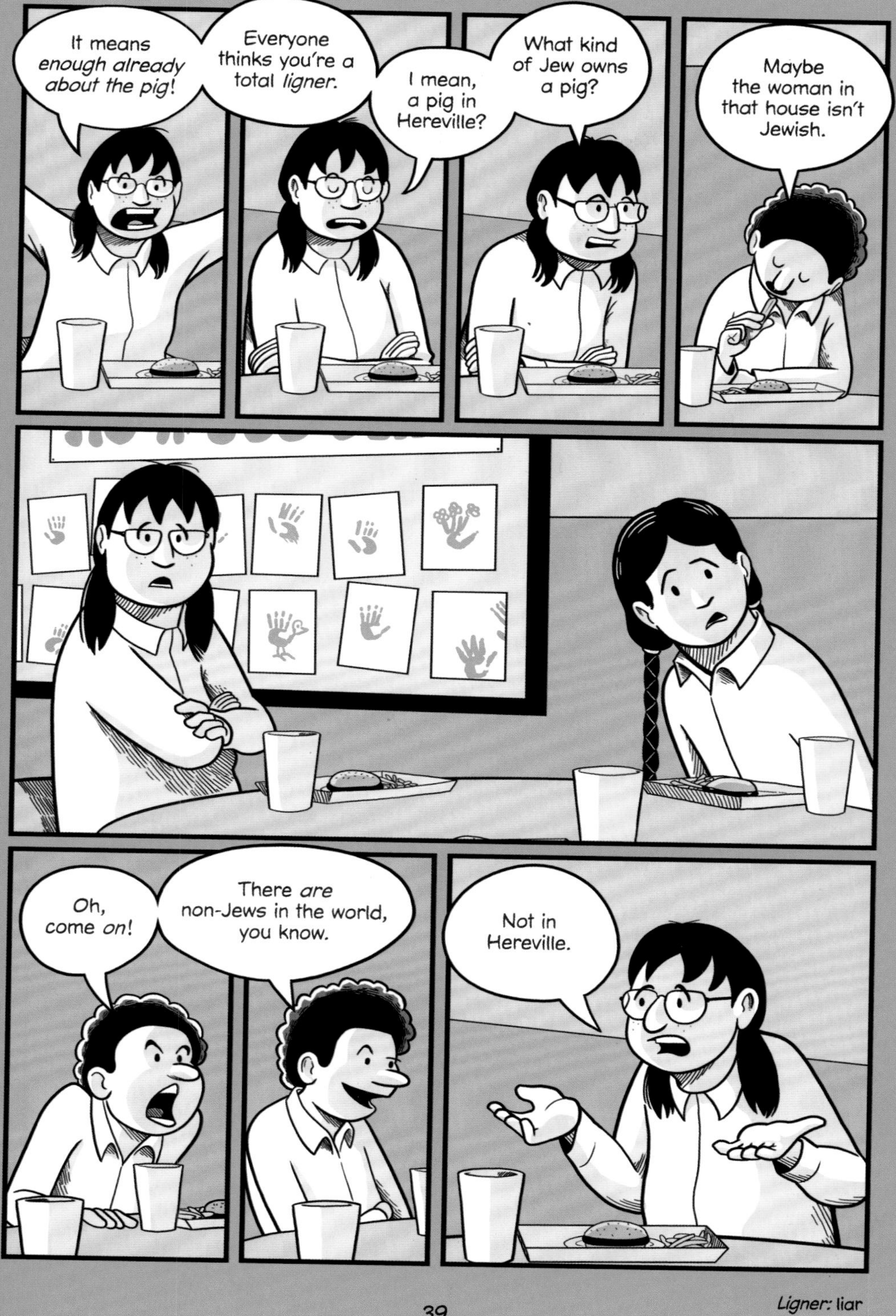
It means *enough already about the pig*!
Everyone thinks you're a total *ligner*.
I mean, a pig in Hereville?
What kind of Jew owns a pig?
Maybe the woman in that house isn't Jewish.
Oh, come *on*!
There *are* non-Jews in the world, you know.
Not in Hereville.

Ligner: liar

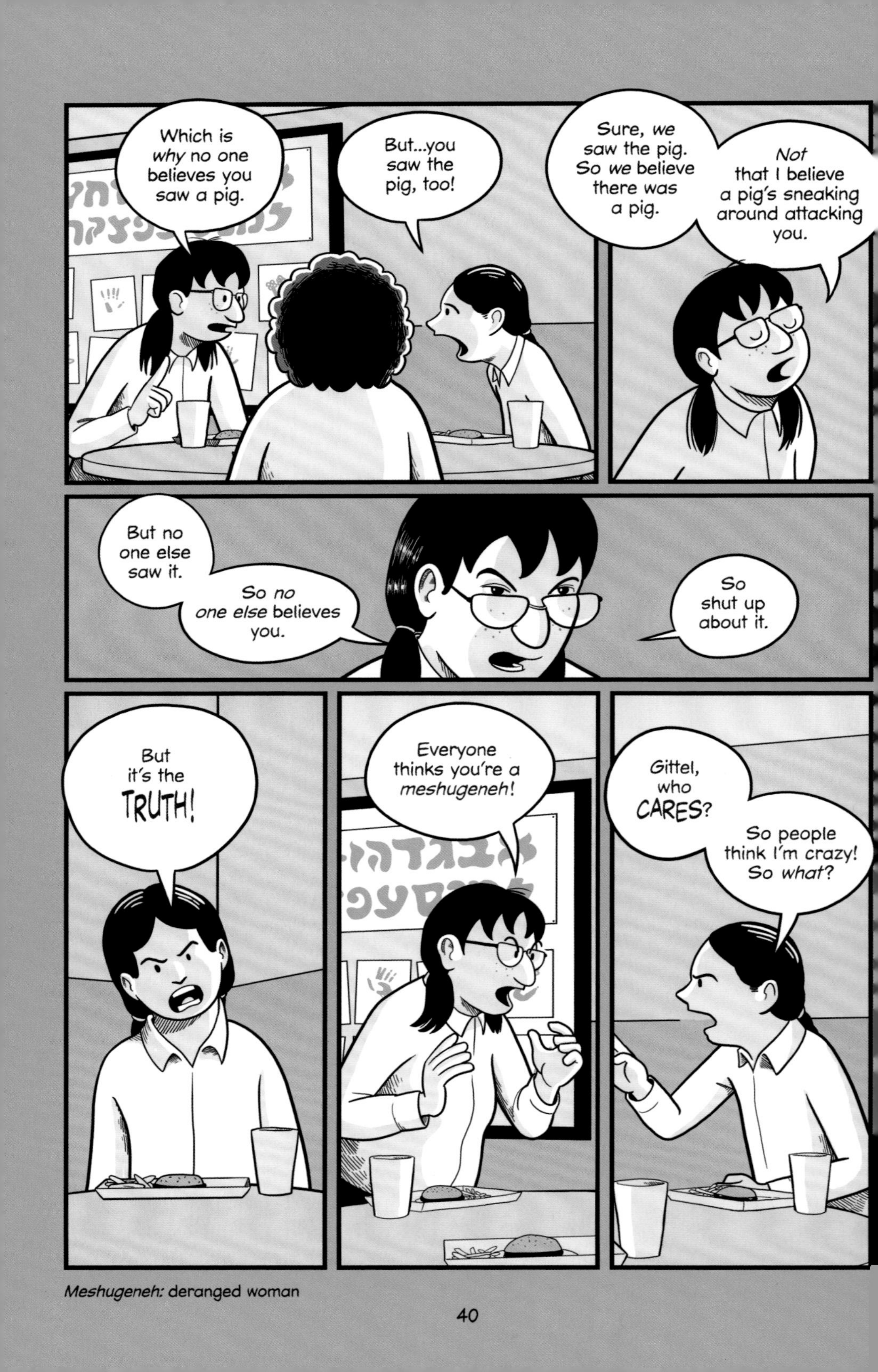
Which is *why* no one believes you saw a pig.
But...you saw the pig, too!
Sure, *we* saw the pig. So *we* believe there was a pig.
Not that I believe a pig's sneaking around attacking you.
But no one else saw it.
So *no one else* believes you.
So shut up about it.
But it's the TRUTH!
Everyone thinks you're a *meshugeneh*!
Gittel, who CARES?
So people think I'm crazy! So *what*?

Meshugeneh: deranged woman

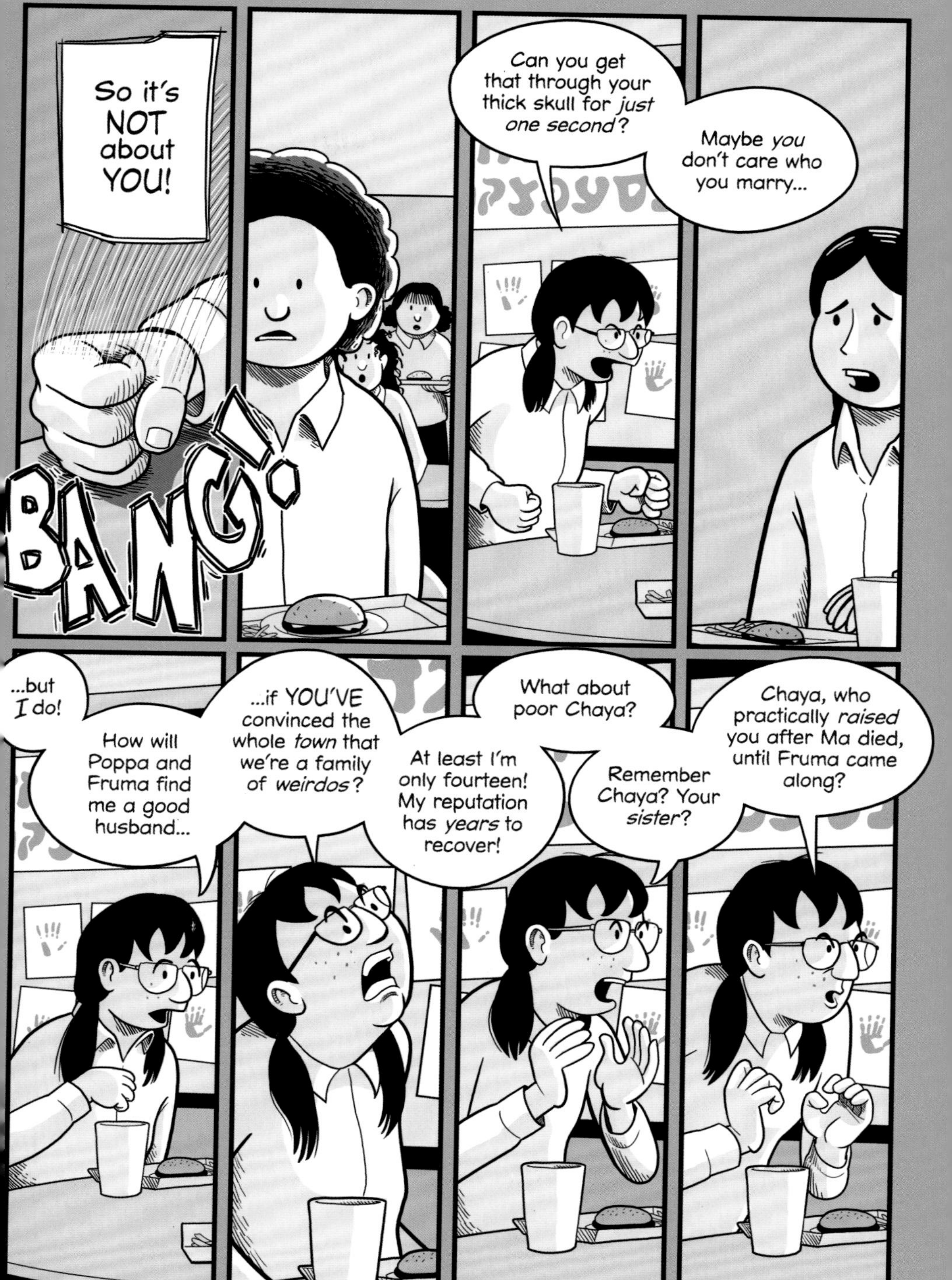
So it's NOT about YOU!
BANG!
Can you get that through your thick skull for *just one second*?
Maybe *you* don't care who you marry...
...but I do!
How will Poppa and Fruma find me a good husband...
...if YOU'VE convinced the whole *town* that we're a family of *weirdos*?
At least I'm only fourteen! My reputation has *years* to recover!
What about poor Chaya?
Remember Chaya? Your *sister*?
Chaya, who practically *raised* you after Ma died, until Fruma came along?

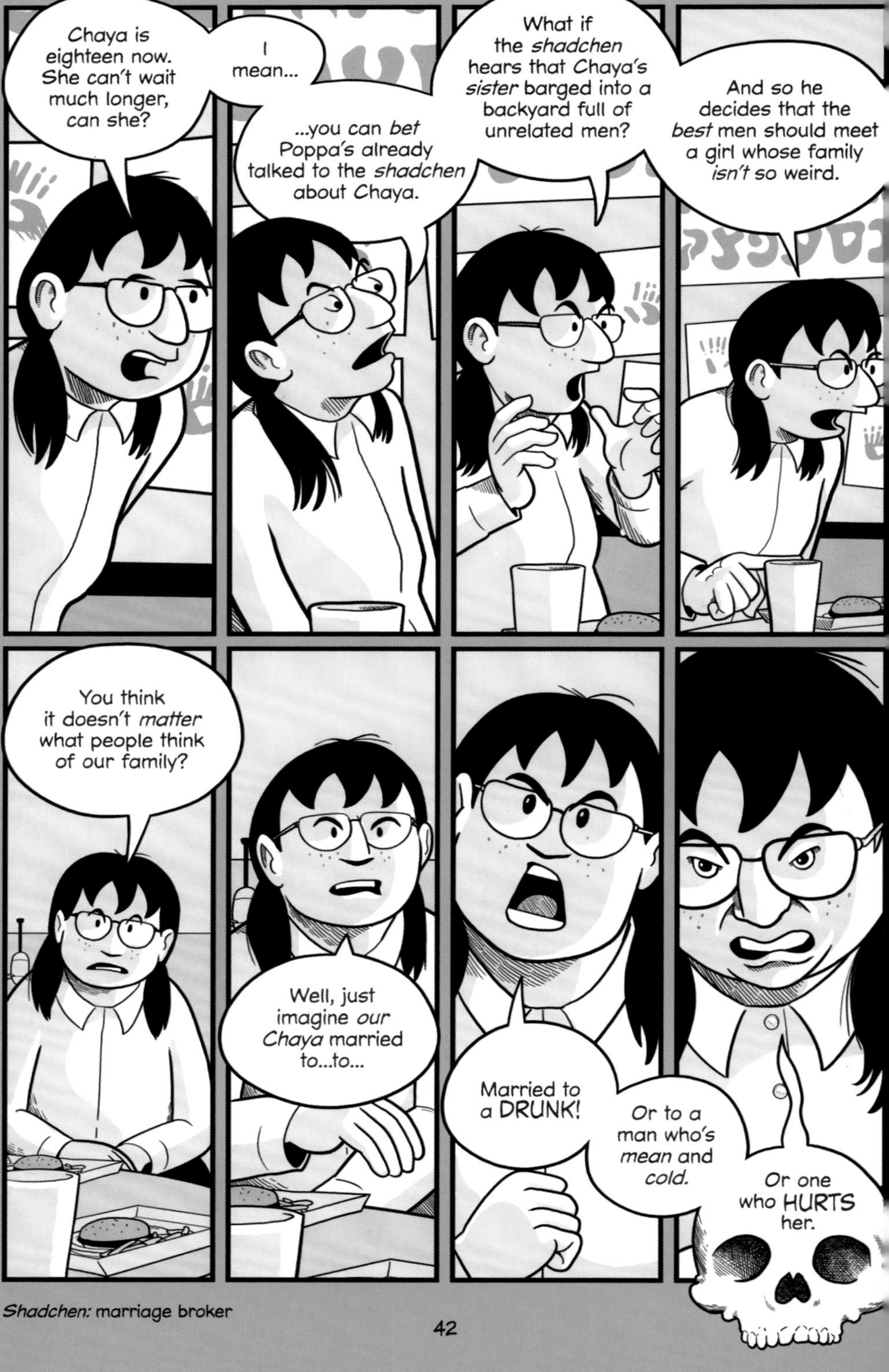
Chaya is eighteen now. She can't wait much longer, can she?
I mean...
...you can bet Poppa's already talked to the shadchen about Chaya.
What if the shadchen hears that Chaya's sister barged into a backyard full of unrelated men?
And so he decides that the best men should meet a girl whose family isn't so weird.
You think it doesn't matter what people think of our family?
Well, just imagine our Chaya married to...to...
Married to a DRUNK!
Or to a man who's mean and cold.
Or one who HURTS her.

Shadchen: marriage broker

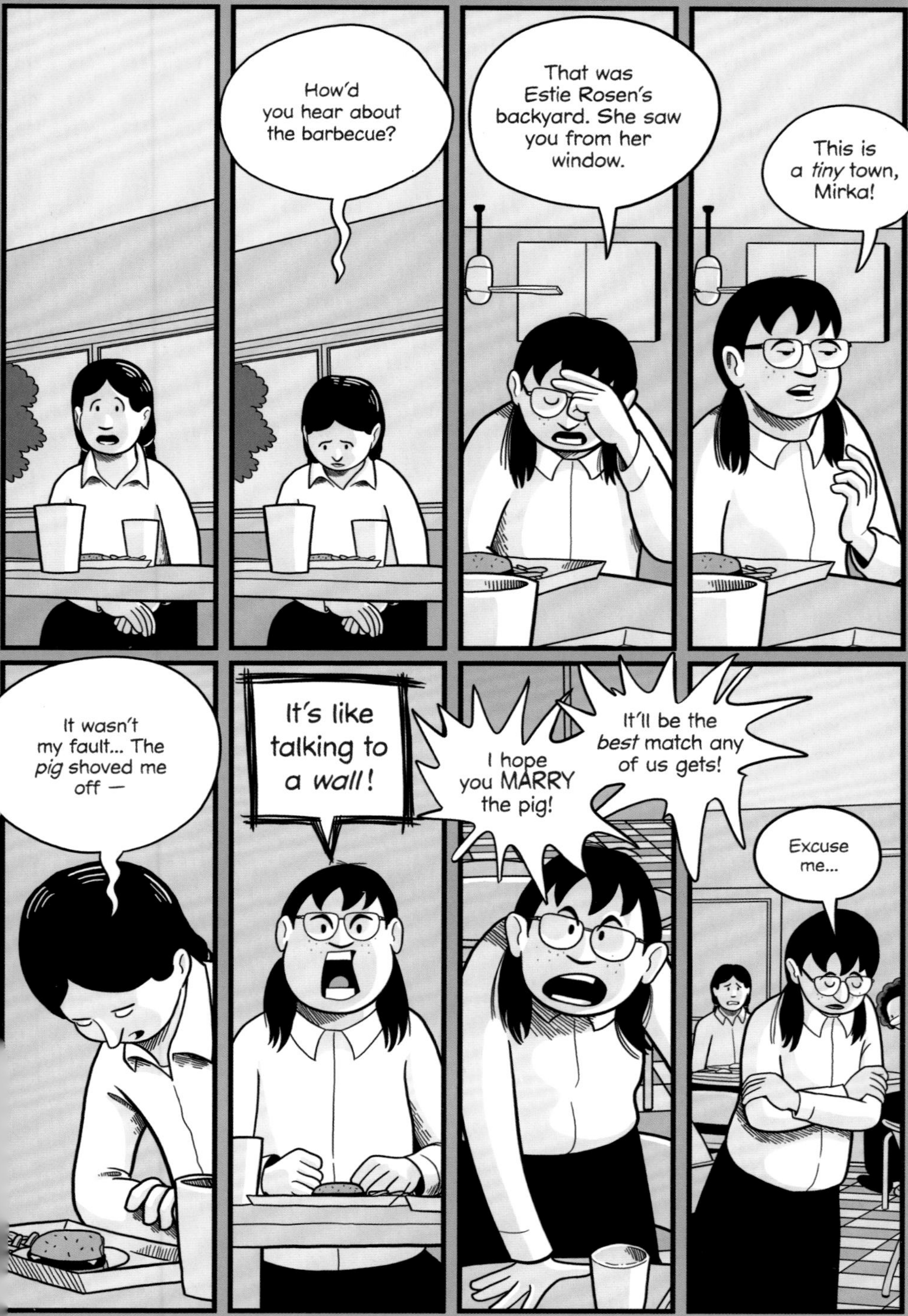
How'd you hear about the barbecue?
That was Estie Rosen's backyard. She saw you from her window.
This is a *tiny* town, Mirka!
It wasn't my fault... The *pig* shoved me off —
It's like talking to a *wall*!
I hope you MARRY the pig!
It'll be the *best* match any of us gets!
Excuse me...

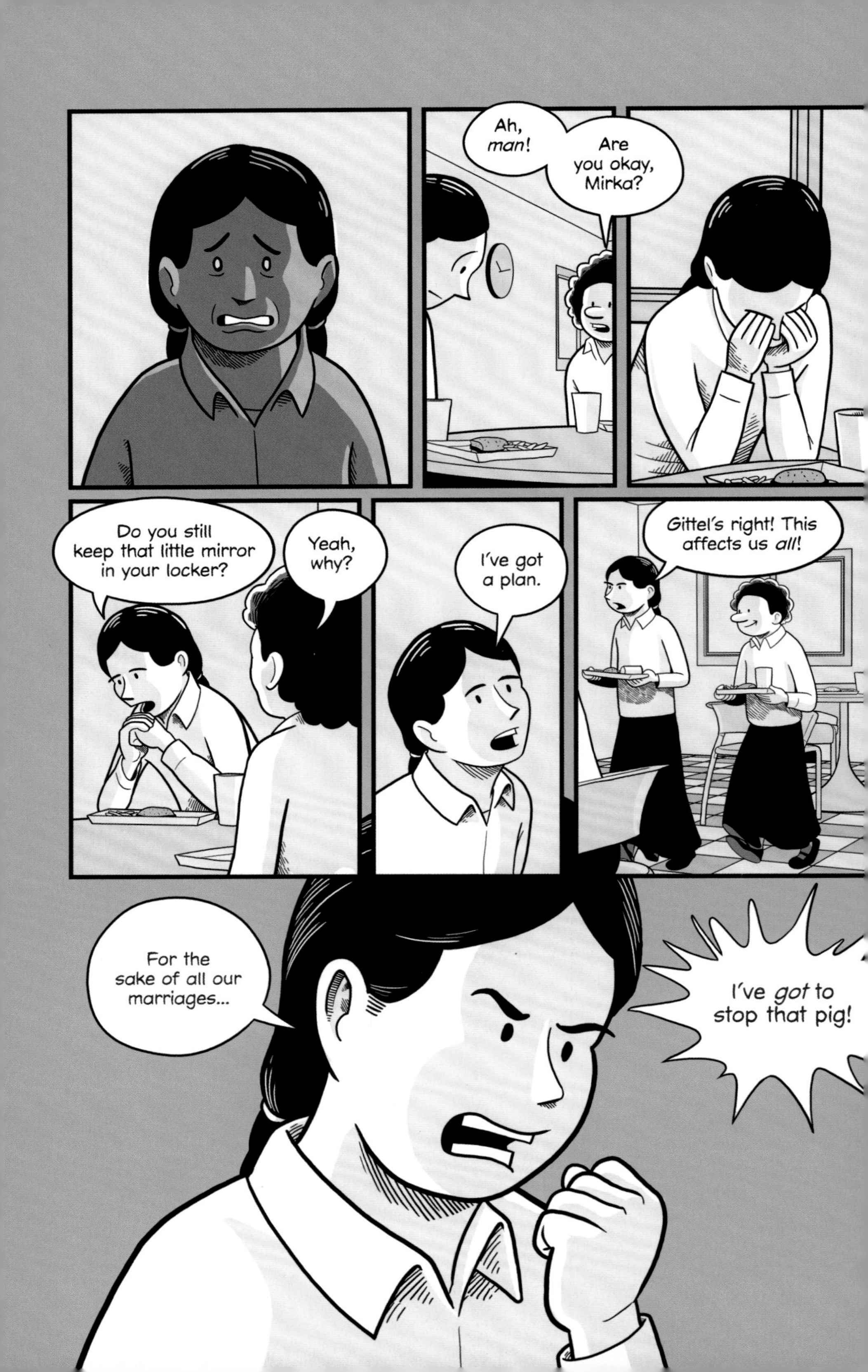
Ah, *man*!
Are you okay, Mirka?
Do you still keep that little mirror in your locker?
Yeah, why?
I've got a plan.
Gittel's right! This affects us *all*!
For the sake of all our marriages...
I've *got* to stop that pig!

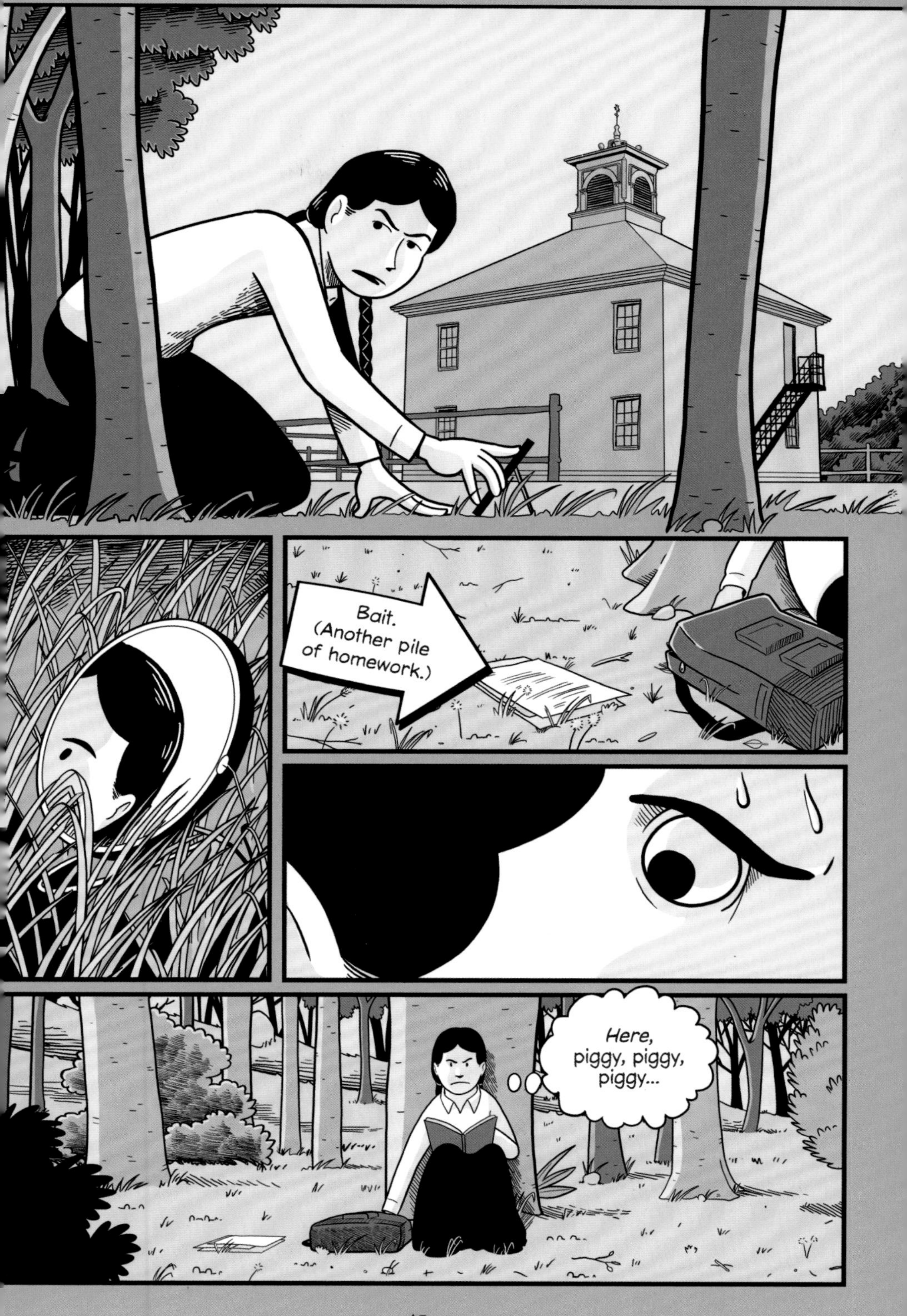
Bait.
(Another pile of homework.)
Here, piggy, piggy, piggy...

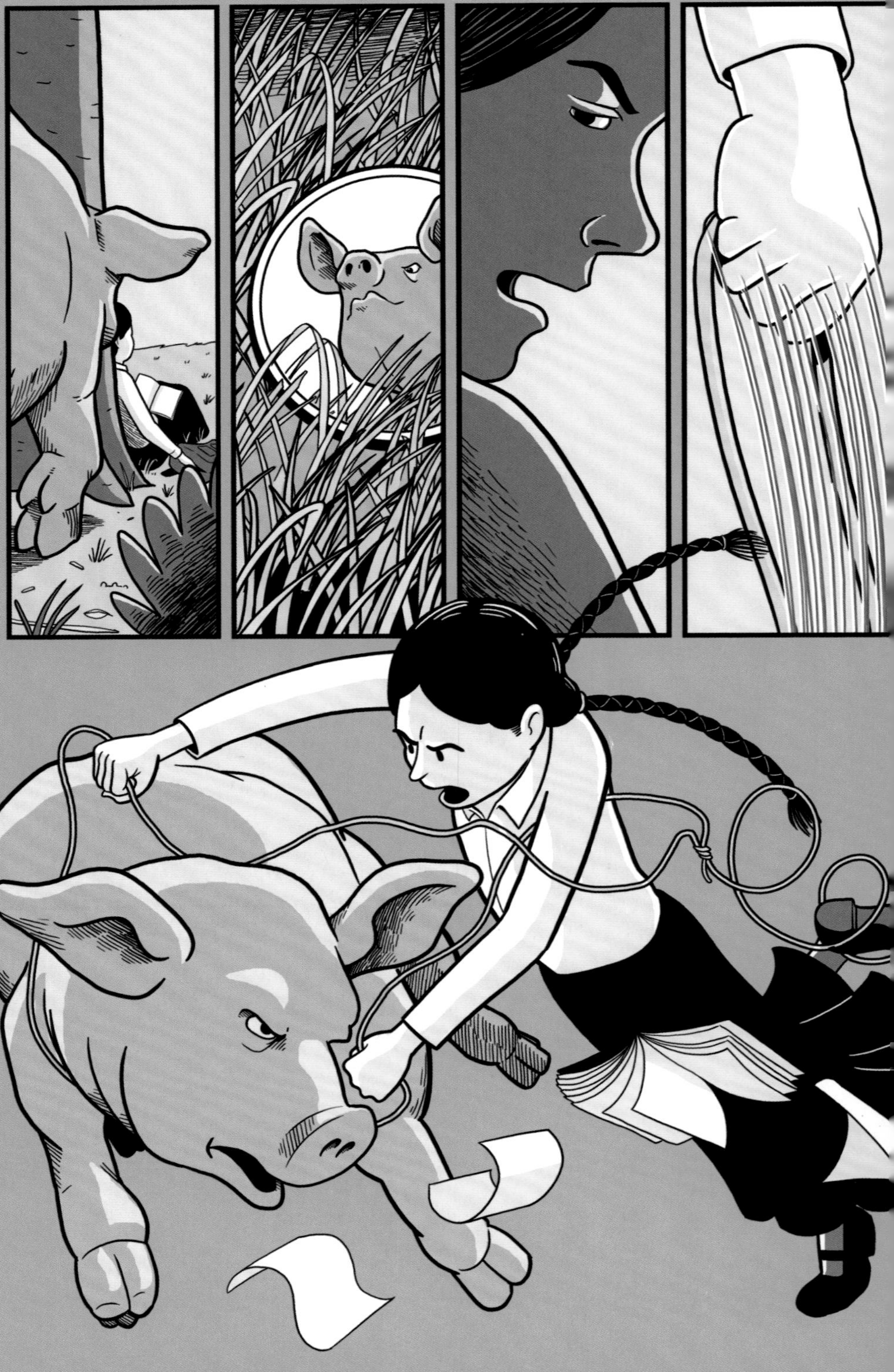

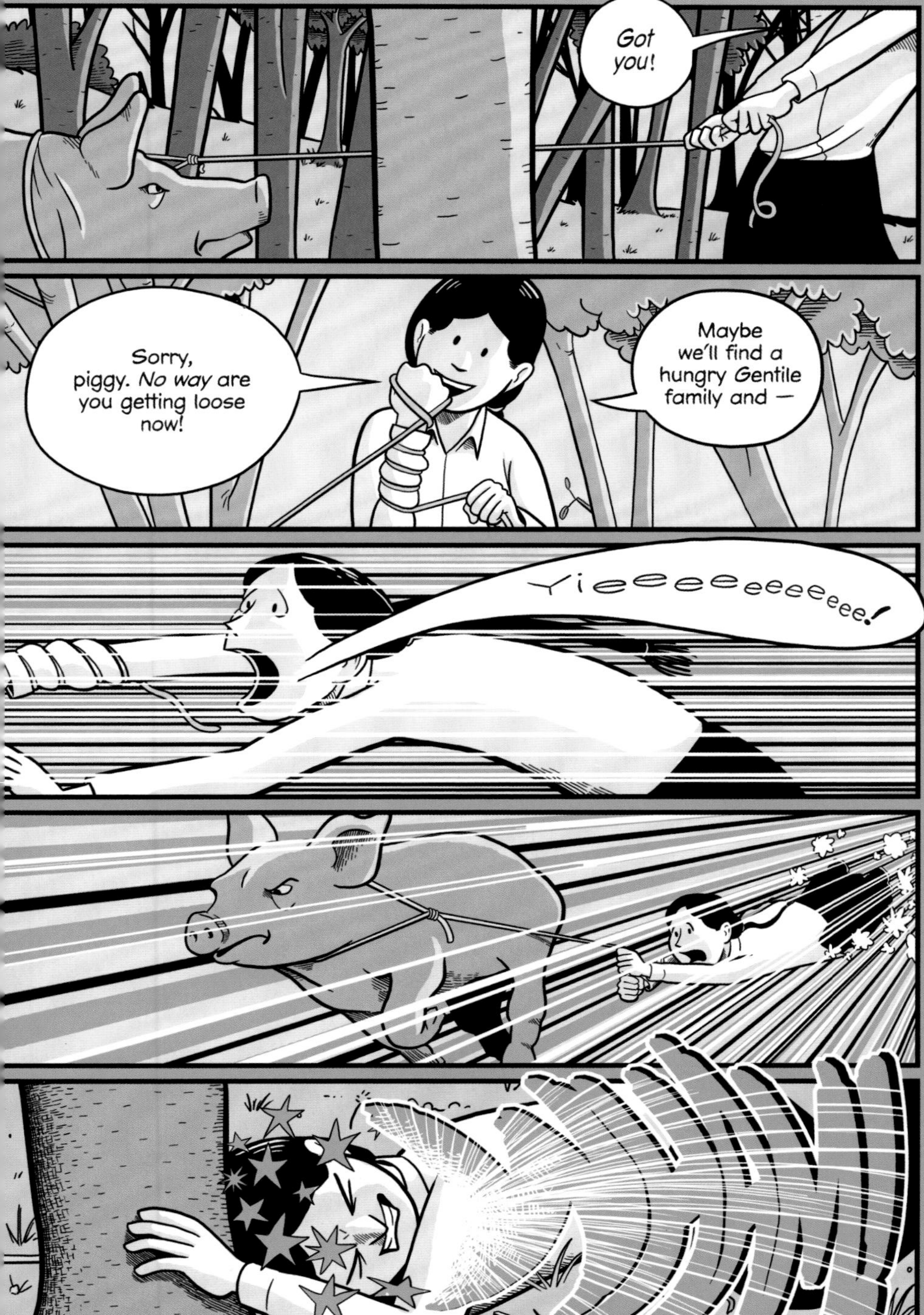

Got you!
Sorry, piggy. *No way* are you getting loose now!
Maybe we'll find a hungry *Gentile* family and —
Yieeeeeeeeeeee!

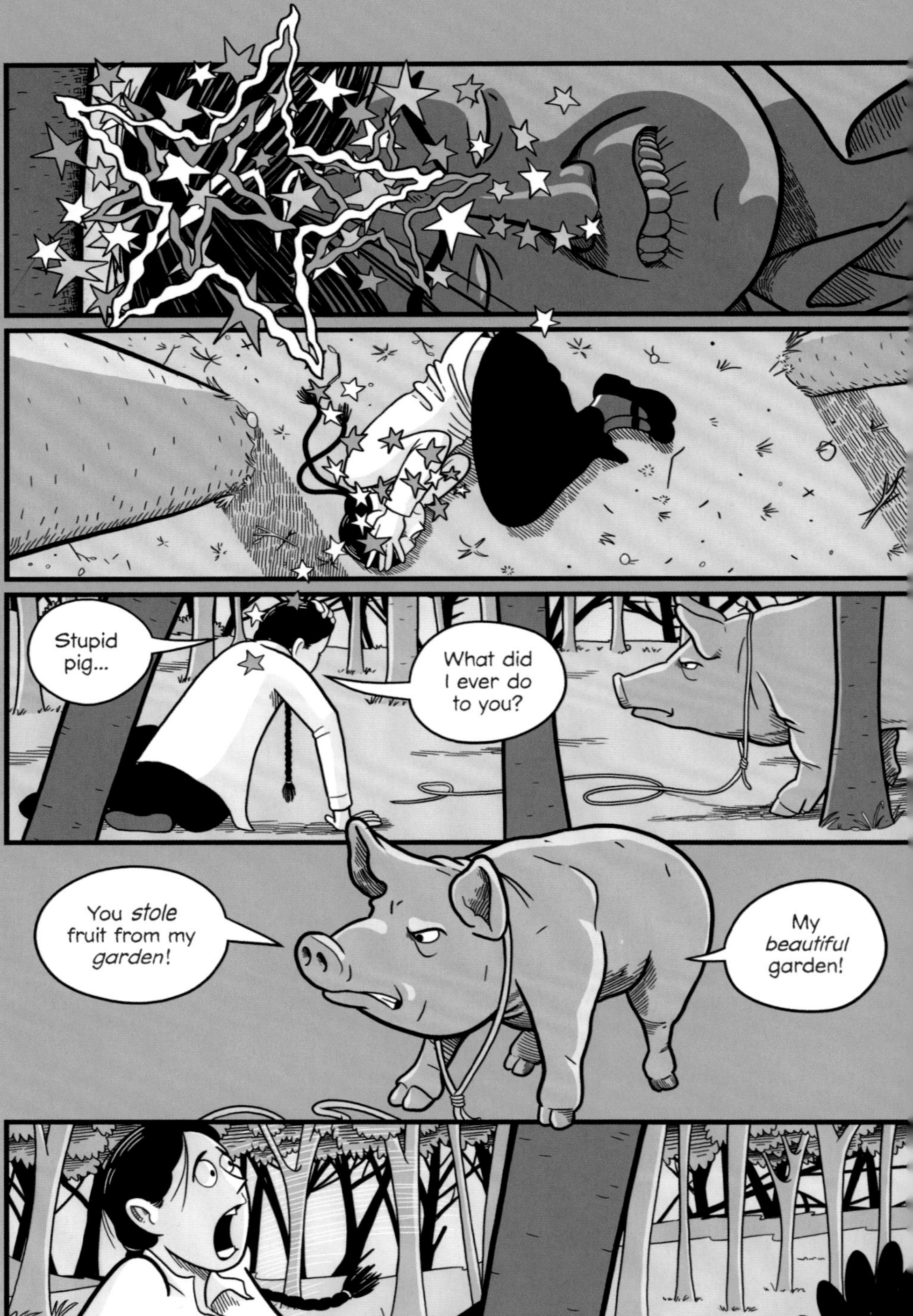

Stupid pig...
What did I ever do to you?
You *stole* fruit from my *garden*!
My *beautiful* garden!

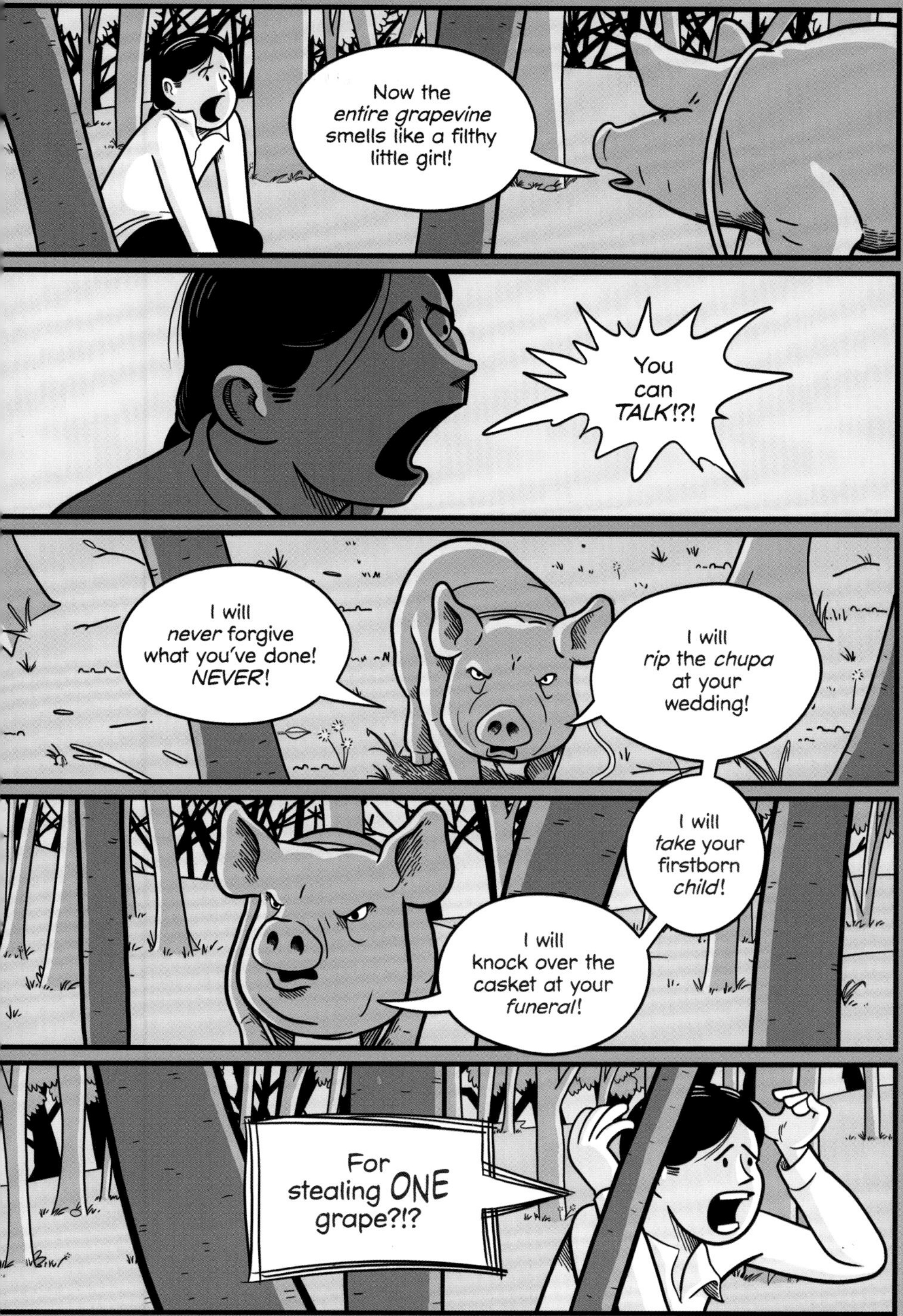

Now the *entire grapevine* smells like a filthy little girl!
You can *TALK*!?!
I will *never* forgive what you've done! *NEVER*!
I will *rip* the *chupa* at your wedding!
I will *take* your firstborn *child*!
I will knock over the casket at your *funeral*!
For stealing ONE grape?!?

Chupa: canopy

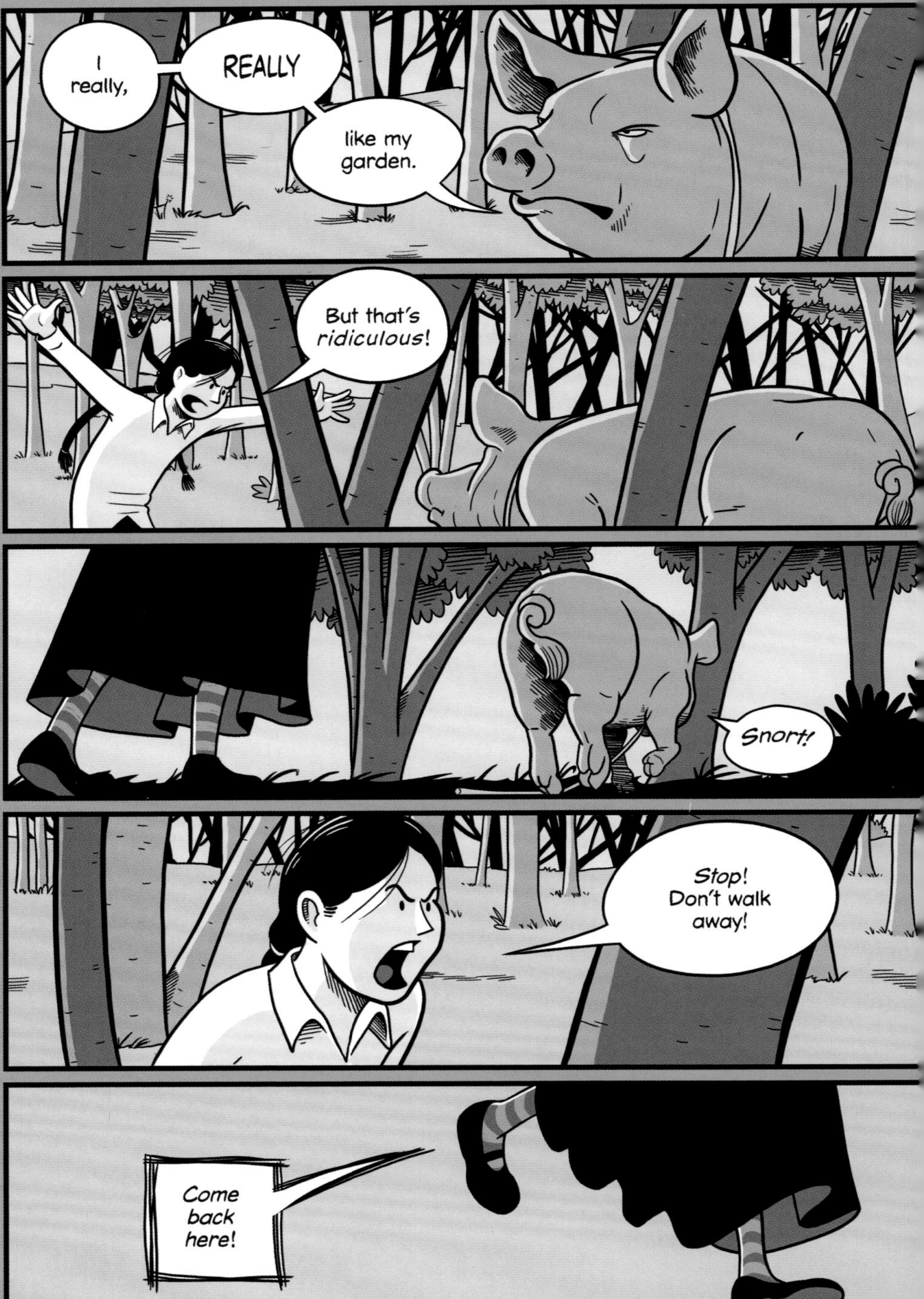
I really,
REALLY
like my garden.
But that's *ridiculous*!
Snort!
Stop! Don't walk away!
Come back here!

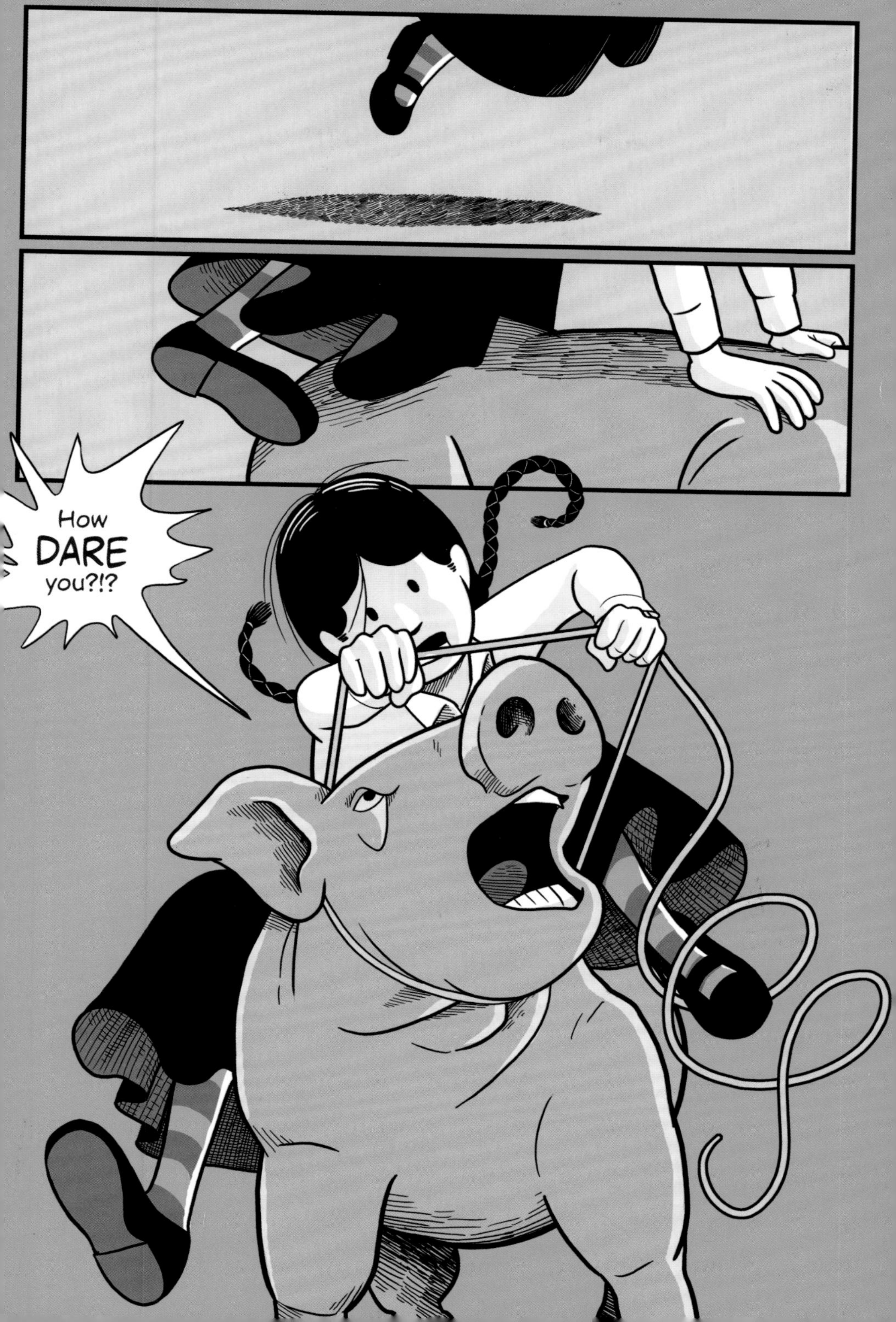
How DARE you?!?

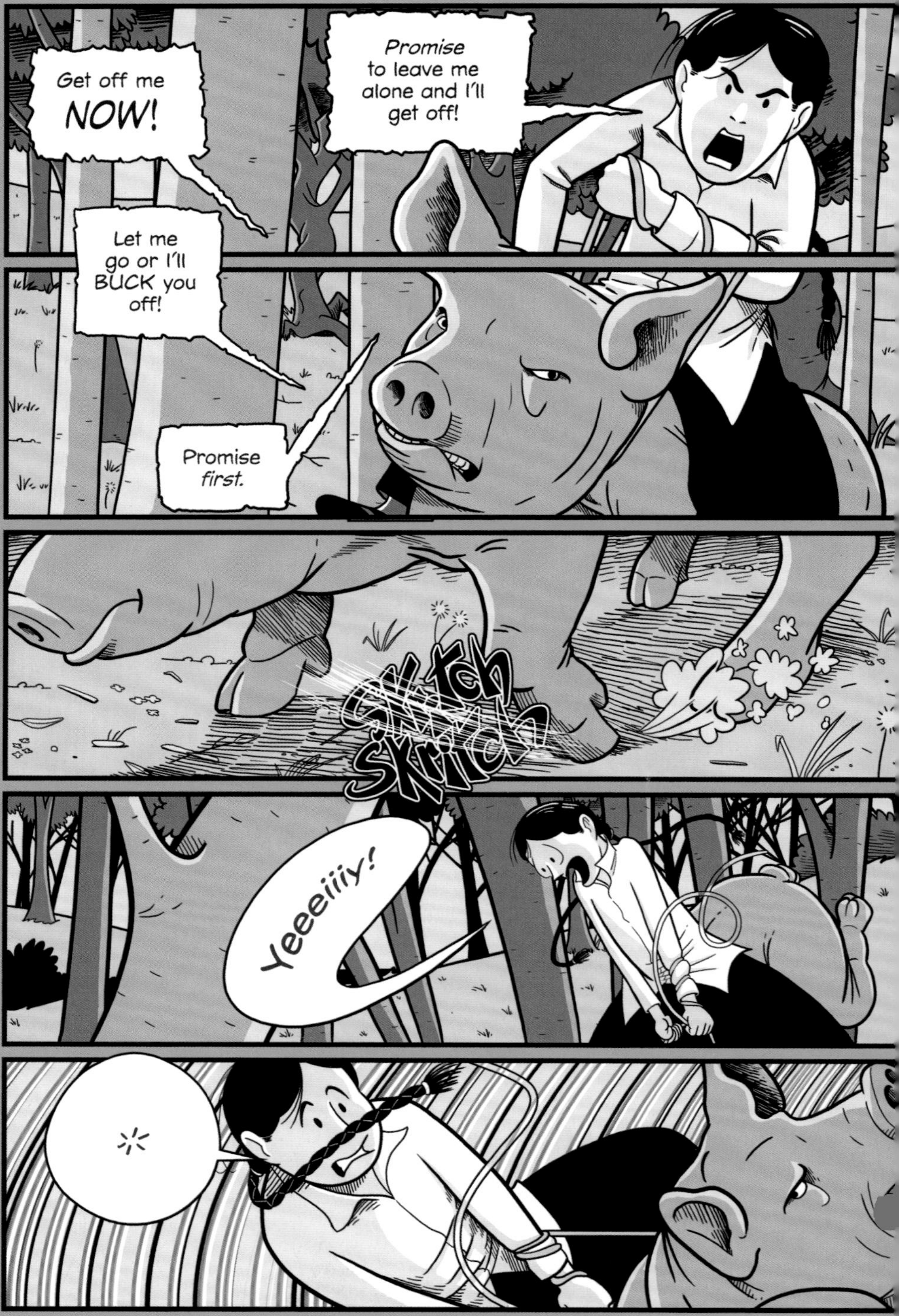
Get off me NOW!
Promise to leave me alone and I'll get off!
Let me go or I'll BUCK you off!
Promise first.
Skritch
Yeeeiiiy!
!

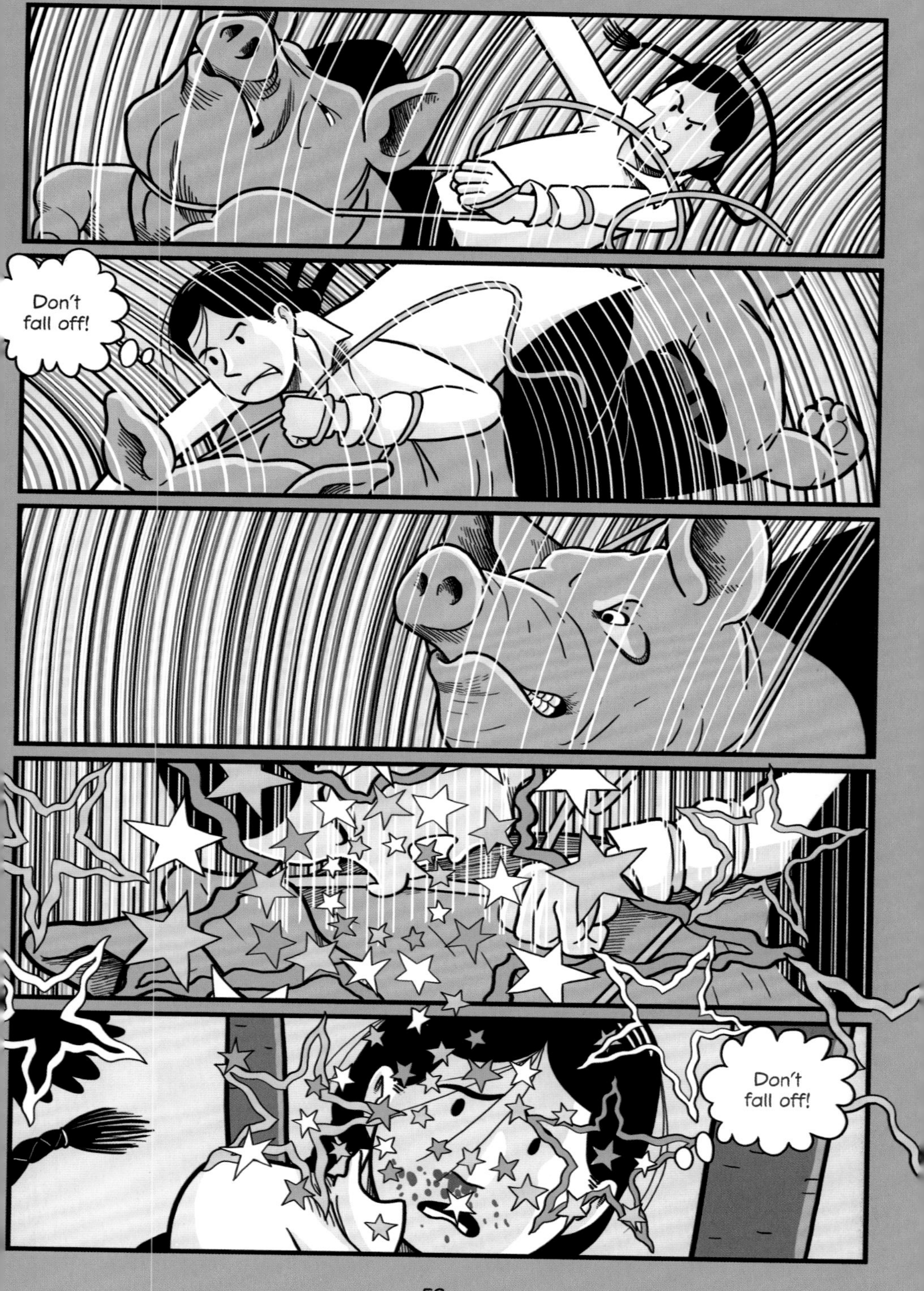
Don't fall off!
Don't fall off!

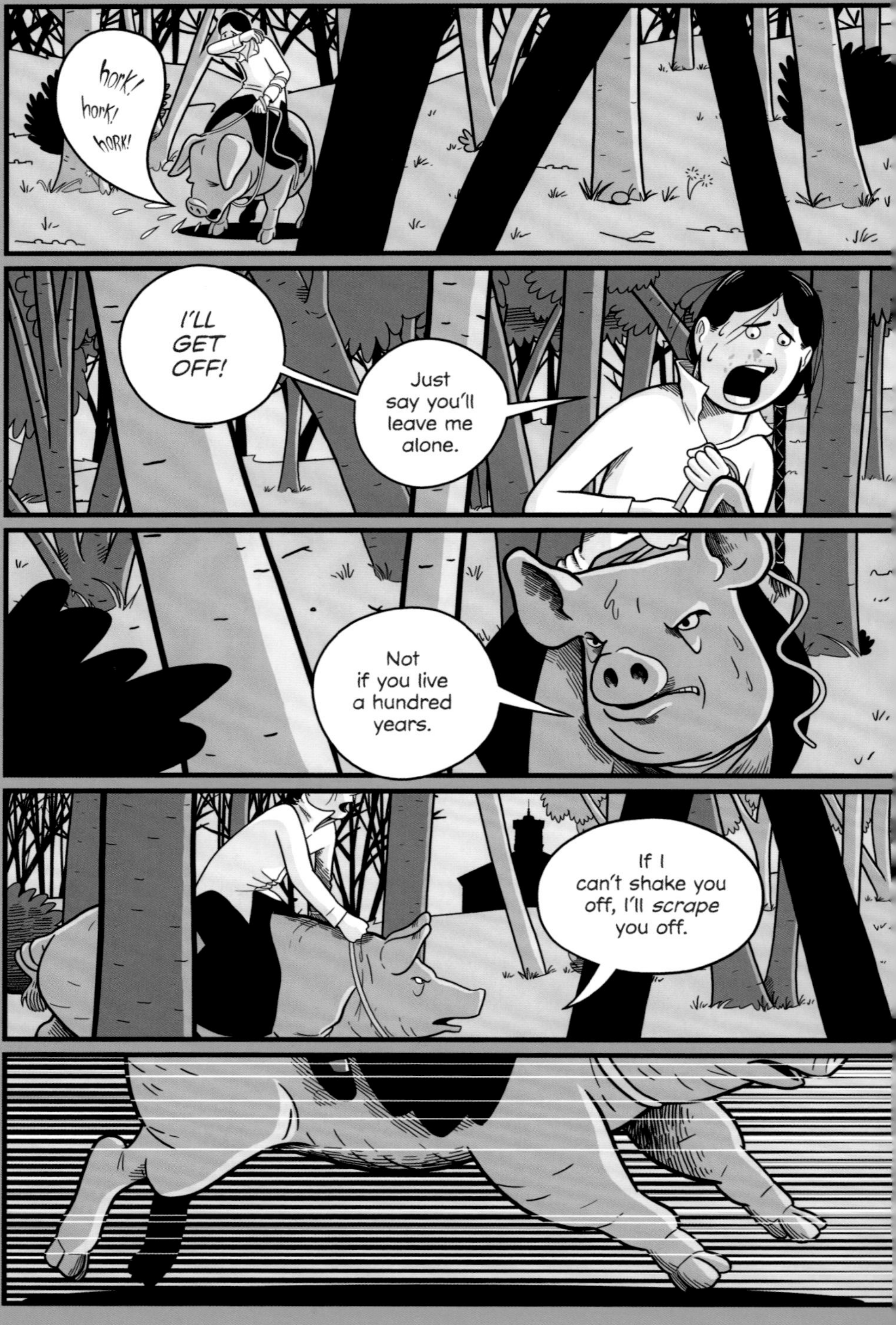
hork!
hork!
HORK!
I'LL GET OFF!
Just say you'll leave me alone.
Not if you live a hundred years.
If I can't shake you off, I'll *scrape* you off.

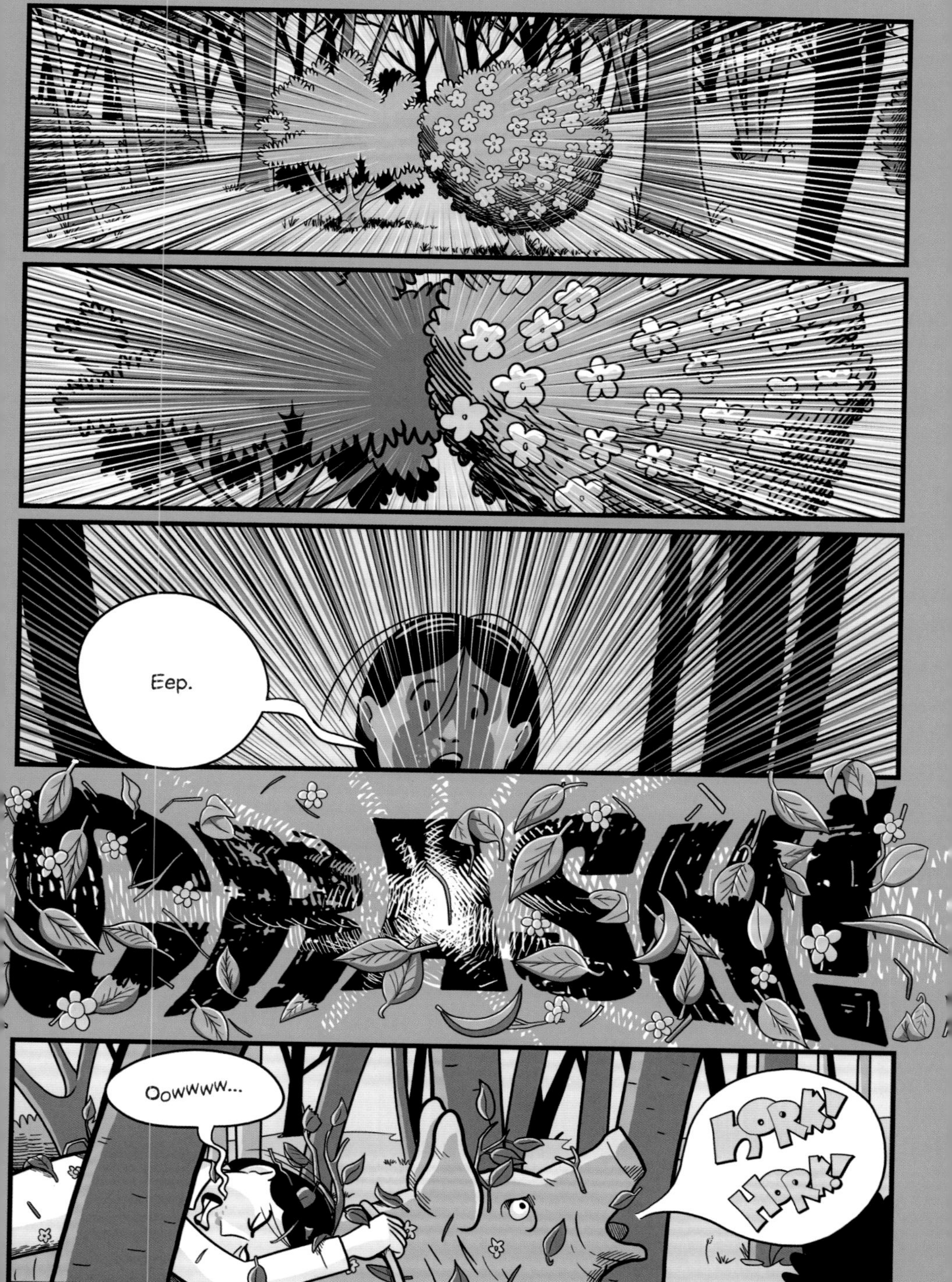
Eep.
CRASH!
Oowwww...
HORK! HORK!

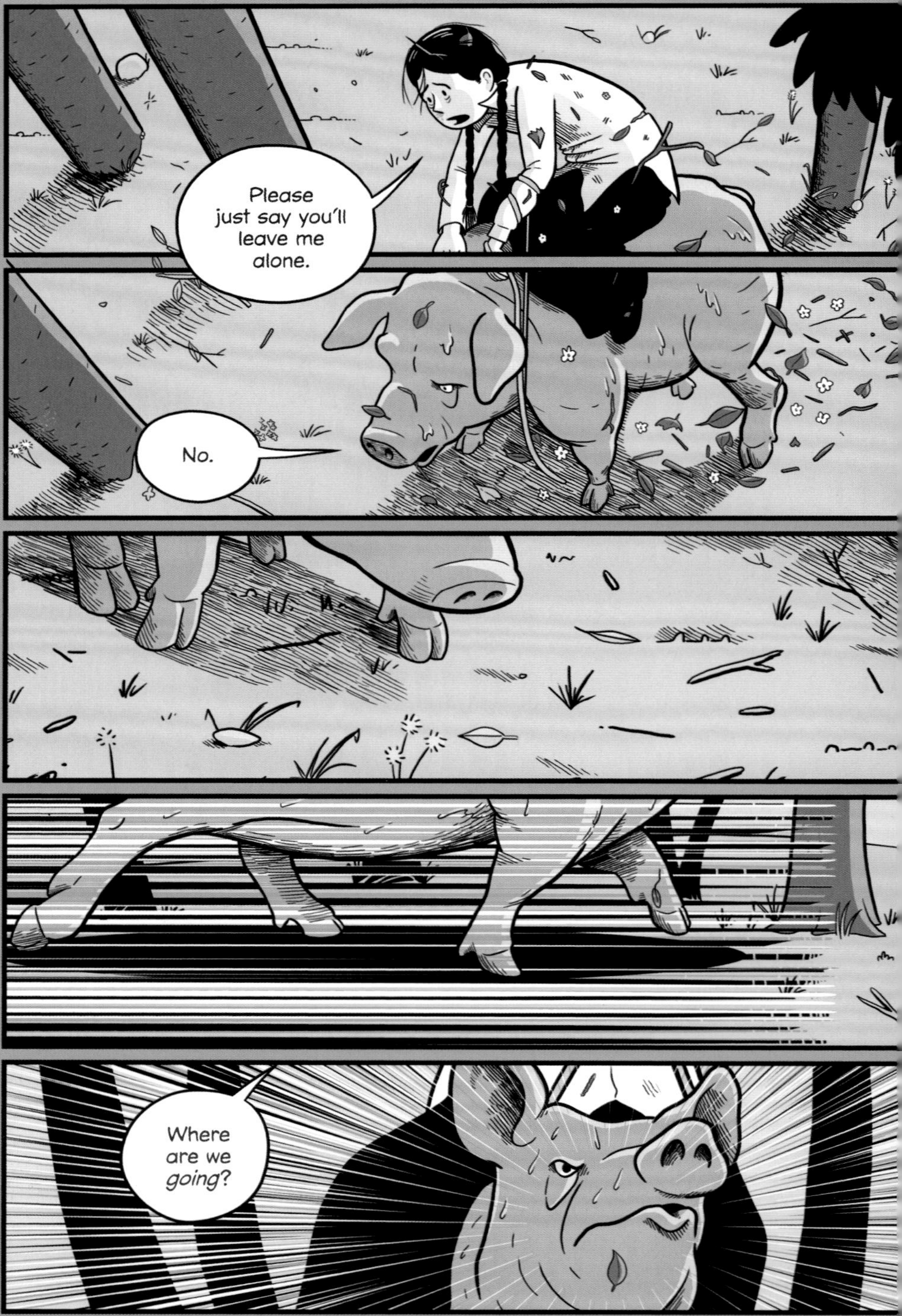
Please just say you'll leave me alone.
No.
Where are we *going*?

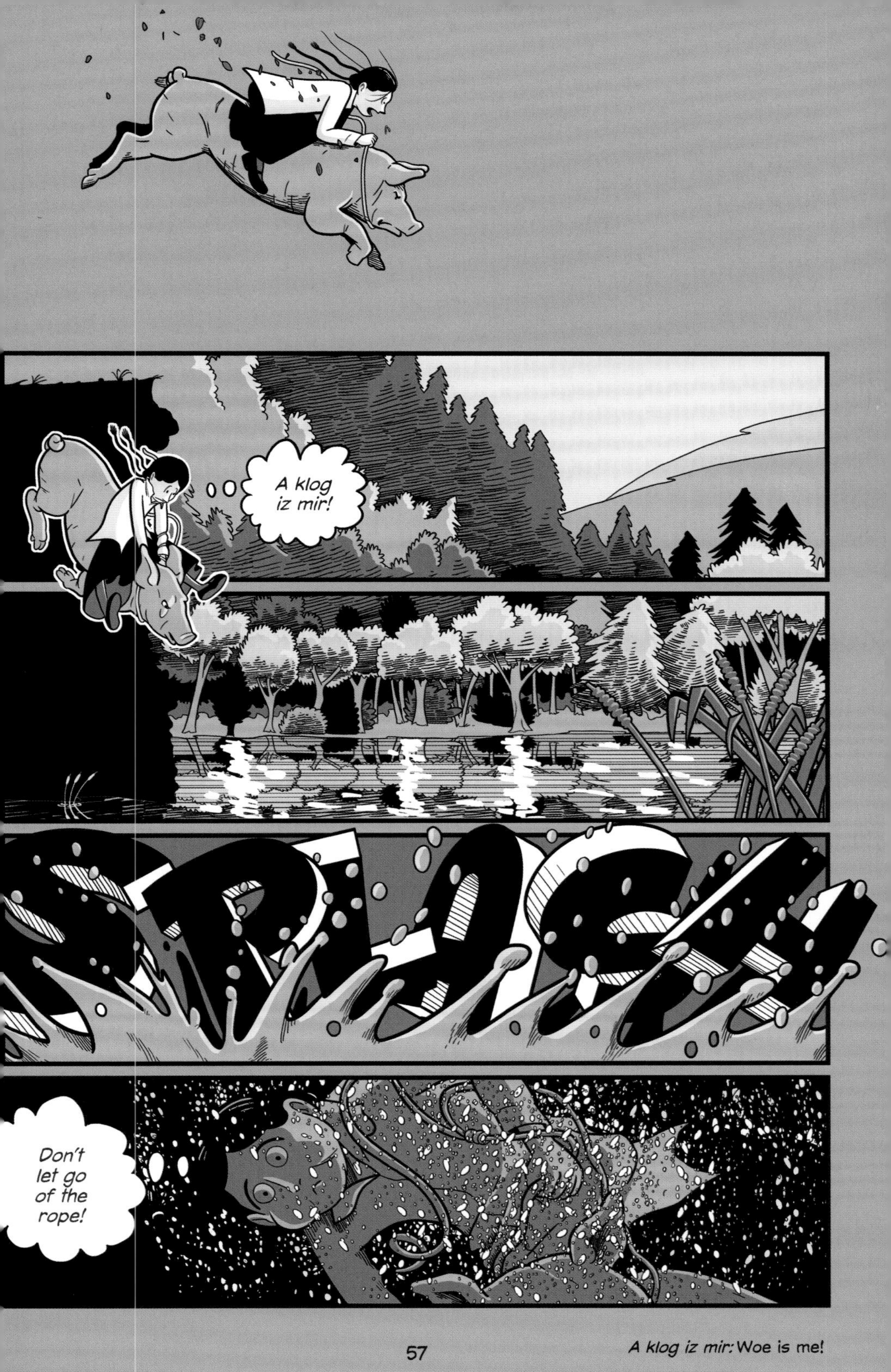
A klog iz mir!
SPLASH
Don't let go of the rope!

A klog iz mir: Woe is me!

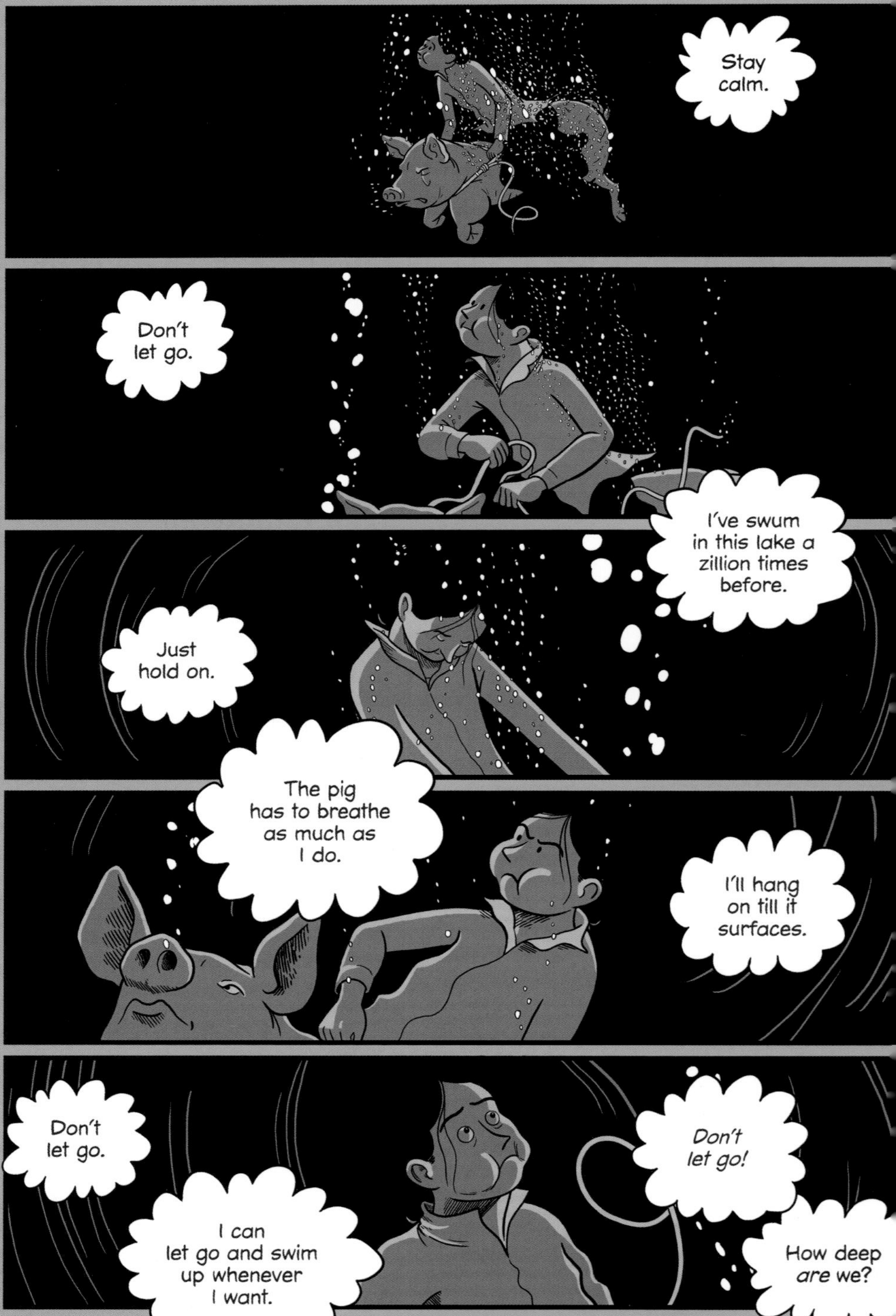
Stay calm.
Don't let go.
Just hold on.
I've swum in this lake a zillion times before.
The pig has to breathe as much as I do.
I'll hang on till it surfaces.
Don't let go.
I can let go and swim up whenever I want.
Don't let go!
How deep *are* we?

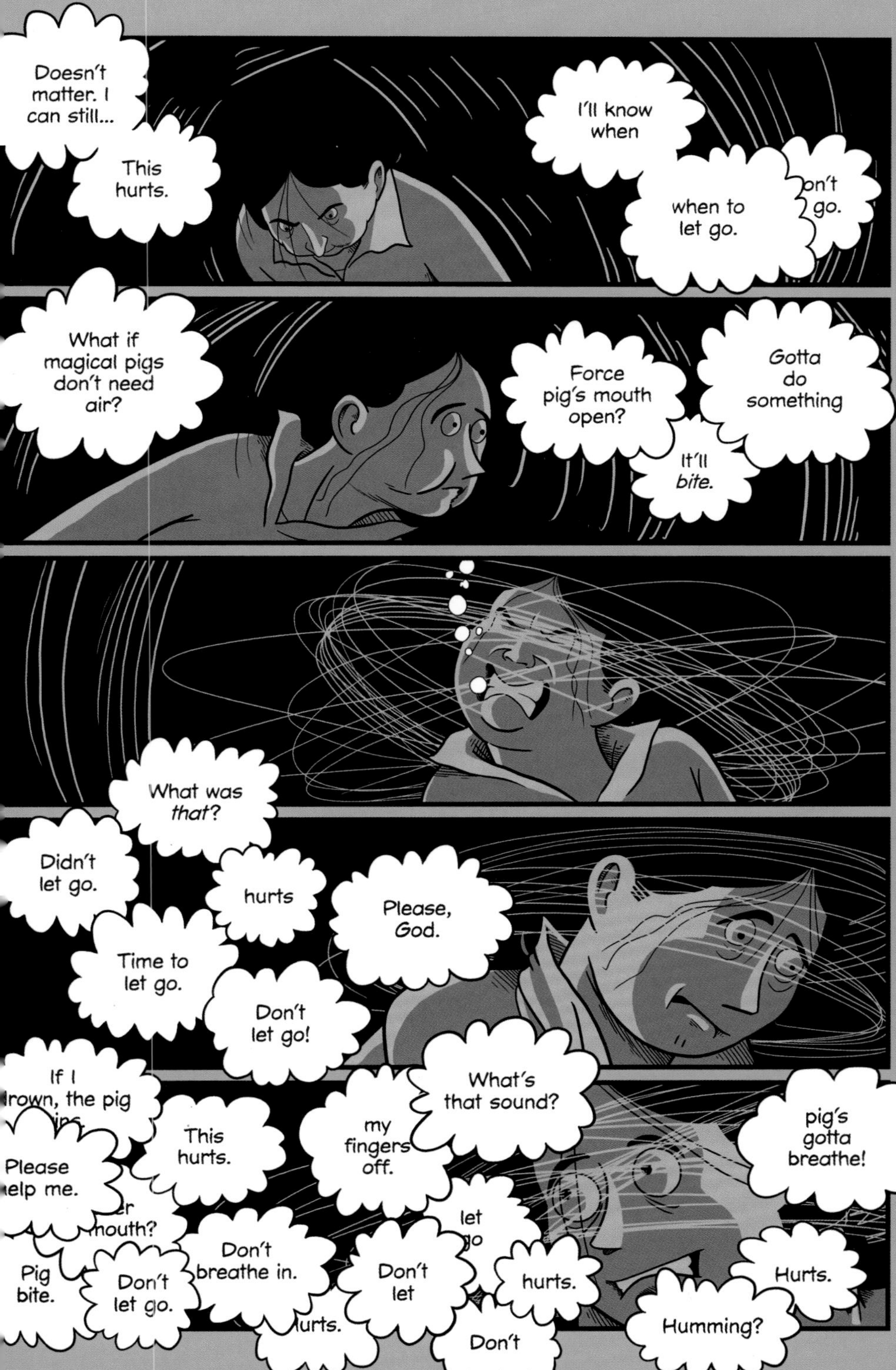
Doesn't matter. I can still...
This hurts.
I'll know when
when to let go.
on't go.
What if magical pigs don't need air?
Force pig's mouth open?
It'll *bite.*
Gotta do something
What was *that*?
Didn't let go.
hurts
Please, God.
Time to let go.
Don't let go!
If I
rown, the pig
Please
elp me.
mouth?
Pig bite.
This hurts.
Don't let go.
Don't breathe in.
my fingers off.
What's that sound?
let
Don't let
urts.
Don't
hurts.
pig's gotta breathe!
Hurts.
Humming?

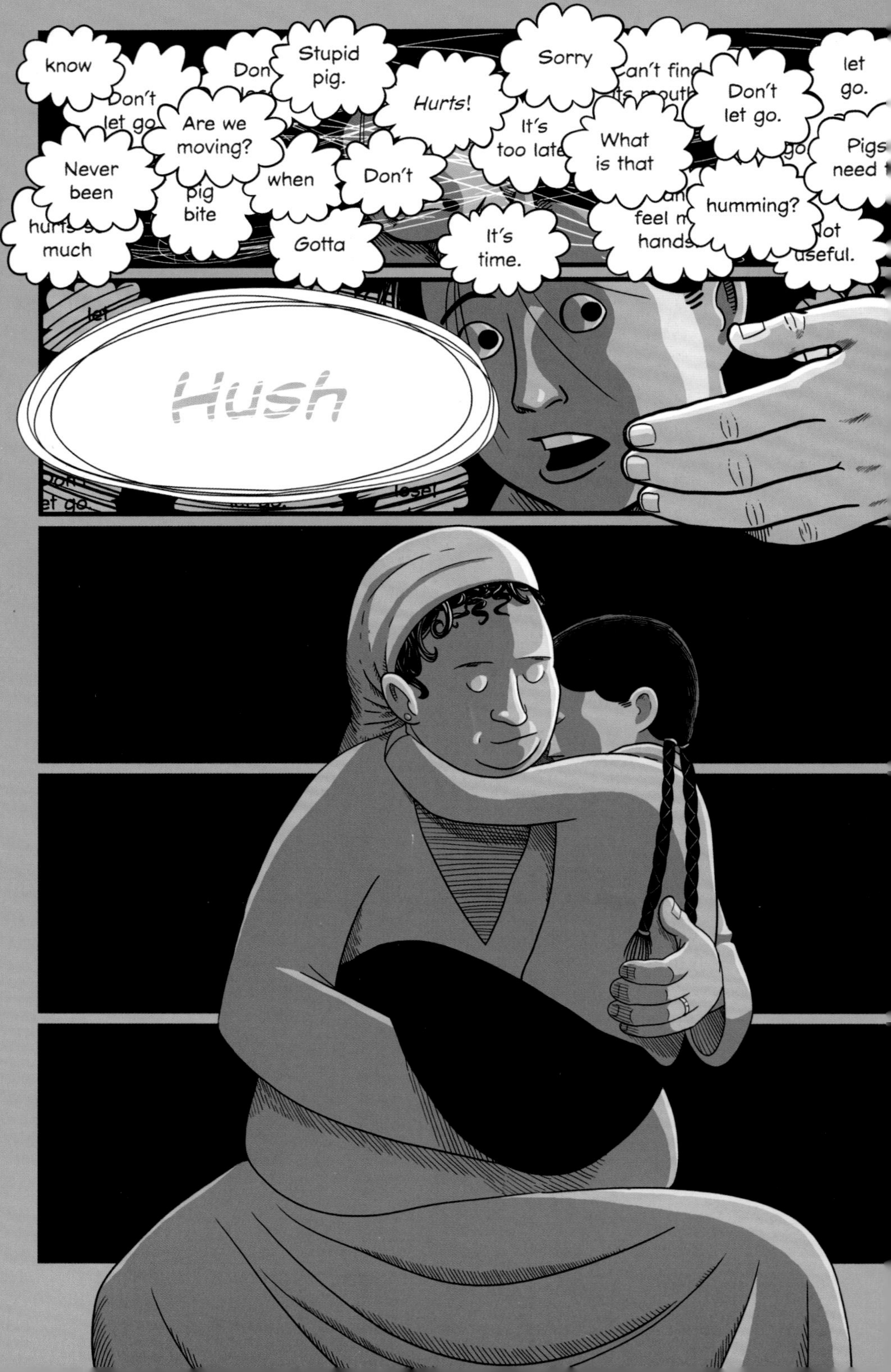
know
Stupid pig.
Sorry
let go.
Hurts!
Are we moving?
Don't let go.
Never been
What is that
when
Don't
Gotta
It's time.
humming?
Hush

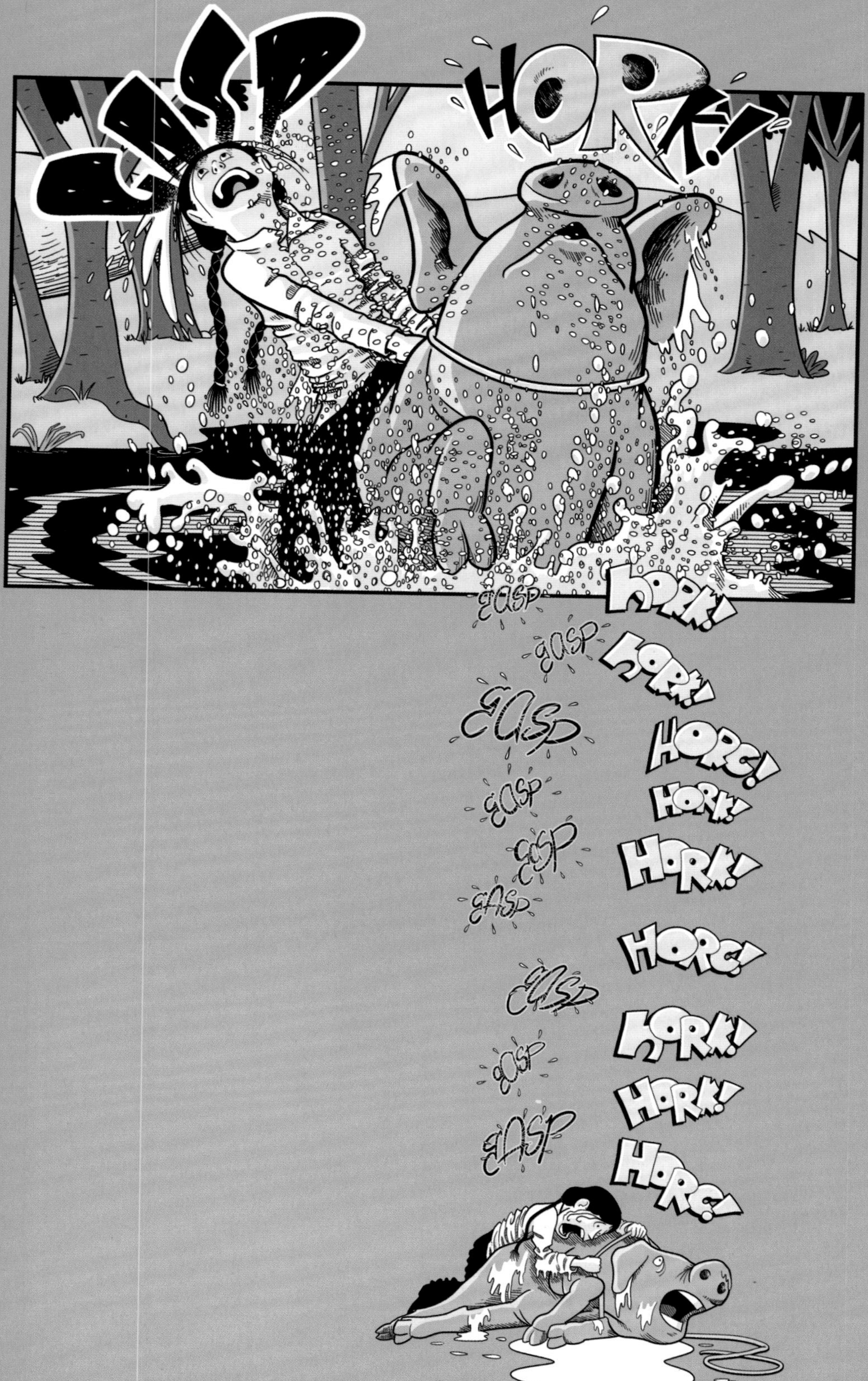
GASP
HORK!
GASP
HORK!
GASP
HORK!
GASP
HORC!
GASP
HORK!
GASP
HORK!
GASP
HORC!
GASP
HORK!
GASP
HORK!
GASP
HORC!

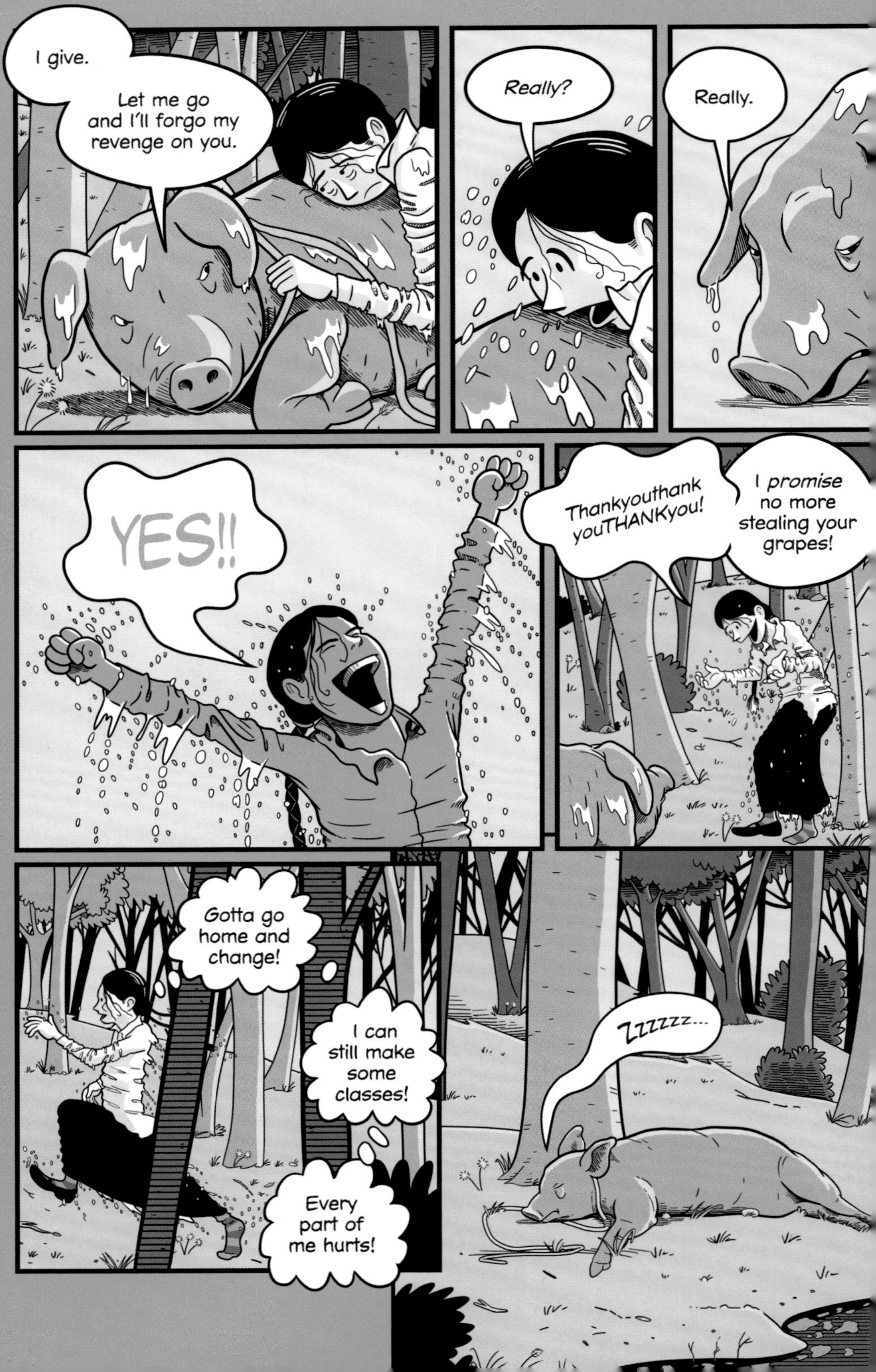
I give.
Let me go and I'll forgo my revenge on you.
Really?
Really.
YES!!
Thankyouthank youTHANKyou!
I *promise* no more stealing your grapes!
Gotta go home and change!
I can still make some classes!
Every part of me hurts!
Zzzzzz...

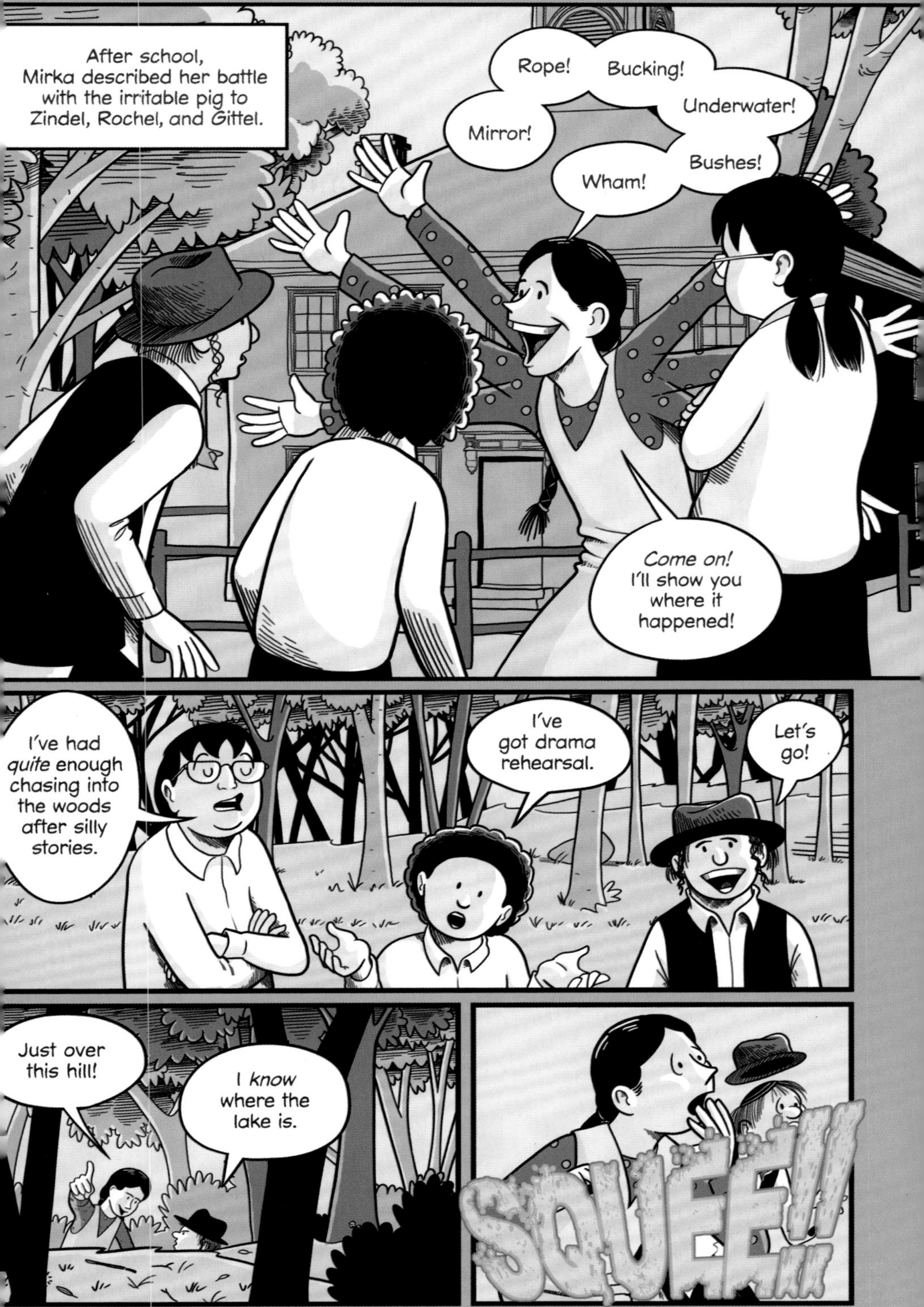
After school, Mirka described her battle with the irritable pig to Zindel, Rochel, and Gittel.
Rope!
Bucking!
Underwater!
Mirror!
Bushes!
Wham!
Come on! I'll show you where it happened!
I've had *quite* enough chasing into the woods after silly stories.
I've got drama rehearsal.
Let's go!
Just over this hill!
I *know* where the lake is.
SQUEE!!

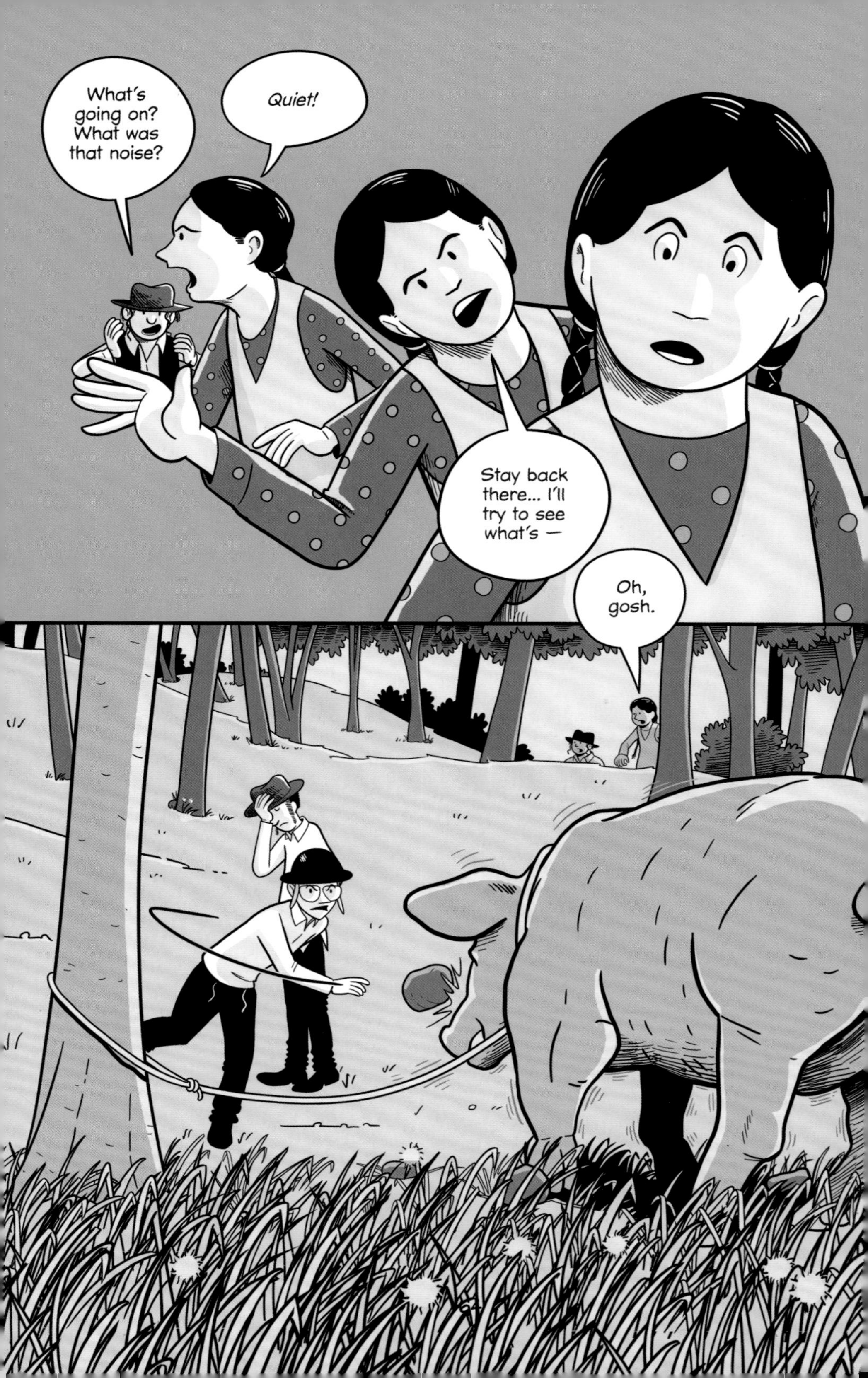
What's going on? What was that noise?
Quiet!
Stay back there... I'll try to see what's —
Oh, gosh.

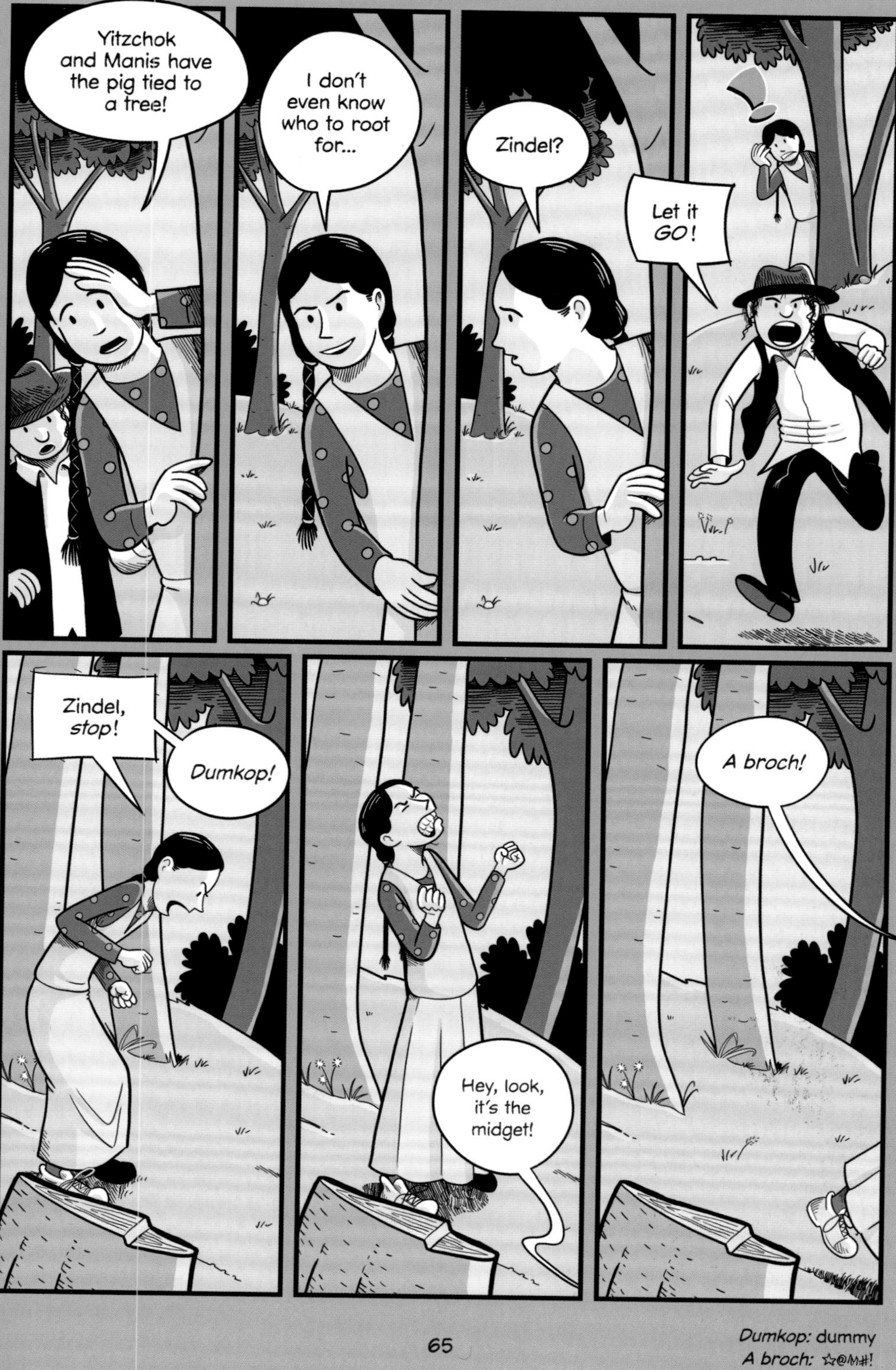
Yitzchok and Manis have the pig tied to a tree!
I don't even know who to root for...
Zindel?
Let it *GO*!
Zindel, *stop*!
Dumkop!
Hey, look, it's the midget!
A broch!

Dumkop: dummy
A broch: ☆@♍#!

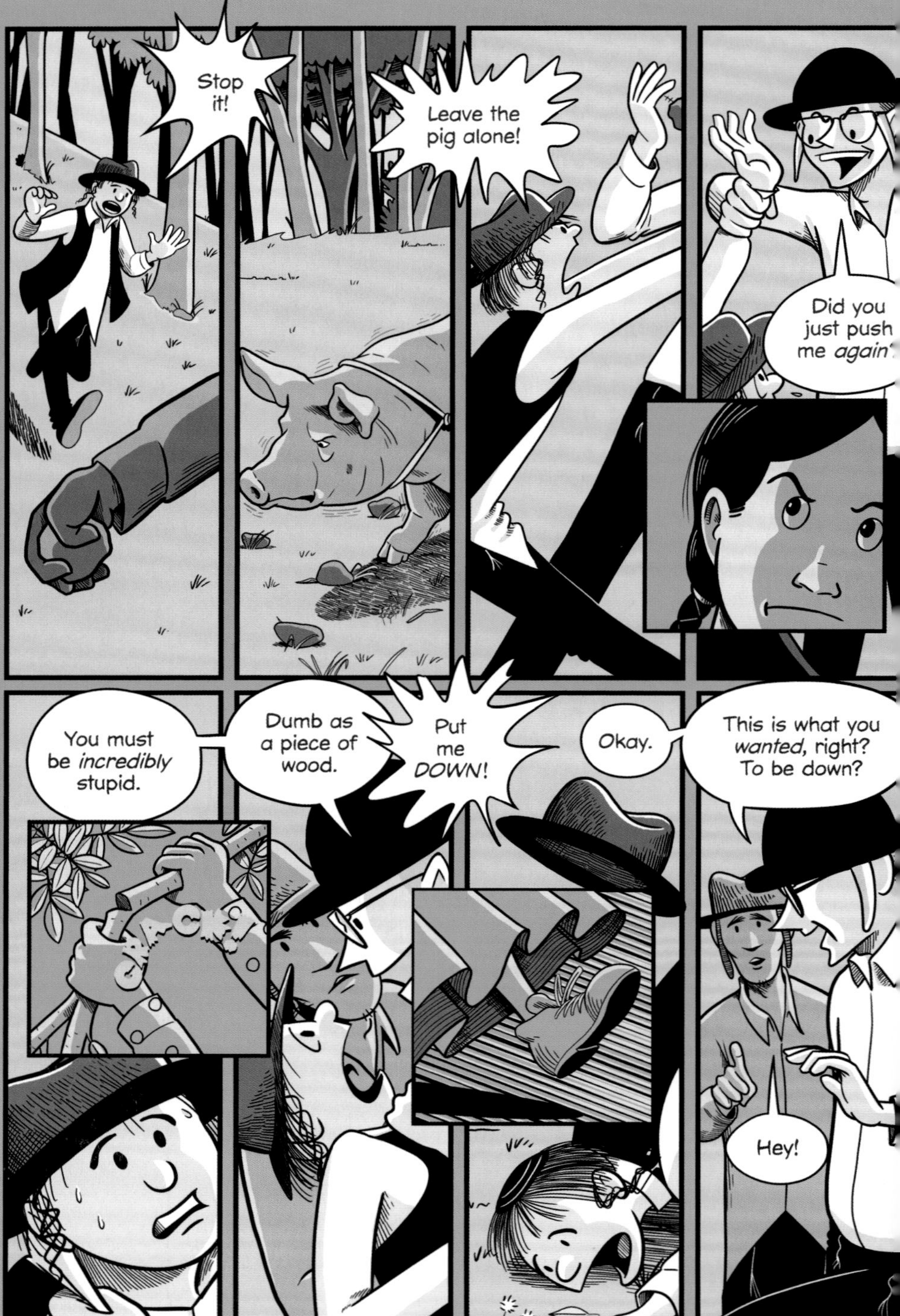
Stop it!
Leave the pig alone!
Did you just push me *again*
You must be *incredibly* stupid.
Dumb as a piece of wood.
CRACK
Put me *DOWN*!
Okay.
This is what you *wanted*, right? To be down?
Hey!

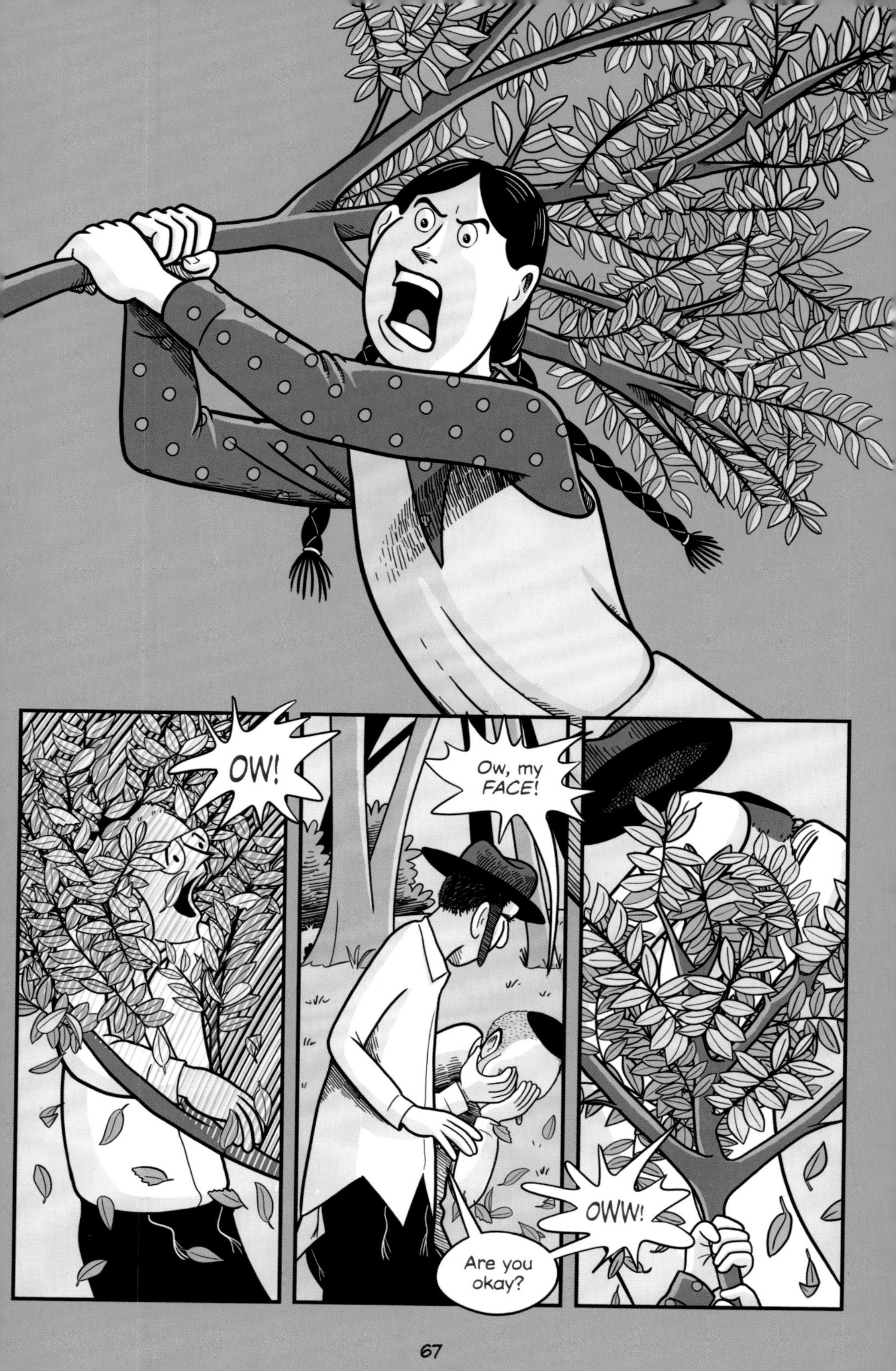

OW!
Ow, my FACE!
Are you okay?
OWW!

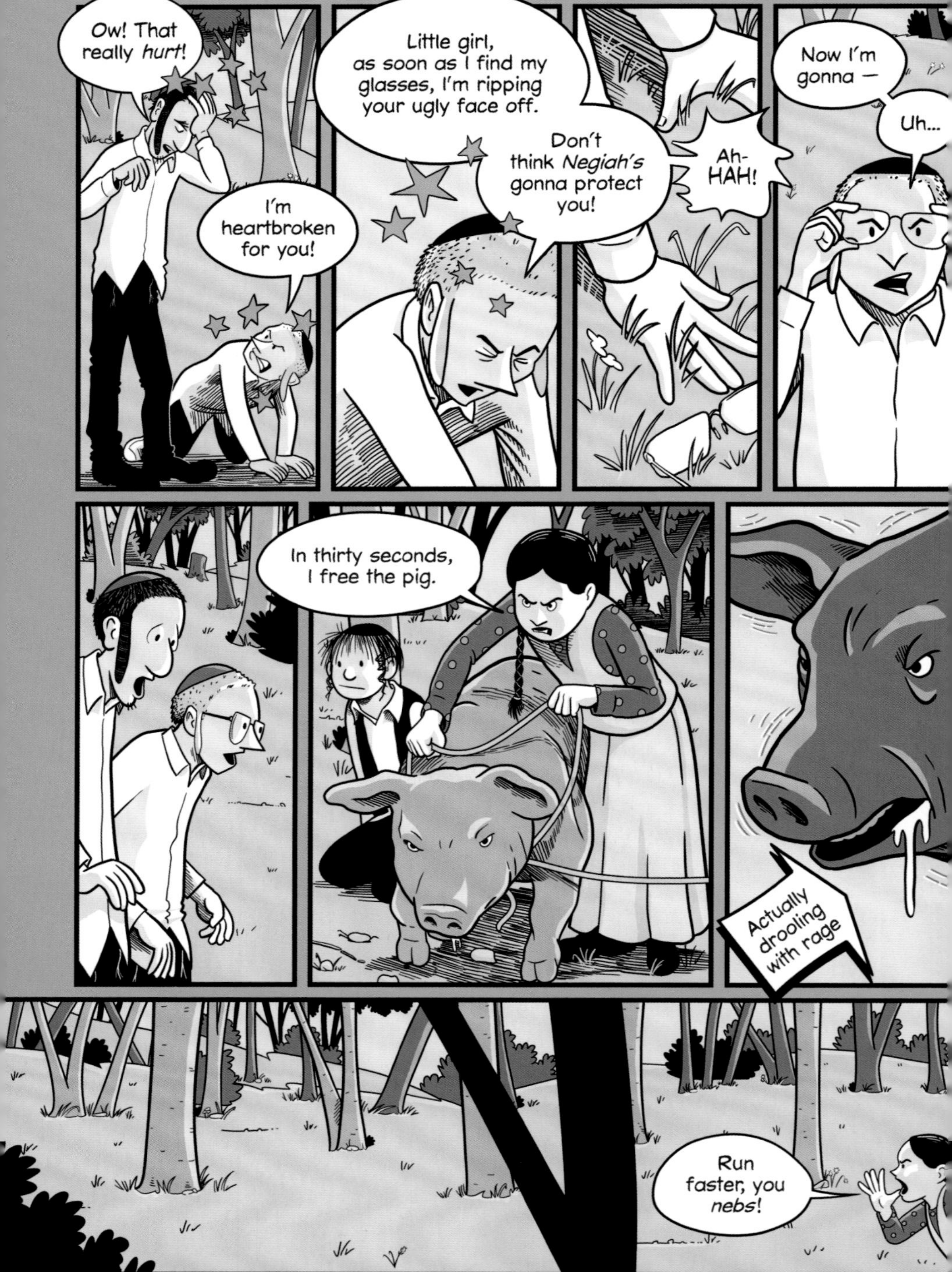
Ow! That really *hurt*!
I'm heartbroken for you!
Little girl, as soon as I find my glasses, I'm ripping your ugly face off.
Don't think *Negiah's* gonna protect you!
Ah-HAH!
Now I'm gonna —
Uh...
In thirty seconds, I free the pig.
Actually drooling with rage
Run faster, you *nebs*!

Negiah: rules forbidding contact between unrelated females and males

Nebs: losers

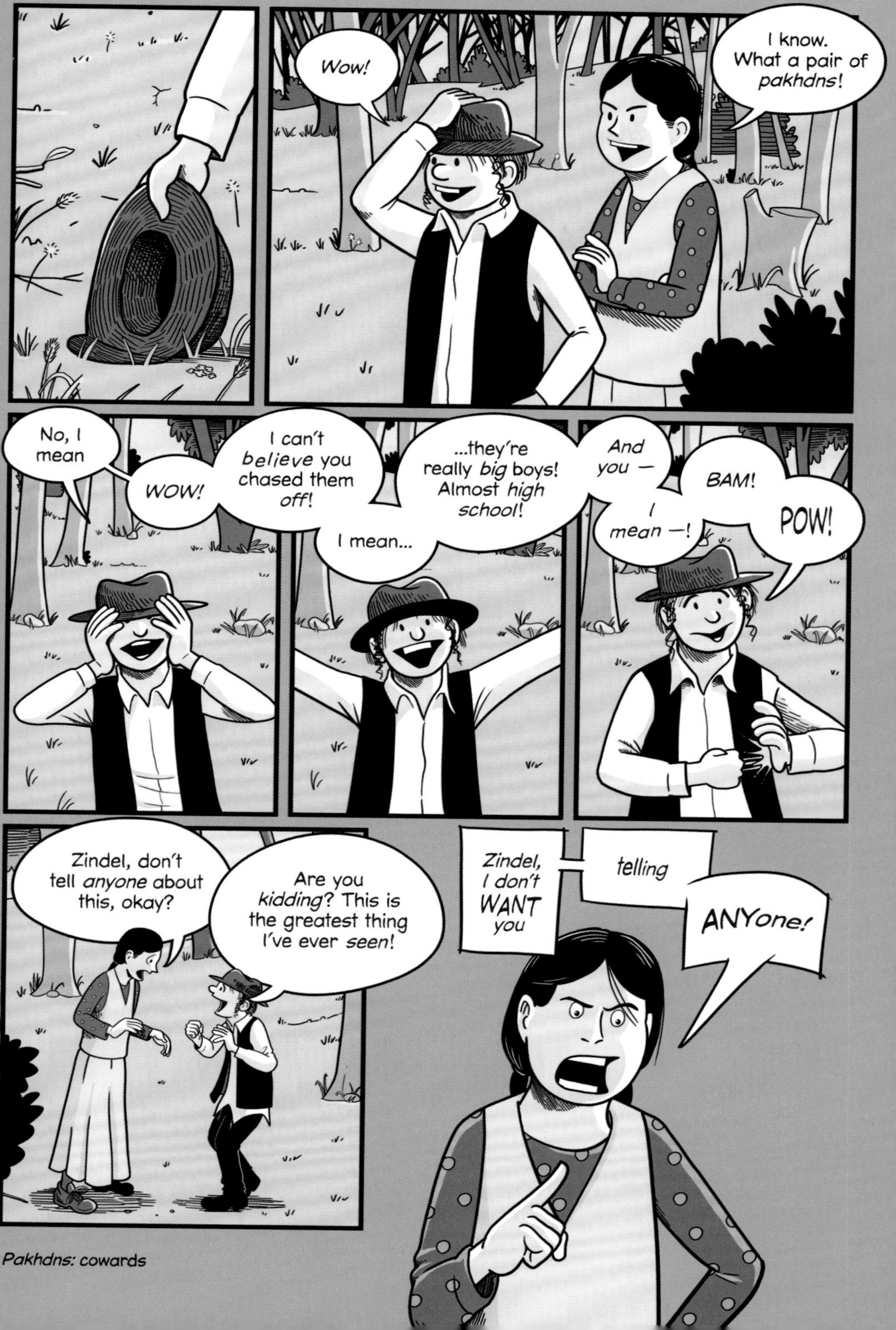
Wow!
I know. What a pair of pakhdns!
No, I mean
WOW!
I can't believe you chased them off!
I mean...
...they're really big boys! Almost high school!
And you —
I mean —!
BAM!
POW!
Zindel, don't tell anyone about this, okay?
Are you kidding? This is the greatest thing I've ever seen!
Zindel, I don't WANT you
telling
ANYone!

Pakhdns: cowards

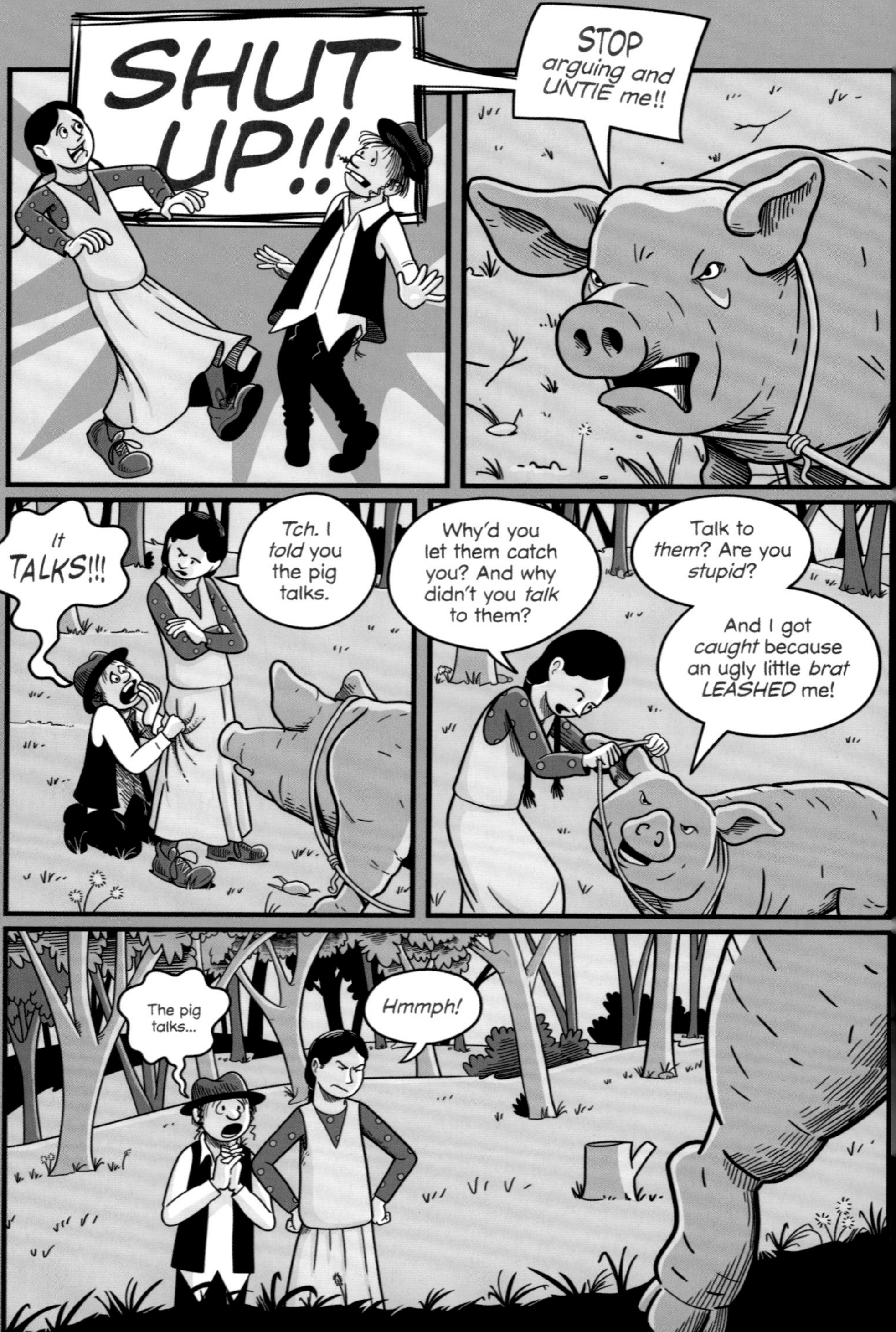
SHUT UP!!
STOP arguing and UNTIE me!!
It TALKS!!!
Tch. I told you the pig talks.
Why'd you let them catch you? And why didn't you talk to them?
Talk to them? Are you stupid?
And I got caught because an ugly little brat LEASHED me!
The pig talks...
Hmmph!

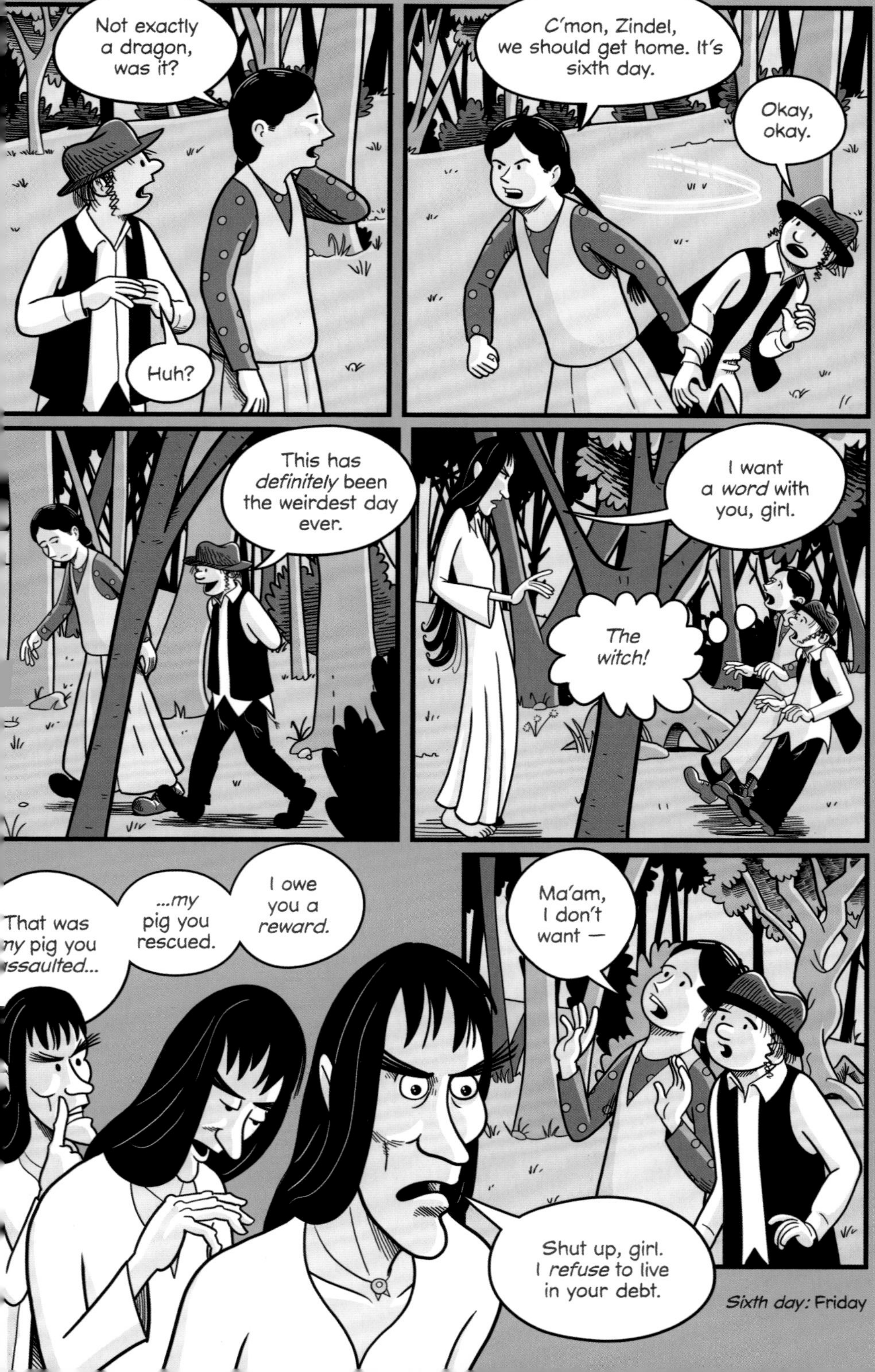
Not exactly a dragon, was it?
Huh?
C'mon, Zindel, we should get home. It's sixth day.
Okay, okay.
This has *definitely* been the weirdest day ever.
I want a *word* with you, girl.
The witch!
That was my pig you assaulted...
...my pig you rescued.
I owe you a *reward.*
Ma'am, I don't want —
Shut up, girl. I *refuse* to live in your debt.
Sixth day: Friday

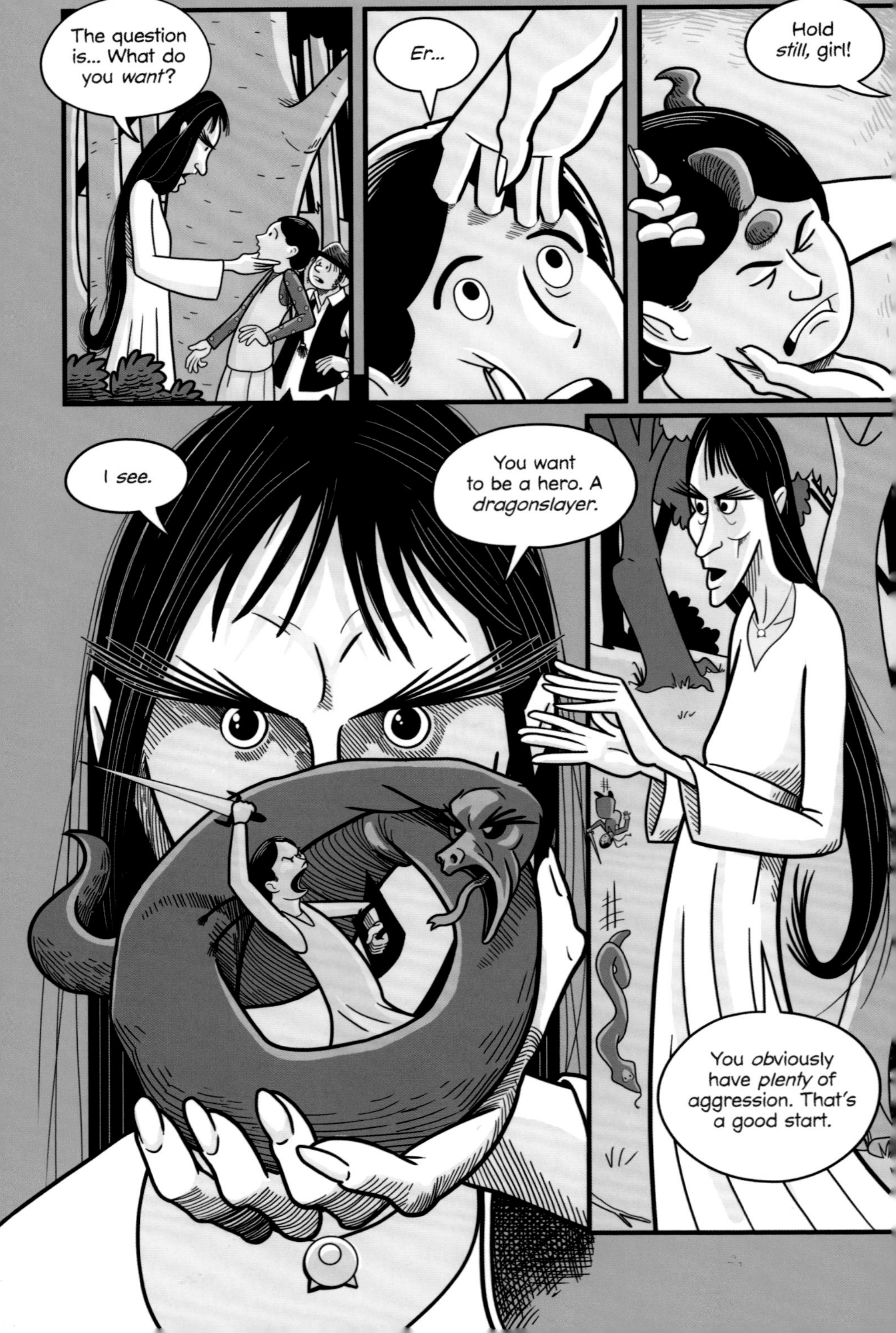
The question is... What do you *want*?
Er...
Hold *still,* girl!
I *see.*
You want to be a hero. A *dragonslayer.*
You *obviously* have *plenty* of aggression. That's a good start.

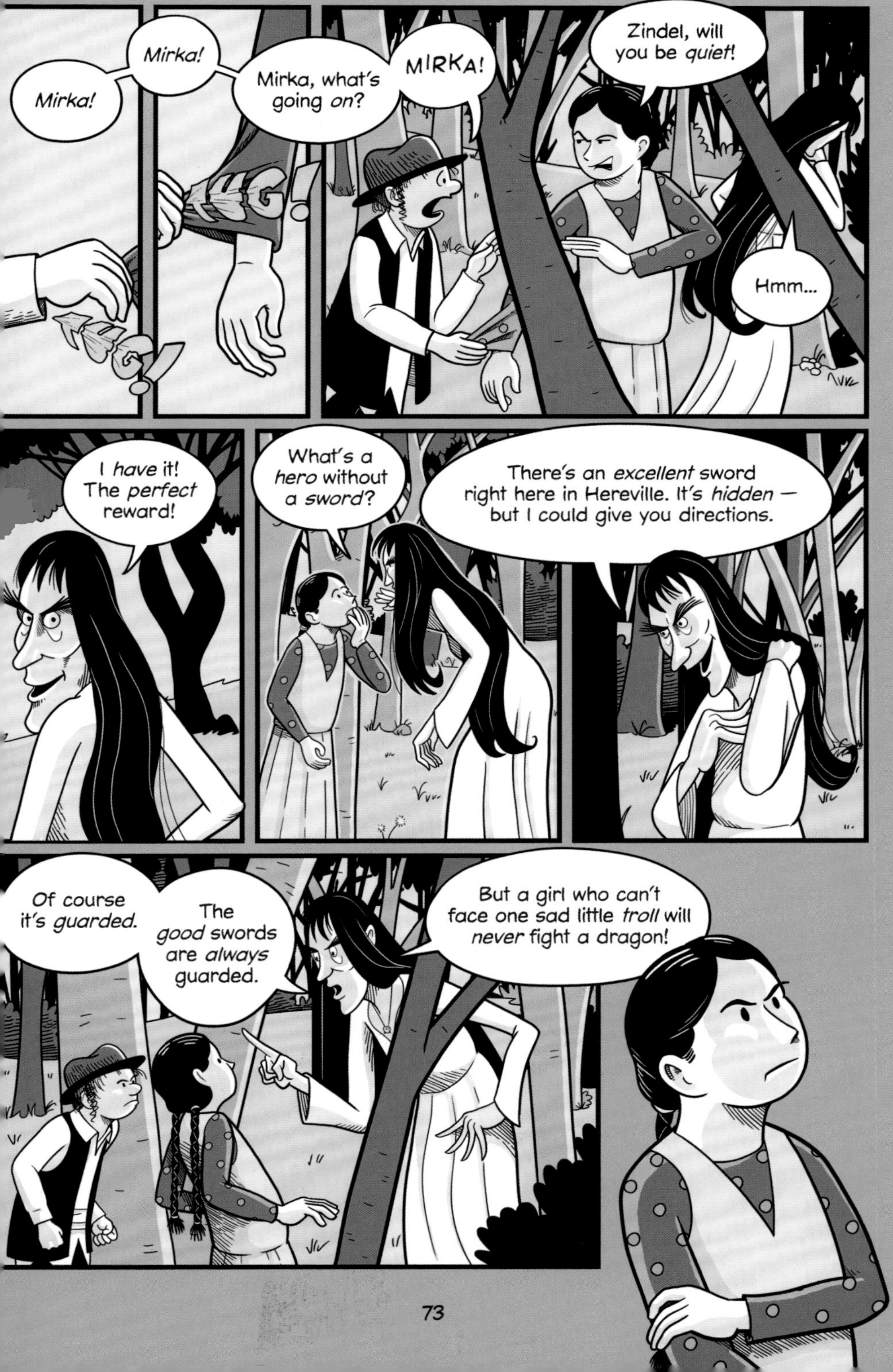
Mirka!
Mirka!
Mirka, what's going on?
MIRKA!
Zindel, will you be quiet!
Hmm...
I have it! The perfect reward!
What's a hero without a sword?
There's an excellent sword right here in Hereville. It's hidden — but I could give you directions.
Of course it's guarded.
The good swords are always guarded.
But a girl who can't face one sad little troll will never fight a dragon!

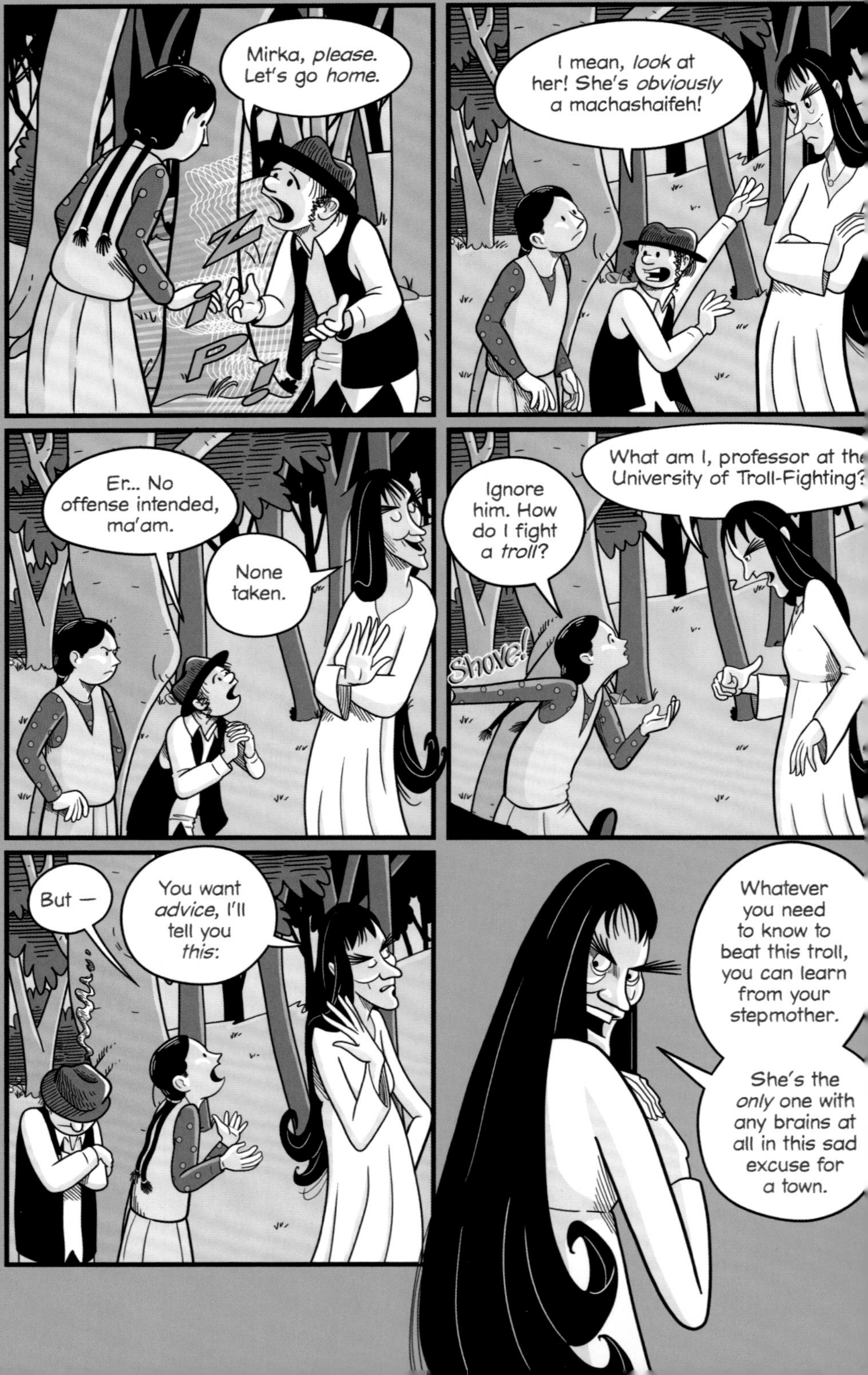
Mirka, *please.* Let's go *home.*
ZZIP!
I mean, *look* at her! She's *obviously* a machashaifeh!
Er... No offense intended, ma'am.
None taken.
Ignore him. How do I fight a *troll*?
What am I, professor at the University of Troll-Fighting?
Shove!
But —
You want *advice,* I'll tell you *this:*
Whatever you need to know to beat this troll, you can learn from your stepmother.
She's the *only* one with any brains at all in this sad excuse for a town.

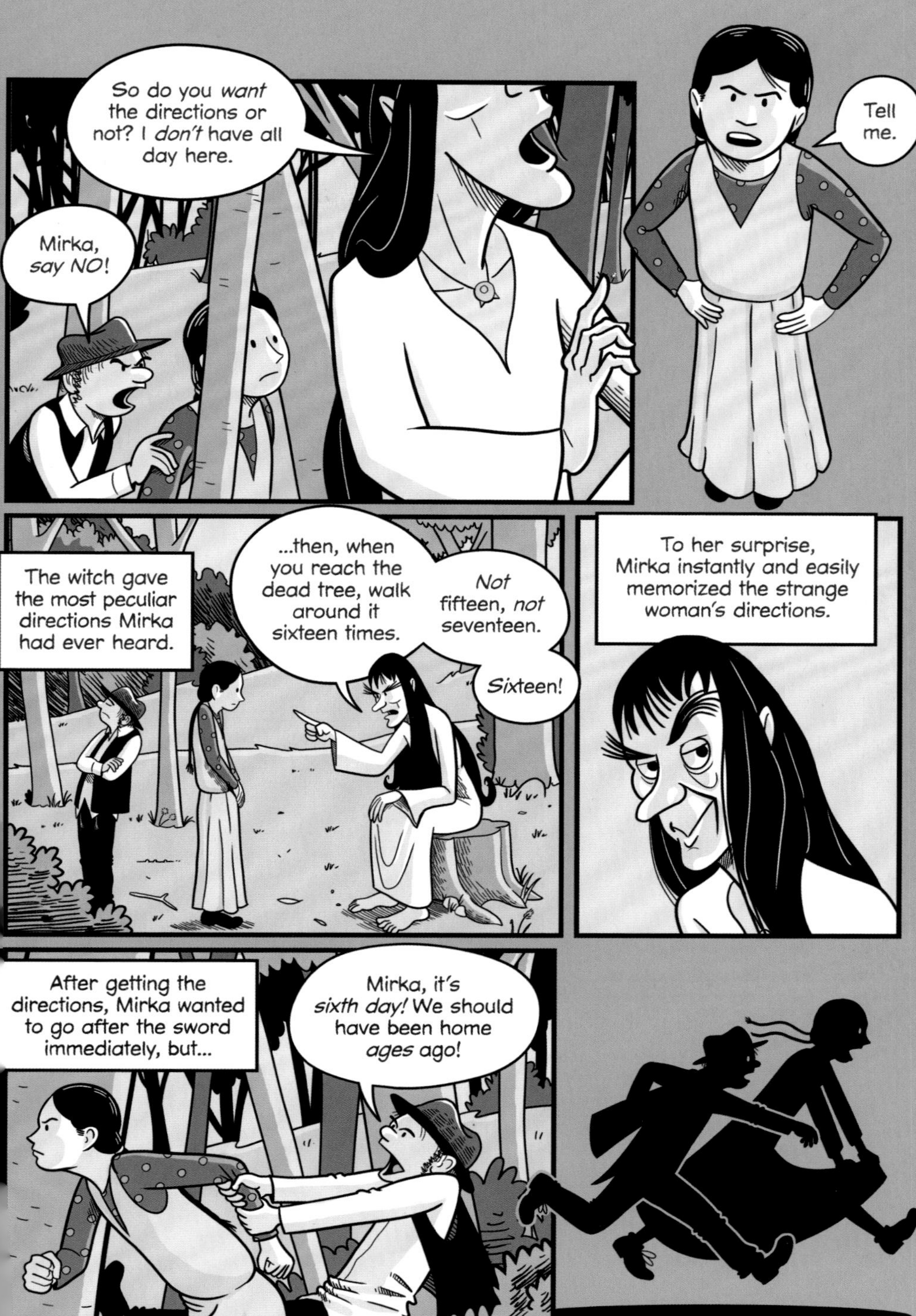

So do you *want* the directions or not? I *don't* have all day here.
Mirka, *say NO!*
Tell me.
The witch gave the most peculiar directions Mirka had ever heard.
...then, when you reach the dead tree, walk around it sixteen times.
Not fifteen, *not* seventeen.
Sixteen!
To her surprise, Mirka instantly and easily memorized the strange woman's directions.
After getting the directions, Mirka wanted to go after the sword immediately, but...
Mirka, it's *sixth day!* We should have been home *ages* ago!

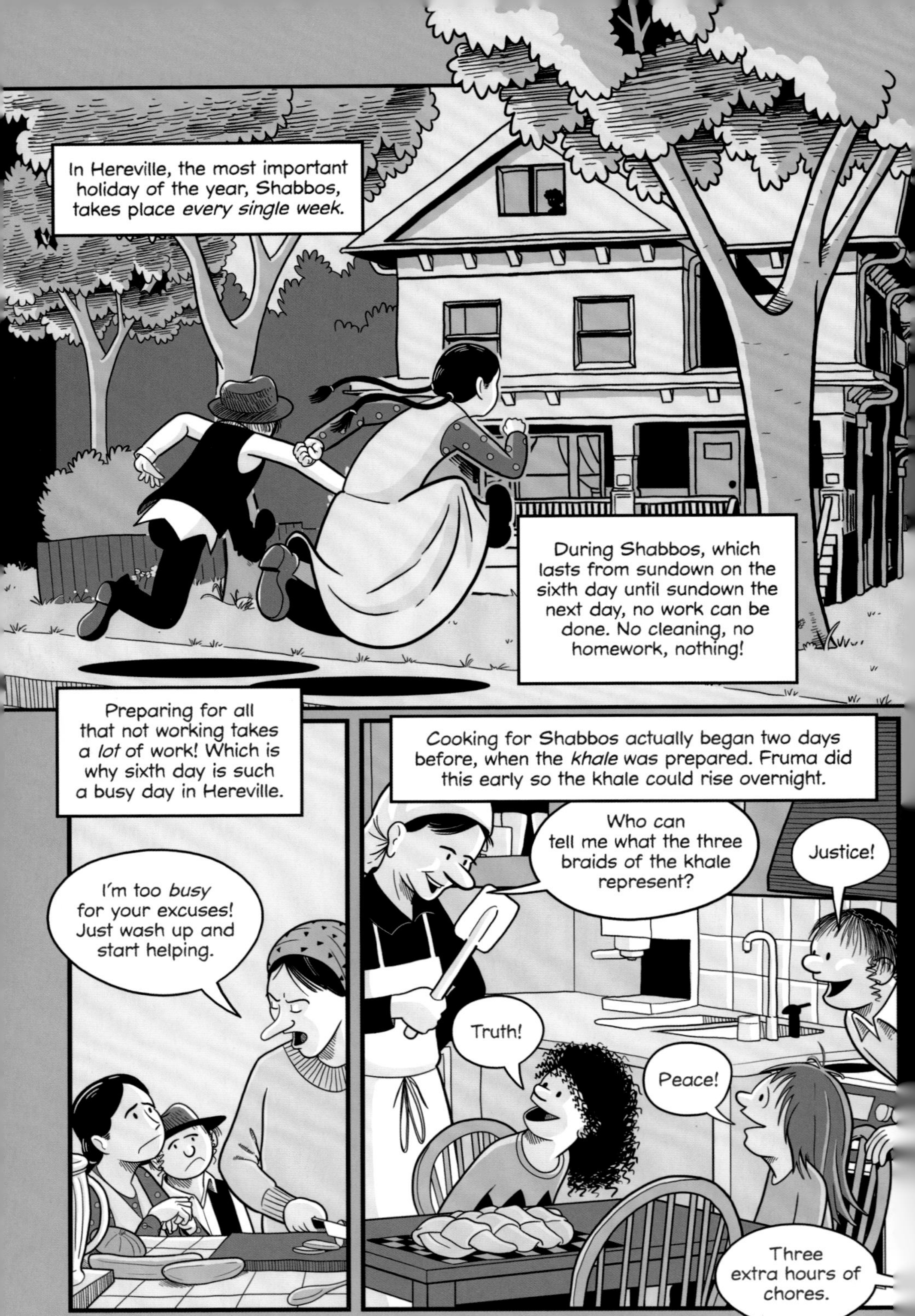
In Hereville, the most important holiday of the year, Shabbos, takes place *every single week.*
During Shabbos, which lasts from sundown on the sixth day until sundown the next day, no work can be done. No cleaning, no homework, nothing!
Preparing for all that not working takes a *lot* of work! Which is why sixth day is such a busy day in Hereville.
I'm too *busy* for your excuses! Just wash up and start helping.
Cooking for Shabbos actually began two days before, when the *khale* was prepared. Fruma did this early so the khale could rise overnight.
Who can tell me what the three braids of the khale represent?
Justice!
Truth!
Peace!
Three extra hours of chores.

Khale: bread

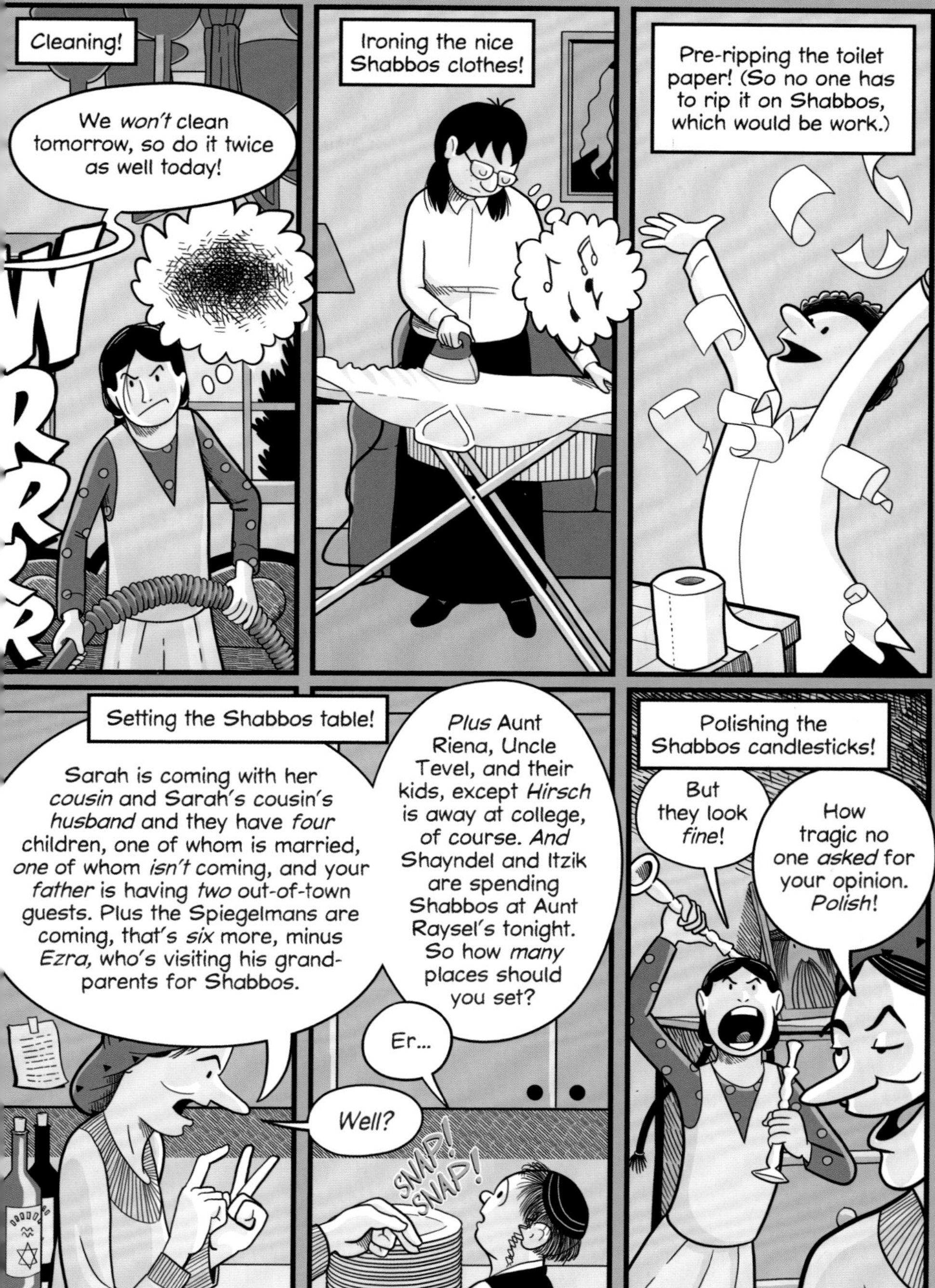
Cleaning!
We *won't* clean tomorrow, so do it twice as well today!
WRRRR
Ironing the nice Shabbos clothes!
Pre-ripping the toilet paper! (So no one has to rip it on Shabbos, which would be work.)
Setting the Shabbos table!
Sarah is coming with her *cousin* and Sarah's cousin's *husband* and they have *four* children, one of whom is married, *one* of whom *isn't* coming, and your *father* is having *two* out-of-town guests. Plus the Spiegelmans are coming, that's *six* more, minus *Ezra,* who's visiting his grand-parents for Shabbos.
Plus Aunt Riena, Uncle Tevel, and their kids, except *Hirsch* is away at college, of course. *And* Shayndel and Itzik are spending Shabbos at Aunt Raysel's tonight. So how *many* places should you set?
Er...
Well?
SNAP! SNAP!
Polishing the Shabbos candlesticks!
But they look *fine*!
How tragic no one *asked* for your opinion. *Polish*!

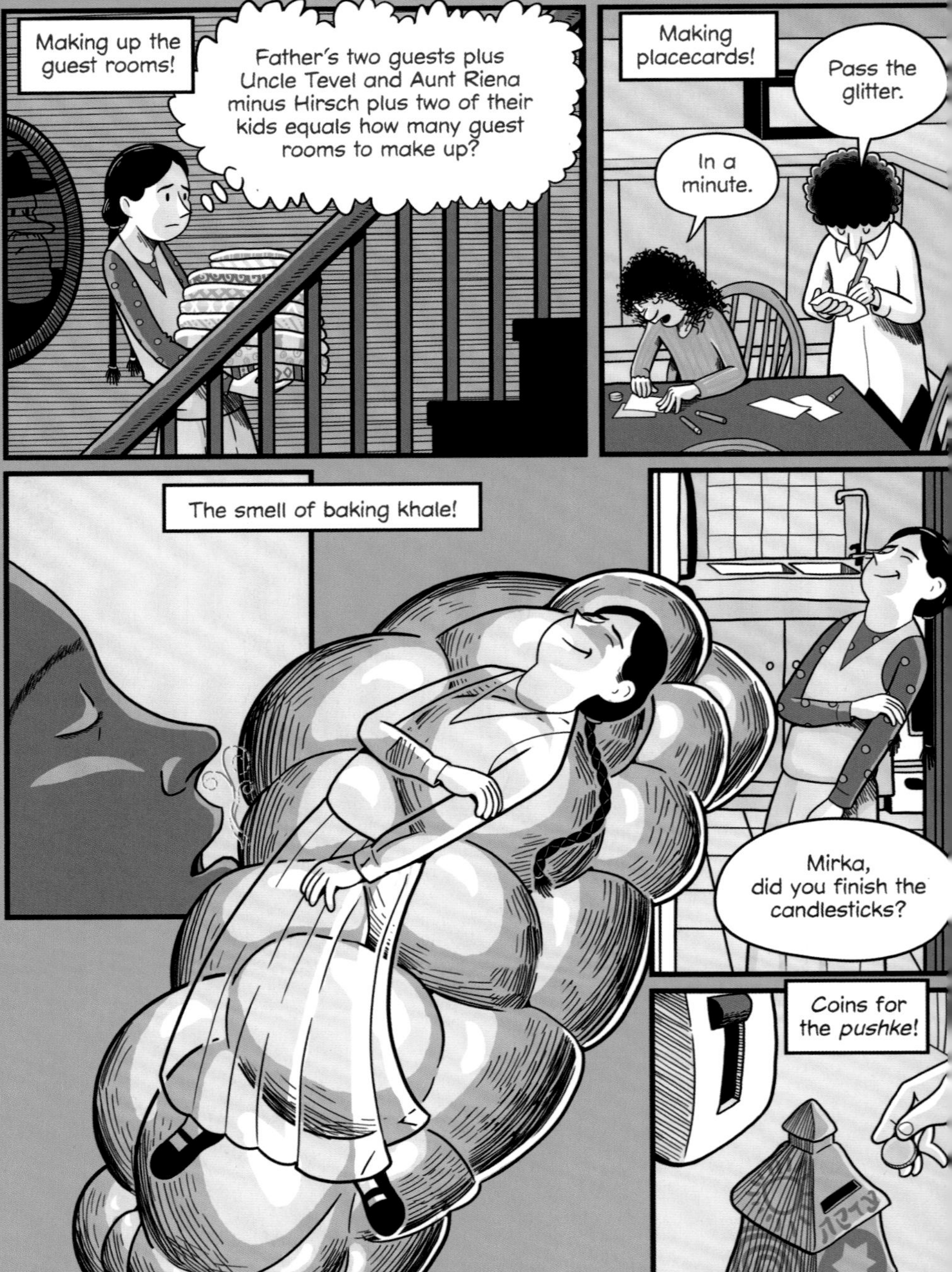
Making up the guest rooms!
Father's two guests plus Uncle Tevel and Aunt Riena minus Hirsch plus two of their kids equals how many guest rooms to make up?
Making placecards!
Pass the glitter.
In a minute.
The smell of baking khale!
Mirka, did you finish the candlesticks?
Coins for the *pushke*!

Pushke: charity box

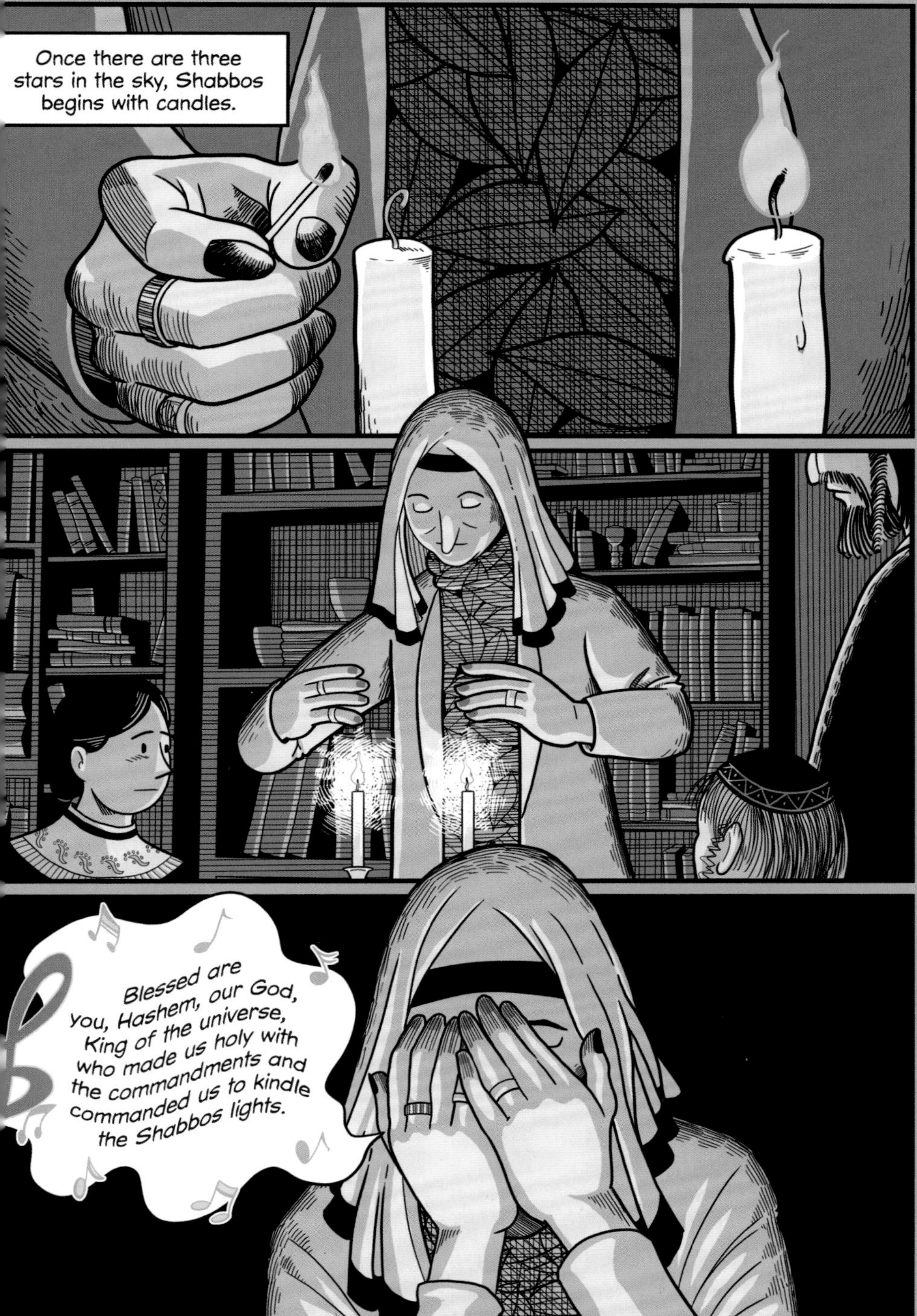
Once there are three stars in the sky, Shabbos begins with candles.
Blessed are you, Hashem, our God, King of the universe, who made us holy with the commandments and commanded us to kindle the Shabbos lights.

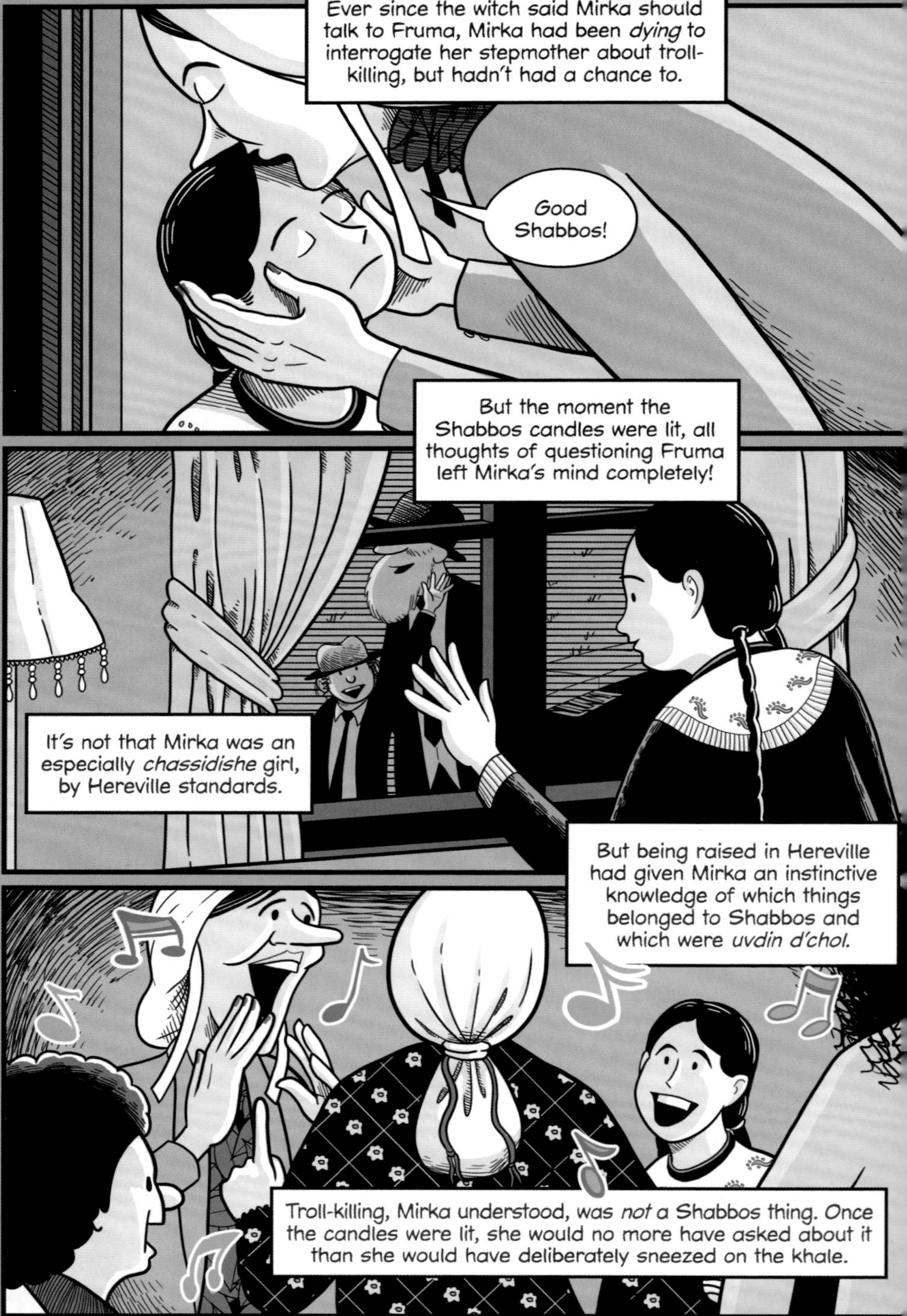
Ever since the witch said Mirka should talk to Fruma, Mirka had been *dying* to interrogate her stepmother about troll-killing, but hadn't had a chance to.
Good Shabbos!
But the moment the Shabbos candles were lit, all thoughts of questioning Fruma left Mirka's mind completely!
It's not that Mirka was an especially *chassidishe* girl, by Hereville standards.
But being raised in Hereville had given Mirka an instinctive knowledge of which things belonged to Shabbos and which were *uvdin d'chol.*
Troll-killing, Mirka understood, was *not* a Shabbos thing. Once the candles were lit, she would no more have asked about it than she would have deliberately sneezed on the khale.

Chassidishe: religiously observant
Uvdin d'chol: weekday things

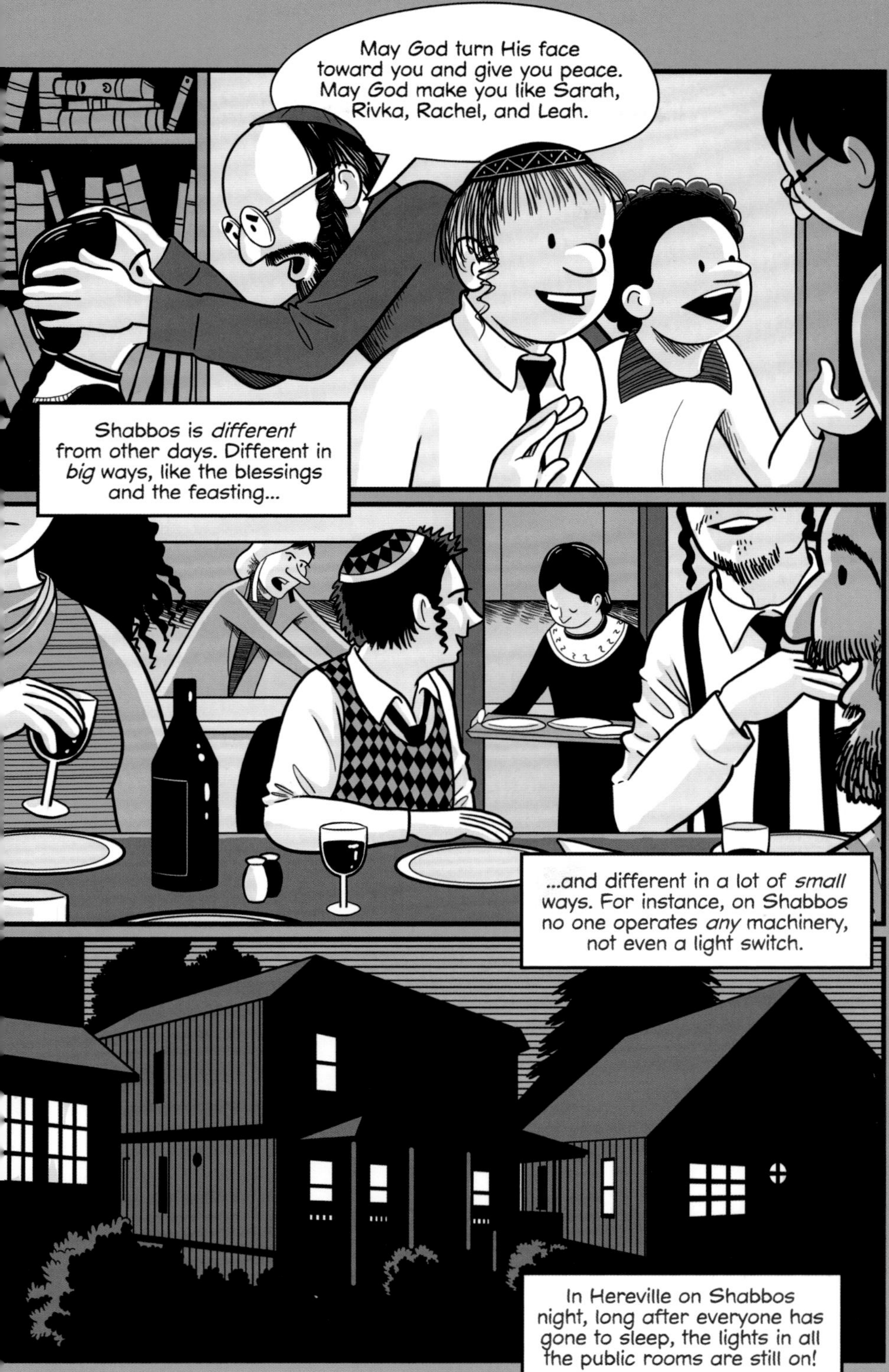
May God turn His face toward you and give you peace. May God make you like Sarah, Rivka, Rachel, and Leah.
Shabbos is *different* from other days. Different in *big* ways, like the blessings and the feasting...
...and different in a lot of *small* ways. For instance, on Shabbos no one operates *any* machinery, not even a light switch.
In Hereville on Shabbos night, long after everyone has gone to sleep, the lights in all the public rooms are still on!

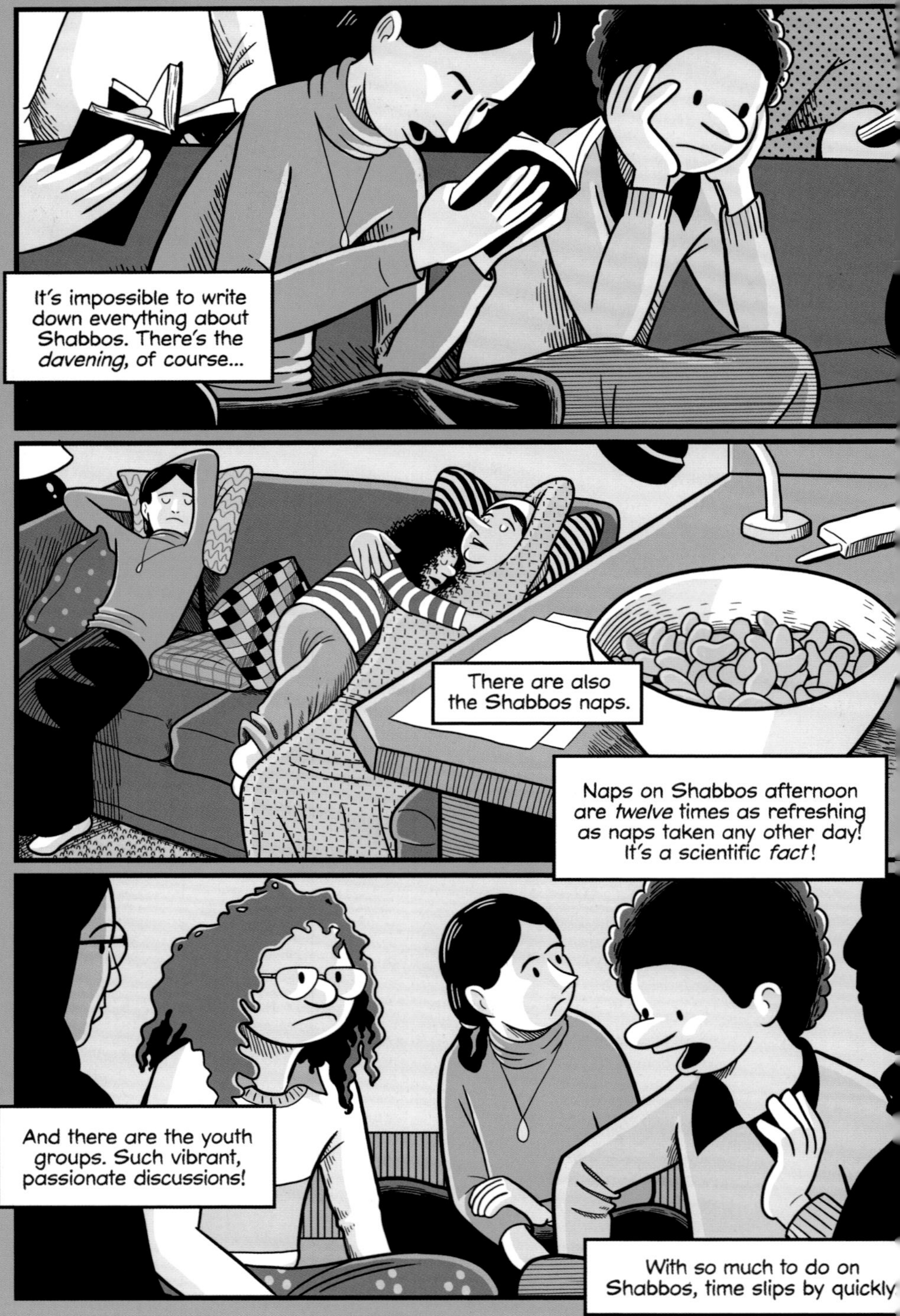
It's impossible to write down everything about Shabbos. There's the *davening*, of course...
There are also the Shabbos naps.
Naps on Shabbos afternoon are *twelve* times as refreshing as naps taken any other day! It's a scientific *fact*!
And there are the youth groups. Such vibrant, passionate discussions!
With so much to do on Shabbos, time slips by quickly.

Daven: pray

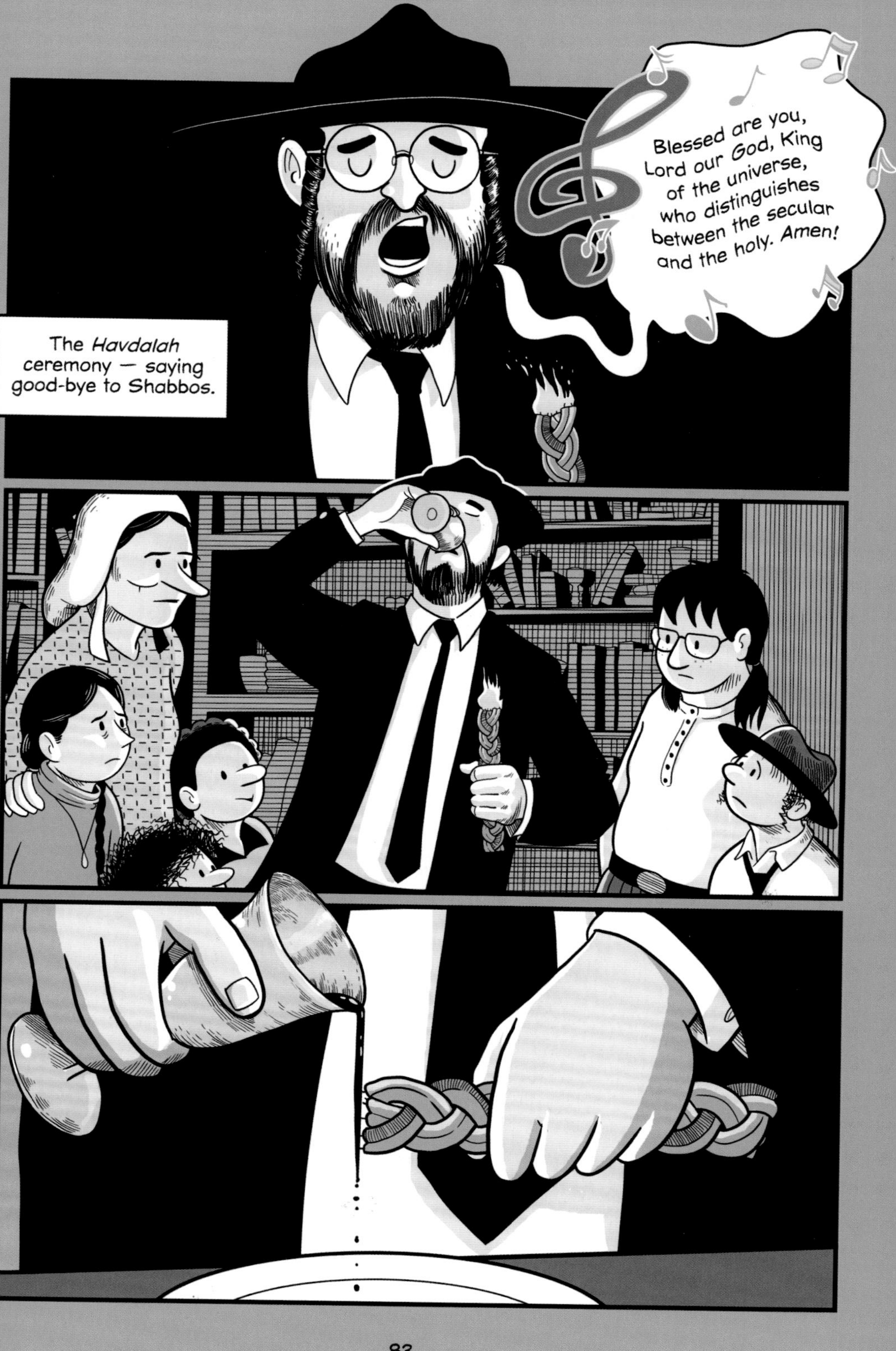

The *Havdalah* ceremony — saying good-bye to Shabbos.
Blessed are you, Lord our *God*, King of the universe, who distinguishes between the secular and the holy. *Amen!*

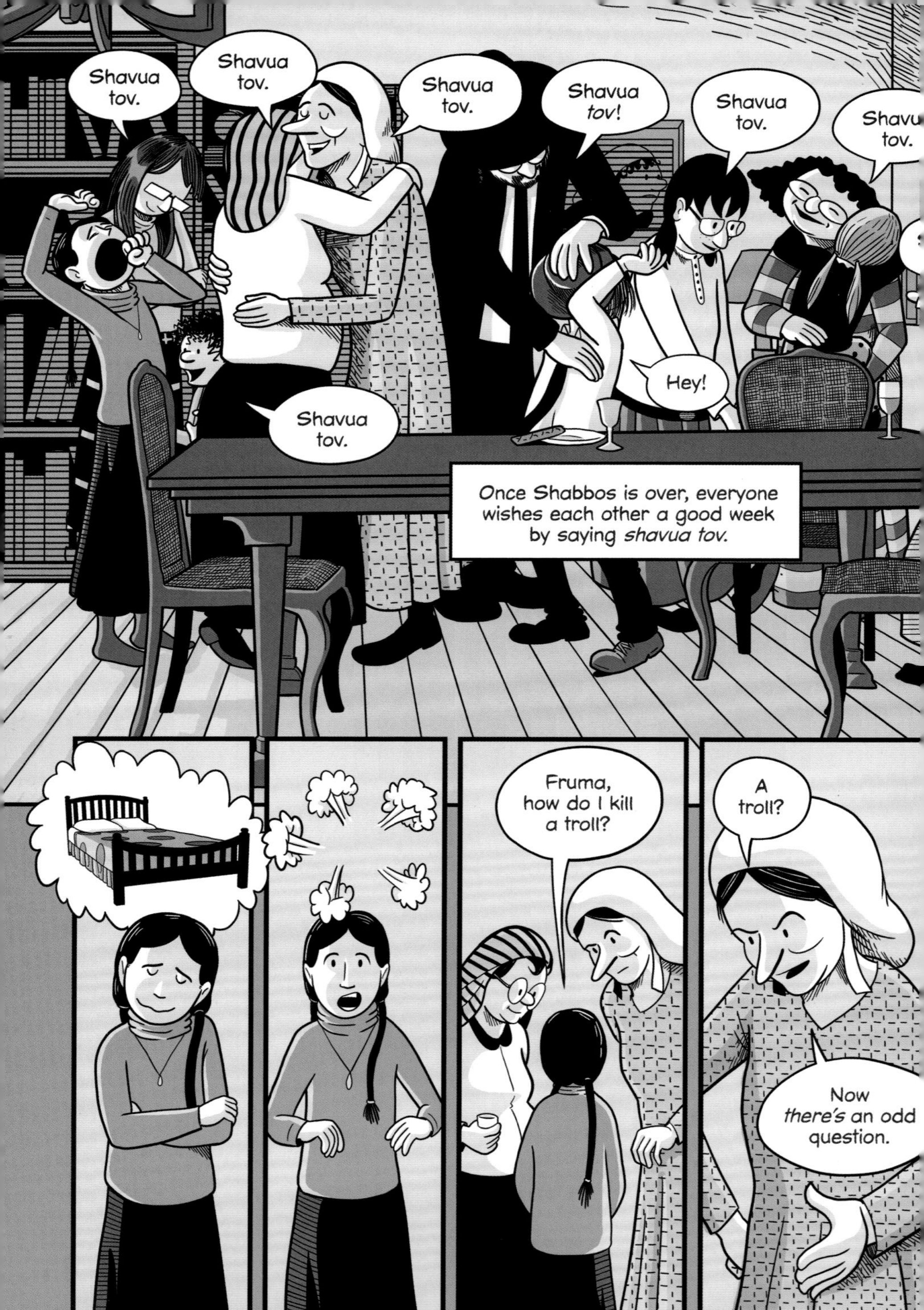
Shavua tov.
Shavua tov.
Shavua tov.
Shavua *tov*!
Shavua tov.
Shavu tov.
Hey!
Shavua tov.
Once Shabbos is over, everyone wishes each other a good week by saying *shavua tov.*
Fruma, how do I kill a troll?
A troll?
Now *there's* an odd question.

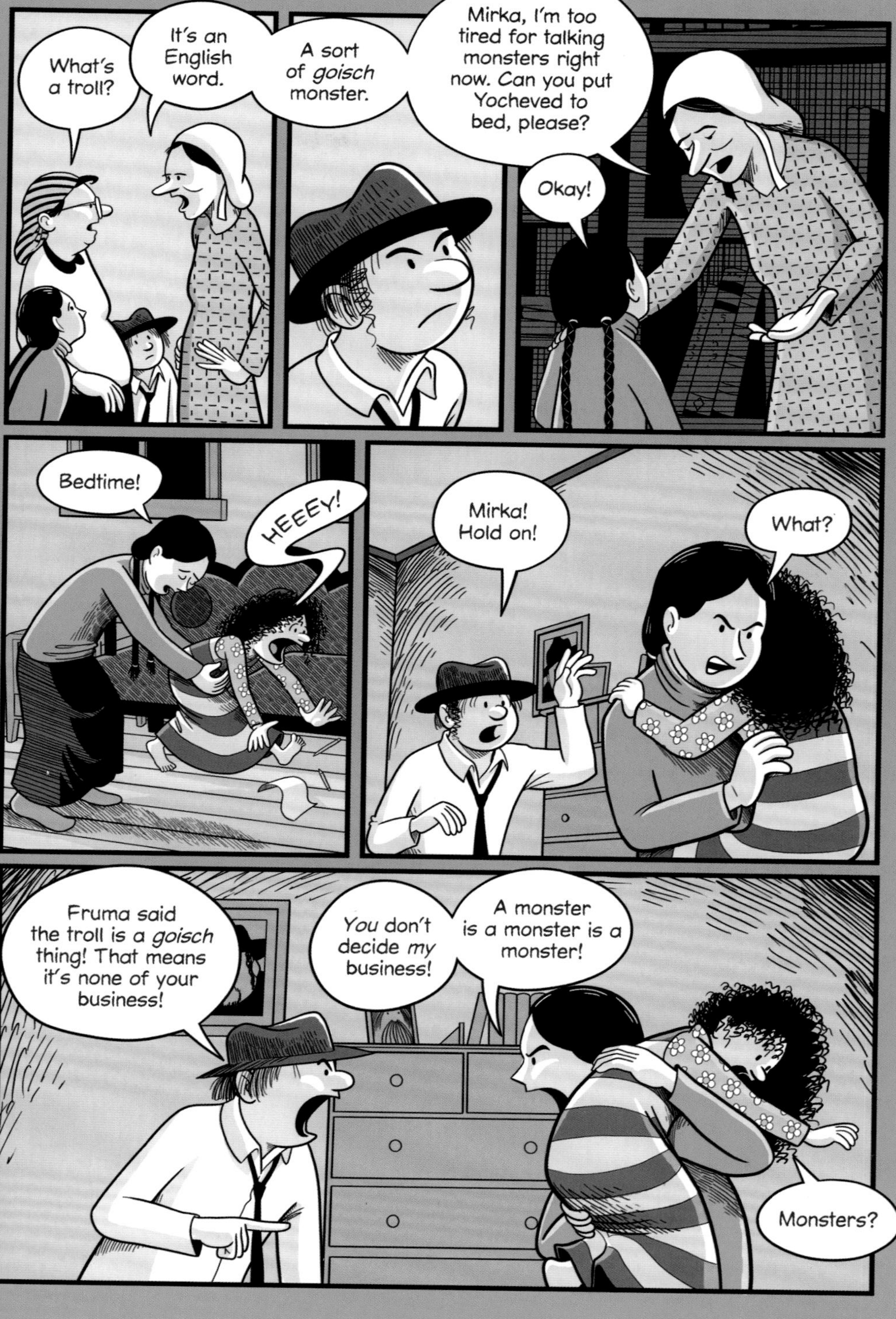
What's a troll?
It's an English word.
A sort of *goisch* monster.
Mirka, I'm too tired for talking monsters right now. Can you put Yocheved to bed, please?
Okay!
Bedtime!
HEEEY!
Mirka! Hold on!
What?
Fruma said the troll is a *goisch* thing! That means it's none of your business!
You don't decide *my* business!
A monster is a monster is a monster!
Monsters?

Goisch: non-Jewish

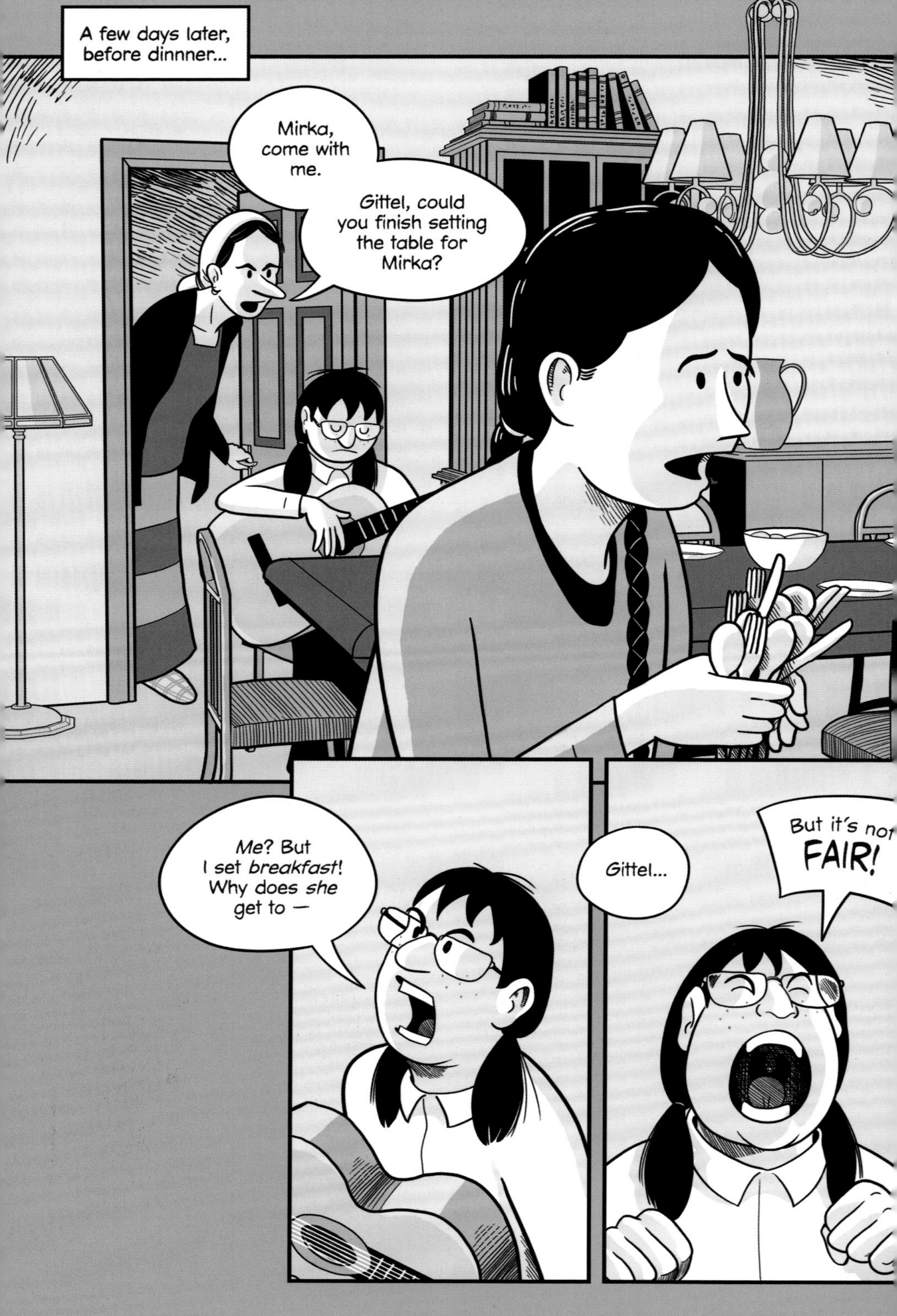
A few days later, before dinnner...
Mirka, come with me.
Gittel, could you finish setting the table for Mirka?
Me? But I set *breakfast*! Why does *she* get to —
Gittel...
But it's not **FAIR!**

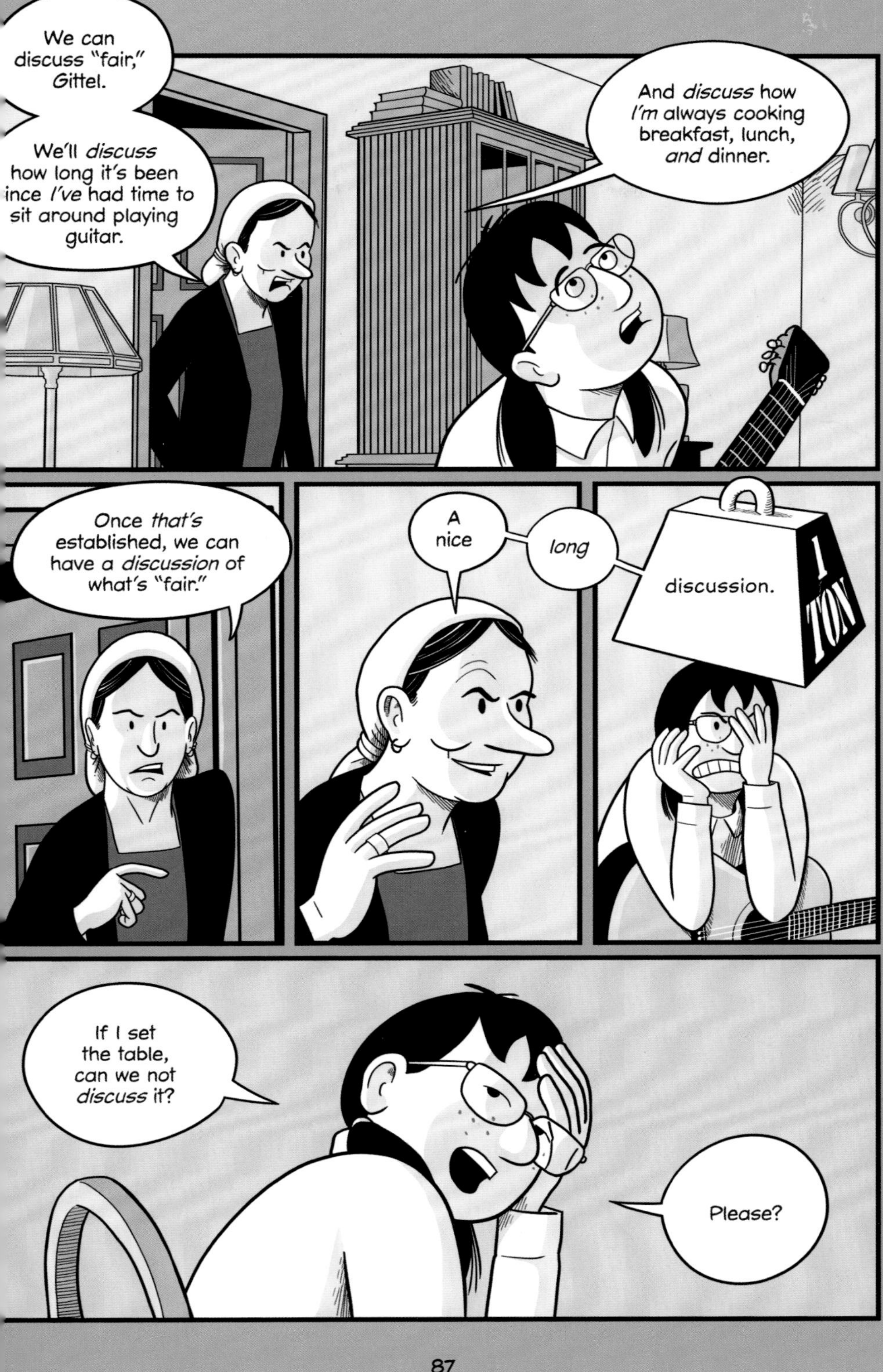
We can discuss "fair," Gittel.
We'll *discuss* how long it's been ince *I've* had time to sit around playing guitar.
And *discuss* how *I'm* always cooking breakfast, lunch, *and* dinner.
Once *that's* established, we can have a *discussion* of what's "fair."
A nice
long
discussion.
1 TON
If I set the table, can we not *discuss* it?
Please?

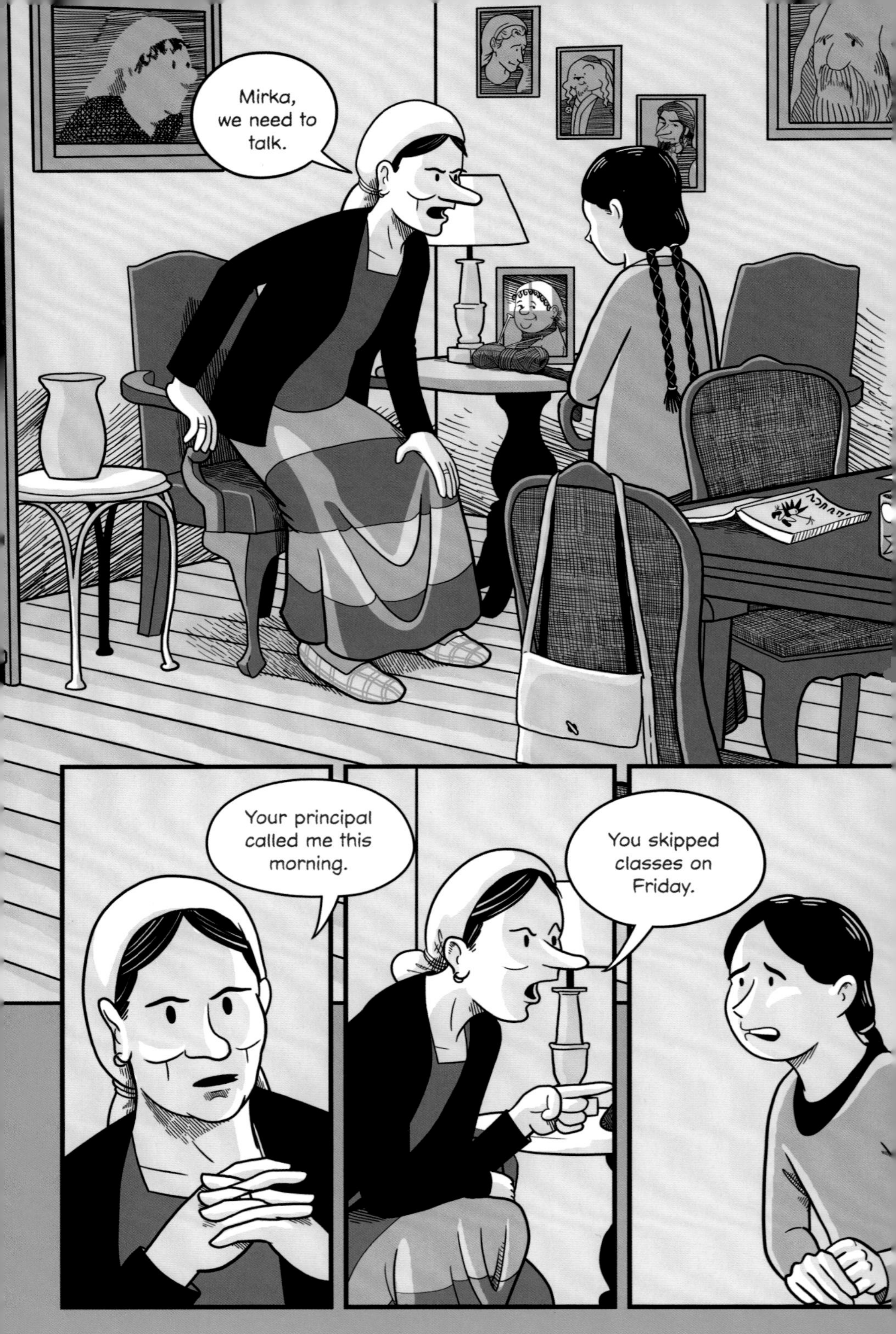
Mirka, we need to talk.
Your principal called me this morning.
You skipped classes on Friday.

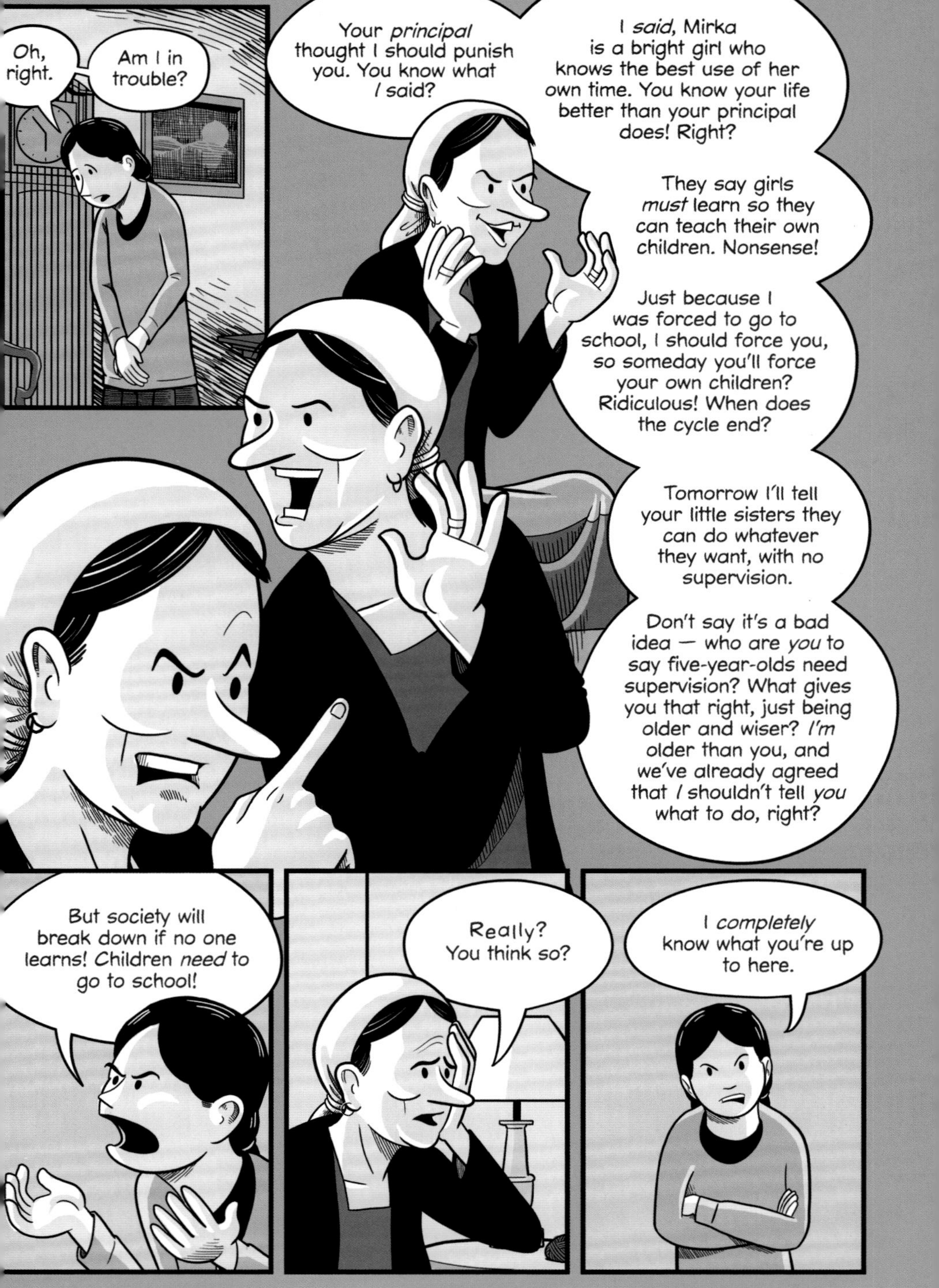

Oh, right.
Am I in trouble?
Your *principal* thought I should punish you. You know what *I* said?
I *said*, Mirka is a bright girl who knows the best use of her own time. You know your life better than your principal does! Right?
They say girls *must* learn so they can teach their own children. Nonsense!
Just because I was forced to go to school, I should force you, so someday you'll force your own children? Ridiculous! When does the cycle end?
Tomorrow I'll tell your little sisters they can do whatever they want, with no supervision.
Don't say it's a bad idea — who are *you* to say five-year-olds need supervision? What gives you that right, just being older and wiser? *I'm* older than you, and we've already agreed that *I* shouldn't tell *you* what to do, right?
But society will break down if no one learns! Children *need* to go to school!
Really? You think so?
I *completely* know what you're up to here.

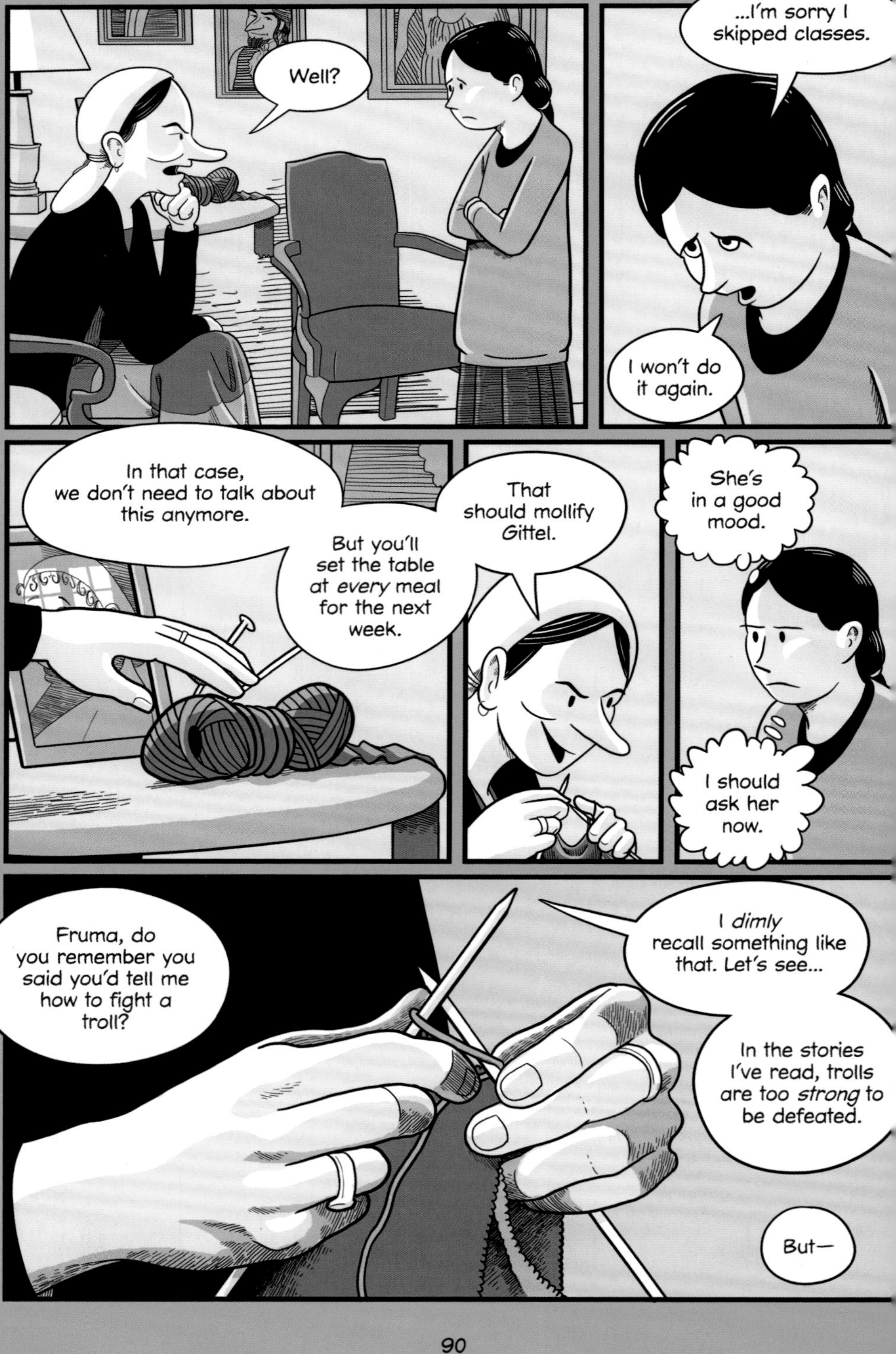
Well?
...I'm sorry I skipped classes.
I won't do it again.
In that case, we don't need to talk about this anymore.
But you'll set the table at *every* meal for the next week.
That should mollify Gittel.
She's in a good mood.
I should ask her now.
Fruma, do you remember you said you'd tell me how to fight a troll?
I *dimly* recall something like that. Let's see...
In the stories I've read, trolls are too *strong* to be defeated.
But—

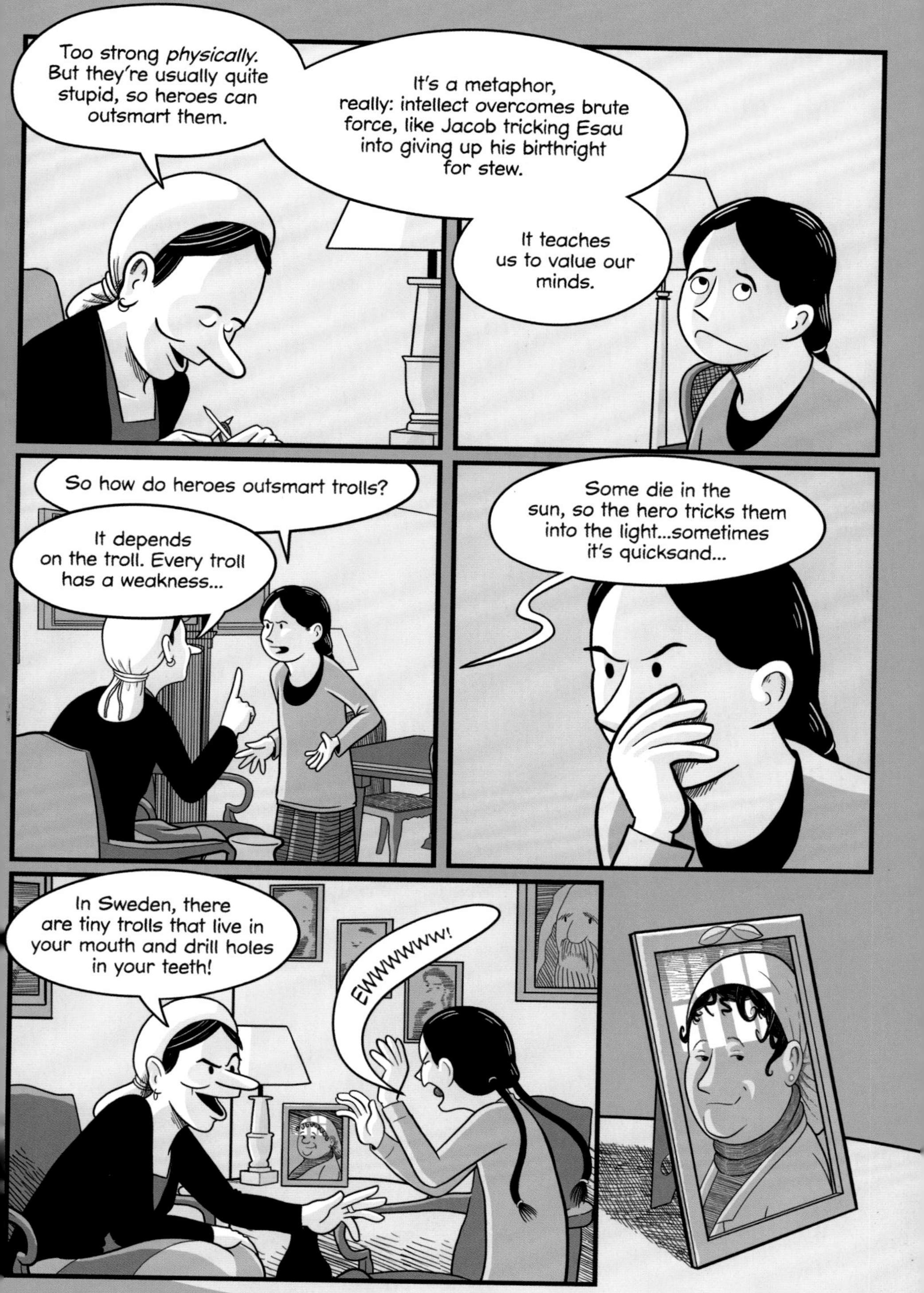
Too strong *physically.* But they're usually quite stupid, so heroes can outsmart them.
It's a metaphor, really: intellect overcomes brute force, like Jacob tricking Esau into giving up his birthright for stew.
It teaches us to value our minds.
So how do heroes outsmart trolls?
It depends on the troll. Every troll has a weakness...
Some die in the sun, so the hero tricks them into the light...sometimes it's quicksand...
In Sweden, there are tiny trolls that live in your mouth and drill holes in your teeth!
EWWWWWWW!

The story of Jacob and Esau is in the Torah, which is one of the founding texts of Judaism.

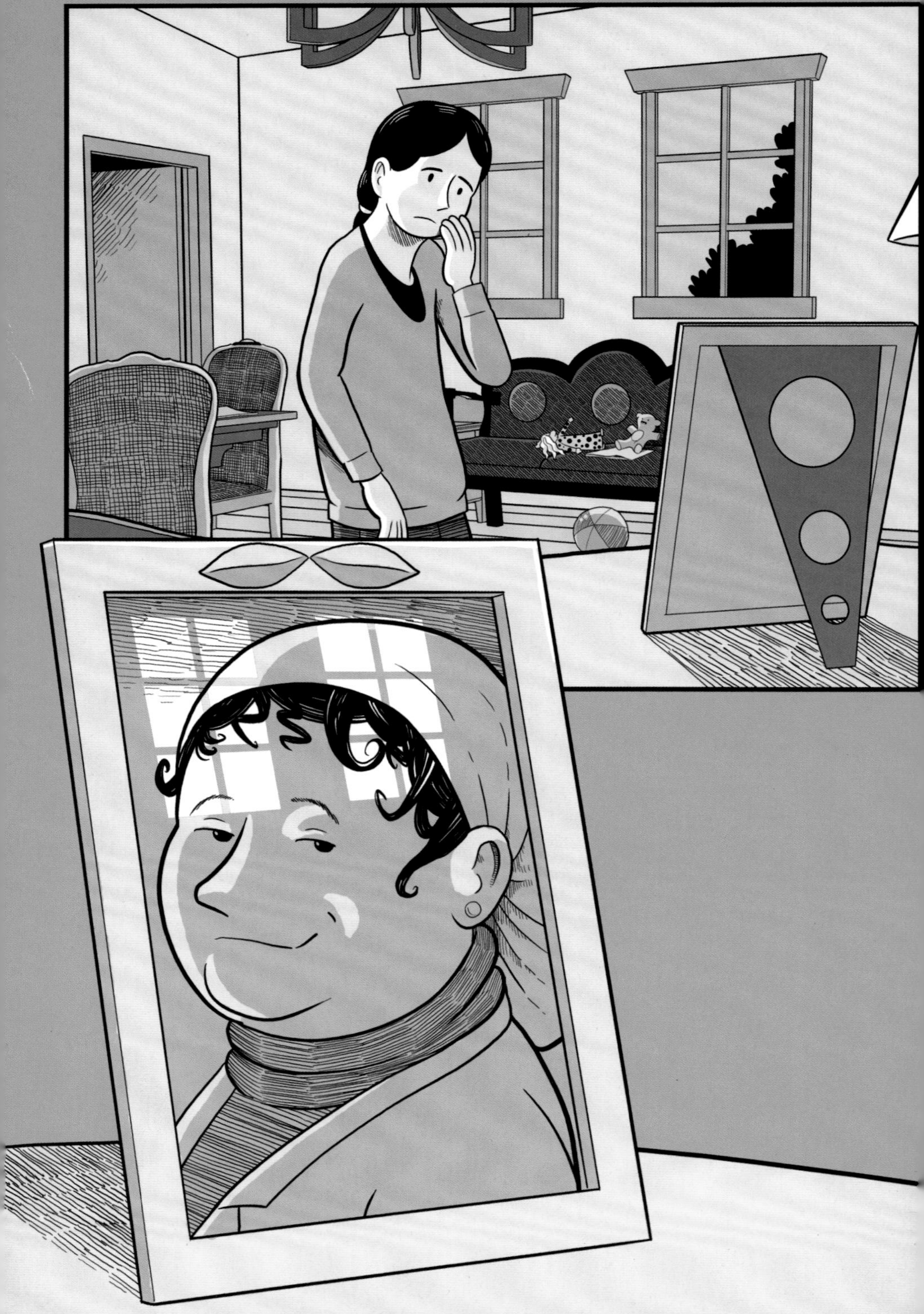

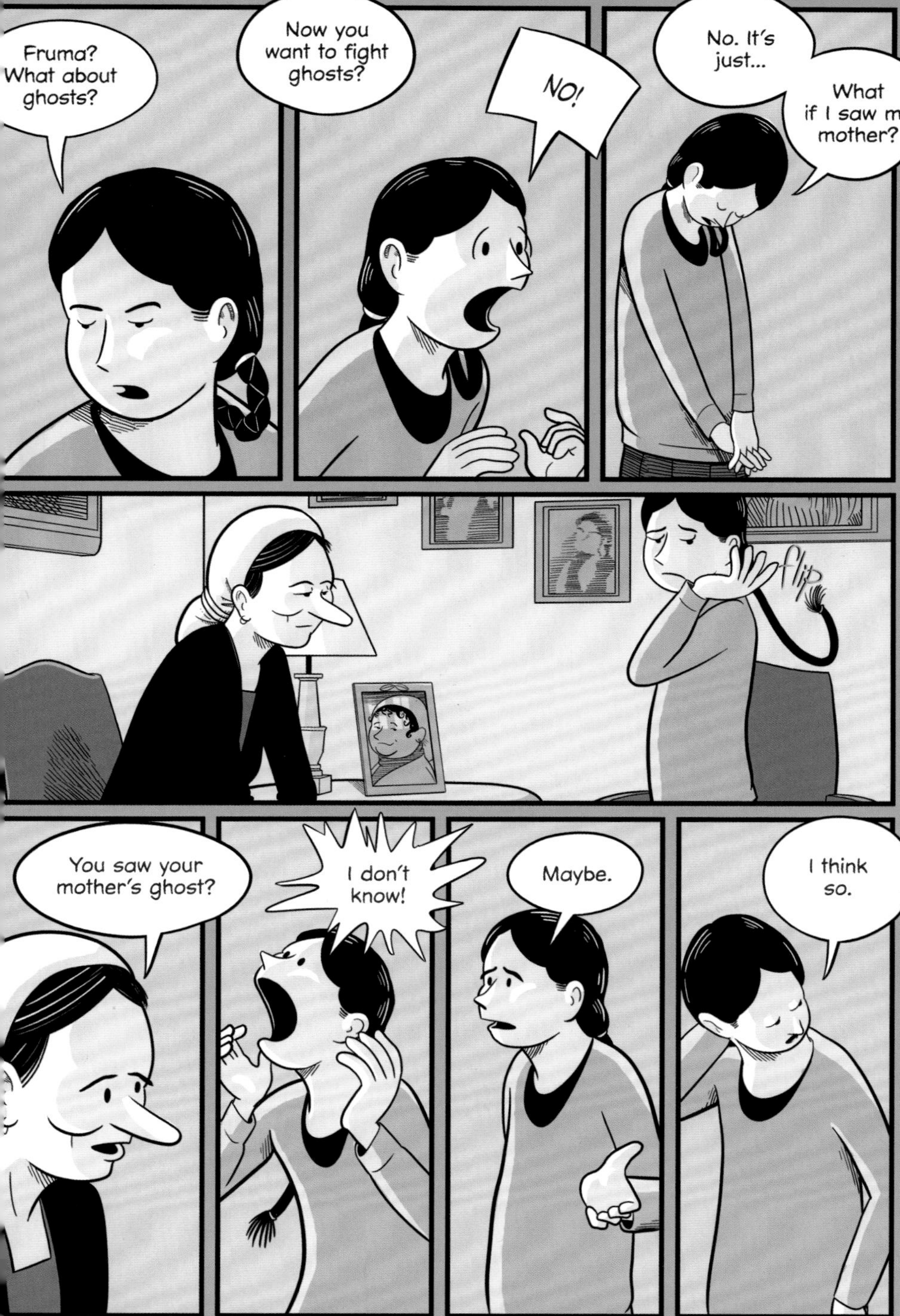
Fruma? What about ghosts?
Now you want to fight ghosts?
NO!
No. It's just...
What if I saw my mother?
flip
You saw your mother's ghost?
I don't know!
Maybe.
I think so.

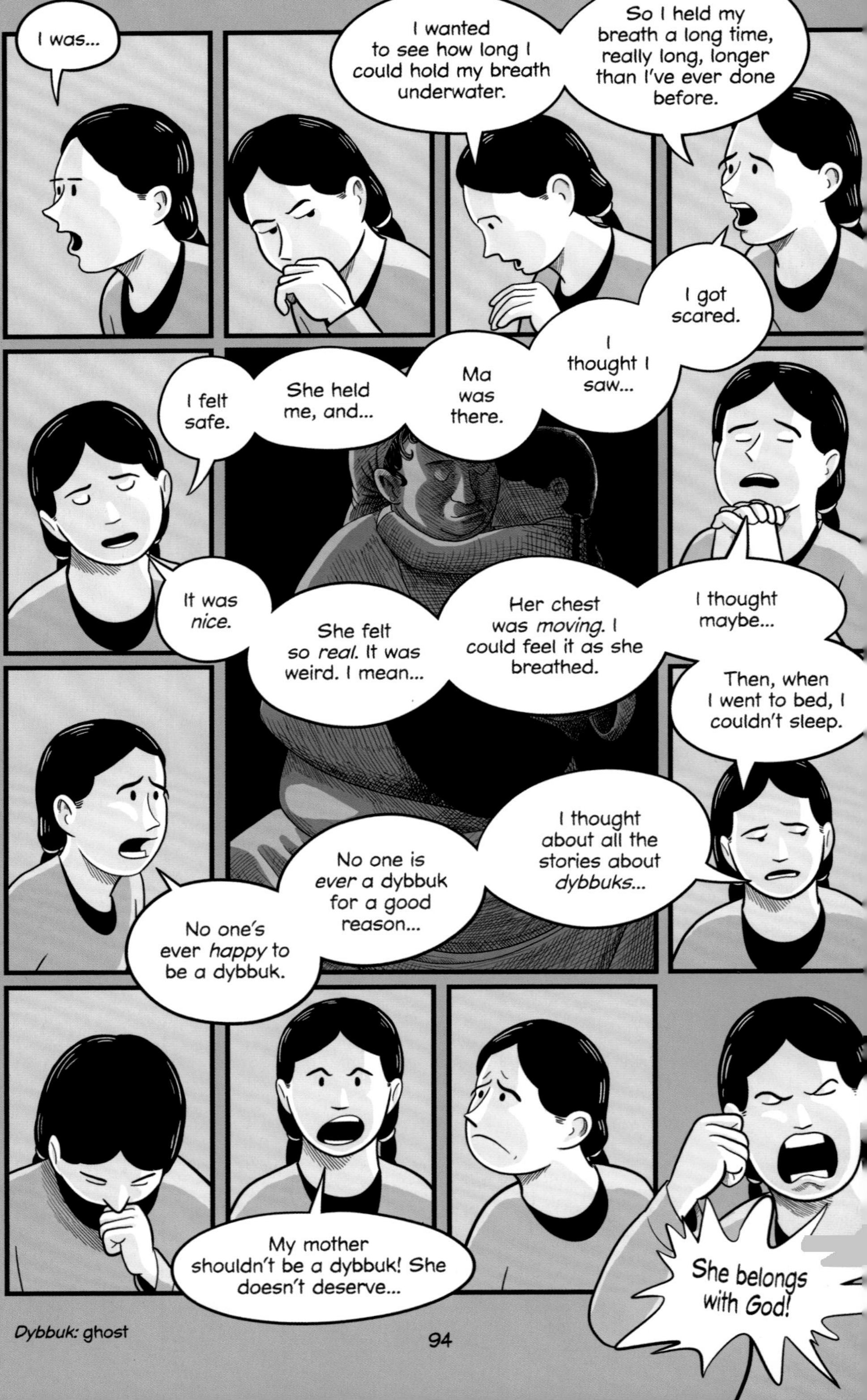
I was...
I wanted to see how long I could hold my breath underwater.
So I held my breath a long time, really long, longer than I've ever done before.
I got scared.
I thought I saw...
Ma was there.
She held me, and...
I felt safe.
It was *nice*.
She felt so *real*. It was weird. I mean...
Her chest was *moving*. I could feel it as she breathed.
I thought maybe...
Then, when I went to bed, I couldn't sleep.
I thought about all the stories about *dybbuks*...
No one is *ever* a dybbuk for a good reason...
No one's ever *happy* to be a dybbuk.
My mother shouldn't be a dybbuk! She doesn't deserve...
She belongs with *God*!

Dybbuk: ghost

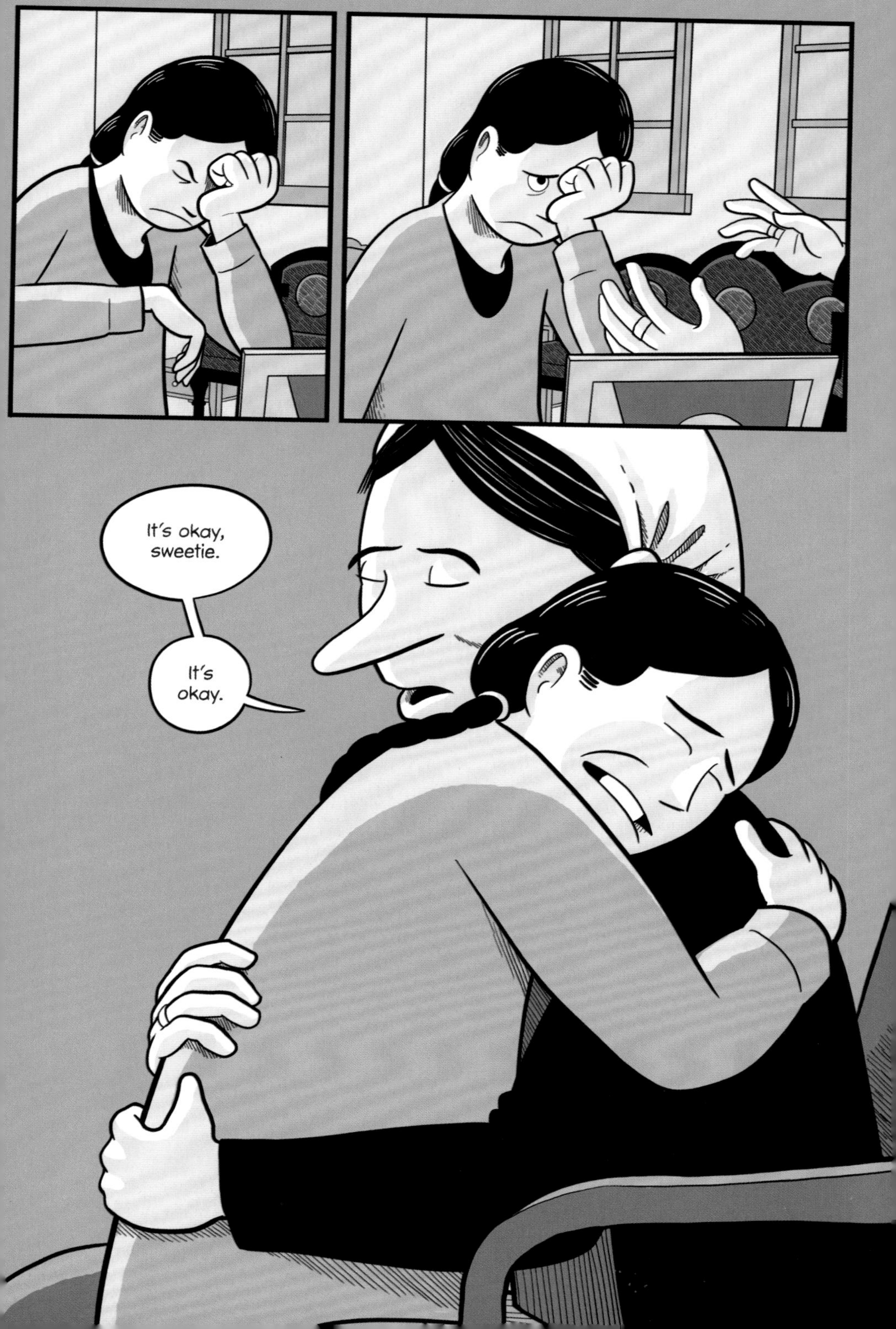
It's okay, sweetie.
It's okay.

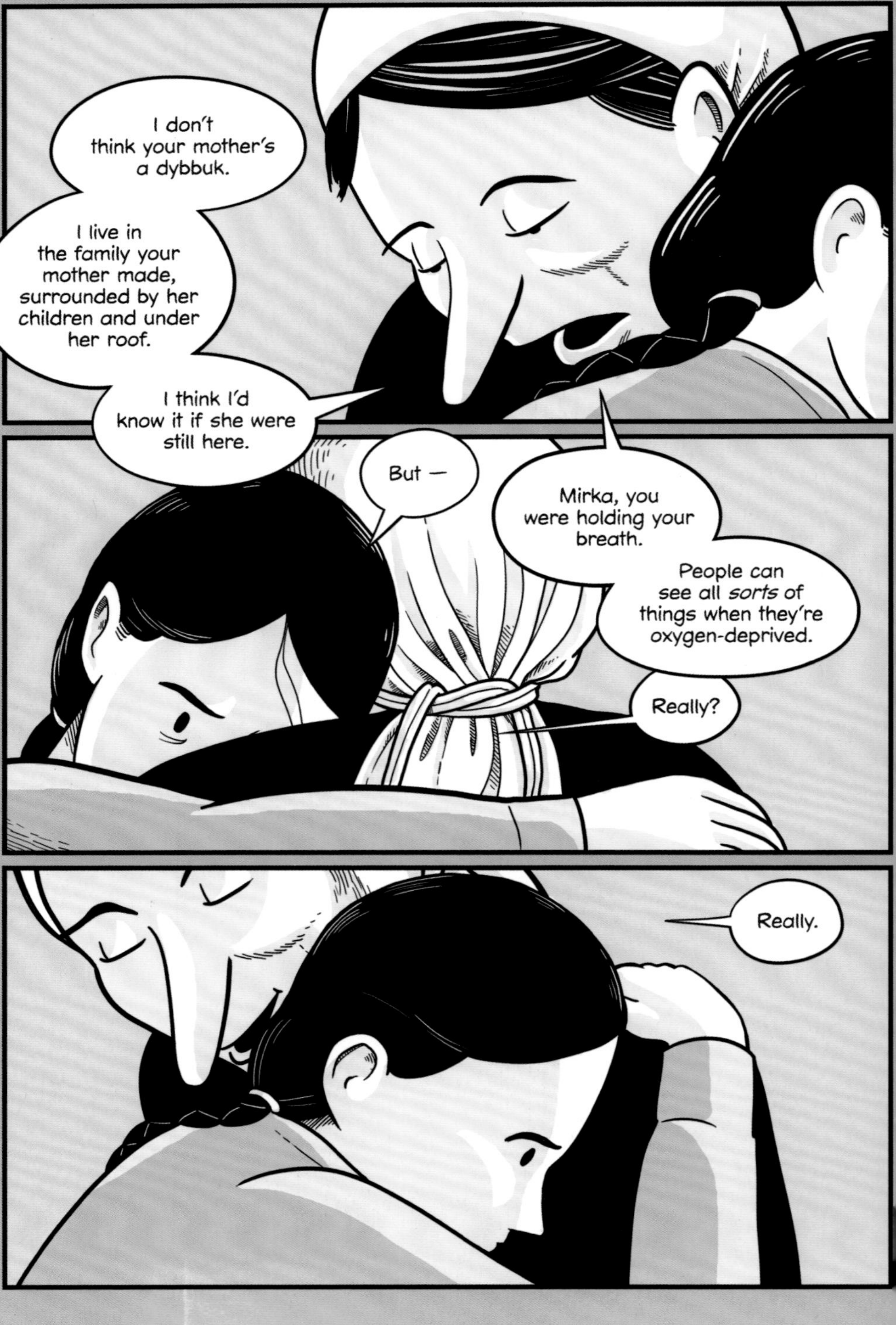
I don't think your mother's a dybbuk.
I live in the family your mother made, surrounded by her children and under her roof.
I think I'd know it if she were still here.
But —
Mirka, you were holding your breath.
People can see all *sorts* of things when they're oxygen-deprived.
Really?
Really.

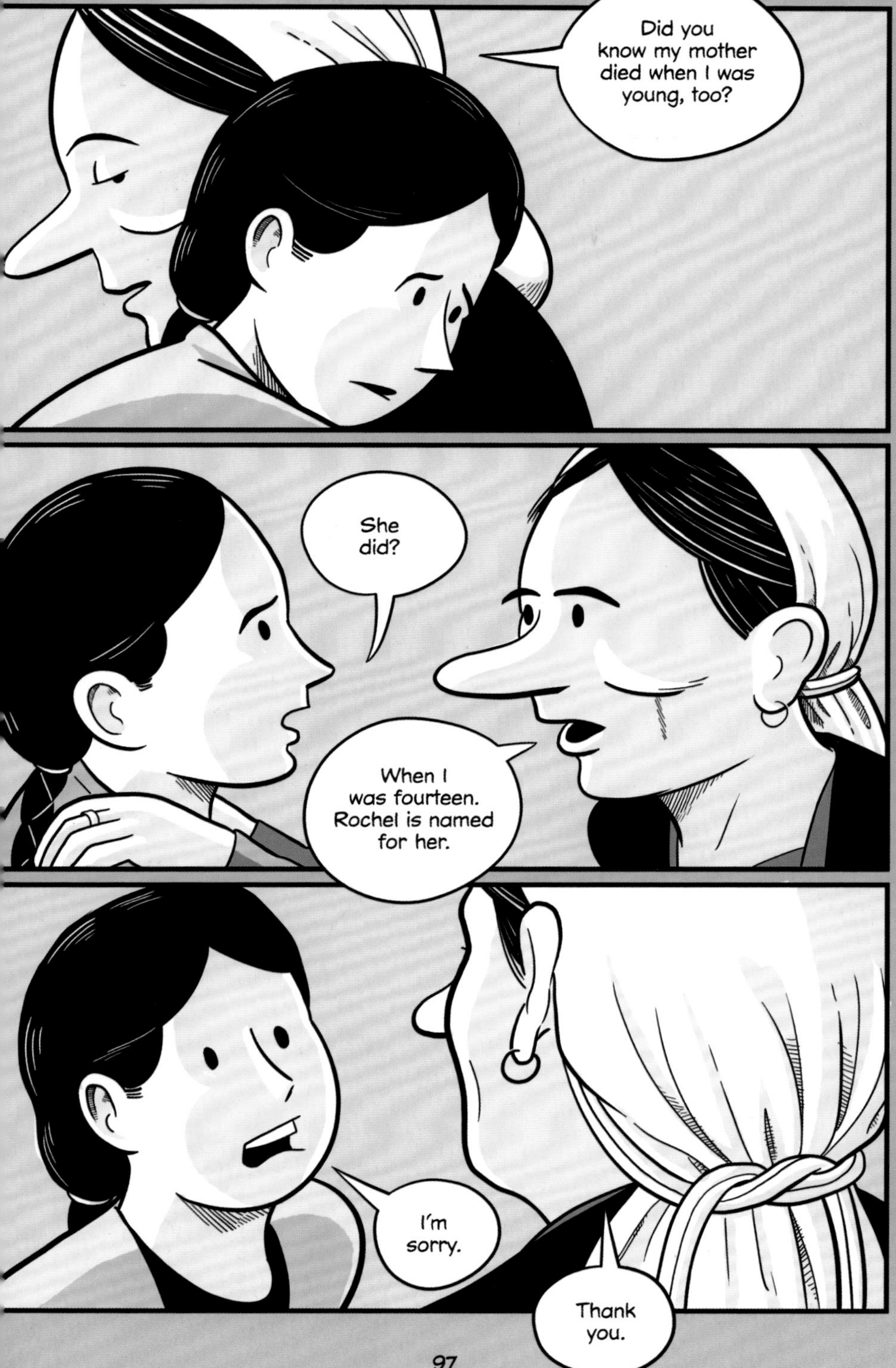
Did you know my mother died when I was young, too?
She did?
When I was fourteen. Rochel is named for her.
I'm sorry.
Thank you.

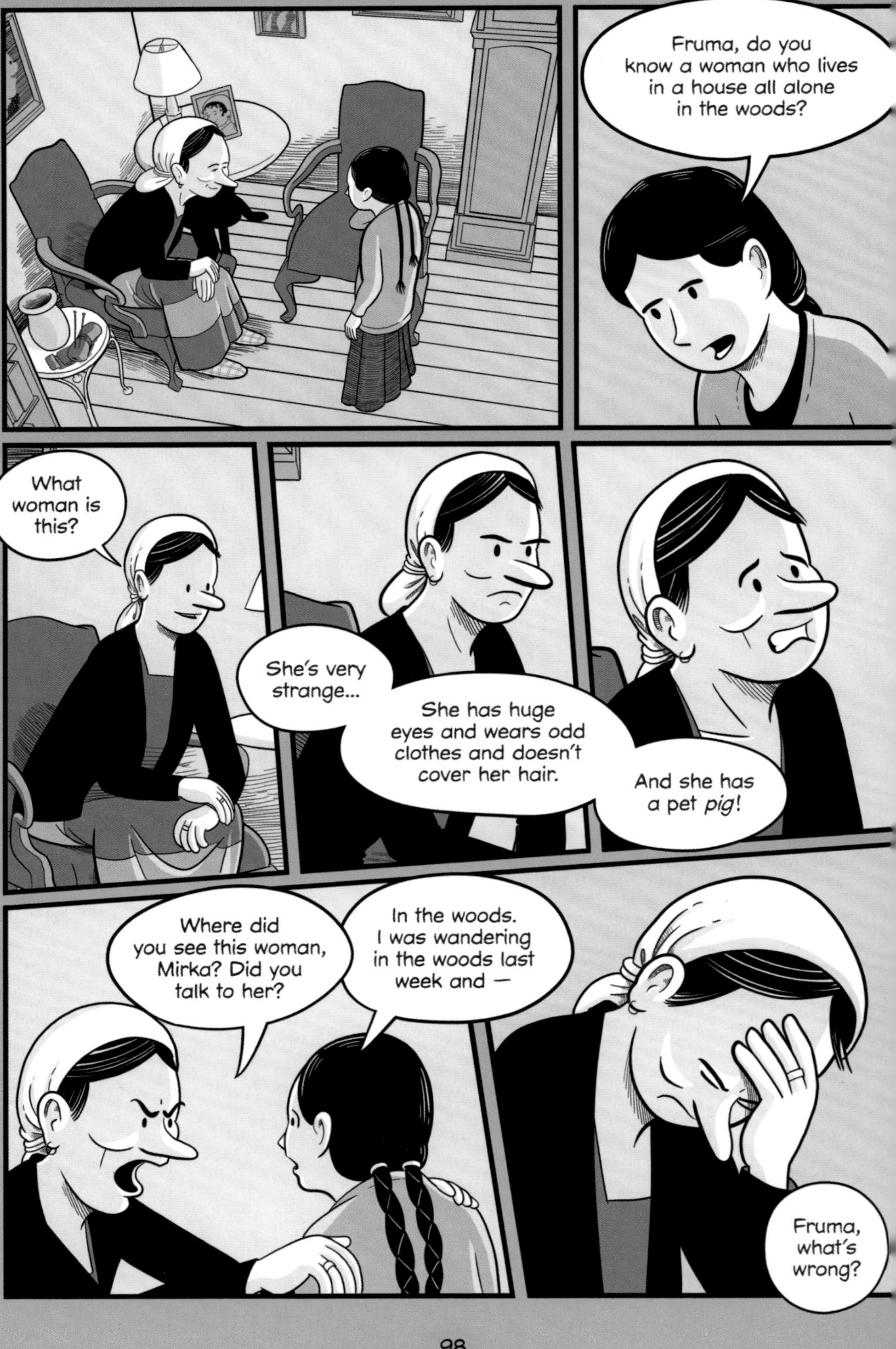
Fruma, do you know a woman who lives in a house all alone in the woods?
What woman is this?
She's very strange...
She has huge eyes and wears odd clothes and doesn't cover her hair.
And she has a pet *pig*!
Where did you see this woman, Mirka? Did you talk to her?
In the woods. I was wandering in the woods last week and —
Fruma, what's wrong?

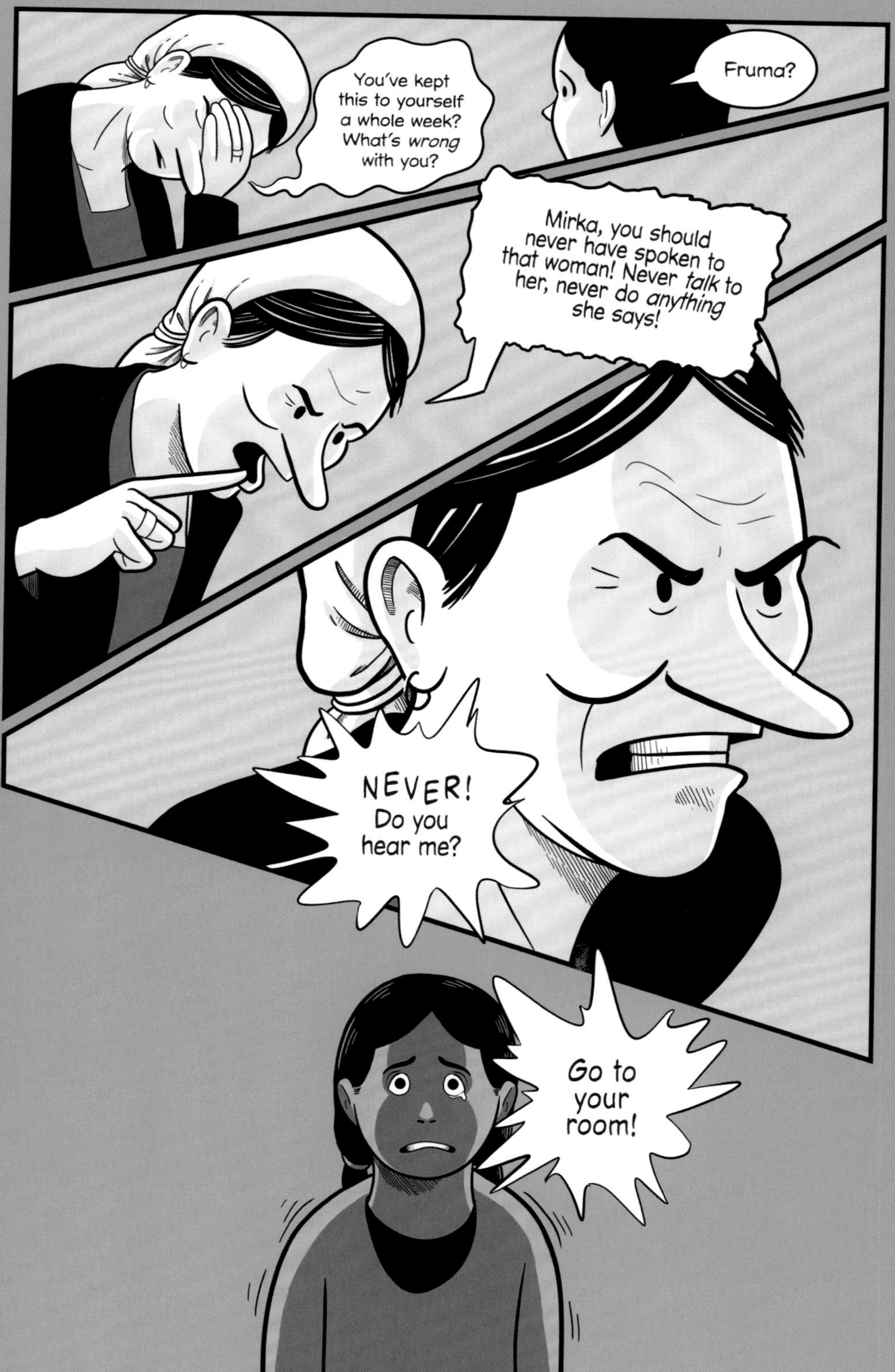
You've kept this to yourself a whole week? What's *wrong* with you?
Fruma?
Mirka, you should never have spoken to that woman! Never *talk* to her, never do *anything* she says!
NEVER! Do you hear me?
Go to your room!

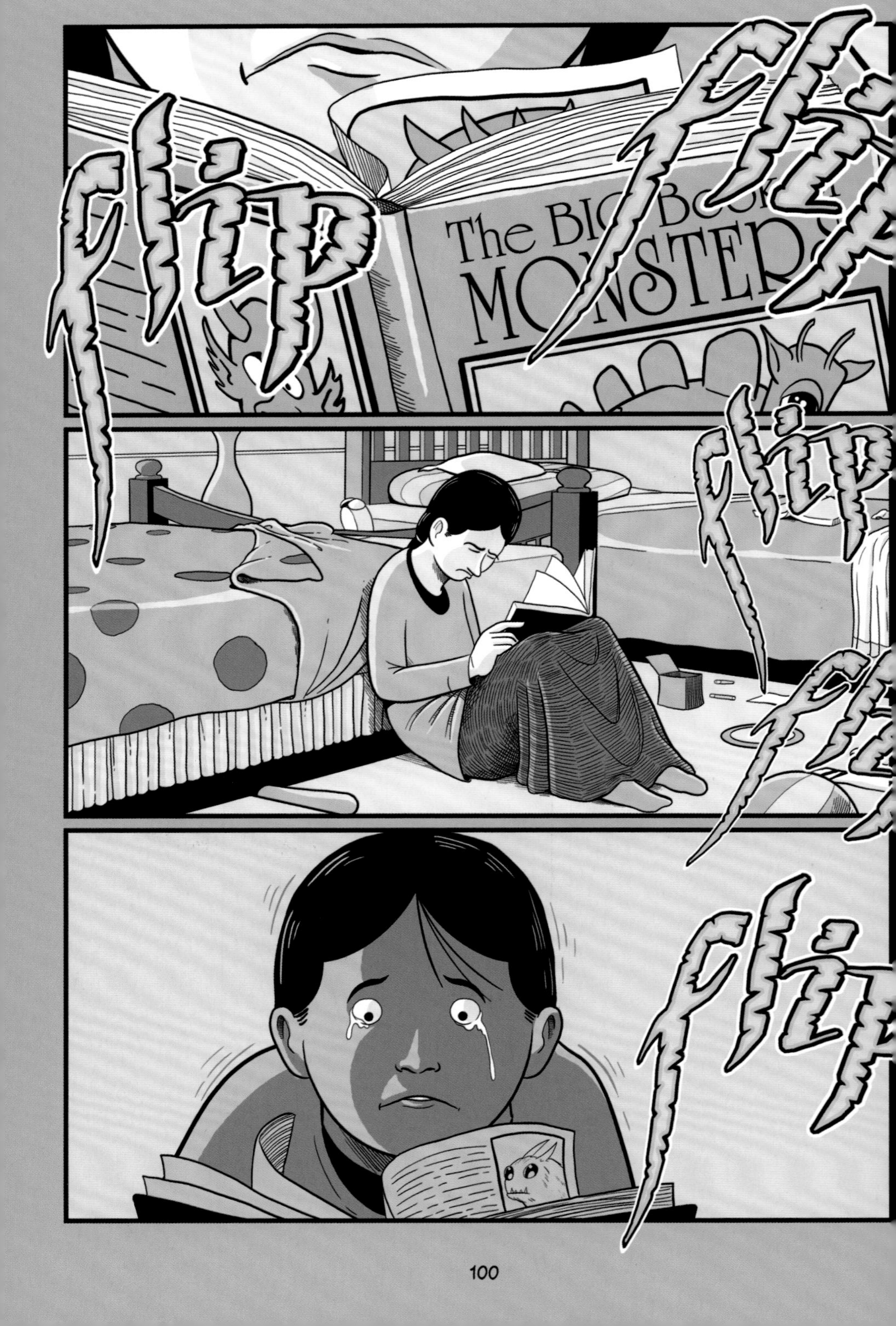
flip
flip
The BI
MONSTER
flip
flip
flip

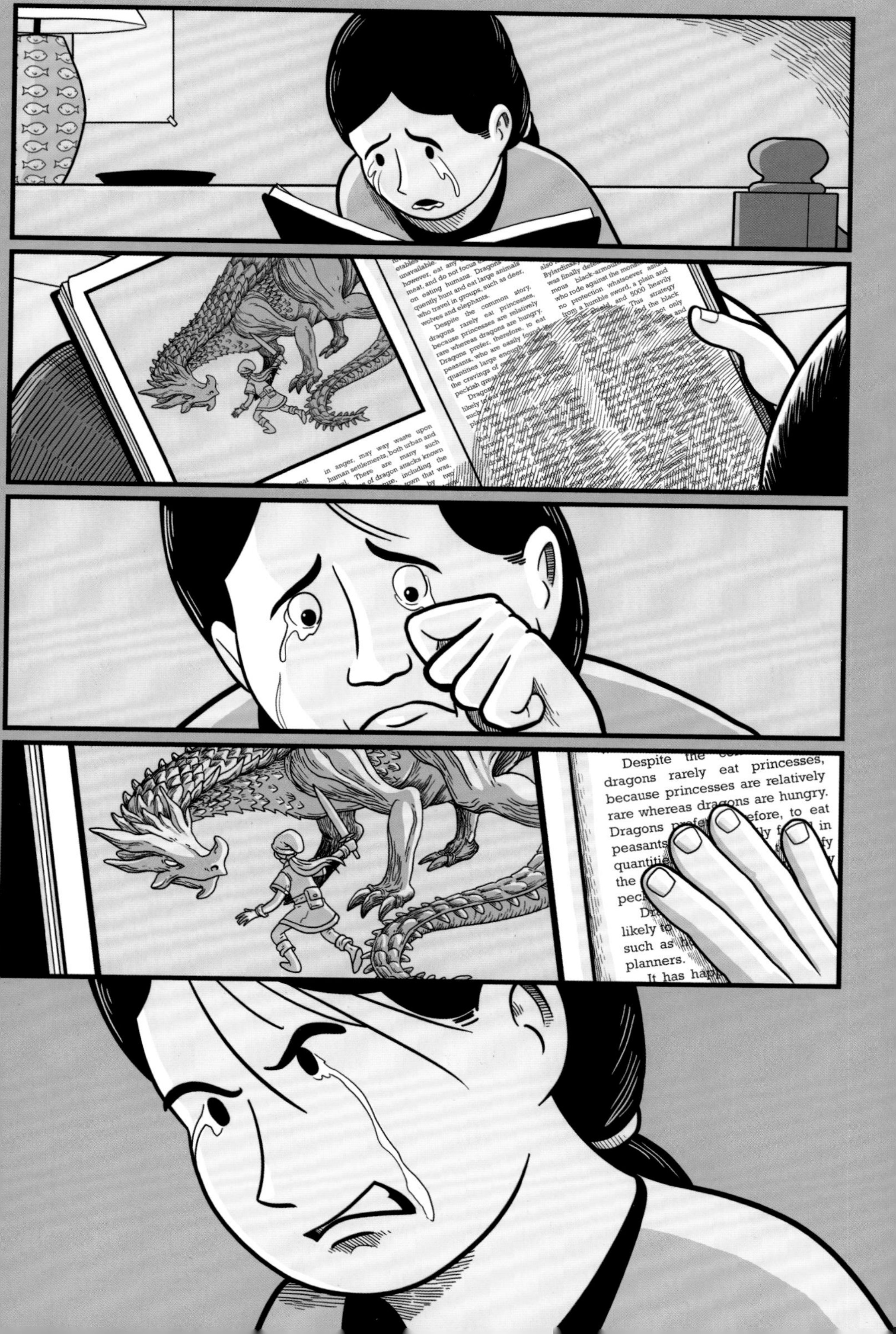

unavailable.
however, eat any
meat, and do not focus
on eating humans. Dragons
quently hunt and eat large animals
who travel in groups, such as deer,
wolves and elephants.
Despite the common story,
dragons rarely eat princesses,
because princesses are relatively
rare whereas dragons are hungry.
Dragons prefer, therefore, to eat
peasants, who are easily found
quantities large enough
the cravings of
peckish great
Bylardinsk
was finally defe
mous black-armou
who rode against the monster
no protection whatsoever aside
from a humble sword, a plain and
simple shield, and 5000 heavily
This strategy
in anger, may way waste upon
human settlements, both urban and
There are many such
of dragon attacks known
including the
town that was
Despite the
dragons rarely eat princesses,
because princesses are relatively
rare whereas dragons are hungry.
Dragons
efore, to eat
peasants
quantiti
the
likely to
such as
planners.
It has hap

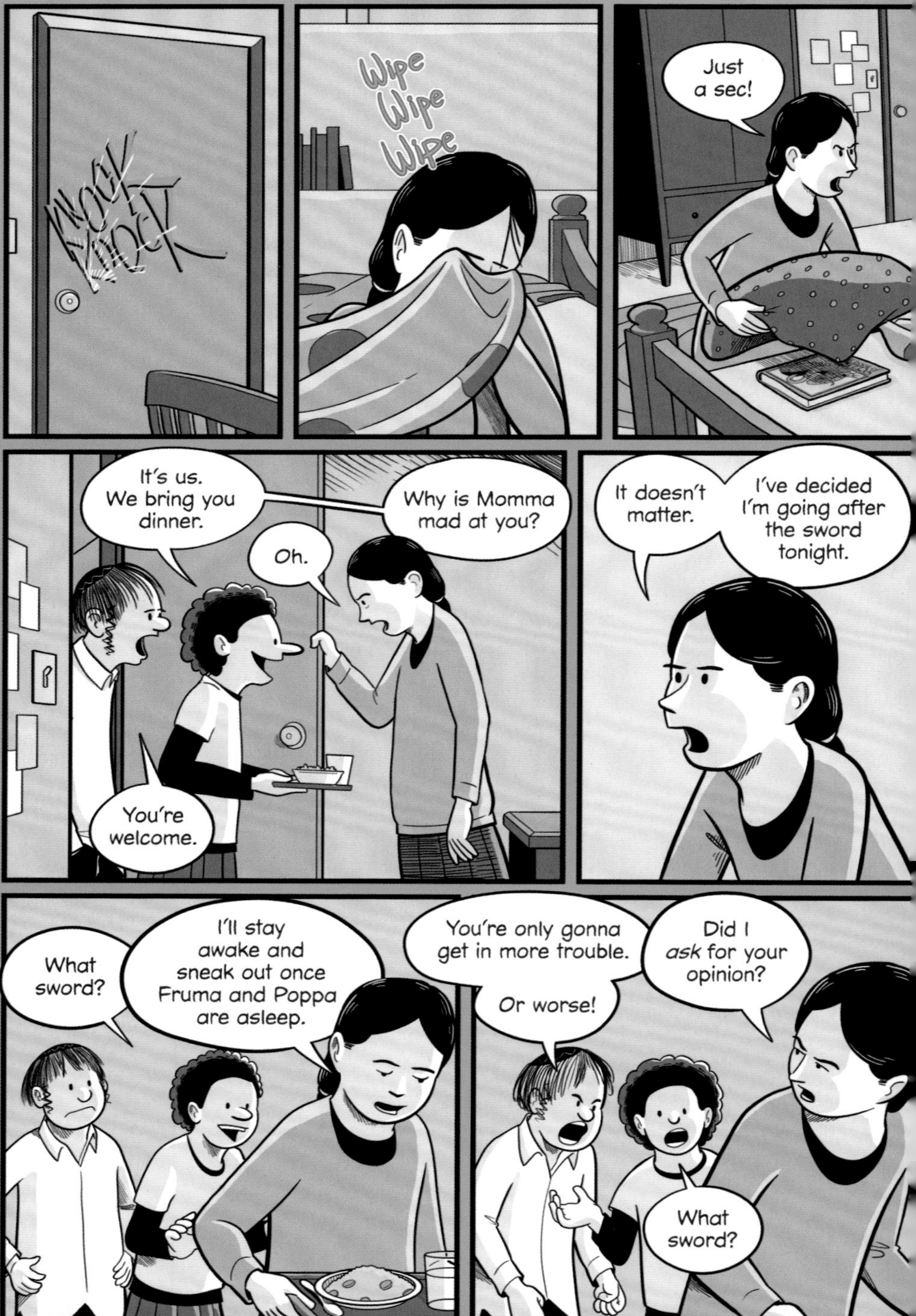
KNOCK KNOCK
Wipe Wipe Wipe
Just a sec!
It's us. We bring you dinner.
Oh.
Why is Momma mad at you?
You're welcome.
It doesn't matter.
I've decided I'm going after the sword tonight.
What sword?
I'll stay awake and sneak out once Fruma and Poppa are asleep.
You're only gonna get in more trouble.
Or worse!
Did I *ask* for your opinion?
What sword?

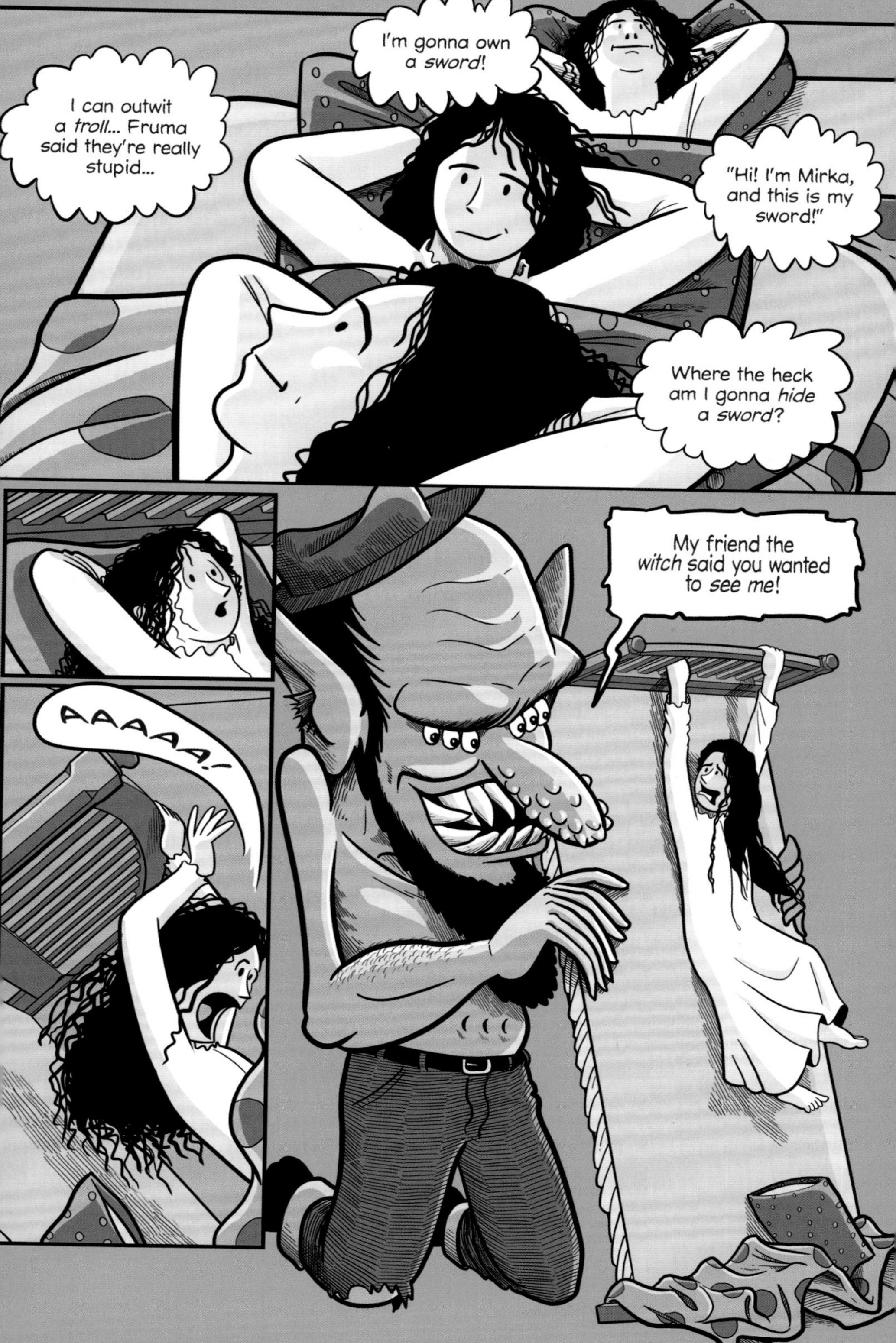
I can outwit a *troll*... Fruma said they're really stupid...
I'm gonna own a *sword*!
"Hi! I'm Mirka, and this is my sword!"
Where the heck am I gonna *hide* a *sword*?
AAAAA!
My friend the *witch* said you wanted to *see me*!

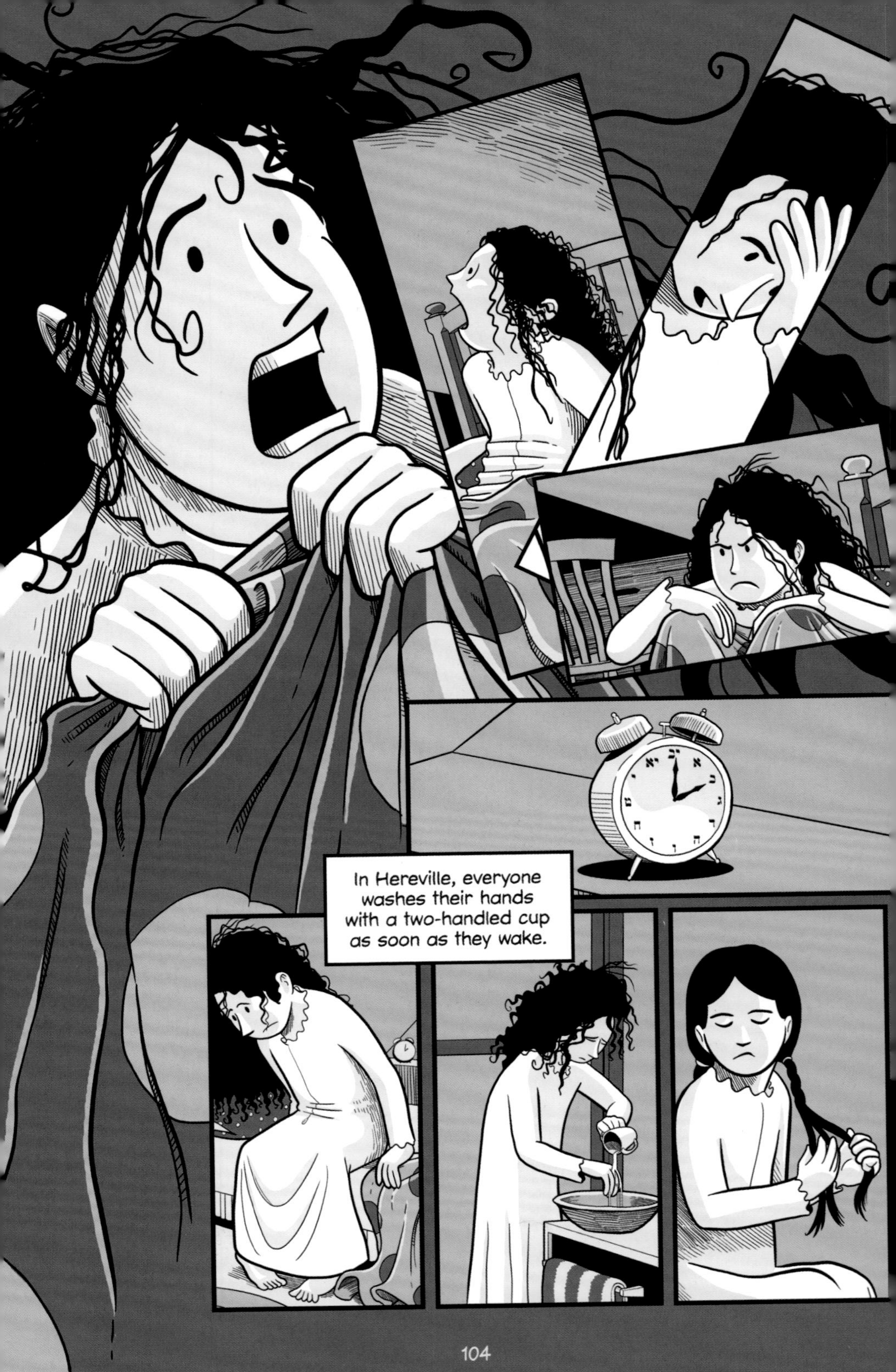
In Hereville, everyone washes their hands with a two-handled cup as soon as they wake.

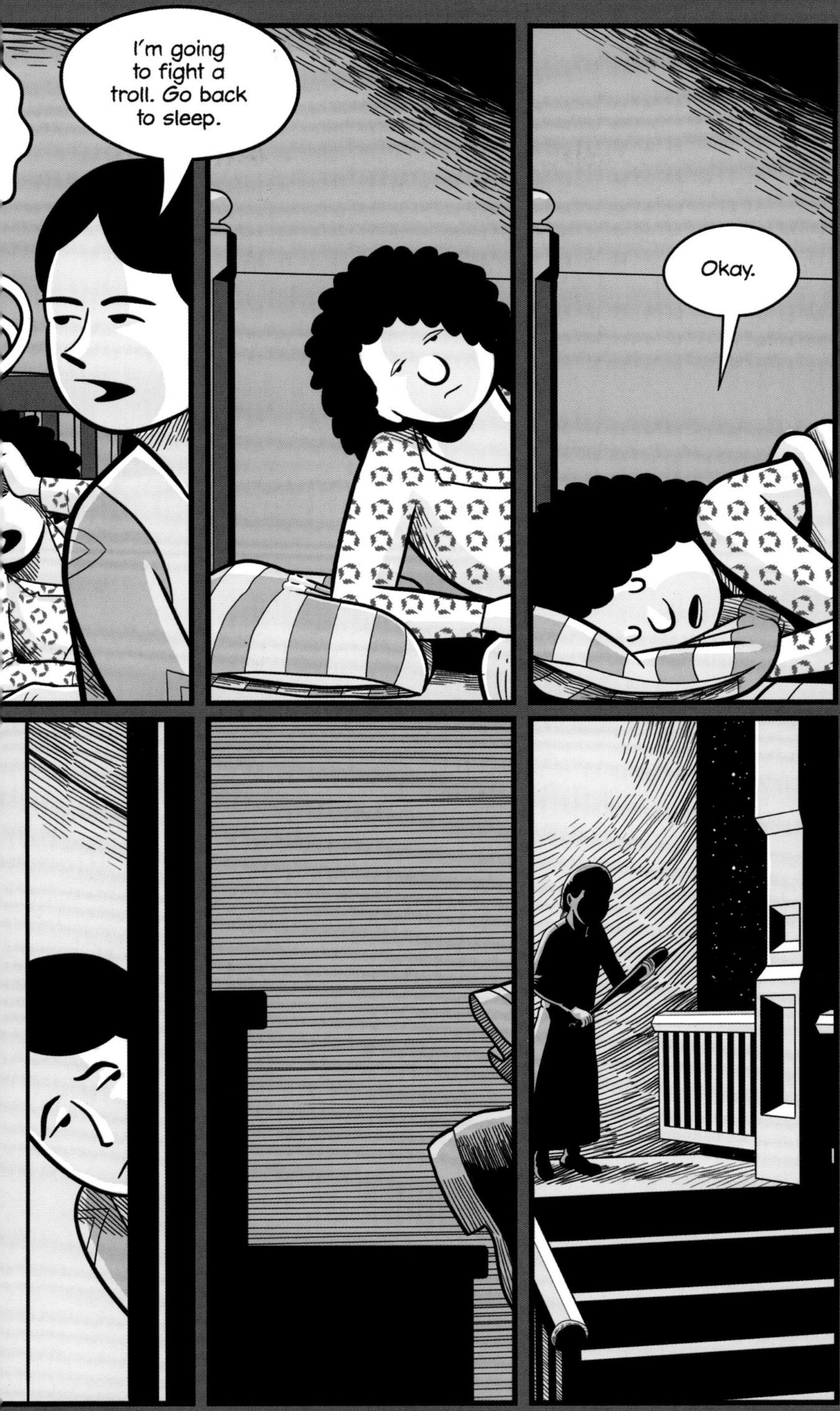
I'm going to fight a troll. Go back to sleep.
Okay.

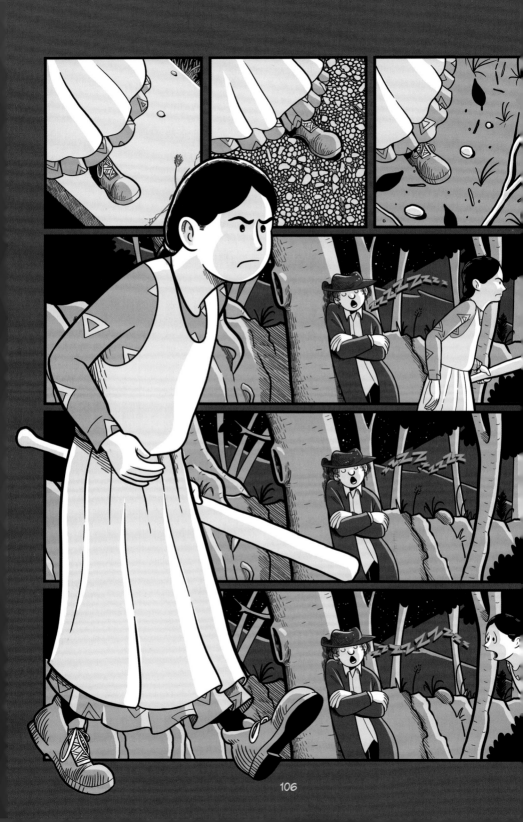

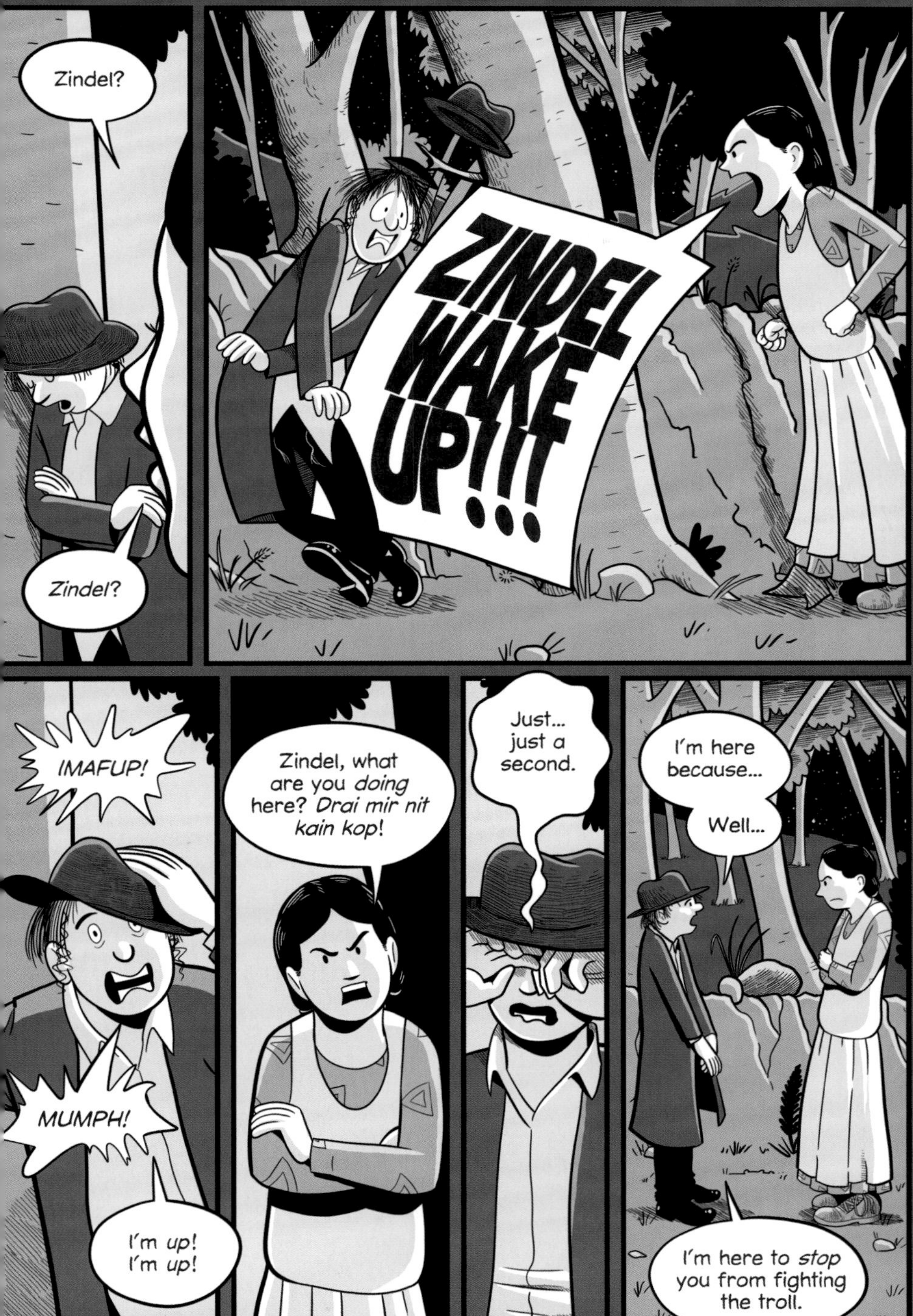
Zindel?
Zindel?
ZINDEL WAKE UP!!!
IMAFUP!
MUMPH!
I'm up! I'm up!
Zindel, what are you *doing* here? *Drai mir nit kain kop!*
Just... just a second.
I'm here because...
Well...
I'm here to *stop* you from fighting the troll.

Drai mir nit kain kop! Don't twist my head!
(Less literal: Stop bothering me!)

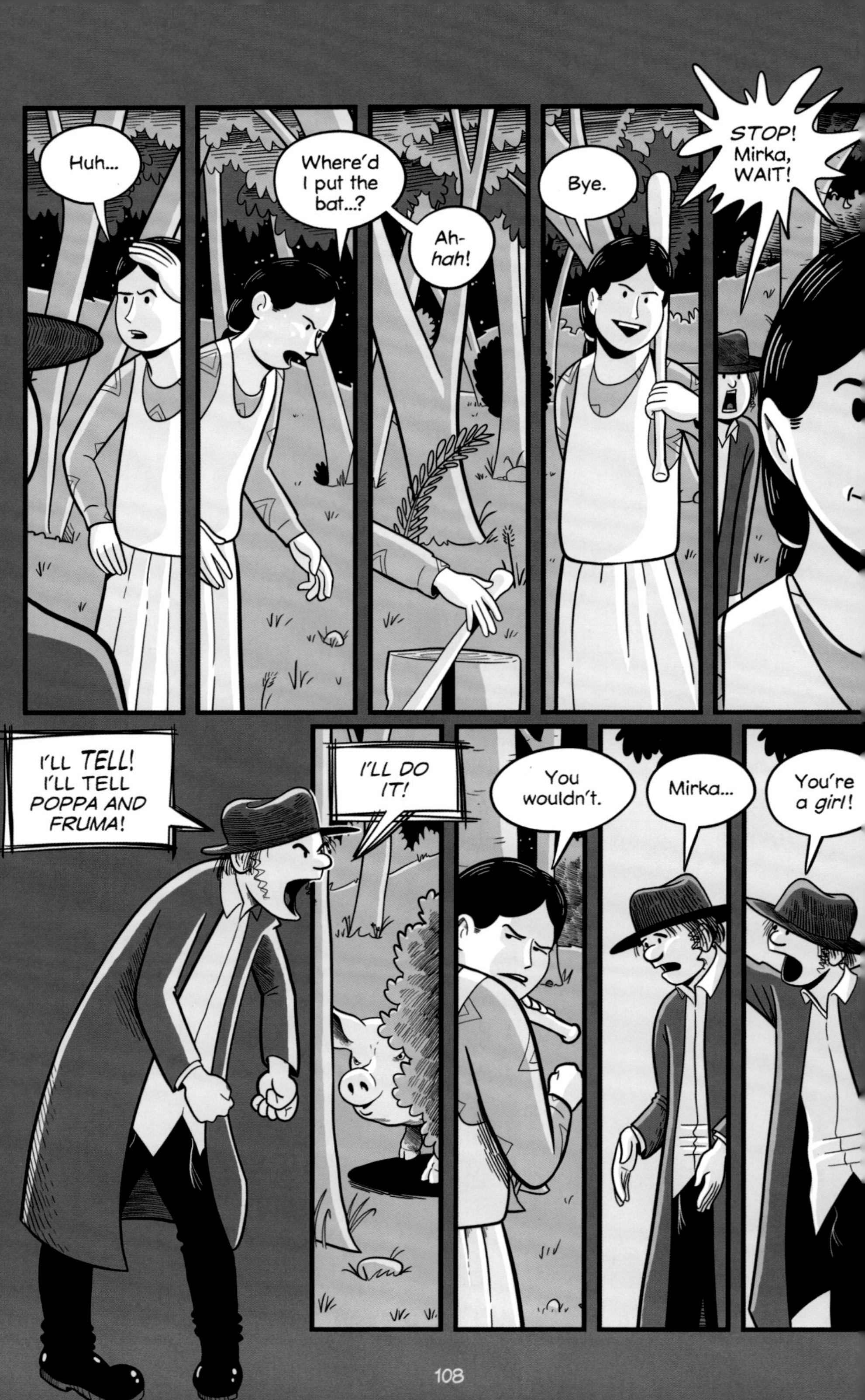
Huh...
Where'd I put the bat...?
Ah-hah!
Bye.
STOP! Mirka, WAIT!
I'LL TELL! I'LL TELL POPPA AND FRUMA!
I'LL DO IT!
You wouldn't.
Mirka...
You're a girl!

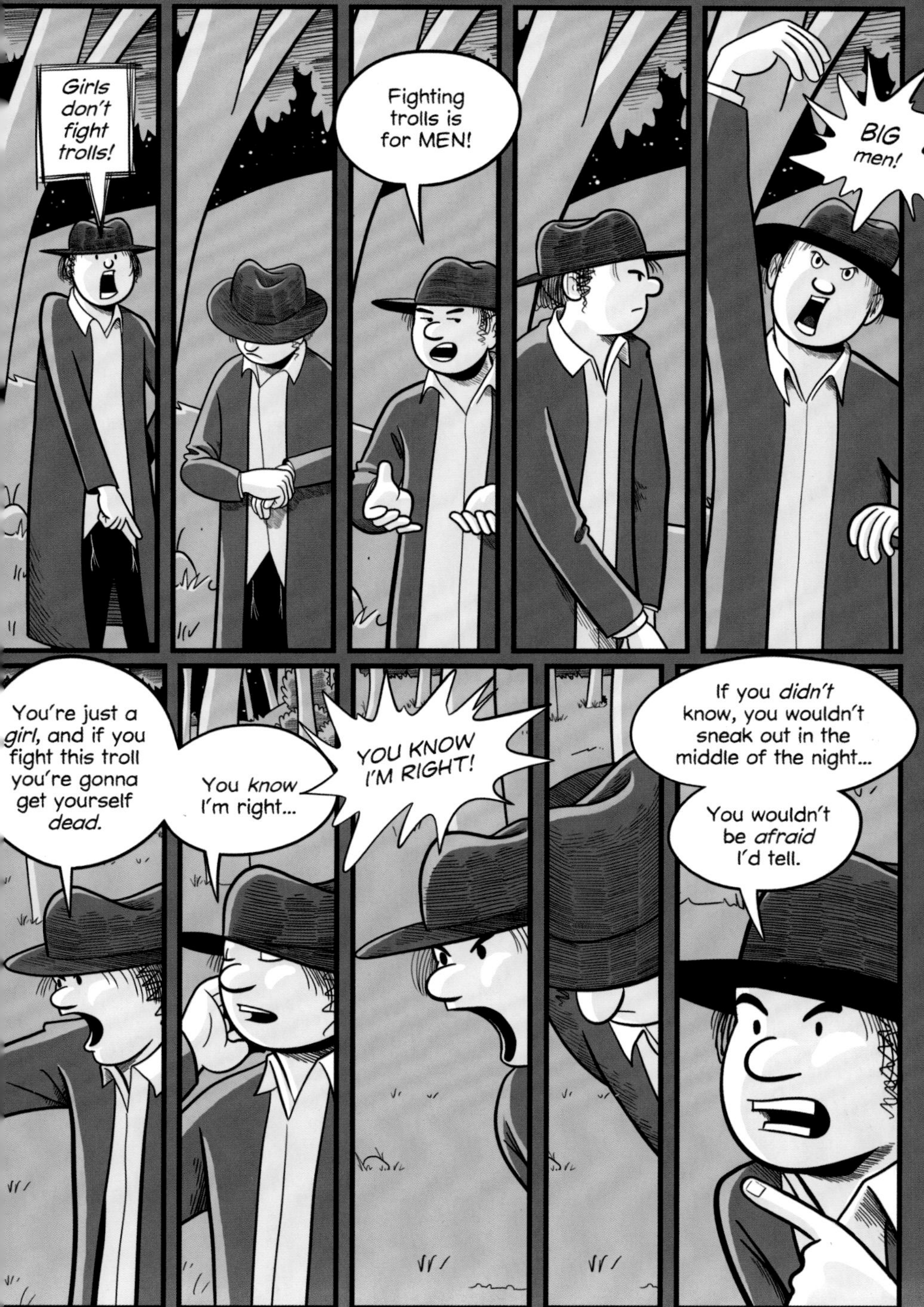

Girls don't fight trolls!
Fighting trolls is for MEN!
BIG men!
You're just a girl, and if you fight this troll you're gonna get yourself dead.
You know I'm right...
YOU KNOW I'M RIGHT!
If you didn't know, you wouldn't sneak out in the middle of the night...
You wouldn't be afraid I'd tell.

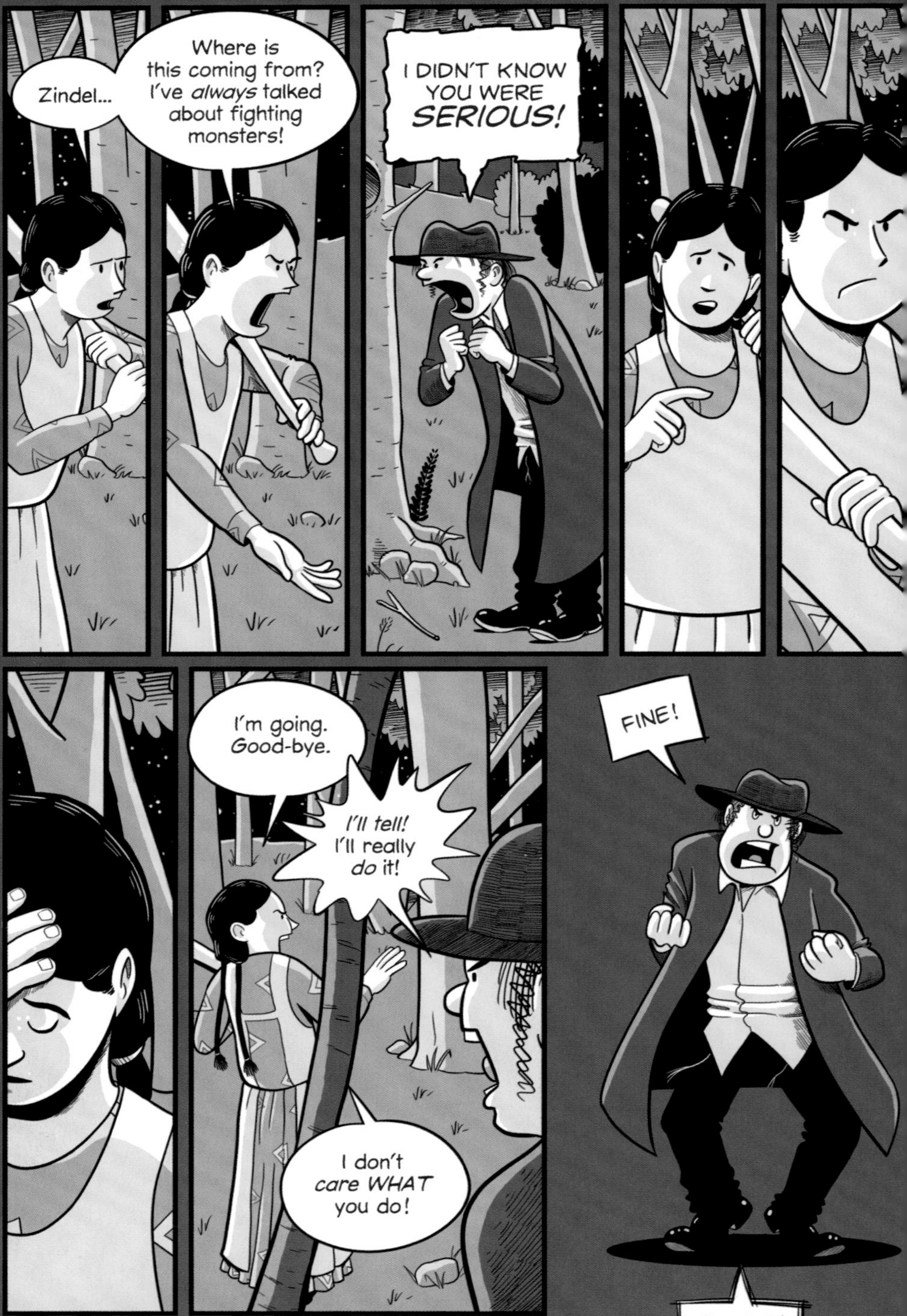
Zindel...
Where is this coming from? I've *always* talked about fighting monsters!
I DIDN'T KNOW YOU WERE *SERIOUS!*
I'm going. Good-bye.
I'll tell! I'll really *do* it!
I don't *care WHAT* you do!
FINE!
FINE!

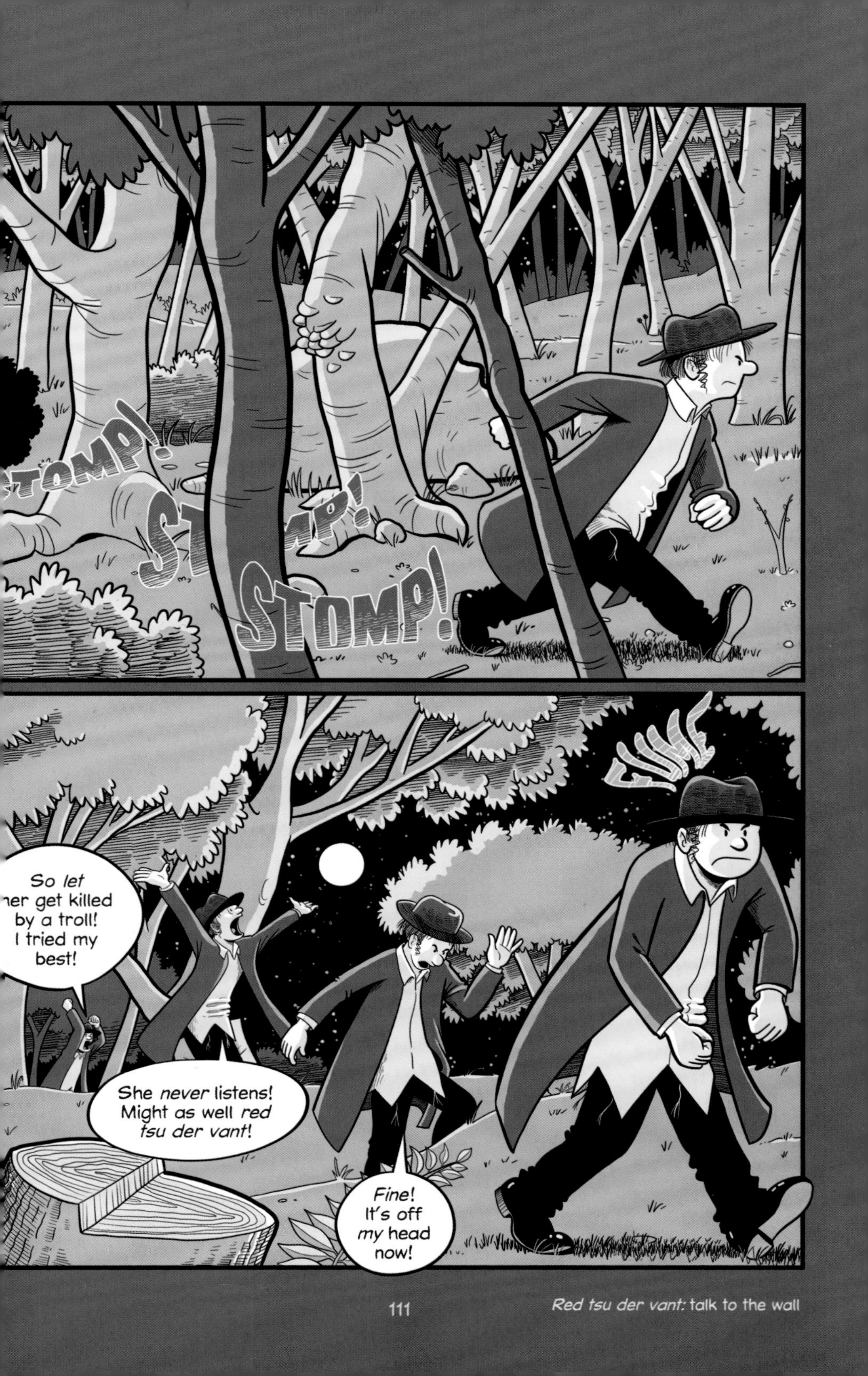
STOMP!
STOMP!
STOMP!
So *let* ner get killed by a troll! I tried my best!
She *never* listens! Might as well *red tsu der vant*!
Fine! It's off *my* head now!

Red tsu der vant: talk to the wall

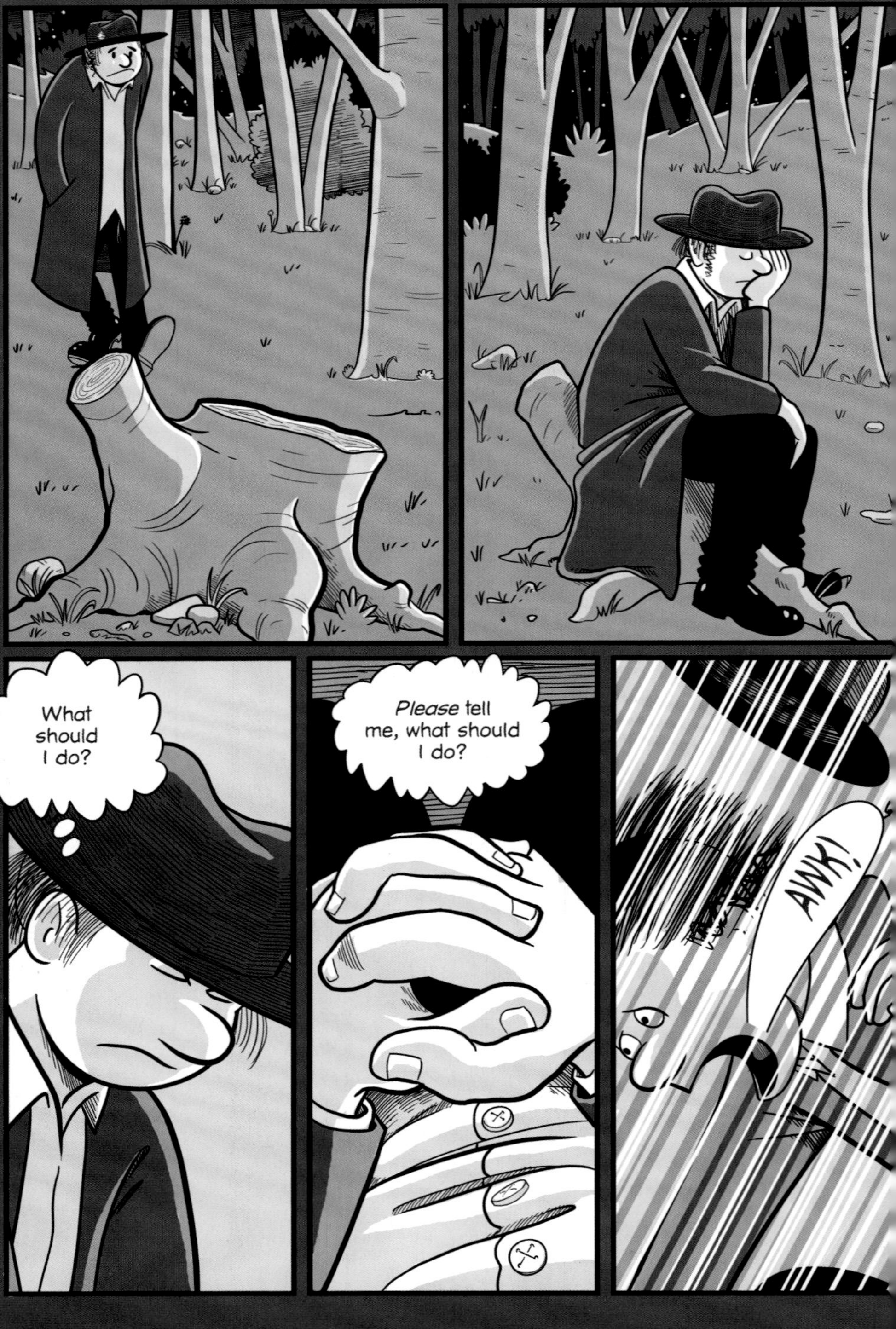
What should I do?
Please tell me, what should I do?
AWK!

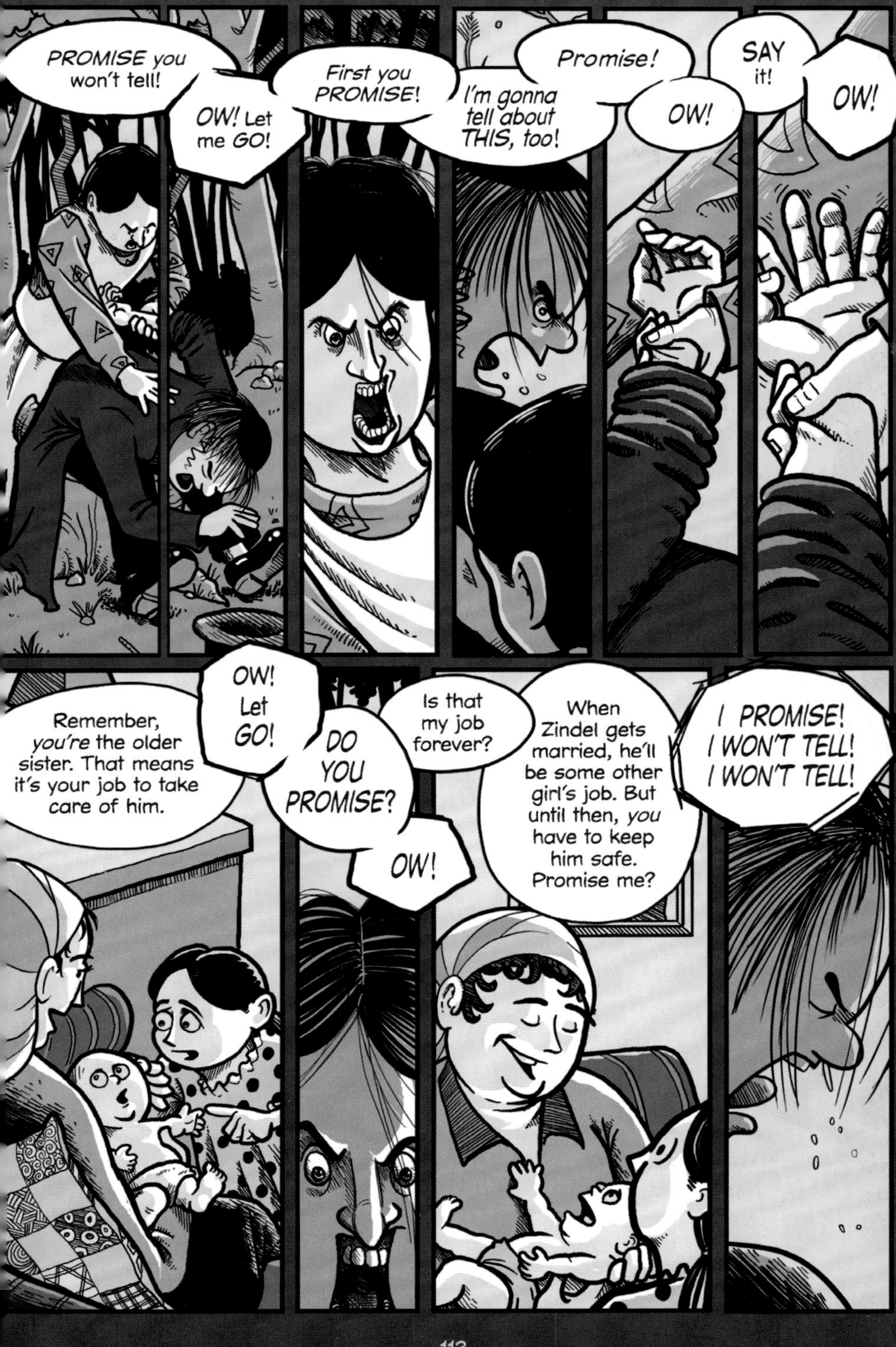
PROMISE you won't tell!
OW! Let me GO!
First you PROMISE!
I'm gonna tell about THIS, too!
Promise!
OW!
SAY it!
OW!
Remember, you're the older sister. That means it's your job to take care of him.
OW! Let GO!
DO YOU PROMISE?
OW!
Is that my job forever?
When Zindel gets married, he'll be some other girl's job. But until then, you have to keep him safe. Promise me?
I PROMISE! I WON'T TELL! I WON'T TELL!

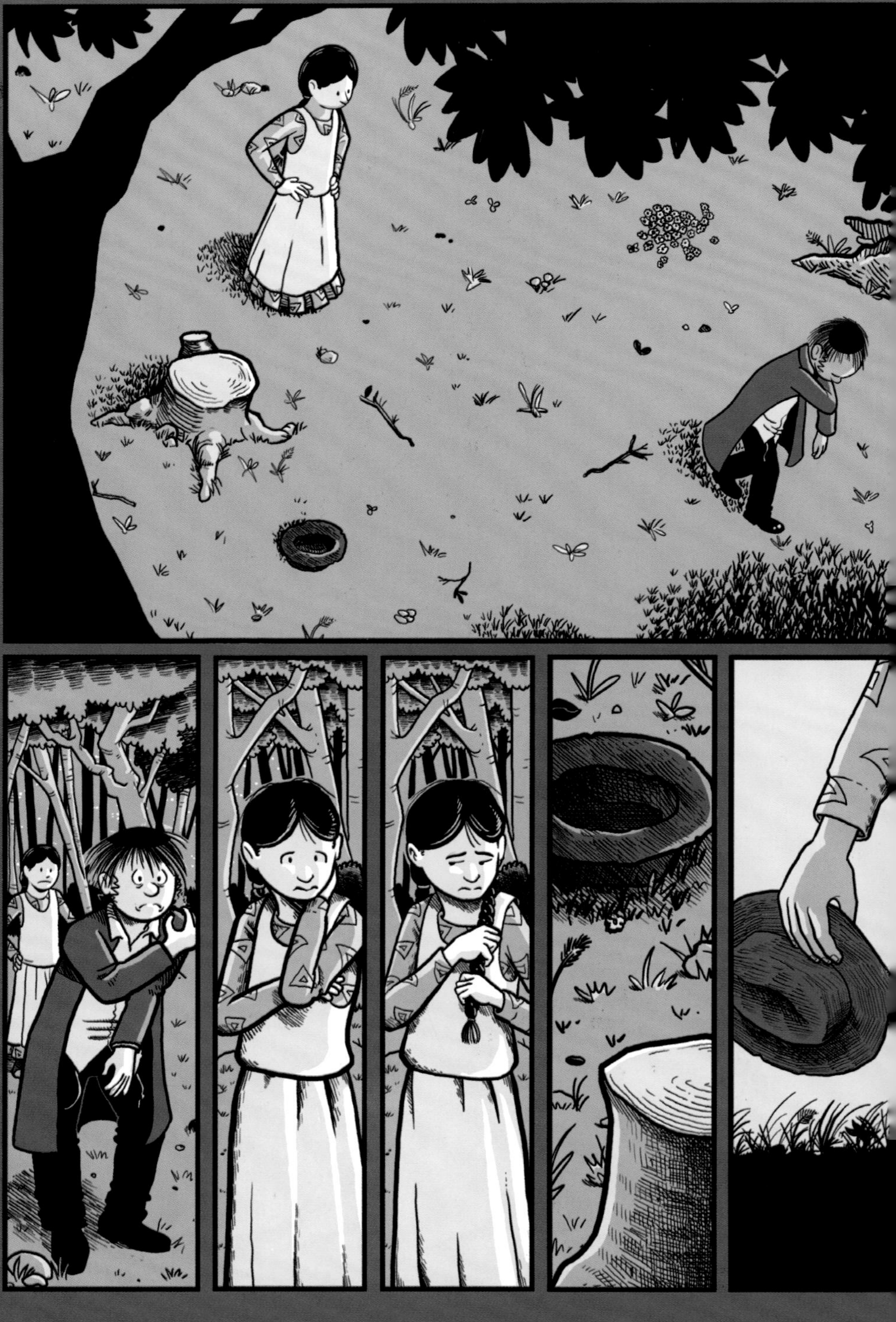

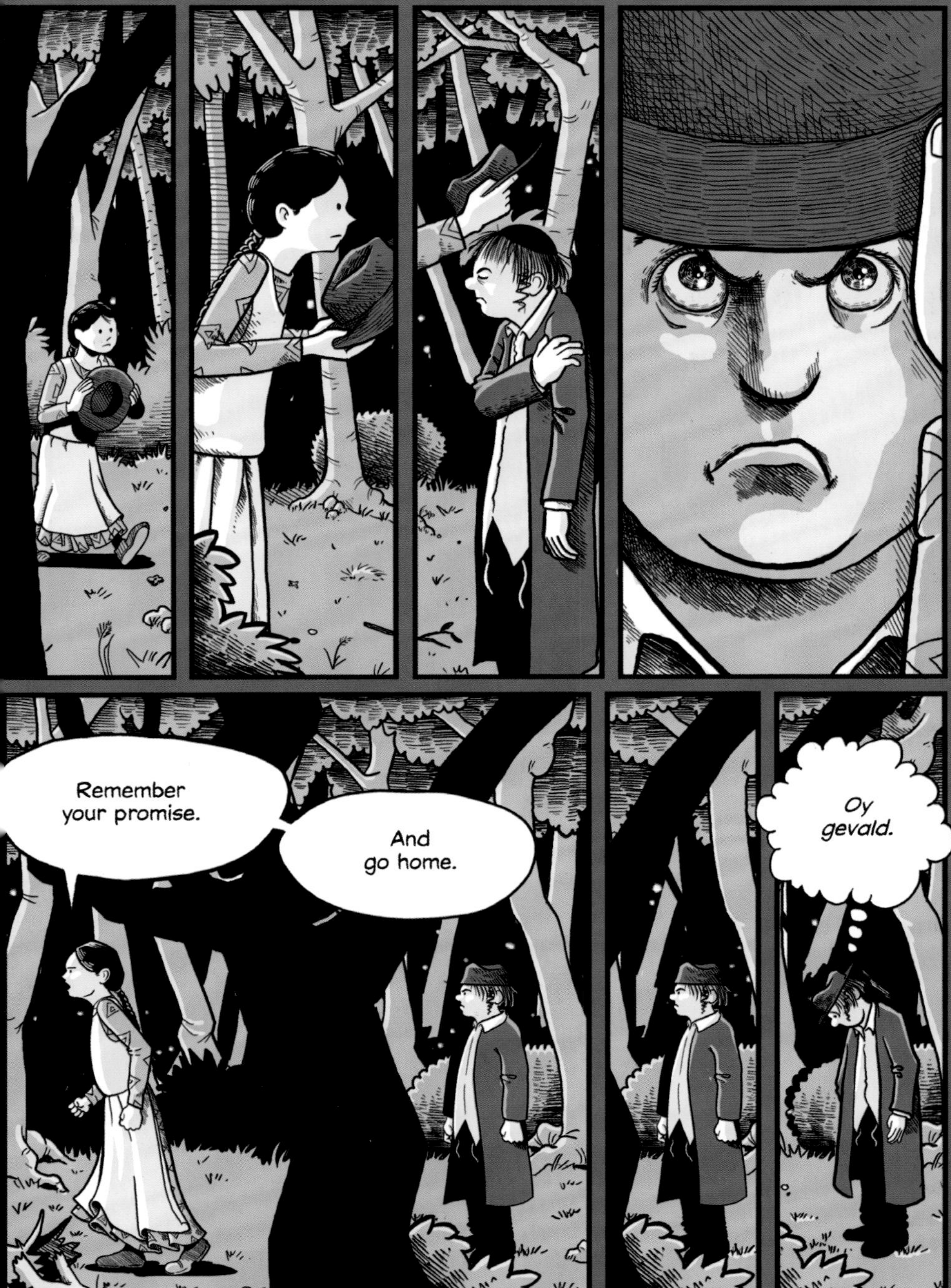
Remember your promise.
And go home.
Oy gevald.

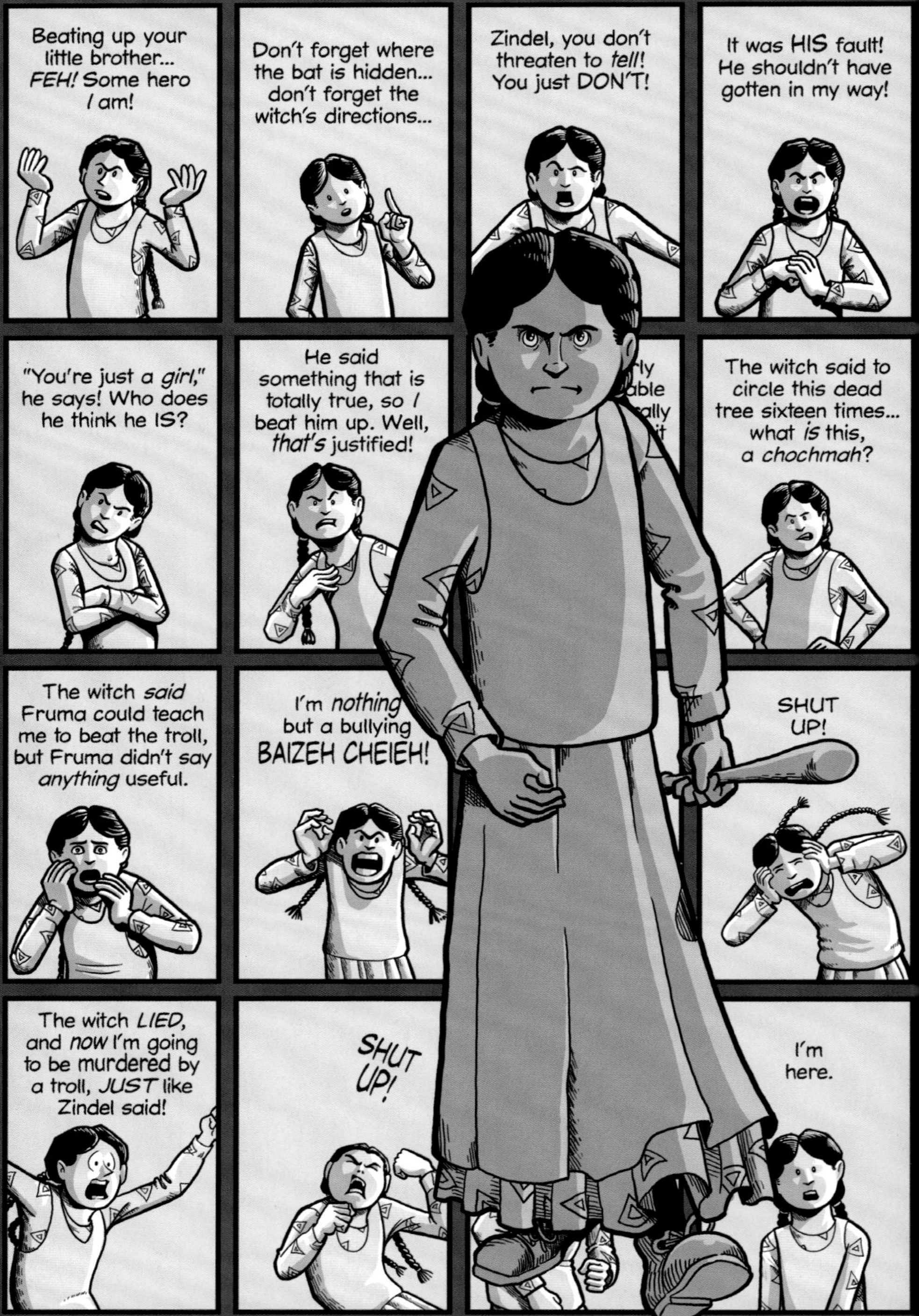
Beating up your little brother... FEH! Some hero I am!
Don't forget where the bat is hidden... don't forget the witch's directions...
Zindel, you don't threaten to tell! You just DON'T!
It was HIS fault! He shouldn't have gotten in my way!
"You're just a girl," he says! Who does he think he IS?
He said something that is totally true, so I beat him up. Well, that's justified!
The witch said to circle this dead tree sixteen times... what is this, a chochmah?
The witch said Fruma could teach me to beat the troll, but Fruma didn't say anything useful.
I'm nothing but a bullying BAIZEH CHEIEH!
SHUT UP!
The witch LIED, and now I'm going to be murdered by a troll, JUST like Zindel said!
SHUT UP!
I'm here.

Chochmah: joke
Baizeh cheieh: vicious animal

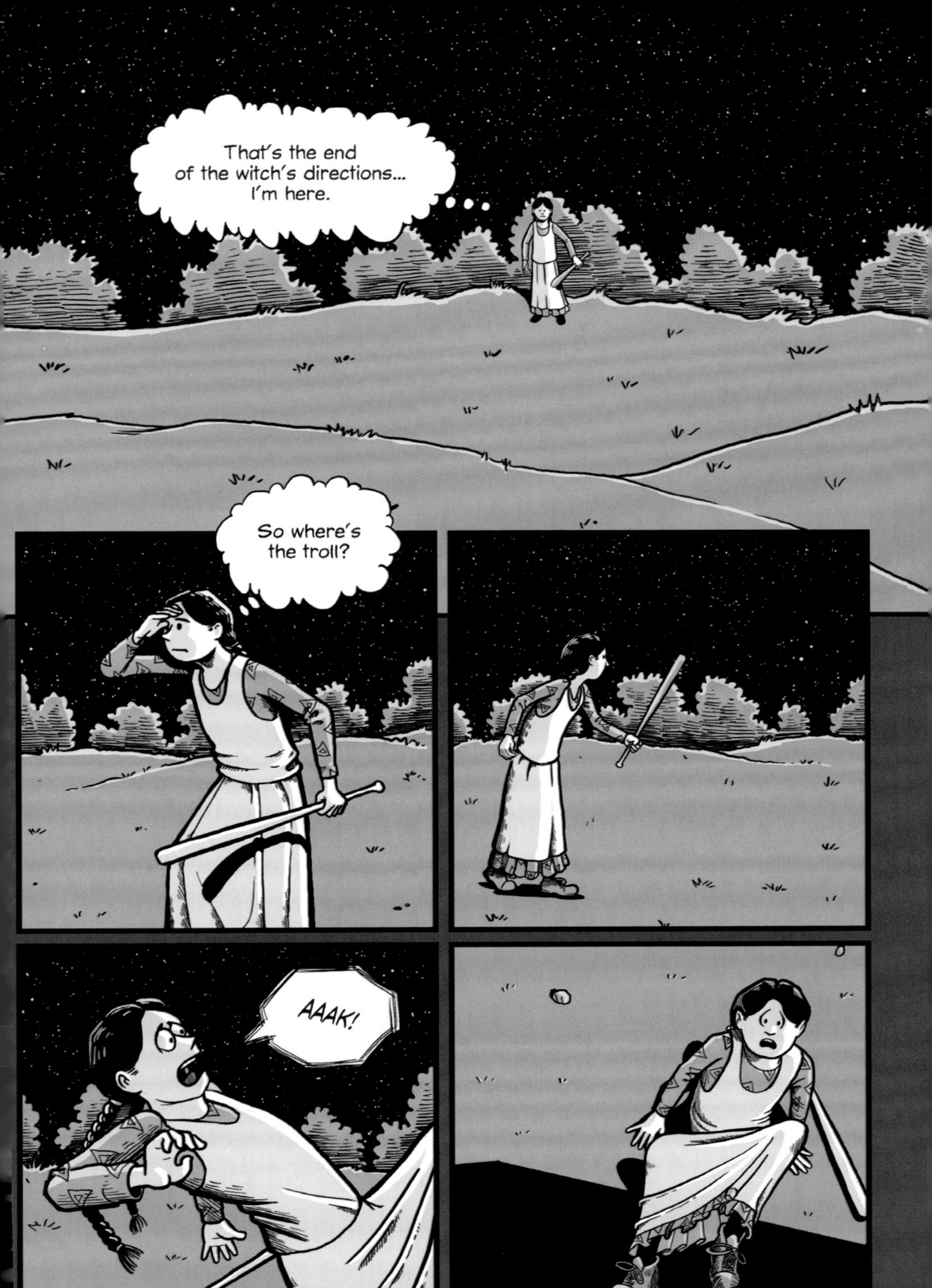
That's the end of the witch's directions... I'm here.
So where's the troll?
AAAK!

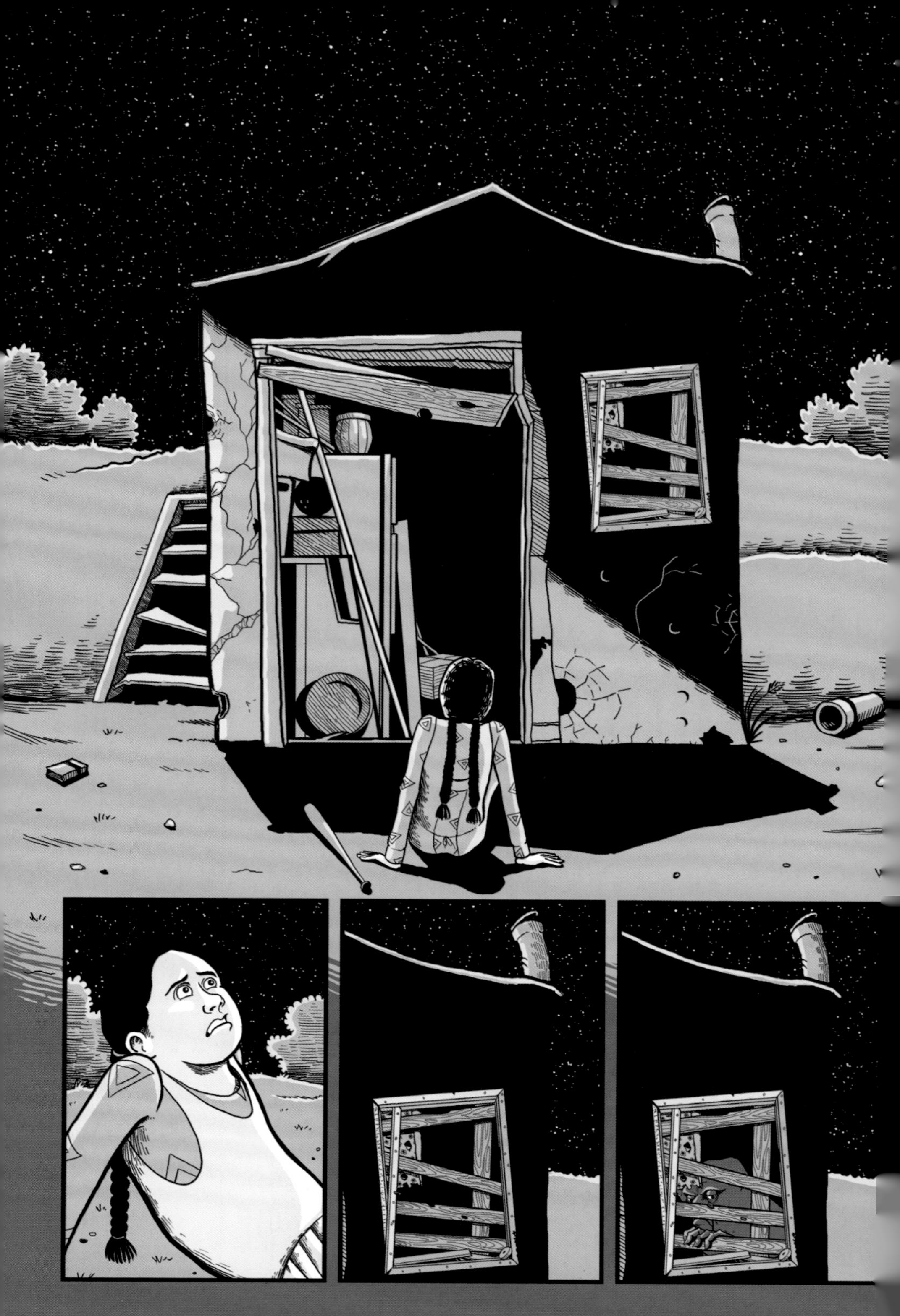

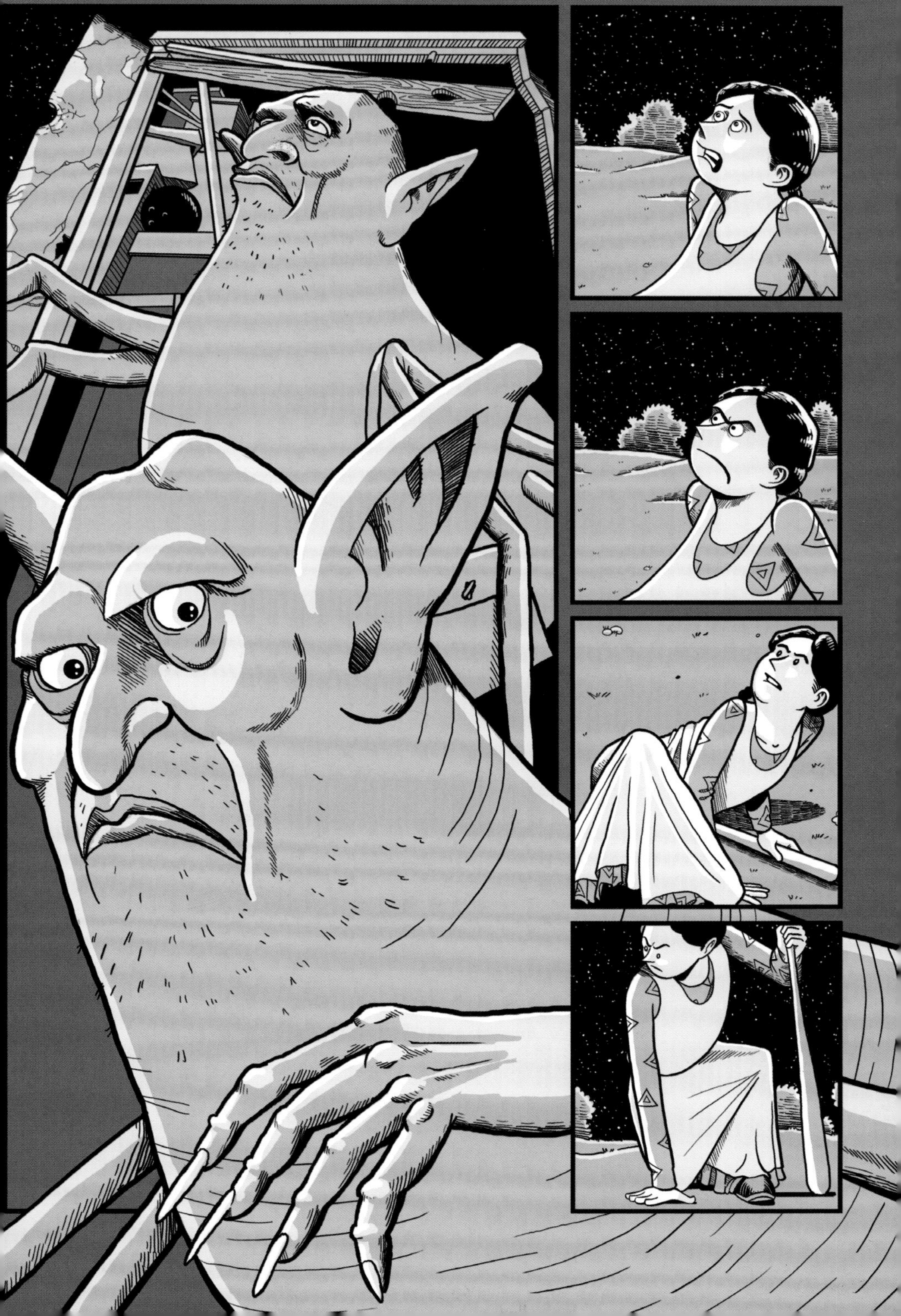

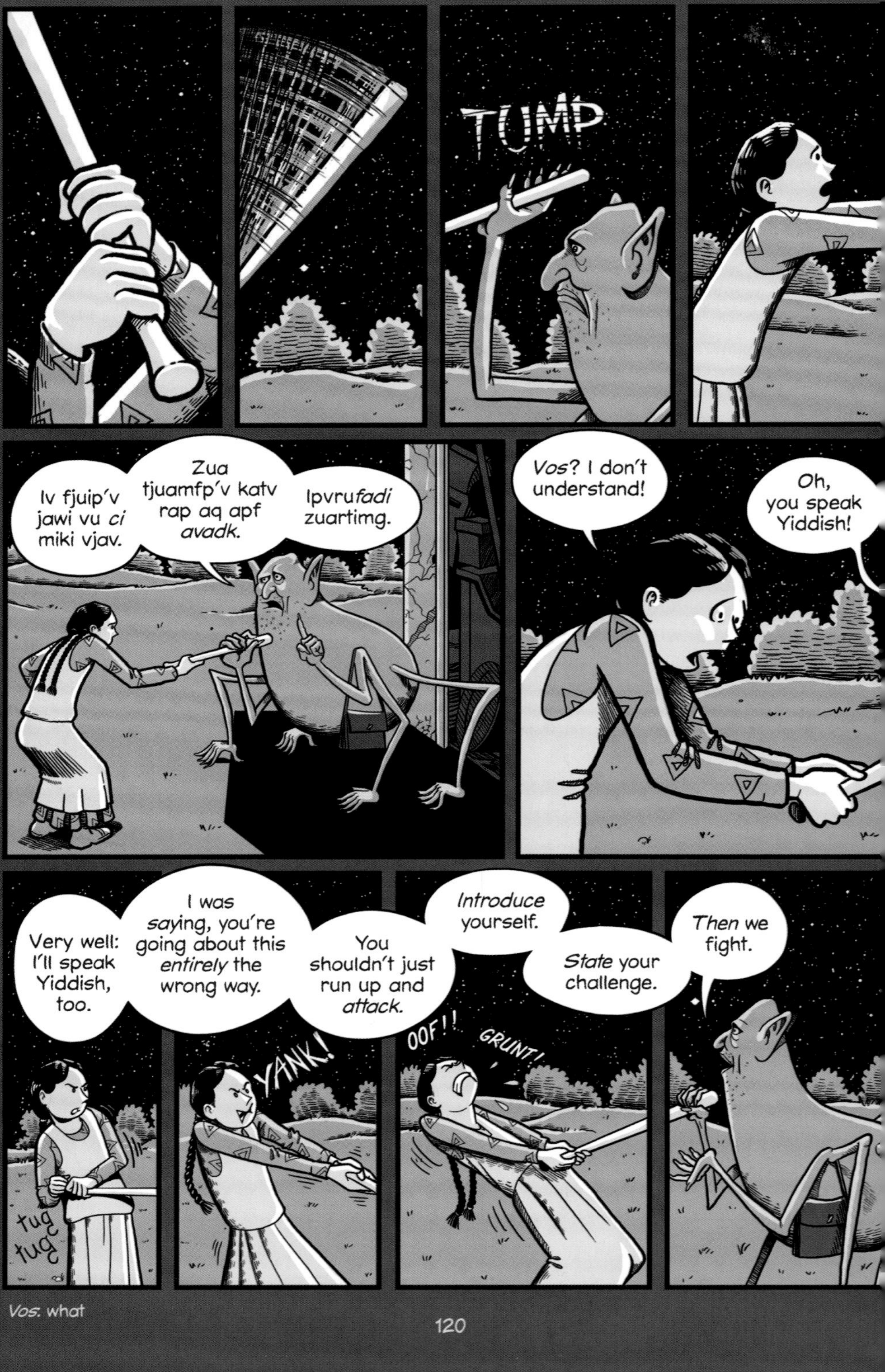
TUMP
Iv fjuip'v jawi vu *ci* miki vjav.
Zua tjuamfp'v katv rap aq apf *avadk*.
Ipvru*fadi* zuartimg.
Vos? I don't understand!
Oh, you speak Yiddish!
Very well: I'll speak Yiddish, too.
I was *saying*, you're going about this *entirely* the wrong way.
You shouldn't just run up and *attack*.
Introduce yourself.
State your challenge.
Then we fight.
tug tug
YANK!
OOF!!
GRUNT!

Vos: what

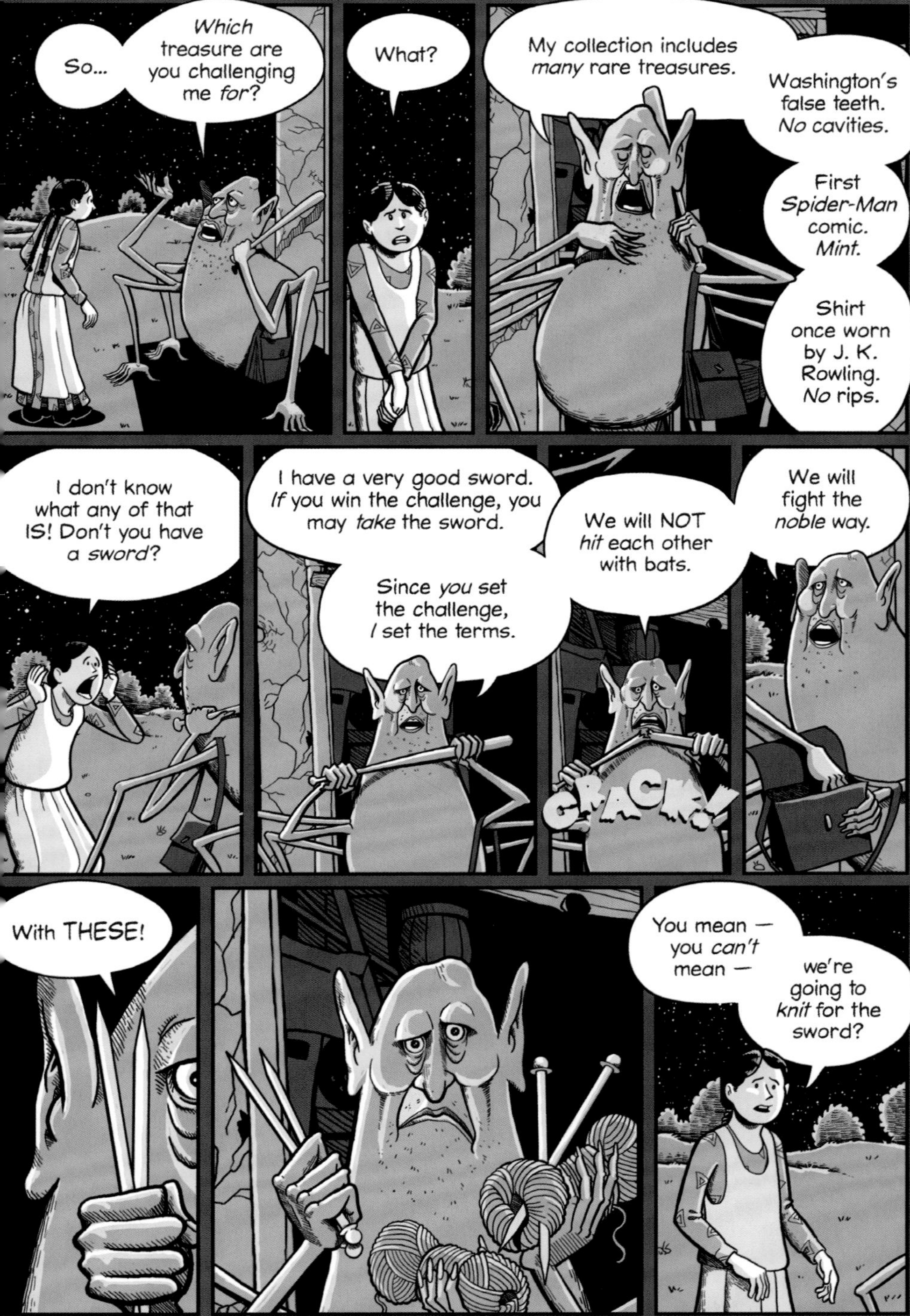
So...
Which treasure are you challenging me *for*?
What?
My collection includes *many* rare treasures.
Washington's false teeth. *No cavities.*
First *Spider-Man* comic. *Mint.*
Shirt once worn by J. K. Rowling. *No* rips.
I don't know what any of that IS! Don't you have a *sword*?
I have a very good sword. *If* you win the challenge, you may *take* the sword.
Since *you* set the challenge, *I* set the terms.
We will NOT *hit* each other with bats.
CRACK!
We will fight the *noble* way.
With THESE!
You mean — you *can't* mean —
we're going to *knit* for the sword?

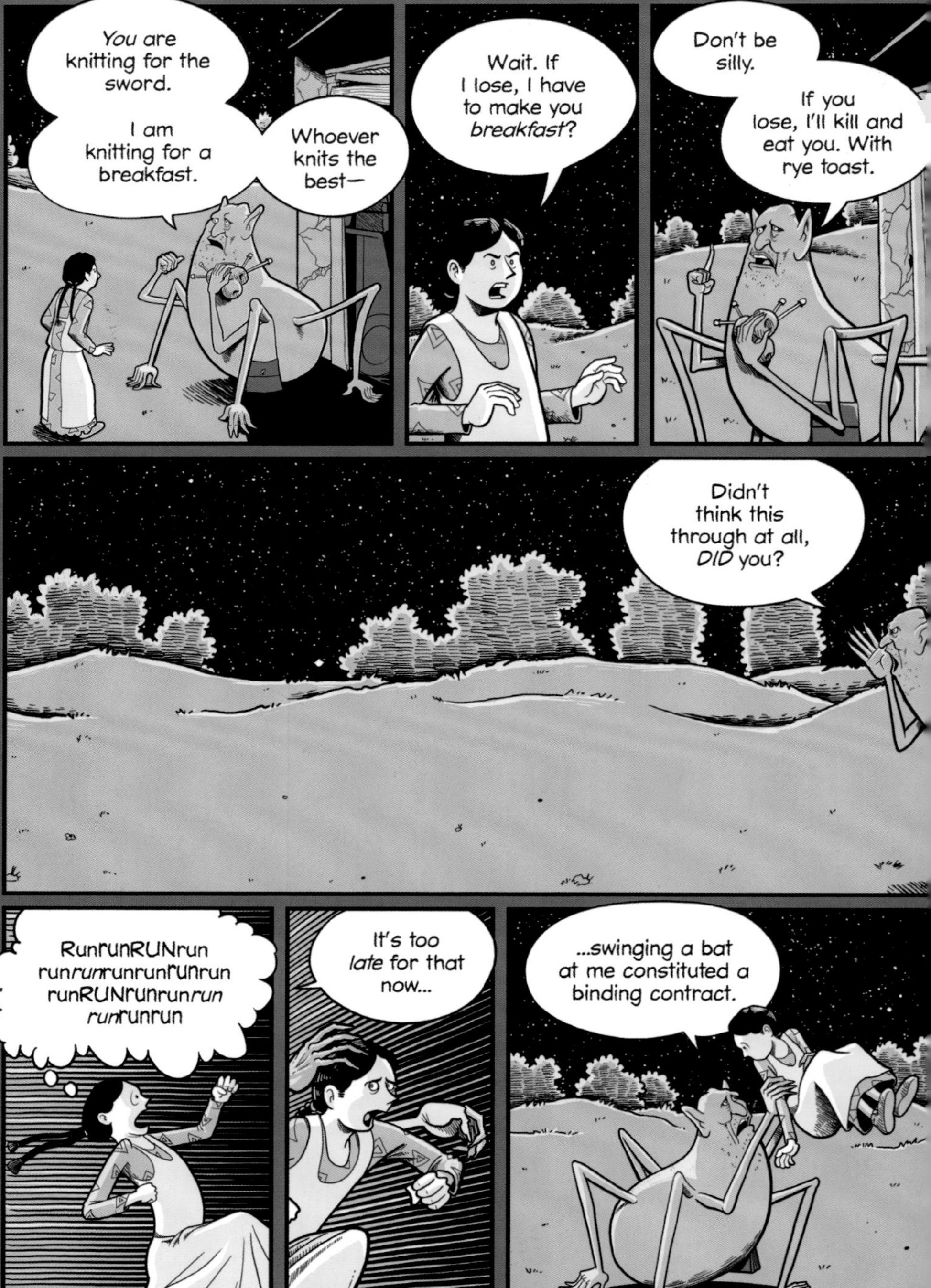
You are knitting for the sword.
I am knitting for a breakfast.
Whoever knits the best—
Wait. If I lose, I have to make you *breakfast*?
Don't be silly.
If you lose, I'll kill and eat you. With rye toast.
Didn't think this through at all, *DID* you?
RunrunRUNrun run*run*runrunrunrun runRUNrunrun*run* *run*runrun
It's too *late* for that now...
...swinging a bat at me constituted a binding contract.

Hmmm...

It's *obvious* I'll win, and I'm *peckish*.

I'll just eat a *few* fingers in advance.

NO! CHALLENGE *FIRST*! CHALLENGE *FIRST*!

Oh, if you *insist*.

Lot of extra bother, if you ask me.

Here. We'll knit until a bit before dawn.

Better sweater wins.

That's only a few hours! NO ONE can knit a whole sweater that fast!

We can. We'll use my *good* yarn.

It's a collector's item.

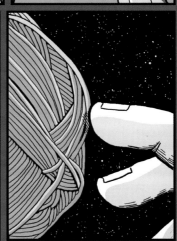

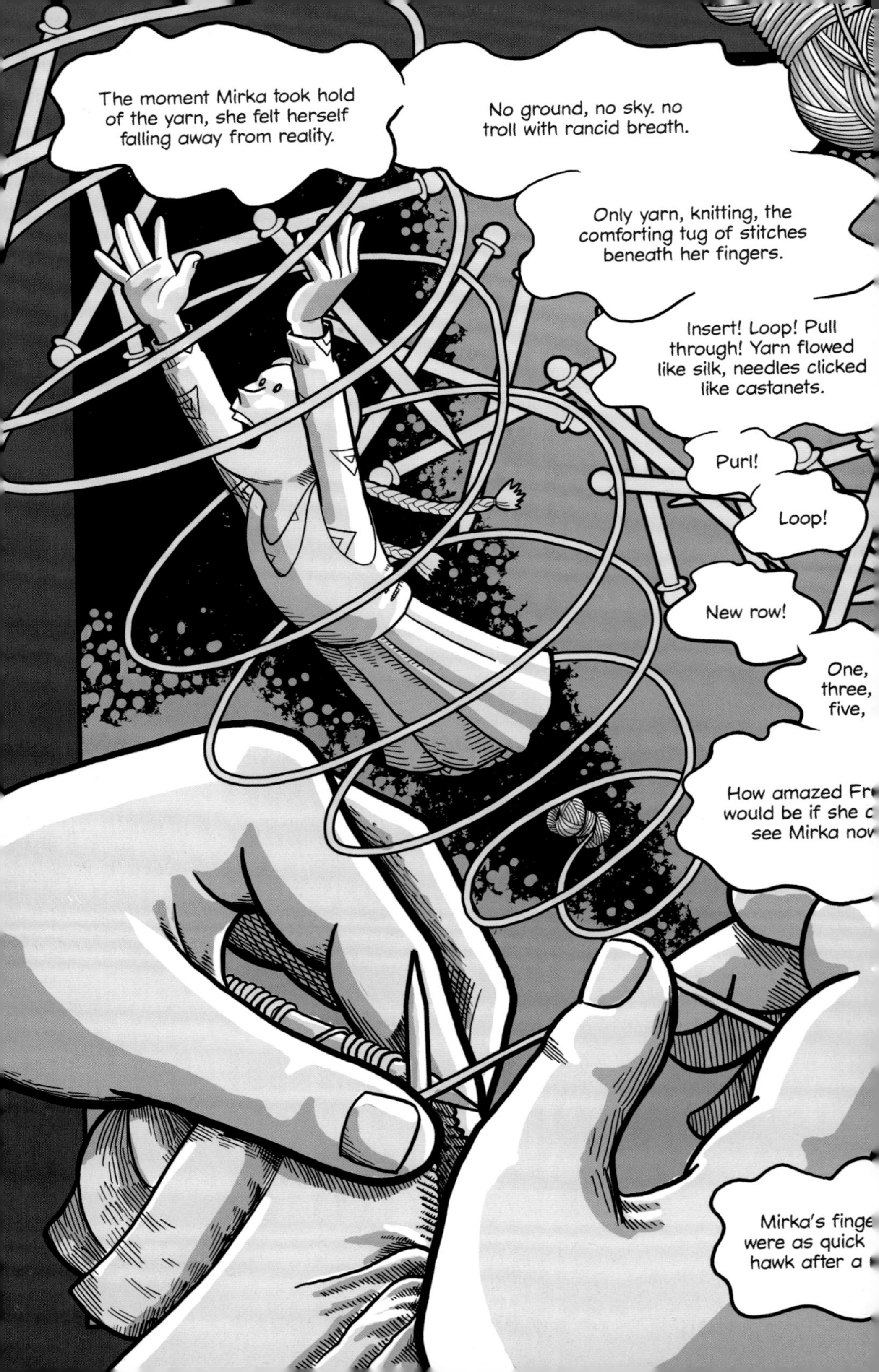
The moment Mirka took hold of the yarn, she felt herself falling away from reality.
No ground, no sky. no troll with rancid breath.
Only yarn, knitting, the comforting tug of stitches beneath her fingers.
Insert! Loop! Pull through! Yarn flowed like silk, needles clicked like castanets.
Purl!
Loop!
New row!
One, three, five,
How amazed Fr would be if she c see Mirka now
Mirka's finge were as quick hawk after a

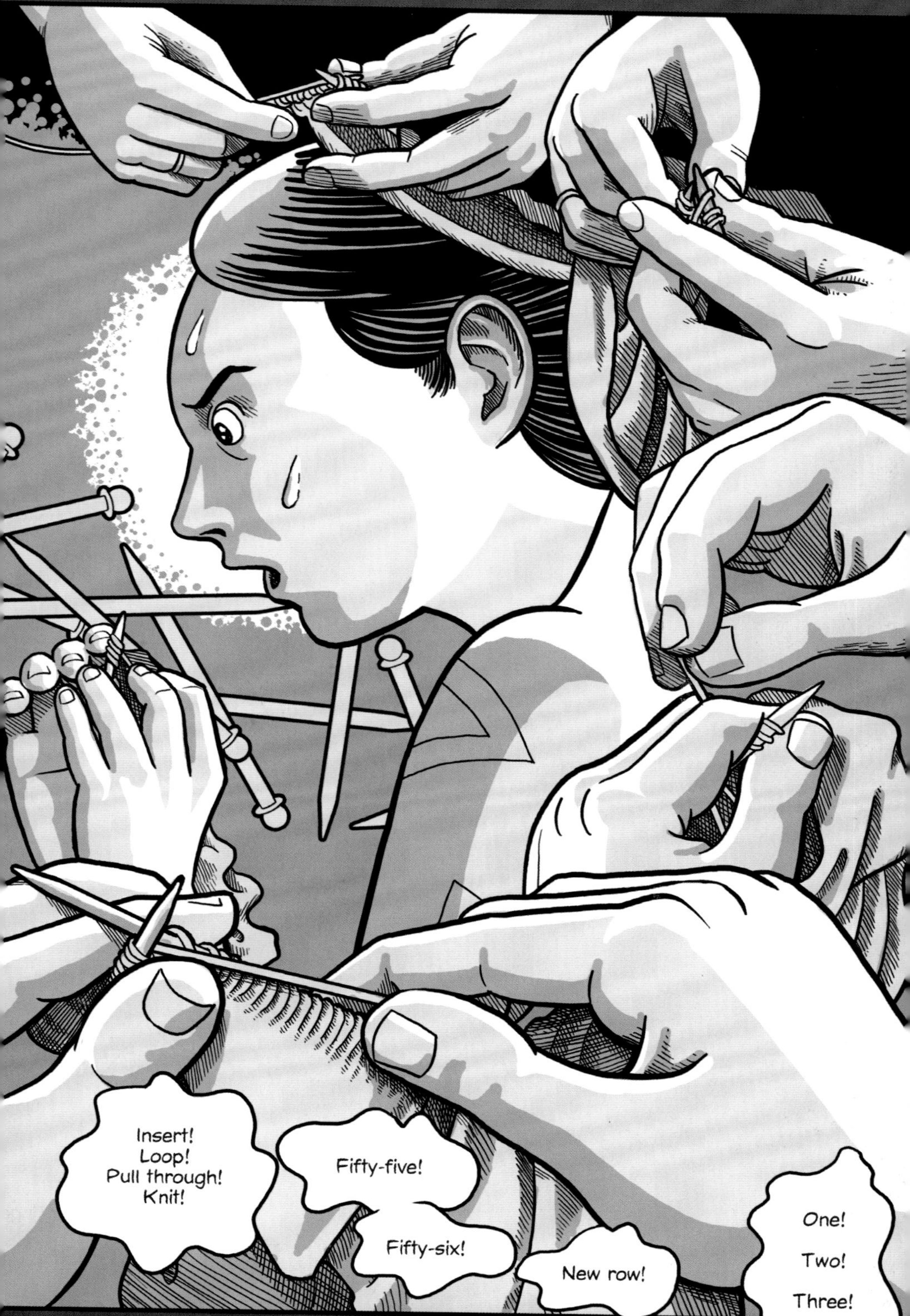
Insert! Loop! Pull through! Knit!
Fifty-five!
Fifty-six!
New row!
One! Two! Three!

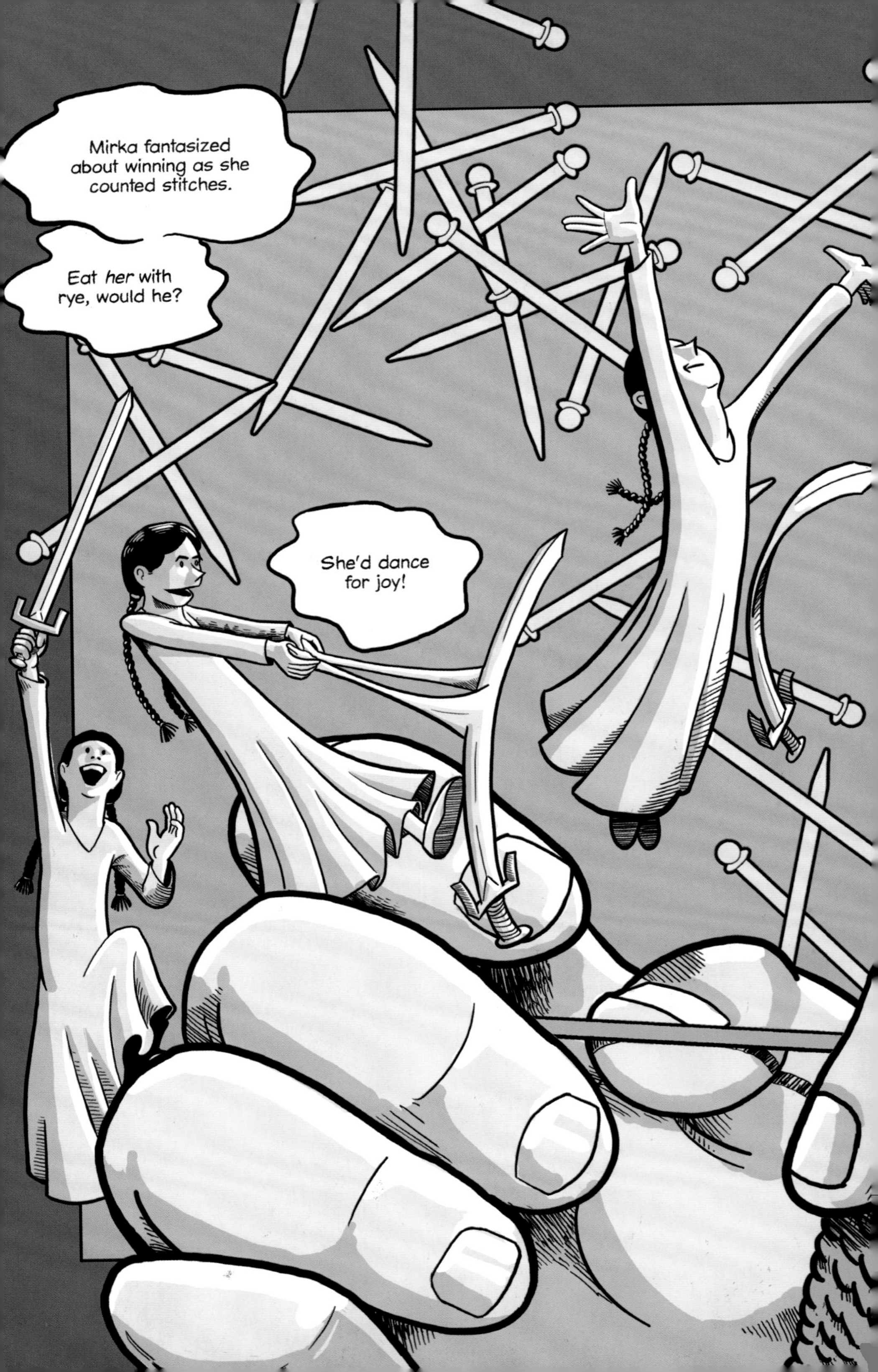
Mirka fantasized about winning as she counted stitches.
Eat *her* with rye, would he?
She'd dance for joy!

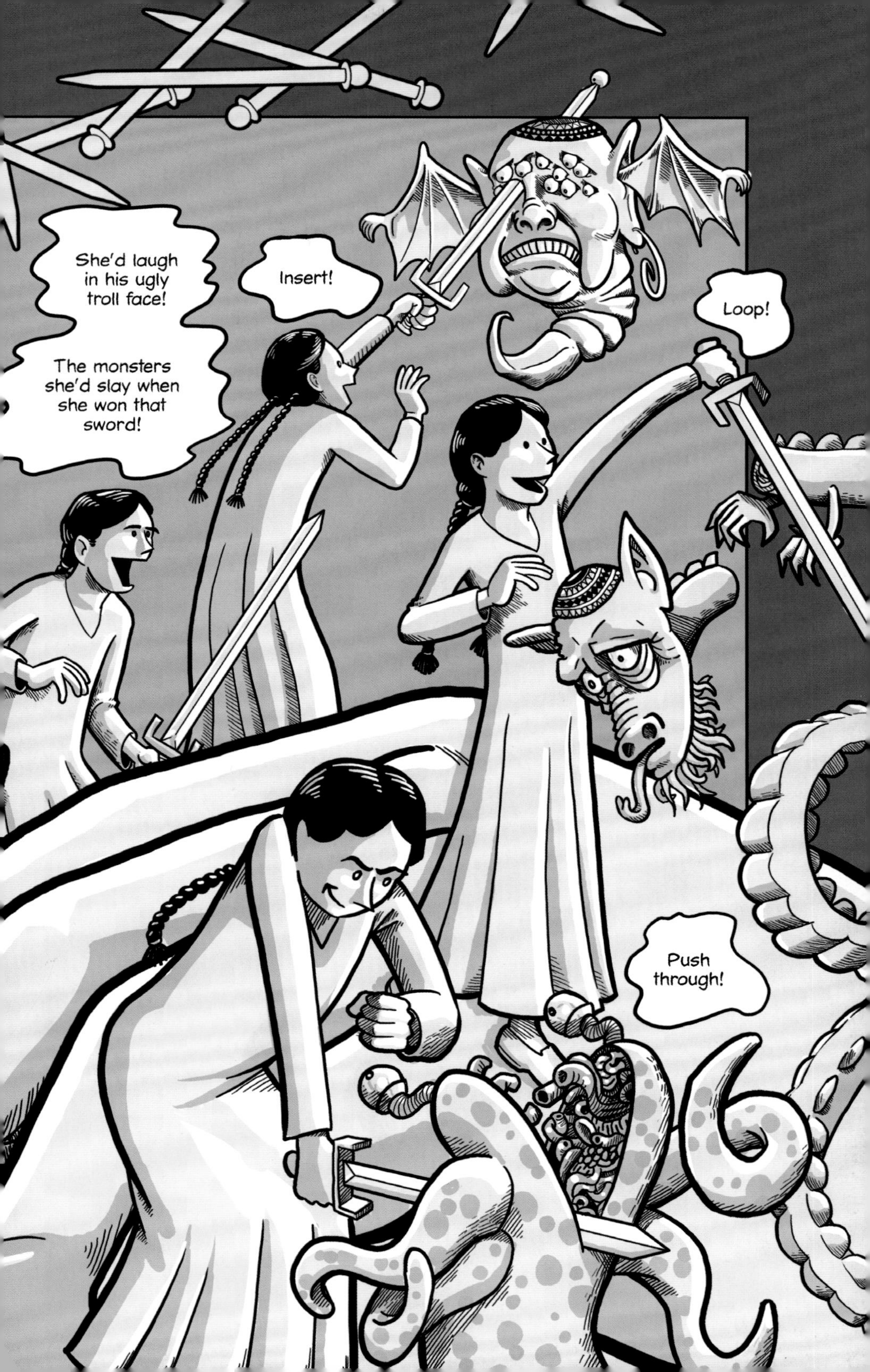
She'd laugh in his ugly troll face!
The monsters she'd slay when she won that sword!
Insert!
Loop!
Push through!

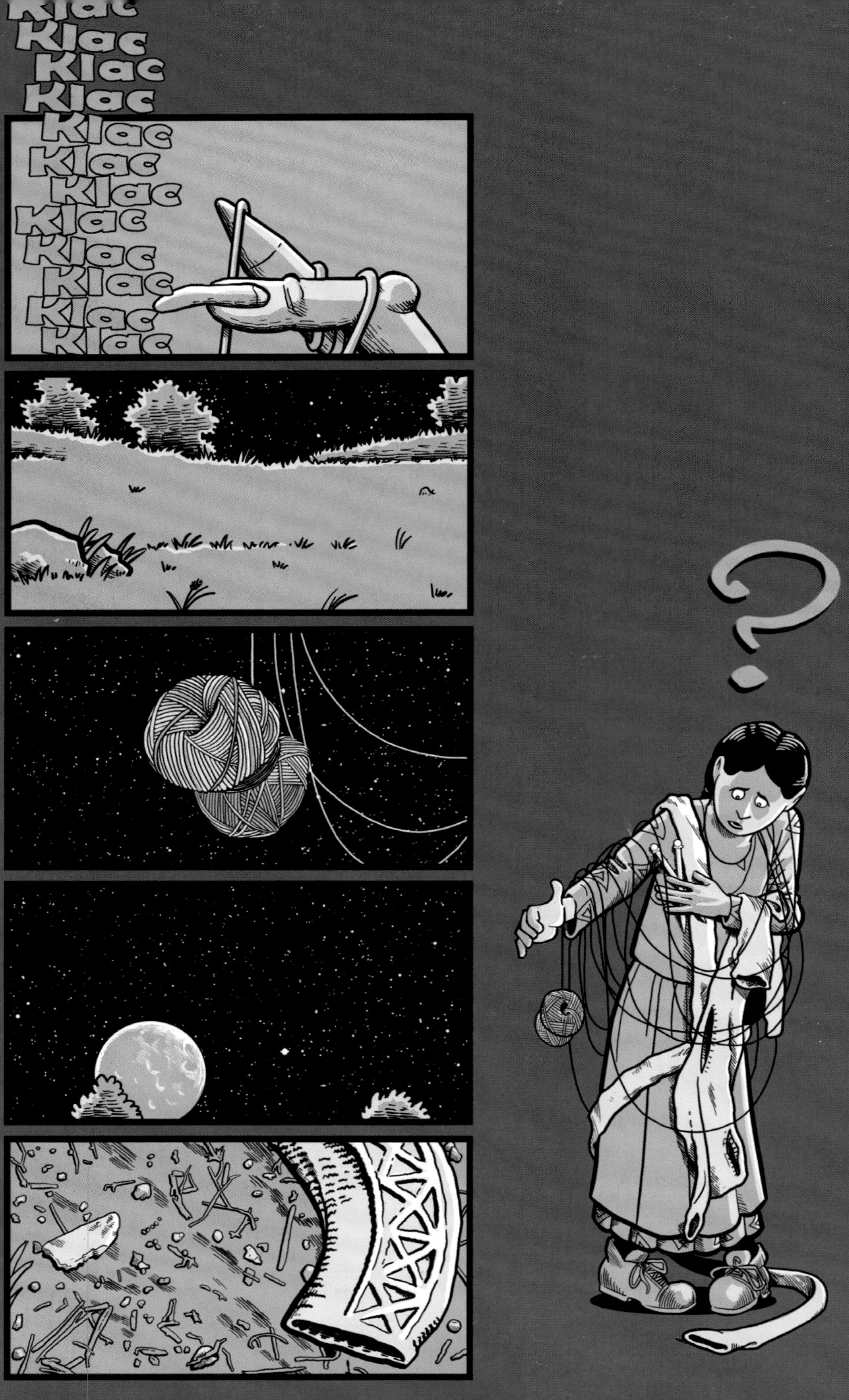
Klac
Klac
Klac
Klac
Klac
Klac
Klac
Klac
Klac
Klac
Klac
Klac

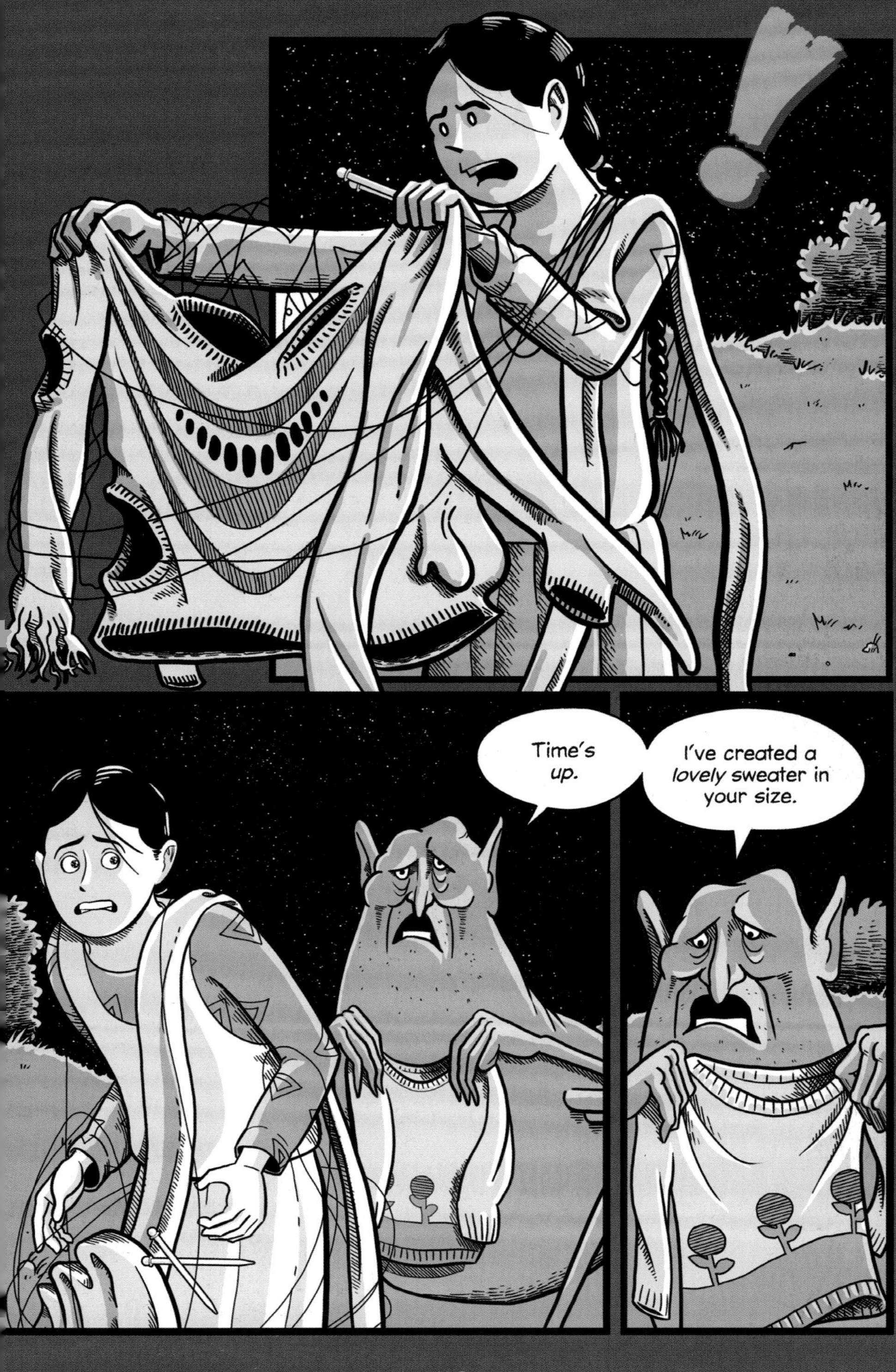
Time's up.
I've created a *lovely* sweater in your size.

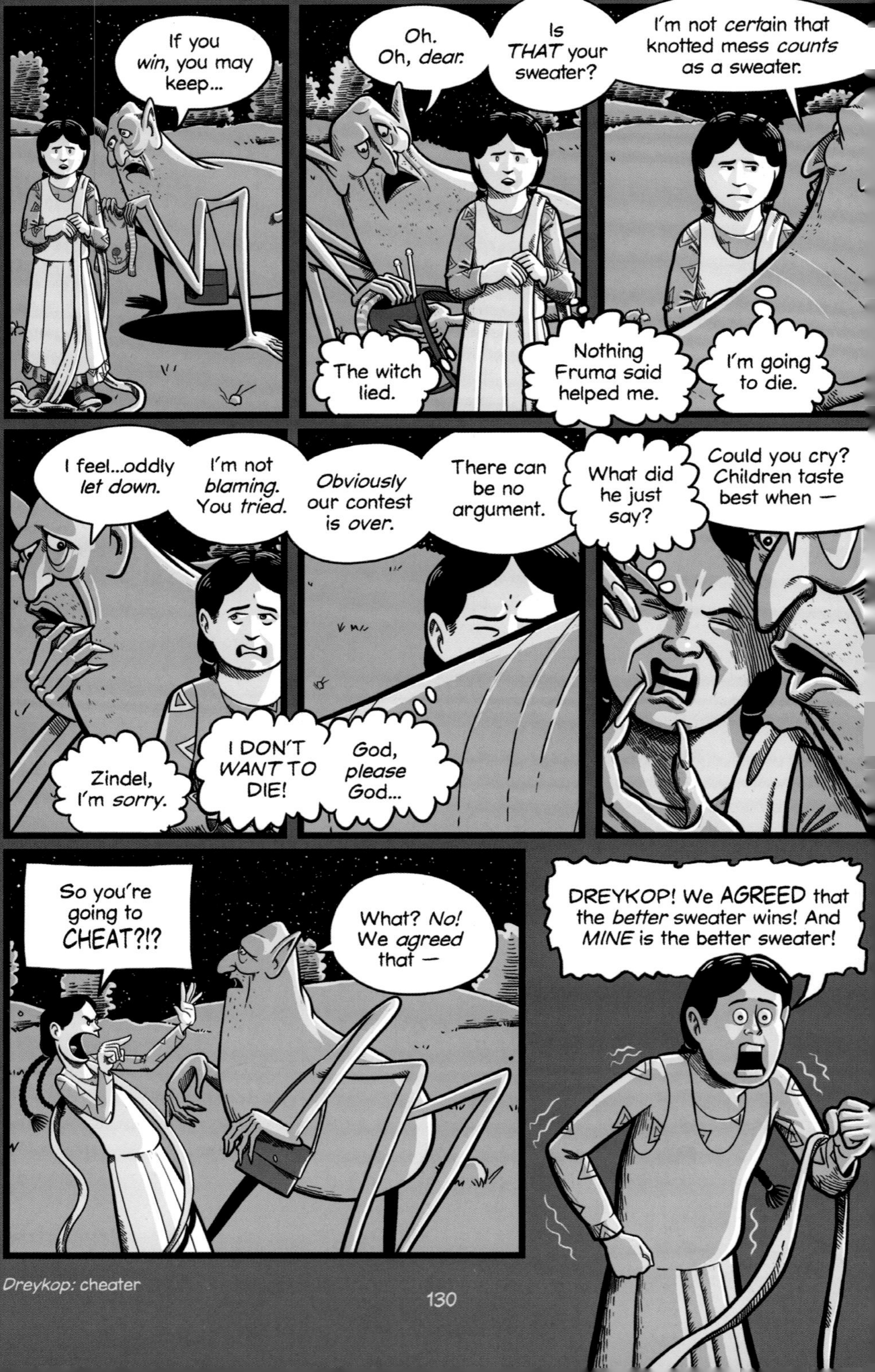
If you *win*, you may keep...
Oh. Oh, *dear.*
Is *THAT* your sweater?
I'm not *certain* that knotted mess *counts* as a sweater.
The witch lied.
Nothing Fruma said helped me.
I'm going to die.
I feel...oddly *let down.*
I'm not *blaming.* You *tried.*
Obviously our contest is *over.*
There can be no argument.
Zindel, I'm *sorry.*
I DON'T *WANT* TO DIE!
God, *please* God...
What did he just say?
Could you cry? Children taste best when —
So you're going to CHEAT?!?
What? *No!* We *agreed* that —
DREYKOP! We AGREED that the *better* sweater wins! And *MINE* is the better sweater!

Dreykop: cheater

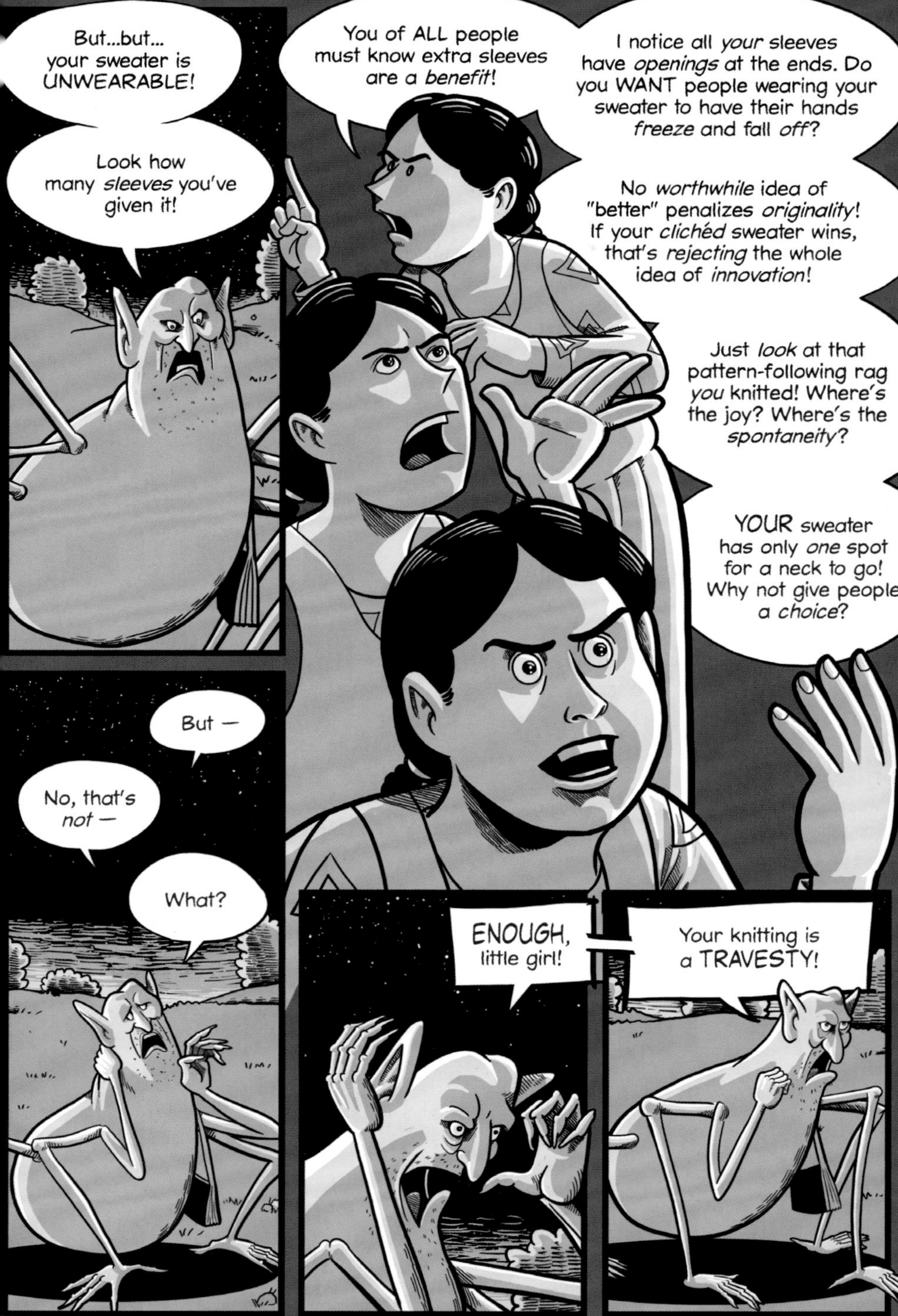

But...but... your sweater is UNWEARABLE!
Look how many *sleeves* you've given it!
You of ALL people must know extra sleeves are a *benefit*!
I notice all *your* sleeves have *openings* at the ends. Do you WANT people wearing your sweater to have their hands *freeze* and fall *off*?
No *worthwhile* idea of "better" penalizes *originality*! If your *clichéd* sweater wins, that's *rejecting* the whole idea of *innovation*!
Just *look* at that pattern-following rag *you* knitted! Where's the joy? Where's the *spontaneity*?
YOUR sweater has only *one* spot for a neck to go! Why not give people a *choice*?
But —
No, that's *not* —
What?
ENOUGH, little girl!
Your knitting is a TRAVESTY!

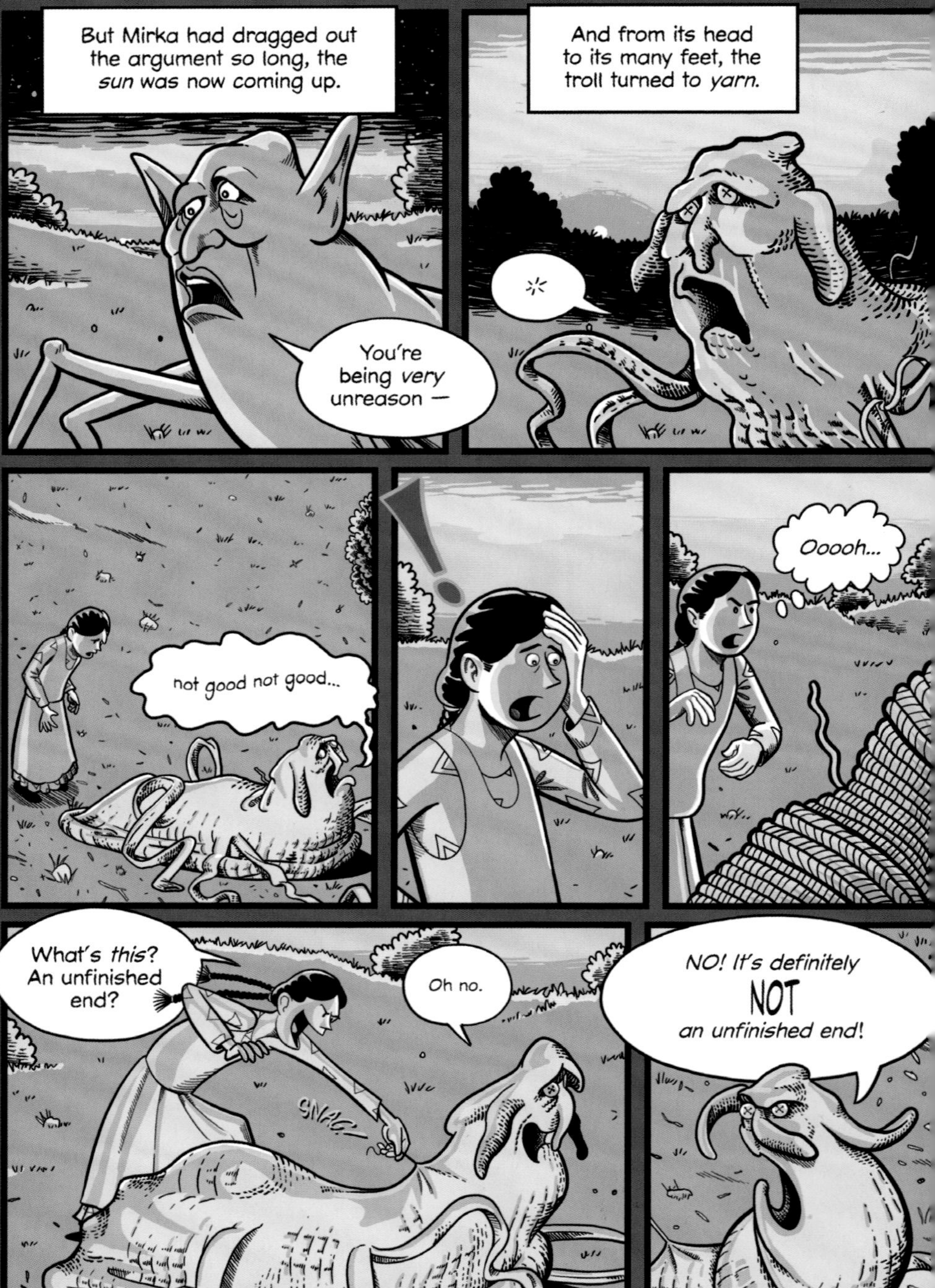

But Mirka had dragged out the argument so long, the *sun* was now coming up.
You're being *very* unreason —
And from its head to its many feet, the troll turned to *yarn*.
not good not good...
!
Ooooh...
What's *this*? An unfinished end?
SNAG!
Oh no.
NO! It's definitely NOT an unfinished end!

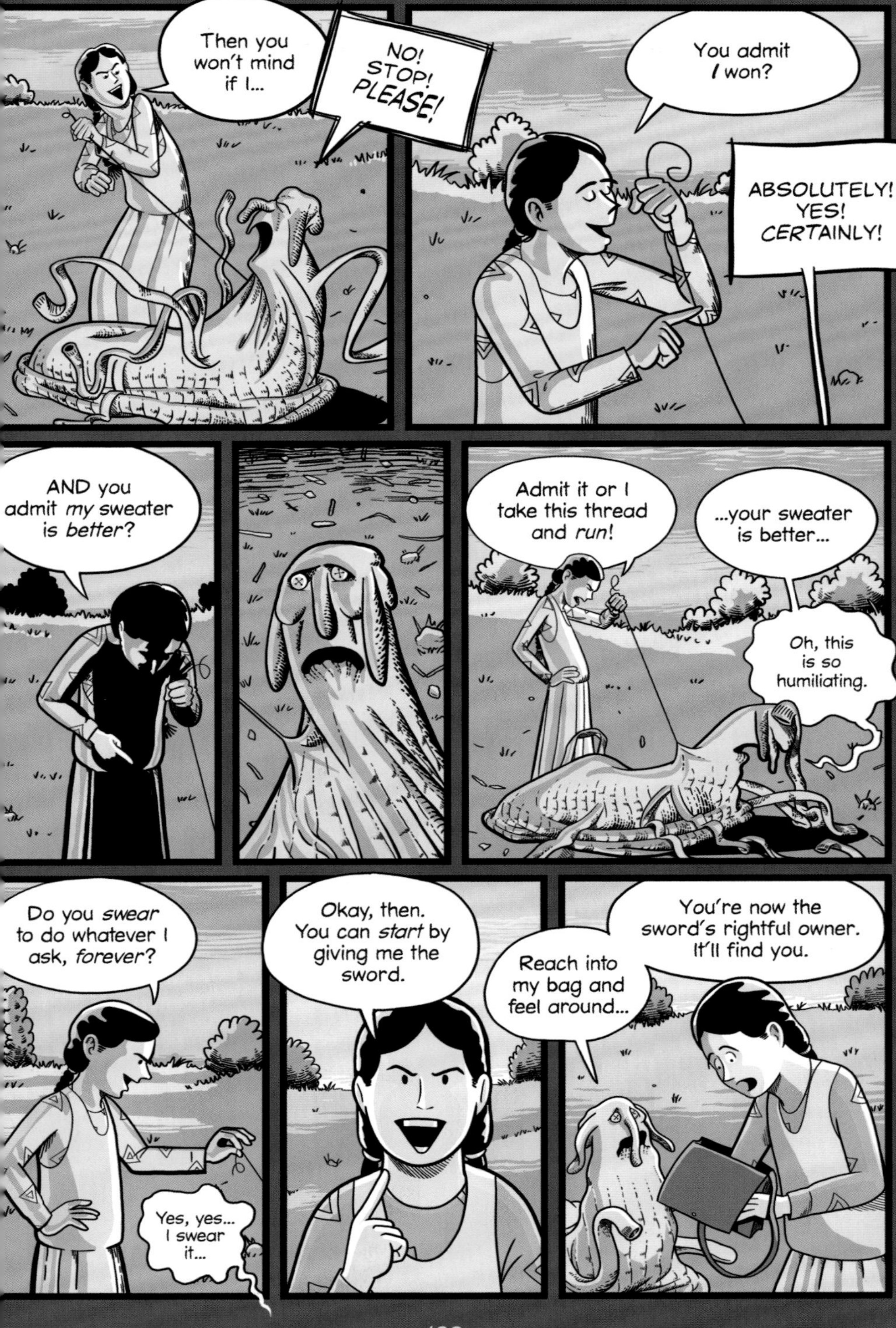
Then you won't mind if I...
NO! STOP! PLEASE!
You admit *I* won?
ABSOLUTELY! YES! CERTAINLY!
AND you admit *my* sweater is *better*?
Admit it or I take this thread and *run*!
...your sweater is better...
Oh, this is so humiliating.
Do you *swear* to do whatever I ask, *forever*?
Yes, yes... I swear it...
Okay, then. You can *start* by giving me the sword.
Reach into my bag and feel around...
You're now the sword's rightful owner. It'll find you.

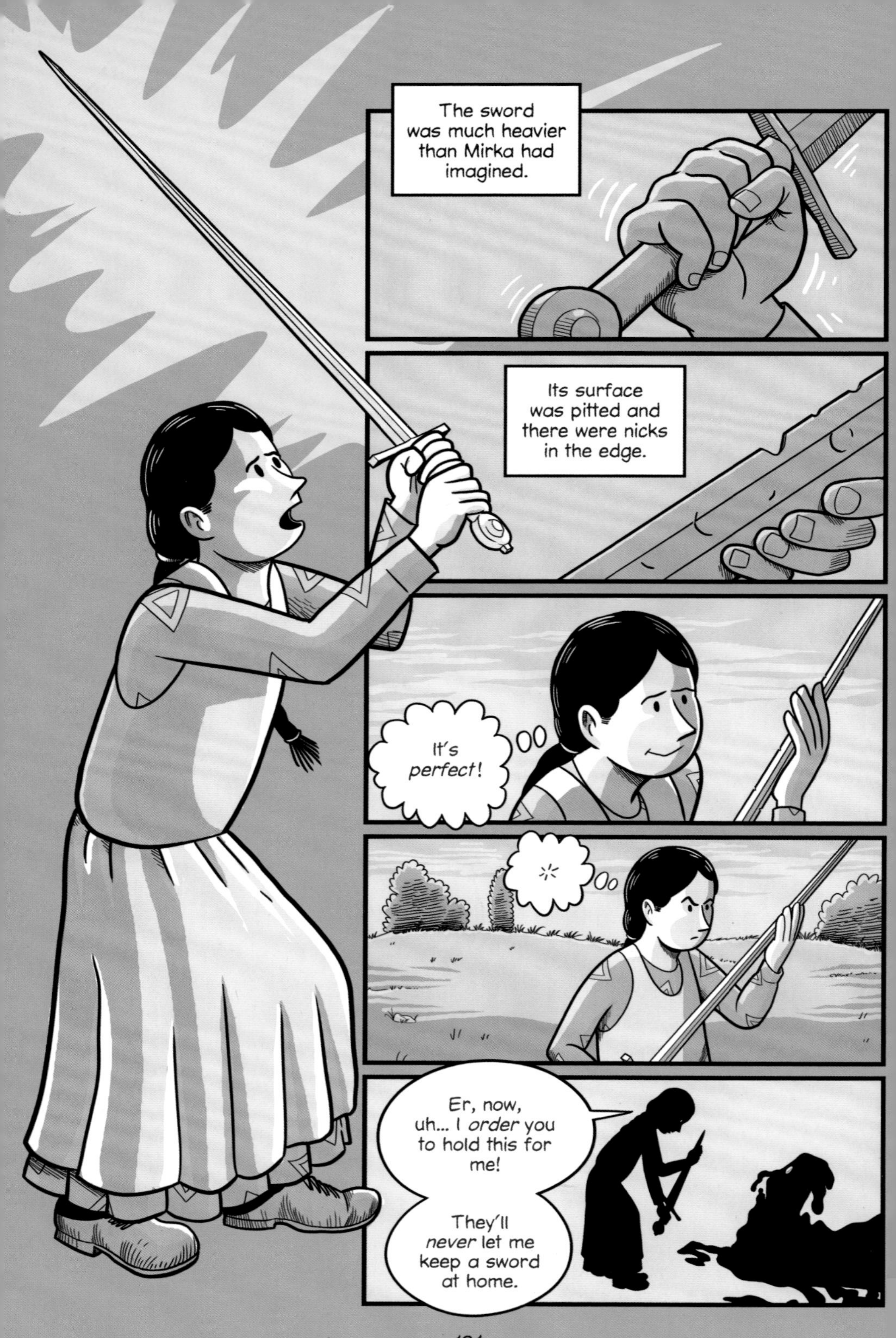
The sword was much heavier than Mirka had imagined.
Its surface was pitted and there were nicks in the edge.
It's *perfect*!
Er, now, uh... I *order* you to hold this for me!
They'll *never* let me keep a sword at home.

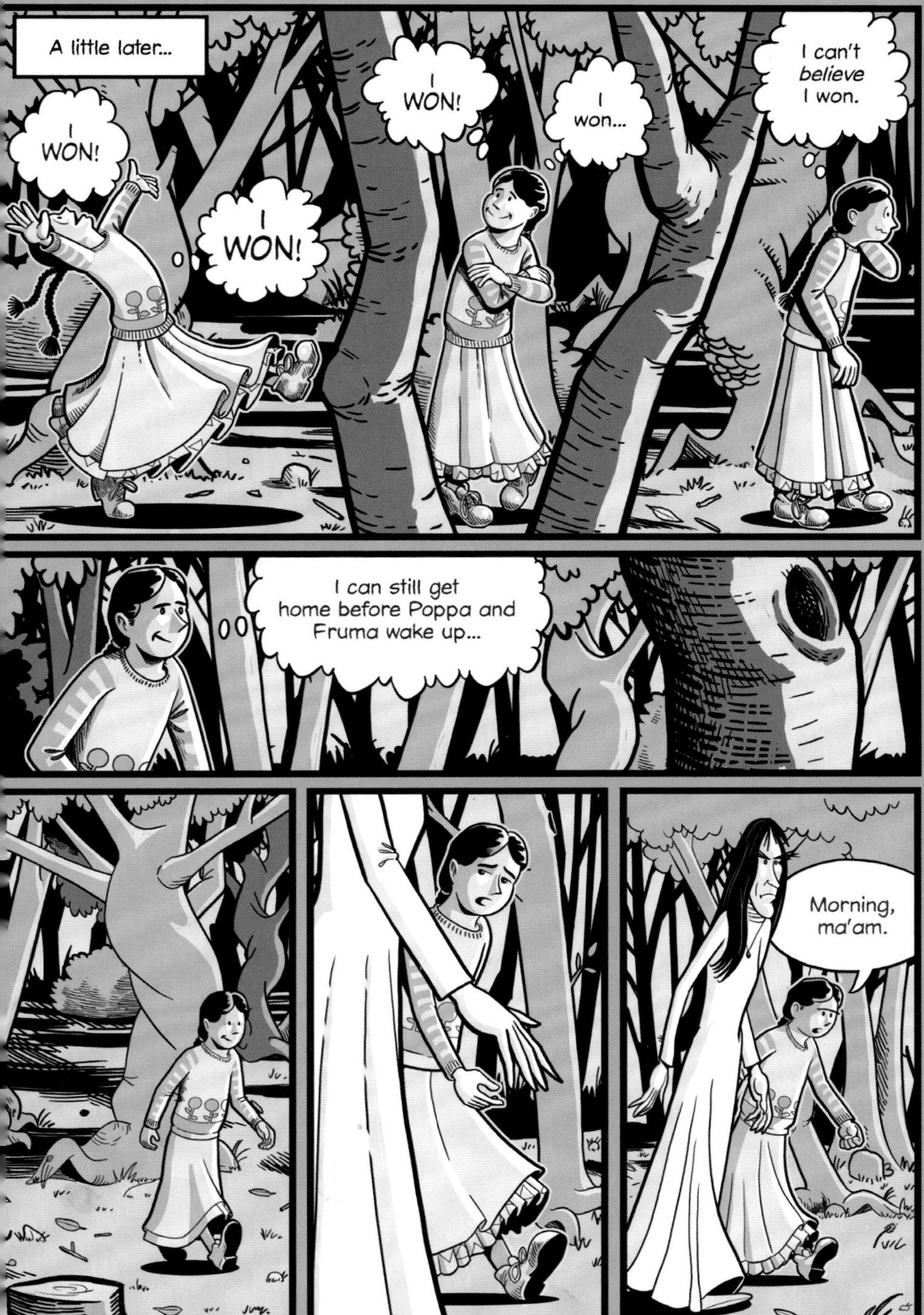
A little later...
I WON!
I WON!
I WON!
I won...
I can't *believe* I won.
I can still get home before Poppa and Fruma wake up...
Morning, ma'am.

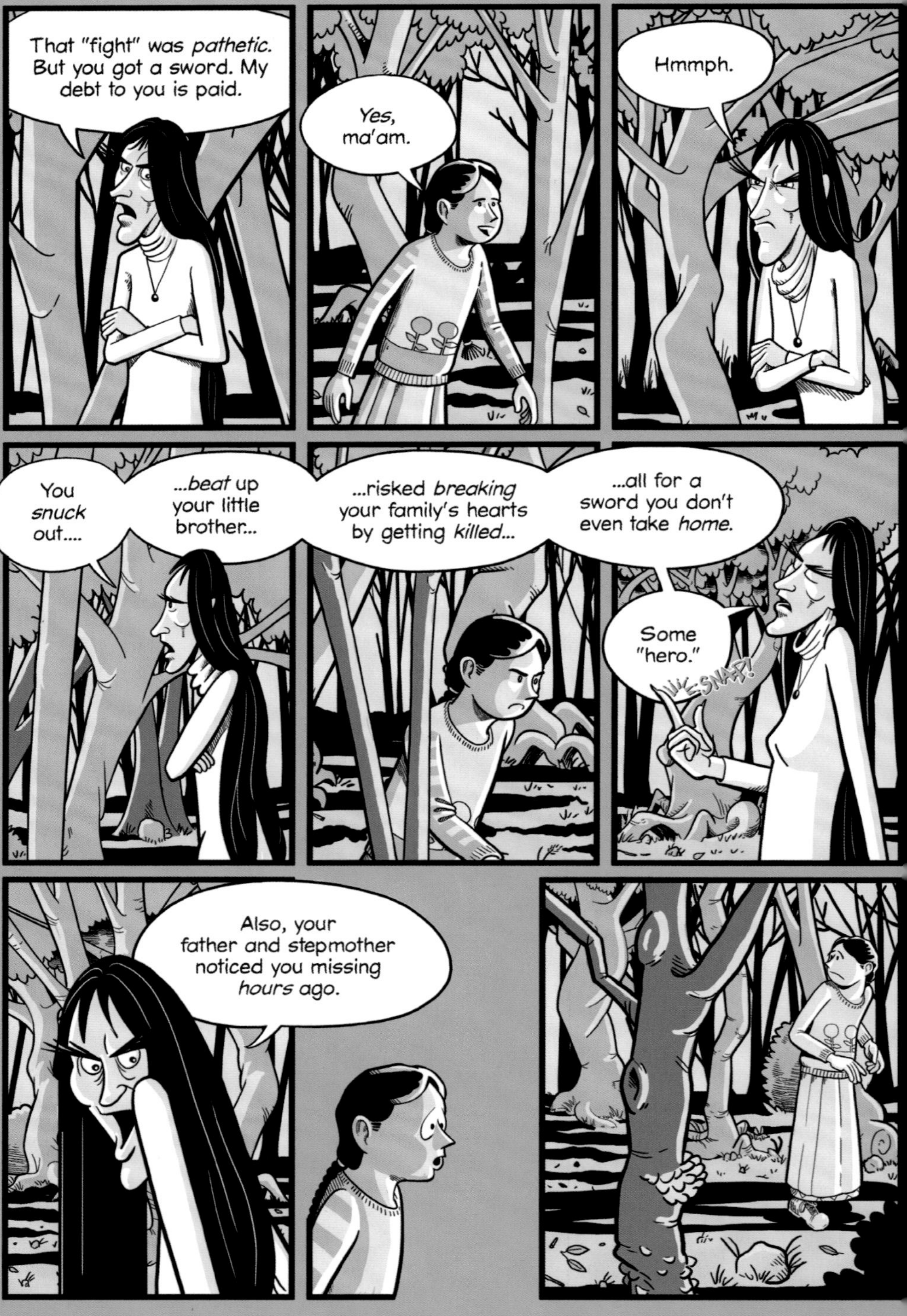
That "fight" was *pathetic.* But you got a sword. My debt to you is paid.
Yes, ma'am.
Hmmph.
You *snuck* out....
...*beat* up your little brother...
...risked *breaking* your family's hearts by getting *killed*...
...all for a sword you don't even take *home.*
Some "hero."
SNAP!
Also, your father and stepmother noticed you missing *hours* ago.

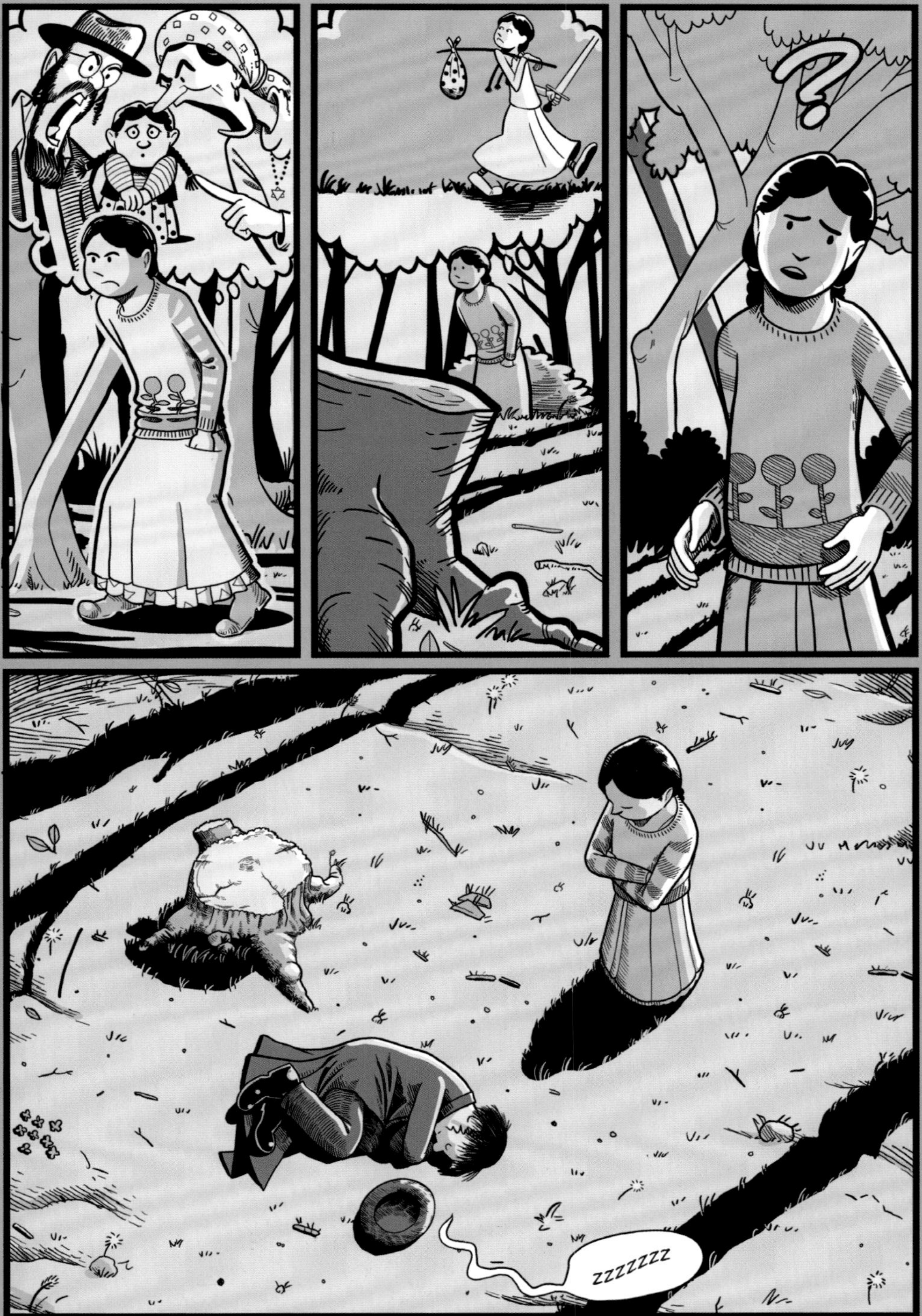
ZZZZZZZ

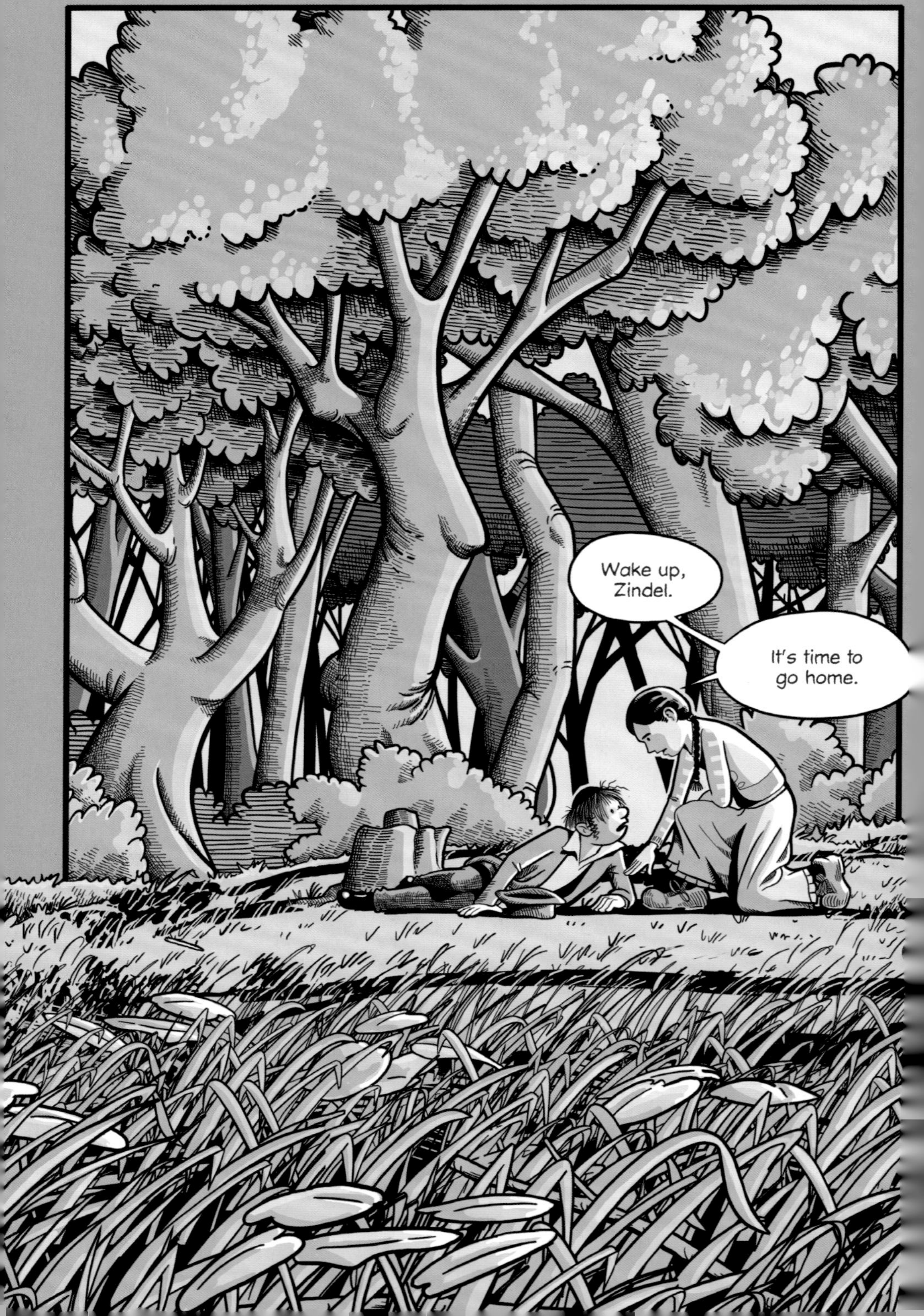
Wake up, Zindel.
It's time to go home.

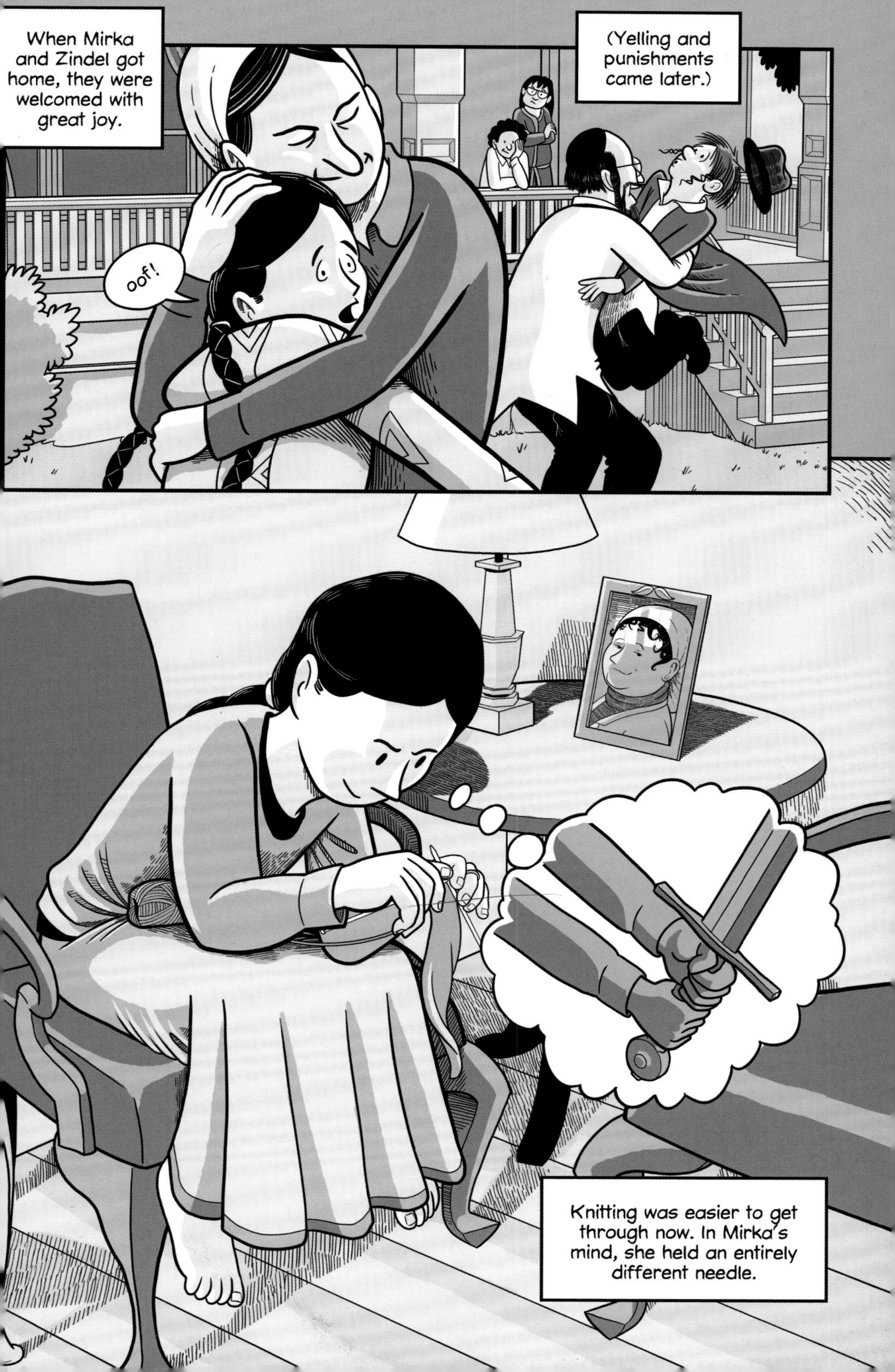
When Mirka and Zindel got home, they were welcomed with great joy.
oof!
(Yelling and punishments came later.)
Knitting was easier to get through now. In Mirka's mind, she held an entirely different needle.

A Hereville Sketchbook

Designing the Troll

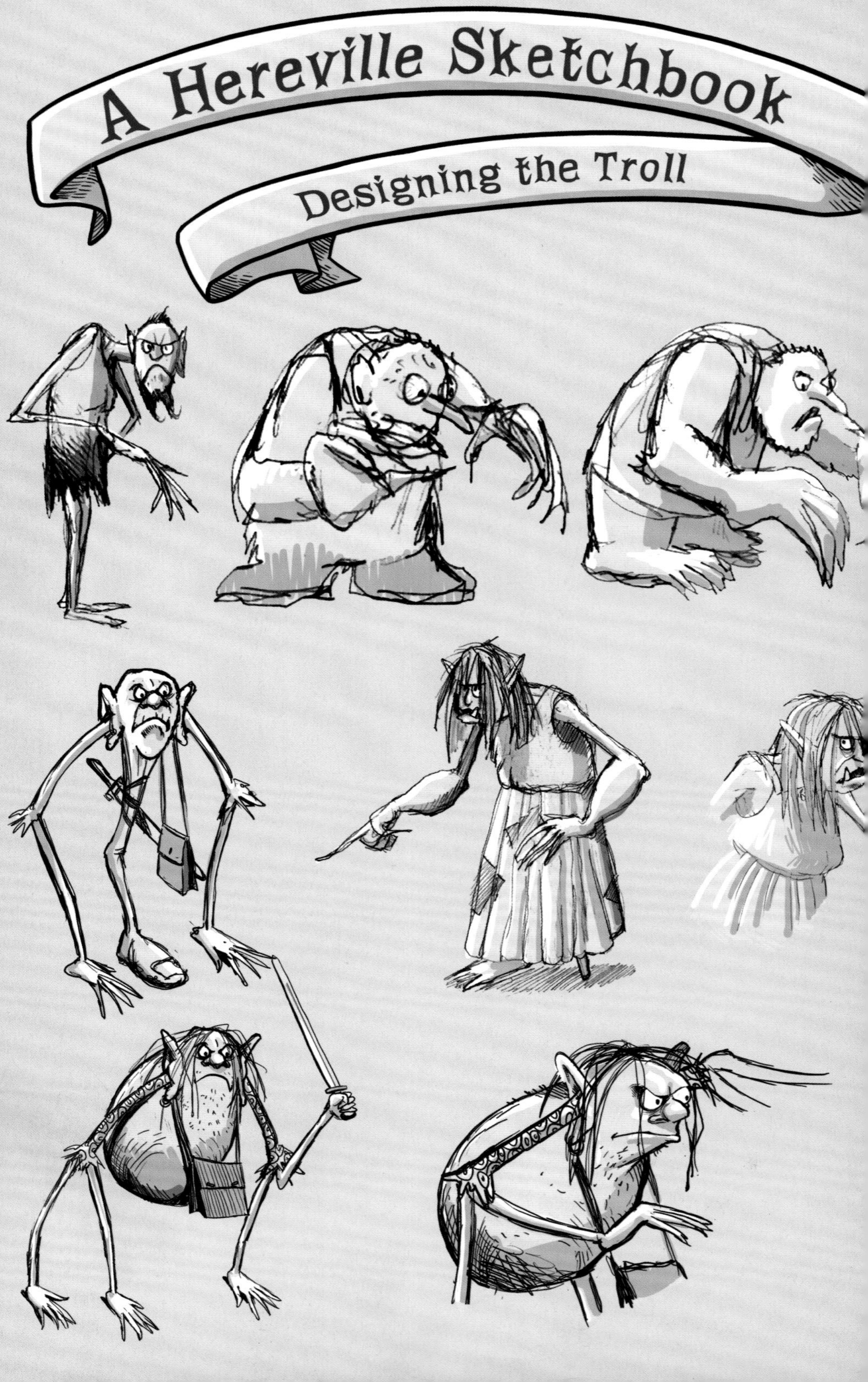

Before I could start drawing *Hereville*, I had to create my characters, which meant thinking about who they are, what they do, and most important, what they look like. That last step meant a lot of drawing and redrawing until a character finally looked "right" to my eyes. Check out these sketches of the troll to see how the process works. For more on how *Hereville* was created, visit me at www.hereville.com.

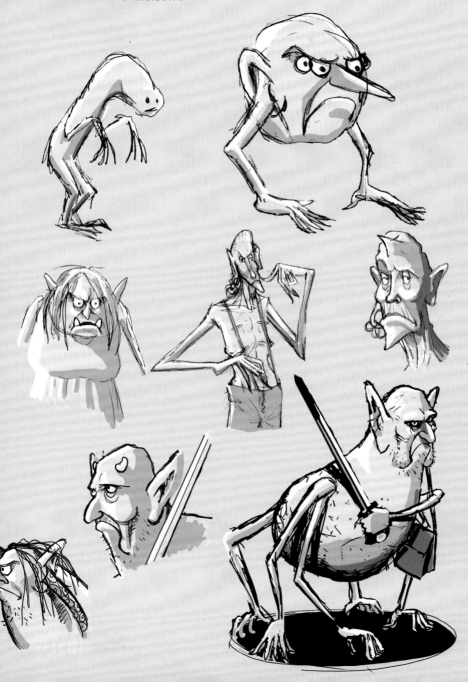

ACKNOWLEDGMENTS

A *sheynem dank* (thank you very much) to Jake Richmond for amazing colors, advice, and calm; Rachel Swirsky, whose contributions are immeasurable; my wonderful agent Judith Hansen; Sheila Keenan, Chad W. Beckerman, Charles Kochman, and the entire Abrams crew; Kim Baker, Toby and Larry Deutsch, Jenn Frederick, Sarah Kahn, Jenn Manley Lee, Kip Manley, Ivy and Scott McCloud, Dylan Meconis, Kevin Moore, Matt Schlotte, and Charles Seaton; girlamatic.com; The Old Church Society; Slate Technologies; and the many more who have helped *Hereville* along the way.

AUTHOR'S NOTE

I drew *Hereville* on my computer using Photoshop and a Cintiq tablet, which is a kind of interactive pen-on-screen tool. Jake, the colorist, also used Photoshop to digitally add color to my black-and-white artwork.

PUBLISHER'S NOTE

Library of Congress Control Number: 2010924236

ISBN 978-0-8109-8422-6

Book and cover design by Chad W. Beckerman and Barry Deutsch

Printed and bound in China
10 9 8 7 6 5 4 3 2 1

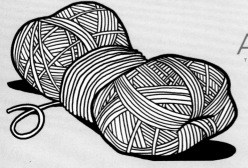

ABRAMS

THE ART OF BOOKS SINCE 1949

115 West 18th Street
New York, NY 10011
www.abramsbooks.com

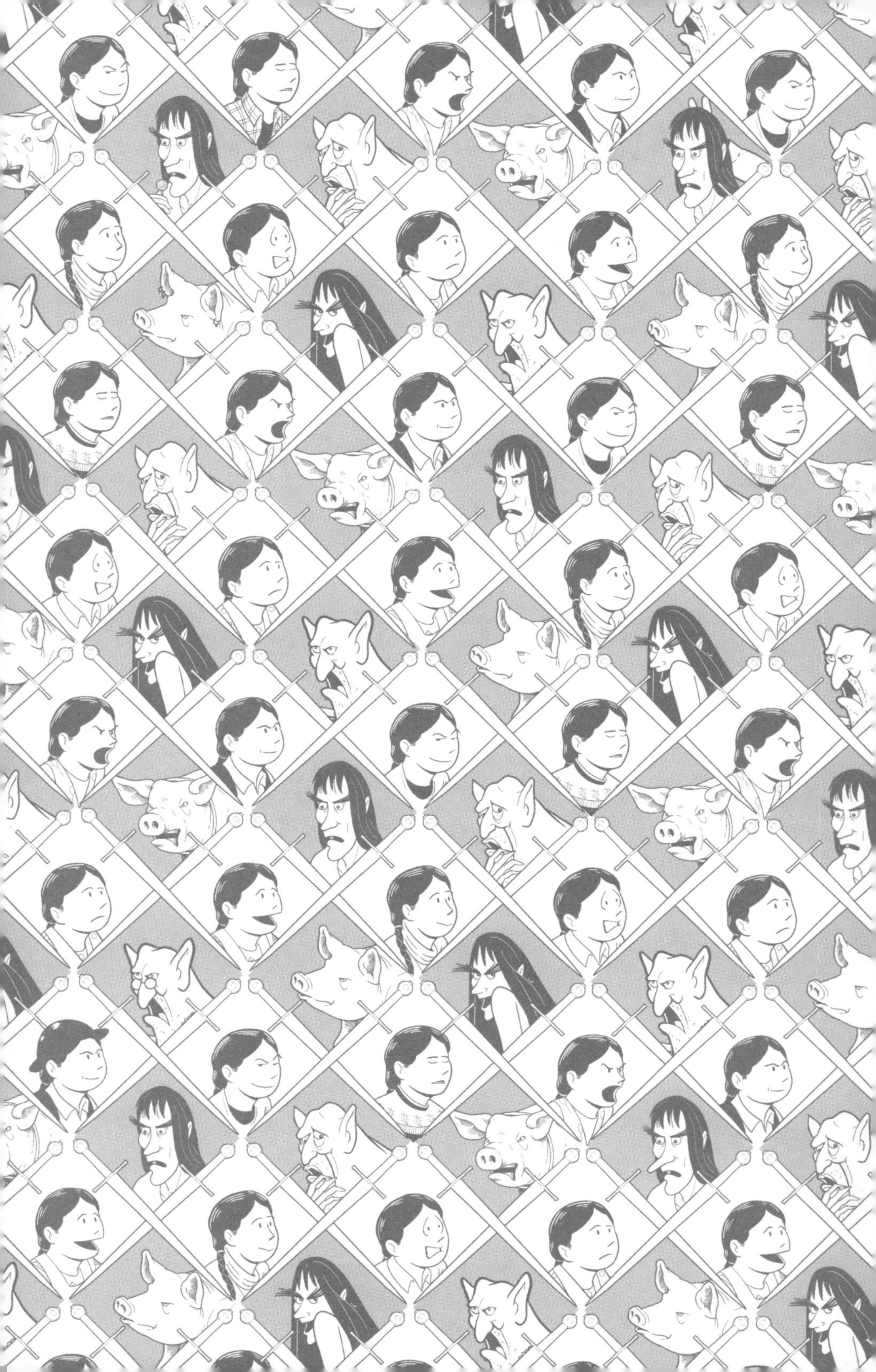

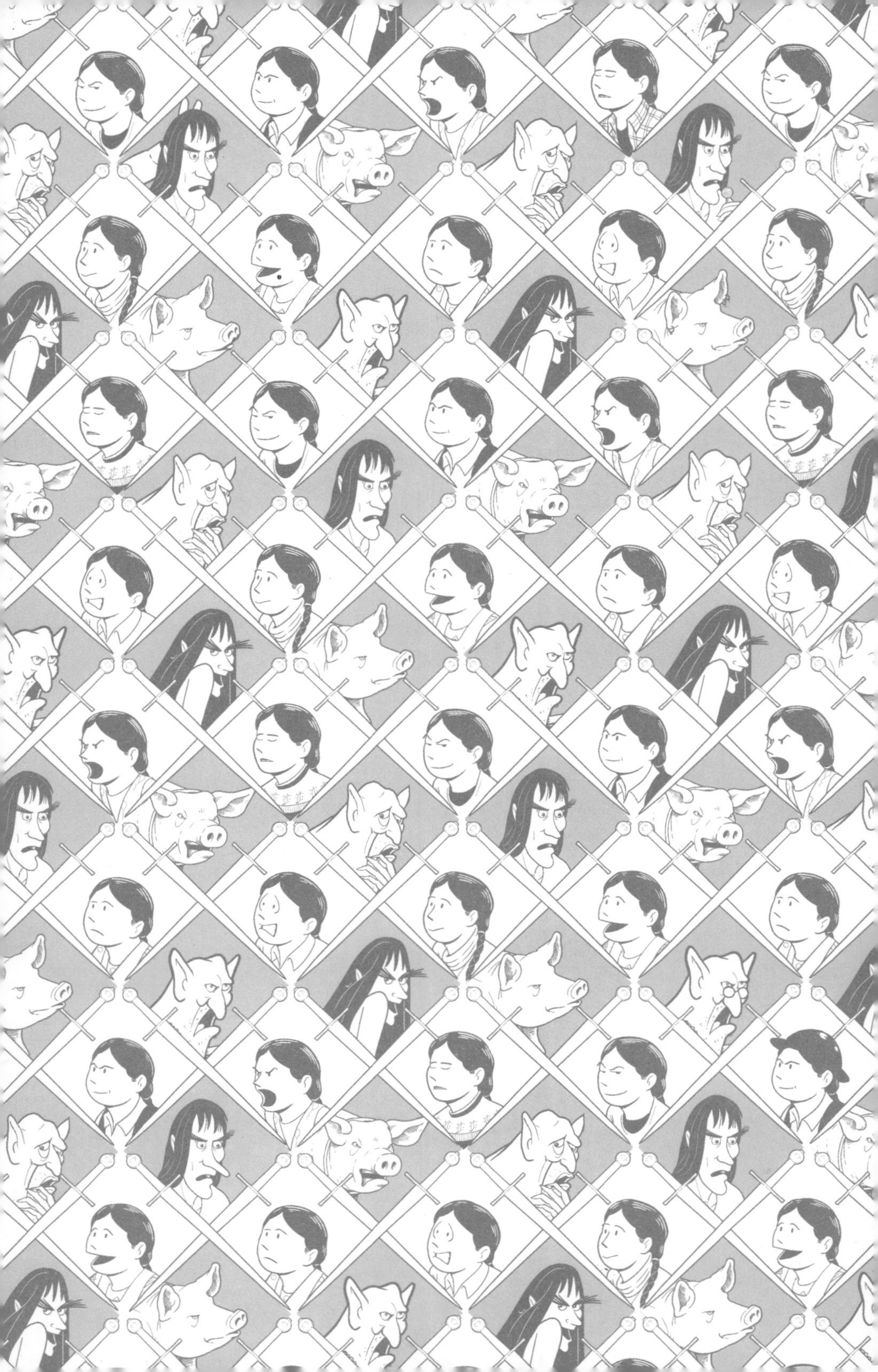